PRAISE FOR *GUNMETAL GRAY*

"Fans of RPG, Hong Kong action films, and high-octane storytelling will love the Gray Man, who battles full-bore through this fast-paced series."
—*The Washington Post*

"Courtland Gentry, also known as the Gray Man, is everything you'd want in a fictional professional killer . . . [He] always gets the job done for the US of A, and he entertains while doing it . . . This one is fat, fast, and fun. Clancy's spirit lives on."
—*Kirkus Reviews* (starred review)

"Outstanding . . . Gray Man fans will close the book happily fulfilled and eagerly awaiting his next adventure."
—*Publishers Weekly* (starred review)

"Nonstop thrills and terrific set pieces make this a strong addition to the series."
—*Booklist*

"From start to finish, *Gunmetal Gray* impresses with a well-laid-out plot and enough action to satisfy even the pickiest thriller fans . . . Nobody is on a hotter streak right now than Mark Greaney."
—*The Real Book Spy*

PRAISE FOR *BACK BLAST*

"Mark Greaney reigns as one of the recognized masters of action and adventure. *Back Blast* is no exception."
—Steve Berry, *New York Times* and #1 international bestselling author

"Fast-paced [and] tightly written . . . A great ride."
—Larry Bond, *New York Times* bestselling author

"Punches with bone-busting power . . . Flesh-and-blood priceless."
—Stephen Templin, *New York Times* bestselling author

continued . . .

"Greaney's unraveling of the *Back Blast* mystery is masterly, but it's the Gray Man's ability to outthink and outgun . . . that will keep readers glued to the pages." —*Publishers Weekly* (starred review)

"[A] high-energy thriller . . . Clancy fans will have a blast." —*Kirkus Reviews*

TITLES BY MARK GREANEY

GUNMETAL GRAY

MARK GREANEY

BERKLEY
NEW YORK

BERKLEY
An imprint of Penguin Random House LLC
375 Hudson Street, New York, New York 10014

ISBN: 9780451489739

The Library of Congress has catalogued the Berkley hardcover edition of this book as follows:

Names: Greaney, Mark, author.
Title: Gunmetal gray / Mark Greaney.
Description: First Edition. | New York : Berkley, 2017.
Identifiers: LCCN 2016037708 (print) | LCCN 2016043046 (ebook) |
ISBN 9780425282854 (hardback) | ISBN 9780698406858 (ebook)
Subjects: LCSH: Assassins—Fiction. | BISAC: FICTION / Espionage. |
FICTION / Action & Adventure. | GSAFD: Suspense fiction
Classification: LCC PS3607.R4285 G86 2017 (print) | LCC PS3607.R4285 (ebook)
| DDC 813/.6—dc23
LC record available at https://lccn.loc.gov/2016037708

Berkley hardcover edition / February 2017
Berkley trade edition / January 2018

Printed in the United States of America
1 3 5 7 9 10 8 6 4 2

Cover design by Steve Meditz
Cover photos: skyscrapers © d3sign/Getty Images; helicopter © Oaker Min/Getty Images
Book design by Kelly Lipovich

For Major (Ret.) Thomas H. Greer
aka Dalton Fury

A good man
(1964–2016)

ACKNOWLEDGMENTS

I would like to thank David Leslie, Scott Swanson, Sean Fontaine, Nick Ciubotariu, Igor Veksler, Darrin Ingram, Mike Cowan, Chris Clarke, Patrick O'Daniel, Lt. Col Hunter Rawlings (USMC), Devon Greaney, Devin Greaney, Dorothy Greaney, Jack Murphy at SOFREP.com, Benedetta Argentieri, Jon Harvey, Nichole Geer Roberts, Dalton Fury, Jeff Belanger, Jay Chase of Houston PD, Chris and David Arrington, Gino and Natalie Debouvry, Mystery Mike Bursaw, James Yeager at tacticalresponse.com, and James Fleming at warfighterconcepts.com.

Special thanks to my agent, Scott Miller, and his great team at Trident Media Group, and my editor, Tom Colgan. Also special thanks to my publicist, Loren Jaggers, and all the talented people at Penguin Random House.

GUNMETAL
GRAY

Stay low, go fast, kill first, die last, one shot, one kill, no luck, all skill.

—*UNOFFICIAL NAVY SEAL SLOGAN*

There is only the trying. The rest is not our business.

—*T. S. ELIOT*

CHARACTERS

Courtland "Court" Gentry: The Gray Man, code name Violator—freelance assassin/contract agent for the Central Intelligence Agency

Matthew Hanley: Director of the National Clandestine Service, Central Intelligence Agency

Suzanne Brewer: Officer, National Clandestine Service, Central Intelligence Agency

Fan Jiang: Chief Sergeant Class 3, cyber intrusion specialist, People's Liberation Army, Unit 61398 (Red Cell Detachment), 2nd Bureau, General Staff Department (3rd Department)

Dai Longhai: Colonel, department director of security and counterintelligence, People's Liberation Army, 2nd Bureau, General Staff Department (3rd Department)

Xi: Major, counterintelligence officer, People's Liberation Army, 2nd Bureau, General Staff Department (3rd Department)

Sir Donald Fitzroy: Director and CEO of Cheltenham Security Services; former handler of Court Gentry

Zoya Feodorova Zakharova: Code name Banshee—officer, Russian Foreign Intelligence Service (SVR)

Oleg Utkin: Code name Fantom—officer, Russian Foreign Intelligence Service (SVR)

Vasily: "Anna One"—paramilitary officer and team leader, Russian Foreign Intelligence Service (SVR), Zaslon (Shield) Unit

Tu Van Duc: Leader of Con Ho Hoang Da (the Wild Tigers), Vietnam-based criminal organization

Bui Ton Tan: Officer, Vietnam People's Police and employee of Con Ho Hoang Da

Kulap Chamroon: Co-leader of the Chamroon Syndicate, Thailand-based transnational criminal syndicate

Nattapong Chamroon: Brother of Kulap, co-leader of the Chamroon Syndicate, Thailand-based transnational criminal syndicate

Song Julong: Major and security officer, People's Liberation Army, People's Republic of China

GUNMETAL GRAY

PROLOGUE

The two bodyguards lay unconscious on the floor, arms and legs splayed, an empty bottle of imported whiskey on the table between them. They'd both lost consciousness within seconds of each other, and then they slid out of their chairs and down to the carpet, wholly unaware they'd been drugged, utterly clueless to the fact that the man they were paid to watch over had spiked their booze with a week's supply of nighttime cold medicine.

And now the culprit sat on the couch across from them in the darkened hotel room, and he stared at the big men on the floor. His hands trembled as he rubbed his knees; bile from his stomach churned up and scorched his esophagus. He forced himself to swallow it back down so he could breathe.

Twenty-six-year-old Fan Jiang made no noise, but his brain screamed, *Go, Fan! Get up and run, now!*

But he could not make himself stand.

When the two men on the floor finally woke, it would take them some time to come to their senses and realize their protectee had fled. Fan Jiang knew they would be slow to comprehend the situation, because it was clear to him Sergeant Liu and Sergeant Chen didn't think that a little shit like him had the balls to make a break for it.

The jury was still out on whether they were right or wrong, because fifteen minutes after the two men dropped, Fan still sat there paralyzed in the dark.

The two Chinese army sergeants were close-protection security officers—bodyguards in the parlance of the trade. But the term had a double meaning when applied to these men watching Fan Jiang. True, it was the job of Sergeants Liu and Chen to protect Fan with their lives, throwing their own bodies between any threat and their protectee, if necessary.

But it was also their job to bring back Fan Jiang's dead body if he ever tried to run.

And now it was time for him to run . . . but he just could *not* fucking get up and go.

It was a rare occurrence when Fan Jiang was allowed to leave the military compound in Shanghai where he worked, but he'd been flown over here to Shenzhen along with his minders so he could attend the annual China Information Technology Expo. Fan was a sergeant in the People's Liberation Army, a computer programmer, and one of the most highly placed cyber intrusion specialists in the nation. From time to time he or others in his unit were sent to see advances in computer tech from international vendors, to ask questions of foreign engineers, and to get a feel for how strong private industry's encryption advances would be three, five, ten years out.

So when he needed to travel, Chief Sergeant Class 3 Fan Jiang traded his uniform for civilian clothes and flew on Air China, with Senior Sergeant Chen and Chief Sergeant Class 4 Liu flanking him at all times, themselves in business suits.

On the flight over, the security protocol called for the two security officers to take the window and aisle seats while Fan got the middle, and one of the protectors even followed Fan to the bathroom, standing just outside the door to make certain he had no unauthorized contacts.

The three men stayed in a suite together at the Sheraton Shenzhen Futian Hotel, a few blocks from the Shenzhen Convention and Exhibition Center, which meant that keeping tabs on Fan was a breeze for Liu and Chen in the off-hours. Each night when the trade show ended they all just went back up to the suite and ordered room service; Fan sat on his bed and ate while his two bodyguards dined on their rollaway beds between Fan and the door, their pistols on or next to their bodies at all times.

But during the exhibition itself, it was all work for the bodyguards; the event lasted three days, and for eight to ten hours each of these days Fan walked the huge exhibition center floor, posing as an engineer for a Chinese computer firm. Liu and Chen acted as Fan's colleagues, but they said nothing while Fan did all the talking, taking business cards and promotional material and asking techie questions of techie types from all over the world. The two quiet men with him were well trained to keep him safe and to keep him in line, competing roles that could both be best managed only by close physical proximity and constant vigilance.

The three days on the conference floor passed without incident, but the last evening in Shenzhen was critical, because Liu and Chen knew that anyone who attempted to go AWOL while traveling would likely do it either the moment they arrived at their destination or on the last night. The last night was prime time for a man to do a runner, true, but meek little Fan had given them no trouble, nor could either of them envision a scenario that had him acting counter to his orders. He was a tiny, frail, bespectacled, fragile little geek, and when it came down to following commands, he was nothing if not a good soldier.

Liu and Chen celebrated the end of the stress of walking the floors of a busy conference full of potential threats for three days, having to guard a man in the presence of literally thousands of foreign actors, by picking up a bottle of Jack Daniel's in a market across the street from the hotel.

Neither of them recognized it at the time, but the Jack Daniel's was the kid's idea in the first place. He said he needed to get some cold medicine, so the three men entered the market. Fan and Chen walked over to the health aisles and the younger man picked out what he needed while Chen looked on and Liu stood at the front counter. Fan stopped at a liquor display, looked it up and down, and commented on how inexpensive the booze was here as compared to the prices he'd seen on the room service card by his bed. With a shrug he suggested to Chen that if they wanted to order a drink tonight with their meal they'd save the Ministry of Defense a lot of yuan by just picking up a bottle here.

Liu and Chen were not allowed to drink on the job; Fan knew this, and he also knew they would see this as a perfect opportunity to subvert their orders and enjoy themselves, without anyone in their command being the wiser.

A minute later the men walked out the door of the market with a bottle of whiskey and a bottle of Coke. Their plan had morphed from a quick room-service meal and then bed before the early flight the next day back to the locked-down compound in Shanghai, to a long evening of drinking and watching television.

Now it was two thirty in the morning and the bottle of Jack was empty, as was the box of cold medicine. Liu and Chen were incapacitated, true, but Fan was positively frozen himself—worried they'd wake tomorrow and he'd still be right here, staring back at them like a stone statue of a terrified and guilt-ridden little man.

Fan took another long look at the two men in the dark. He had nothing against Liu and Chen; they were not nice to him in any respect but they were government security men—Fan had been around the type since university, and he'd yet to meet one who'd treated a protectee of his low rank with any sort of deference or even kindness. But he knew that they had *their* job to do and he had *his*, and if Fan got away, he knew they'd probably be placed in front of a firing squad for their failure.

But Fan rationalized this away—this wasn't his fault. He didn't *want* to run.

He *had* to run.

Finally he forced himself to stand, to collect his things, and to heave his backpack over his shoulder. With this newfound momentum he moved as softly as he could across the room and opened the hallway door. He shut it behind him with even more care, then tiptoed away from the hotel room and up the carpeted hall, heading for the stairs.

On the way there he did one last thing. With his heart pounding so hard he felt certain he could hear it echo off the walls around him, he reached out, put his hand on the fire alarm . . . and pulled it down.

Alarm bells screamed in the still hall, and Fan ran for his life.

It was on; there was no turning back.

Three hours before the first light of day, Chief Sergeant Class 3 Fan Jiang of the People's Liberation Army, Unit 61398, 2nd Bureau, General Staff Department (3rd Department), one of the most talented computer hackers on Earth and one of only a few entrusted with the virtual keys to China's digital kingdom, left through the side entrance of the Sheraton in the middle of a large group of guests that overwhelmed hotel security: a fast-moving mass of humanity reacting to the fire alarm. When Fan was clear of the crowd on the street, he turned to the south and then headed off through the city, in the general direction of mainland China's border with Hong Kong.

CHAPTER

ONE

The sleek executive jet descended out of the gray clouds just three miles west of runway 07 Left. As it lowered its landing gear, a set of binoculars focused on the plane, watching it streak over the water on its final approach.

"I've always wanted to kill a CIA officer. With my own hands. I've dreamed of the day, wrapping my fingers around his throat, squeezing the life from him, watching his eyes bug out and then go blank."

The comment was in Mandarin, and it came not from the man with the binoculars but from his partner, on his left. Both stood on the roof of an airport outbuilding, doing their best to ignore the stifling morning heat. The man with the binoculars also did his best to ignore his colleague, and he kept his focus on the approaching aircraft.

He replied in Mandarin, as well. "Dassault Falcon. Might be a model Seven X. This should be our target."

"Can you read the tail number?"

"Negative. Still too far."

"Killing a CIA man won't be anything like that guy I strangled Monday. I predict a CIA man will have real muscles in his neck. He'll be a real fighter."

With a muted sigh, the man with the binoculars said, "Why are you talking like this, Tao?"

"Because if someone gets off that plane, I predict Control will order us to terminate them. What do you think?"

"I think you are almost as crazy as Control."

The man behind the Pentax binos kept his gaze fixed on the airplane as it touched down, then slowed on the runway. He checked the tail number now that it was close enough to make out through the ten-power lenses.

"It's a match."

"Good."

Both men were relieved to see that the intelligence reports about the arrival of the plane had been accurate. The aircraft from America was right on time, and this meant the duo wouldn't have to stand around up here on the hot roof all damn day.

While the man with the optics watched carefully, the aircraft taxied to the customs ramp, then over to the tarmac in front of Hong Kong Business Aviation Center, a fixed-base operator popular with high-end corporate jets visiting the city. Both Chinese nationals lowered their bodies to low squats to decrease any faint chance they could be detected from a cabin window. They didn't expect to be spotted, because they did this sort of thing all the time and were confident in their skills, but the target today was likely to be someone adept in surveillance detection and countersurveillance measures, so they took no chances.

As intelligence officers with China's Ministry of State Security, Wang Ping Li and Tao Man Koh were, by law anyway, precluded from working here without notifying the authorities in the Special Administrative Region of Hong Kong of the People's Republic of China. The mainland had its rules, and HK, officially speaking, followed a different set of rules when it came to security matters. But these men were spies, and spies rarely followed the rules, and these two even less so, because they weren't just *any* spies.

Their real mission in Hong Kong, the reason Tao and Wang and two dozen other men like them were here in the first place, meant they wouldn't be checking in with the local authorities. They were ghosts, smoke.

They were assassins.

Wang didn't like this morning's pedestrian work, but he understood the situation. Airplanes operated by known CIA front companies landed at Hong Kong International Airport from time to time, but never this particular jet, so these two intelligence officers had been sent to check it out. It was a distraction, but orders were orders and they'd been ordered here.

That these were the only men close enough to respond to the request by the Ministry of State Security was unfortunate for them. Their real job here was for the Ministry of Defense; it was high-end wet work, and if it turned out getting an ID of the passengers of the Falcon took more than a couple of hours, their MOD control officer would hear they were off *his* job, and he'd ride them hard about it, their orders from Beijing be damned.

Because, in the viewpoint of these two men, MOD Control was *fucking* nuts, and getting crazier by the day.

Wang and Tao both had their long-range cameras out when the aircraft's main hatch opened, and a black Mercedes S-Class pulled up in front of it. A rear door opened on the far side of the car, and both intelligence operatives focused their lenses there, assuming the Mercedes would disgorge a passenger. But the opposite happened. A man carrying his own luggage stepped down the jet's stairs quickly and disappeared into the front passenger seat behind the smoked glass of the Mercedes.

"Shit! Did you get him?" Wang asked quietly.

"I'm not a photographer. If I had a sniper rifle, he'd be dead now."

"Not what I asked."

"I was focused on the back door of the Mercedes. I thought someone would come out. You?"

"I'll check." Wang looked back at the digital images on his camera. "I don't have a clear image of the face; he's shielding the sun with his hand. Dark hair, beard, gray suit, sunglasses. He's Western, for certain. Gold wedding band on his left hand. Roll-aboard luggage and a backpack."

"Whoever he is, he'll be dead by sundown."

Wang stowed his camera in his backpack. "Would you stop with that, already? Let's get to the car."

"That limo service is geotracked. We can see the movements of each car in their fleet from my laptop. Wherever the Mercedes takes him, we'll know."

"And if this man should get out along the route?"

The two walked quickly along the roof towards the stairs, their suits sticking to them with perspiration. Tao asked, "Why would he do that?" Wang replied, "Because he is CIA and trained in countersurveillance." Tao felt some shame in not thinking the situation through. He made up for his humiliation by being the first to arrive at the stairs and the first to make it down to the black Toyota Aurion, an Australian-made vehicle that blended in well with the traffic here in the city of nearly eight million.

With Tao behind the wheel they fell in behind the black Mercedes as it left the front gate of the Hong Kong Business Aviation Center and entered the busy morning traffic of Chek Lap Kok Road.

While he drove, Tao said, "Colonel Dai is going to find out we're off tailing some guy who has nothing to do with our assignment for MOD, and he's going to order us to terminate him. Or else Dai will take it out on us, give us the crap jobs, a reprimand. The Americans have a saying." He switched to English because both men spoke it well. "Shit runs downhill."

Wang sniffed. "That's not a saying. That's physics." And then he continued, "If anything, Colonel Dai will get us to rough him up, interrogate him, scare him out of town. This won't go lethal."

With that, Tao took his eyes off the road in front of him and looked to his passenger. "Disagree. Dai had us kill the man at the border, and he had Su and Lin kill the two Triads in Shek Kong. Fan Jiang's bodyguards were executed the day after he ran in Shenzhen, and Dai gave that order, as well. The colonel is in a killing mood on this job, you must admit. I say Dai will have us terminate this CIA boy and dump his body in the harbor and then lie to Beijing about it." Tao sniffed. "Dai is mad."

"Stark raving," Wang agreed. "But a dead CIA officer in Hong Kong will just make his operation *more* complicated, not less."

Tao was unyielding in his opinion. "Complicated for us. Not for him. Colonel Dai doesn't give a damn. Beijing has given Dai free rein, so *that* man in *that* Mercedes will be dead by midnight. There are no fucking rules for Dai in Hong Kong these days." After a dry little chuckle in the back of his throat, he added, "The streets of this city will be running rivers of blood before this one's over."

CHAPTER

TWO

Courtland Gentry sat in the front passenger seat of the Mercedes, much to the confusion of his driver. Normally passengers sat in the back and their luggage rode in the trunk, but Court had hurried off the aircraft and into the front of the car to disrupt any potential surveillance at the FBO, and since the driver didn't know anything about tradecraft, he thought this American to be some kind of a weirdo.

Court hadn't seen the two men on the roof, but he saw them now, or at least he saw the black Aurion varying between six and ten car lengths behind his Mercedes, always there, despite the turnoffs, red lights, and off-and-on gridlocked traffic of a Hong Kong workday.

Court had picked up a tail and he hadn't even been on the ground here in HK for ten *fucking* minutes.

Terrific.

He considered bailing out of the Mercedes somewhere en route to his destination to lose the surveillance detail, but he figured this driver was probably an informant for Chinese intelligence, and the man would just pass on the fact that his passenger had, with no warning, dived from his hired car and dashed up some alley.

Nope, that wouldn't do. Court's cover for status had to be maintained, which meant Court would just pretend like he didn't see the black car lurking behind him.

He'd been here to HK before, but only once. To the extent he had a regular beat, East Asia certainly wasn't it, so he did his best to push the tail car out of his mind and instead spend his time doing all he could to observe the fabric of life on the streets around him. He noted what the police cars looked like, where the street signs were located, the flow of traffic, and the manner of dress of the commuters. He made a mental note of the cardinal positions of several major buildings in view. He'd spent hours of his flight over from the States prepping for his op here, but he'd not had time to digest more than a thumbnail sketch of this area of operations—and as he had learned countless times in the past, not only was the map not the territory, but most preconceived notions about a place were dead wrong.

You really had to experience a location to know it at an operational level.

Court had a lot of work to do to get up to speed, but his assignment here was as time sensitive as they came, so he'd have to work out the atmospherics of this AO while on the job.

His car drove onto the Tsing Yi Bridge, and he glanced back in the passenger-side mirror to confirm that the black Aurion continued to follow. It was in a reasonable position for a tail car; Court gave these boys credit for knowing their stuff, but he had been either the tailer or the tailee thousands of times in his life, so sniffing out a car on his six was nothing to him.

Both vehicles left the bridge, continued south along the water, and finally entered the Hong Kong district of Tsim Sha Tsui, on the southern tip of Kowloon. The black sedan was still back there, which meant to Court this tail on him was a simple affair. There were no teams of vehicles in radio contact leapfrogging all around, which was what he would have expected if mainland China's Ministry of State Security was working here and had ordered up a large surveillance package on him. Either the guys in the tail car were working for some group not tied to the Chinese intelligence services, or else Chinese intel found him more of a curiosity than a real concern, so they just sent a couple of men to see where he was heading and what he was up to.

Looking away from the mirror, he got his first glimpse of his hotel. The five-star Peninsula Hong Kong sat at the southern tip of Kowloon, just across the street from the harbor ferry terminal. He was anxious to get into his room—not so he could rest after the two-leg, nineteen-hour flight from the United States; rather so he could whip out his encrypted phone and call his handler. He would let her know about the surveillance, and he would let her have it, because this bullshit wasn't his damn fault, and it could ruin this mission before it began.

No, Court told himself. This wouldn't hurt the op. It *couldn't*, because his assignment here was possibly the most important of his life. The potential for gain was exponentially larger than any intelligence haul he'd ever heard of short of wartime.

And lives were on the line, including the life of a man who had saved Court Gentry years ago.

Court told himself he would not fail. Regardless of the hurdles ahead, he would see this through somehow, even if he had these Chinese mother-fuckers breathing down his neck for the duration of his assignment.

The Mercedes drove around the fountain in front of the Peninsula and stopped under the awning. A bellman opened the back door, but Court climbed out of the front seat with barely a nod to his driver. He handled his own luggage and passed the attentive bellmen with a curt nod, like he was a businessman who did this every day of his life.

A stunning fleet of green Rolls-Royce Phantoms, eight in total, were lined up near the entrance to the hotel, and Court pretended to give a damn about them, just as a foreign businessman might. He knew the cars were here to take the well-heeled guests to and fro around Hong Kong, and he wouldn't mind going for a ride in the back of a luxurious classic car, but this wasn't going to be that type of assignment. No, he figured he'd likely spend his time skulking alone in shady alleys and cracking heads in opium dens and strip clubs.

Despite the nice hotel and his nice suit, he fully expected to find himself serving as a low-grade ground pounder on this gig, not a high-flying cock-tail circuit spook.

After slowing a moment to fulfill his cover by looking over the Rolls-Royce fleet approvingly, he returned to his brisk pace and entered the lobby.

Five minutes later he was checked into his twenty-fifth-floor room. It wasn't a suite but it was roomy and ornate. It came with a dramatic floor-to-ceiling view of Victoria Harbor. Beyond the congested waterway, the massive skyscrapers of Hong Kong Island shot skyward. Past the stunning urban landscape, lush hills dwarfed the buildings, and Victoria Peak, the highest point in HK, was completely hidden by the low cloud ceiling.

Court took in the view just for a moment before dropping his roll-aboard and his backpack on the bed, fishing in his luggage for his mobile phone and its battery, and reassembling the device.

He turned on his room's impressive stereo system, made sure the surround-sound speakers were each playing with the "all channel" stereo mode to remove the chance that a hidden surveillance mic happened to be positioned near a speaker that was only blaring music intermittently, and then he chose a station playing some annoying techno that was sure to madden anyone who might be eavesdropping. Court then entered the spacious bathroom and turned on the spigot in the tub. The sounds of water moving through pipes in the walls would play havoc on a microphone positioned nearby.

More than once in his own career he'd had to yank headphones from his ears and throw them across the room to save himself from the roar of a filling tub or the thunder of a flushing toilet.

Court's mobile was encrypted with nonproprietary, off-the-shelf software that had been tweaked to improve the performance of the encryption but not augmented with any gadgetry that would give away the fact that Court got it from the Science and Technology Division of the CIA. It would withstand examination by experts at even top-tier intelligence organizations. If they ever got their hands on it, he'd seem like a paranoid businessman, an anti-surveillance technology geek, but he would *not* look like a government spy.

Gentry's primary cover was as an American businessman, but his secondary cover was that of a freelance assassin—a hit man without portfolio—and he wasn't about to give that away by using gear with the Agency's fingerprints on it.

It took a moment for his phone to establish a connection, but when it went through, the call was answered on the first ring.

"Brewer."

Court checked his watch and saw that it was ten p.m. in Langley, Virginia, and he wondered if Suzanne Brewer was still in her office.

He said, "Violator."

"Identity challenge, Roadster." He heard a hint of relief in her voice. Court knew she'd been anticipating his call.

"My response is Renaissance."

"Challenge response confirmed. I assume your operation is proceeding nominally."

"Not even close. There's a problem."

"A *problem*? By the clock on my desk you should just now be arriving at your hotel. Is your bed too lumpy?"

"I've got a tail."

"Oh." A pause. "Are you—"

Court interrupted. "Yes, I'm sure."

"How the hell did you manage to pick up a tail?"

"My plane landed, and there was a surveillance team waiting for me in a car as I left the airport."

Another pause. "That's problematic."

"*Problematic?* At Langley, yeah, I guess that's how it looks. Here, from my angle, it looks like an utter clusterfuck. How am I supposed to do this job with eyes on me?"

Brewer remained detached and professional. "I understand your concern, Violator. I'll begin a review immediately, look into the aircraft, see if there is a chance—"

"Who knows about this operation?"

Brewer answered without hesitation. "You, me, and Hanley. Full stop."

Matthew Hanley was the CIA's new director of the National Clandestine Service. Court had a long history with Hanley, whereas his relationship with Suzanne Brewer was less than twenty-four hours old. But she was his handler, his single contact, his *one* lifeline with the Agency on this operation. He had to work with her, and to some extent, he had to trust her.

But Court wasn't a trusting guy. "You're sure about that?"

"Absolutely certain. Look, this isn't about you. *Can't* be. Whoever it is that's following you doesn't know who you are. They must just somehow know the plane belongs to us, so whoever climbed off the plane is now their target."

"I hope you're right."

Brewer said, "I'm always right. We just met, so you can't know that yet, but you will learn soon enough."

"You sure as hell weren't right about the jet."

"That wasn't *my* jet. That was the transport Hanley arranged. I'm as new to this op as you are." She thought a moment. "If the Chinese know it's an

Agency asset, then we won't use it again. When the job is done, *I'll* fly you out of there on a clean aircraft, I promise you that."

Court gazed out the window and down at the harbor, twenty-five floors down. Dozens of different watercraft of all sizes and types were in sight. "Maybe I'd be safer on one of these old junks bobbing in the harbor."

"That's your call, but until you complete your op, no slow boats for you. The clock is ticking. You know what's at stake here."

Court breathed into the phone for a moment. "The men tailing me. Do they pose a physical danger?"

"How can I answer that? I don't even know who they are."

"I only spotted one vehicle, but the surveillance was competently conducted. I'm guessing they are MSS. My question is: have any Chinese intel operatives killed any Agency operatives in the past . . . I don't know, ten years?"

Brewer was unequivocal in her response. "Negative. It's been more than twenty years, actually. And you're in Hong Kong, not Beijing. Hong Kong has autonomy, in theory, anyway. If MSS is roving around there in force, it would only happen after the Chinese broke a lot of rules."

"But it *could* happen."

Brewer walked back her last comment. "Sure. We know MSS is there in Hong Kong, obviously. Your entire operation is based on the presumption that the Chinese are conducting intel ops in HK. I'm only saying it isn't the same as it would be if you were on the mainland, in Beijing or Shanghai. Also there are transnational criminal groups in HK—the Triads, a few of whom China holds some sway over."

"So you're saying the MSS might send some local gang to target me."

She thought this over before answering. "I guess it's possible if they felt they had to. But you won't give them a reason, now, will you?"

Court lay back on the bed, staring at the ceiling. "For some reason, I tend to find my way to people's wrong side."

"Then I guess you'll have to be on your best behavior."

Court blew out a sigh. "Look, I'm going below radar."

"What does that mean?"

"It means I need to lose these guys, to shake any possible compromise. I won't be checking in for a while."

Brewer took her time responding. Then she said, "Well, you are certainly experienced in working alone."

"And I'm sure you are experienced in conducting reviews of company failures." It was a shitty thing to say. Court knew he didn't need to get off on a bad foot with Suzanne Brewer, but he'd been on his own for five years and was unaccustomed to this bullshit. He was back with the Agency for the first time in a half decade, in a thin quasi relationship, anyway, and he wasn't a team player who knew how to pick and choose his battles.

Brewer could have gotten her hackles up, Court realized, but instead she remained professional and even contrite. "Remember, you aren't there on a direct-action mission. You make contact with your target, garner as much intel as you can about the situation, then report in and get out of there. This isn't you against the bad guys." She added, "Sorry about the glitch here at the beginning."

Court Gentry softened. "It's not your fault. I'll check in down the road." He hung up, then listened to the techno music for a minute more. Soon he climbed off the bed, crossed the room, and turned that shit off.

Twenty-five floors below, Wang Ping Li and Tao Man Koh sat in a conference room in the administrative suite of the Peninsula hotel, watching silently while the day manager stood and left the room. The man had been angry about informing on one of his guests, and he'd made a show about demanding Wang's and Tao's credentials, but it was only a show, and while both operatives knew they could have filed a report on the manager's recalcitrance, they weren't here in HK to gauge the party loyalty of hoteliers.

And anyway, after a little huffing and puffing, the manager *was* playing ball. He'd already told them that the guest who'd arrived in the Mercedes was traveling under the name Roger Hartley, and he was ostensibly a businessman from Ohio in the United States. The intelligence officers didn't have the man's passport to look at; hotels here in Hong Kong, unlike in China proper, were under no obligation to take their guests' passports, and the five-star properties like the Peninsula distanced themselves from China by not doing so.

But even though on the surface the Peninsula acted high minded about guests' rights, in truth Roger Hartley's room was already bugged with listening devices; most four- and five-star hotels in HK maintained rooms wired by MSS as a matter of course, though the bugs weren't turned on unless there was a specific need. Tao would make a call to initiate twenty-four-hour monitoring of Hartley's room now that he had the room number, and he'd follow up hourly with the listeners for updates.

The manager returned with a pair of key cards and handed them over without a word. This would give Tao and Wang access to the room directly across the hall from Hartley; as it happened it had been vacant, but if a guest had been staying there, the annoyed hotel manager would have moved them out under some emergency-repair ruse. Through a pinhole camera Wang and Tao would attach to their door's peephole they would have a perfect view of Hartley's door, and through the motion-detector setting on the device they'd be sure they wouldn't miss him leaving his room.

The manager had also handed over extra copies of cards that would get them into Hartley's room itself, in case they wanted to make entry when the man was out.

After passing over the key cards, the manager walked the two intelligence operatives out of the conference room and back into the lobby. He bid them an insincere good day, then turned and went back inside.

Tao looked to Wang. "He was disrespectful."

"No time to make trouble for him. He gets a pass for now. Let's go to the room."

Tao nodded, then said, "Should we call in more eyes to assist?"

"Who? Everyone else here is working for Ministry of Defense. When Colonel Dai finds out we've been pulled off his operation, he'll be angry enough. If we start removing others to help us, he'll lose his mind."

The two men headed for the elevators. As soon as the door closed, the mobile phone rang in Tao's jacket. He looked at the incoming number, then immediately handed the phone over to Wang.

"It's him."

Wang took the phone from Tao and answered with a report, not even waiting to be asked where the hell they were. *"Way, ni hao, Shangxio."* Yes, hello, Colonel. "We were ordered by our Beijing Control to divert from your operation here and proceed to the airport. An American CIA Dassault Falcon Seven X, tail number—"

Wang stopped talking abruptly and just listened; Tao could tell he'd been interrupted. The elevator stopped and the two men headed up the hall.

Wang spoke again, more softly now. "Yes, sir. Our orders were made clear to us. We then followed our subject to the Peninsula, and we have taken a room across from—"

He stopped speaking again; Tao could hear the voice of the man through the phone at Wang's ear.

The two men were already in their room with the door shut when Wang spoke again. "I understand, sir. But this came from our department . . . not yours. Apologies, but despite our seconding to you, our chain of command retains authority to—"

For a third time Wang was interrupted. Tao looked on while Wang listened, nodded compliantly, and ended the call. He looked uncomfortable but made no remarks to his junior colleague.

"What did he say?" Tao finally asked.

"What do you think? He's mad we left his op to follow the MSS directive, as if we had a choice."

Tao was the junior man, but he chanced a comment. "Colonel Dai has his own ass on the line on this operation for some reason. The next call we get from him will be the one ordering us to terminate the subject."

Wang took off his suit coat, still a little damp from his time on the hot roof at the airport. "He's after a promotion, or maybe, as you suggest, there is some other reason for his personal involvement. If Dai fails here, it will be men like us who will suffer."

Tao held up a finger. "No. Not men *like* us. It will be us, exactly. That's why we should terminate the CIA man and—"

Wang waved a hand in the air. "I've been doing this longer than you, Tao. Get it out of your head. We're here on a surveillance job for MSS, and then we will go back to being two more good little soldiers for Ministry of Defense. Nobody is killing anybody until we find Fan Jiang, or until someone gets in our way."

Tao said, "Roger Hartley is in Dai's way already. And Colonel Dai doesn't mess around."

CHAPTER

THREE

C ourt had spent almost all of the past nineteen hours in the air, and he'd worked through nearly all of the flight. He'd known nothing about his assignment when he boarded the Falcon, not even if he would accept it, but before the plane took to the sky he'd read his eyes-only orders and he was fully on board with the mission. And by the time the plane had reached its cruising altitude, Court had sketched out a mental to-do list for the long flight ahead of him.

The flight attendant, herself a CIA employee, had brought him dinner and offered him drinks, but he ate lightly and drank nothing but water and coffee, knowing he needed a plan of action to hit the ground running in HK more than he needed a buzz, a heavy stomach, and some shut-eye.

Now he knew that both jet lag and hunger would kick in before long, but he had more work to do. He opened his carry-on and his backpack and dumped everything out onto the bed. He went through each item slowly and carefully, because he'd not packed these bags himself and none of these belongings were his.

He'd already been through this gear on the plane, but he wanted to go over it again. In addition to clothing and toiletries, it had all manner of mission-specific items, from encrypted mobiles to infrared scopes masked as binoculars. He'd taken only a small portion of the equipment left for him on the Falcon, and now he decided to pare this down even more. Most anything could have a GPS tracker in it these days, and he didn't want the CIA knowing his exact whereabouts, just in case someone in the CIA had passed on the tip about the plane's identity and arrival here in the first place.

Now he sat on his bed and searched everything that came off the plane with him. He found nothing that raised an eyebrow, so he thought it likely that Brewer was right—the aircraft itself had been compromised.

He knew what he had to do to get back on track. Tonight he would lose his tail, and tomorrow, when no one knew he was the guy who got off that CIA aircraft, he would intentionally pick his tail back up again, because those were his orders from Langley.

This was going to be a weird op, of this he was certain.

He'd come to meet with a man who had been detained by the Chinese, and since he didn't know where this man was, the only way to find him was to make the Chinese aware of who he was and who he was looking for.

But they could *not* know he was here on a mission for the CIA, or this whole operation would fall to pieces.

He grabbed a pillow from the bed, stepped into the closet, lay down on the carpet, and fell asleep while the hot Hong Kong day raged on outside.

everal hours later Court sat at the bar at the Felix, an ultra-chic Philippe Starck–designed restaurant on the top floor of the hotel. The view over the harbor was breathtaking; the lights of Hong Kong Island to the south looked like the Manhattan skyline as seen by a helicopter from just a few hundred yards away. In fact, in many ways it was more dramatic; HK was the world's tallest urban agglomeration, with one building reaching 118 stories and 312 buildings standing at least 150 yards high, many more than in New York City.

While Court ate a steak and drank a beer at the bar with his back to the windows, forty-four buildings on both sides of Victoria Harbor flashed colors synchronized to music in the nightly Symphony of Lights show. Well-dressed men and women stood at the windows of the Felix and marveled at the spectacle, even though it happened every evening.

Court didn't turn and look at the lights, and neither did one other man in the room. Tao Man Koh sat at a table near the window high above the harbor and sipped a glass of wine. Through the reflection in the glass next to him he could see the back of the American, and he kept eyes out for anyone who might try to communicate with him in a clandestine fashion.

So far he'd not seen a thing that gave him any impression that Roger Hartley was anything other than a businessman here having a meal, but he continued his covert surveillance, careful not to give himself away.

While Tao watched the target, his partner Wang Ping Li stood in the middle of the hotel room of the man he knew as Roger Hartley, checking the area carefully one more time. He'd done this an hour earlier upon his arrival in the room, scanning for anything out of the ordinary, thinking that if Hartley was CIA, he might have prepped his room with hidden cameras or listening devices of his own, or he might have placed objects in specific ways so that he'd know immediately if anything had been tampered with. It was tradecraft 101, and while Wang worked these days as a direct-action operative for the Ministry of State Security, he'd been trained as a simple spook and he knew how to scan a room for telltales.

Wang had spent an additional half hour going through the man's luggage, taking apart his laptop, and looking through the top dozen places someone might hide items in a hotel room. He took the drawer out of the desk, unscrewed heating ducts, searched below trash can liners, behind wall art, under the mattress, even in the toilet tank.

He didn't find a single item of interest.

The phone buzzed in Wang's pocket, and he checked it quickly; it was Tao.

Wang answered in a whisper. "He's moving?"

"Negative. No movement. He ate dinner and he is just sitting and drinking a—"

"I don't give a shit what he's drinking. You are to inform me when he leaves."

Tao asked, "Anything in his room?"

"Nothing. Unless he has something on him right now, he is clean. We might find ourselves following this son of a bitch for days waiting for him to meet someone."

"Doubt it."

Before Wang could respond, his phone told him another call was coming. "Shit. It's Dai now."

"Let me know what he—"

Wang hung up and rejected the new call. He wasn't going to talk to Dai from his target's room. Instead he left and went across the twenty-fifth-floor hallway to his own room, where he immediately hit redial.

Dai answered after several rings. "Still on your little errand for Beijing?"

"Yes, sir."

"What do you have to report?"

"Our target is sitting in the Felix bar at the top of the Peninsula."

"What is he doing?"

"He had dinner, and now he's drinking. Just sitting there. We think he may be waiting to meet someone, but perhaps he's just jet-lagged and lingering over dinner. I have searched his room, but I've found nothing to indicate why he is here."

"I didn't bring you and Tao to Hong Kong to sit in a bar all night. Your real target here could be slipping out of the city at this very moment."

"I understand, sir, but I saw no way to avoid my orders from the Ministry of State Security, which supersedes your command at the Ministry of Defense. I report first to—"

"Wang, let me ask you . . . when I snap your neck the next time I see you, will *that* supersede your orders from State Security?"

Wang just gazed at the floor of his hotel room. Finally he said, "What do you want me to do, sir?"

"Has MSS ordered you to move on the target?"

"No. Just investigate and report contacts."

"How long is the target registered at the hotel?"

Wang hesitated, knowing his answer was going to send Colonel Dai into orbit. "Eight days, sir."

As Wang fully expected, Dai screamed at him. "You aren't sitting in a *fucking* hotel for eight days!"

"Sir, if you would like to speak with MSS I am sure they can send in another team from Beijing and—"

"They already have more assets here in Hong Kong than they are comfortable with! They won't send anyone else!"

Wang had no answer to this so he just sat there, his phone to his ear.

"You will confront the target. Immediately."

"I'm sorry, sir, I don't understand."

"I am ordering you to end this wasted journey and take him. I'm not telling you to terminate the subject. You have drugs to obtain information, do you not?"

"You issued them to each of us the day we arrived."

"Use them. Find out who he is, what he wants. Those drugs will render his memory foggy, so he won't have any idea you questioned him. Then throw him in his bathtub, turn the shower on, and break his leg with the heel of your shoe. When he wakes he'll be too fucked-up to know what happened and too injured to continue his mission here."

Wang spoke the truth now, but his heart wasn't in it. He knew he would lose. "Colonel, you have no authority to order me to circumvent my orders from my divisional director."

"My op here is a national priority mission! I will pull rank on you and change your orders. Call your masters at MSS in exactly fifteen minutes and you will see that your mandate and rules of engagement have been updated. But after that, return to Beijing, don't come back to me. I'll have no use for you or your partner after you challenge my authority. I have thirty-four other men here who would not dare this insubordination that you seem so comfortable with."

Wang knew this was bullshit. Dai was just being petulant.

But Wang also knew Dai had the capacity to make his life hell if he disobeyed him.

Wang said, "No need to contact Beijing, sir. We will comply immediately." Wang didn't need enemies at MOD, especially not someone who could make or break everyone in his family. And on top of this, Wang wouldn't mind roughing up the CIA officer. He'd never done that before.

"Very well," Dai said.

"I will do as you say and report back to you with what we found out."

Dai snapped back. "No. You can tell MSS all about your American; I don't care about him. I only care about my target here in HK. I want you back on *my* job first thing in the morning."

"Shi de, xian sheng." Yes, sir.

Wang hung up and called Tao.

Tao answered with, "Target has asked for the check."

"Our plans have changed." Wang explained Dai's orders.

When Wang finished, Tao asked, "Rules of engagement?"

"We force compliance. We meet resistance with escalating resistance."

"Up to?"

A pause. "Up to everything."

"Told you."

"You *told* me this would be an assassination. It's not that. We take him as he returns to his room. Overpower him, tie him up, drug him, get the intel, and bust him up. Dai wants us back with him in the morning."

"I hope this guy is a fighter." Tao chuckled. "I'll get my check and head down."

Court didn't really want the third beer; he'd barely sipped it, spending most of his time fiddling with his wedding band and pretending to surf the Internet on his phone. He only wore the band for the op; he wasn't married, but the Agency had put it in his backpack on the plane, and he'd recognized it for what it was, so he slipped it on, along with a set of designer eyeglasses that did nothing for his vision but used a special refracted glass to break up the outline of his face to hamper facial recognition software.

Court took his time lounging here at the bar, for the simple reason that he wanted the lookout seated behind him to report to whoever was in his room right now that the coast was clear.

He'd ID'd the watcher minutes after sitting down, pegged him as likely to be one of the men who'd followed him from the airport, because this still felt like a small op. If he was right about that, then there would just be a few other men involved, and they would be conducting a site exploration in Court's room three floors below right now. If this was, indeed, the case, Court wanted to give them plenty of time to do their work.

It wasn't that Court was afraid to confront a couple of guys in his room. The fact was he didn't need the aggravation. He wanted to give the Chinese the time they needed to go through his belongings so he could convince them he was no one worth following, or at least that they didn't need to call in any backup.

He'd decided to simply check out of his hotel tomorrow morning and lose his tail then, but for now he just wanted to look as sedentary, nonthreatening, and downright boring as possible to the men watching him.

Finally he paid his bill, then went to the bathroom here at the Felix to take a leak, giving the men downstairs even more time to clear out of his room. He stood at a space-age-looking urinal in front of floor-to-ceiling windows that looked out and down twenty-eight floors, which Court found bizarre and a little silly, but it was a decent distraction for a man taking his time while taking a piss, and as far as bathrooms went, this one was indeed memorable.

He headed for the elevator. The watcher was gone from his seat by the windows, which Court hoped meant his surveillance team had pulled the plug for the night.

Court fiddled with his key card outside his door for a moment, then slid it into the lock, all the while hoping like hell the sweep had been completed and the man performing it had done a decent job hiding evidence of his search. If it was obvious his belongings had been disturbed, he'd need to report it to hotel management, just to continue along with his ruse that he was like any other Western businessman here. It would be in keeping with his cover that he'd freak out if someone went through his stuff while he was at dinner, so if the goons who searched his room couldn't be bothered to refold his clothes and zip his luggage back up, then Court would have to make a scene.

As soon as Court entered his room, his shoulders sank. Down the little entry hall, past the bathroom ahead on his left, he could just see the front edge of his king-sized bed. His laptop was lying open there; cords, chargers, and socks were strewn about, hanging down to the floor.

Shit, his room had been tossed. He'd have to call the front desk and throw a fit, to pretend he thought housekeeping had rummaged through his belongings.

As he moved forward into the room, he knew the bathroom on his left was a blind spot, and there was a chance a member of the site exploration team was still in there, either working or hiding. The chance was small considering the lookout in the bar had been given ten minutes to warn anyone in his room, but if these guys sucked so bad at their job they didn't even try to clean up after themselves, it was also possible their comms were down.

But even though he thought it possible he might be about to disturb someone in the act, he knew he had to remain in cover. He couldn't just fly into the room and waylay anyone standing there. That wasn't the normal behavior of a businessman who had just downed a steak dinner at a swanky bar.

If it turned out there *was* someone in there squeezing out Court's toothpaste into a rubber glove, Court would just feign shock and confusion, then adopt a posture of nervous anger.

He passed the bathroom and looked in matter-of-factly, and suddenly his already thumping heart began to pound harder. An Asian man in a black tracksuit and dark wraparound sunglasses sat on the toilet seat, and he held a pistol with a suppressor on the end, leveled at Court's chest.

This Court had not expected.

He slowly raised his hands.

Now he heard a key card placed in the door behind him, and then a second man entered. Court looked back over his shoulder to confirm that it was the man in the suit and tie from the bar. He wore dark glasses now, as well.

So, still just the two guys, he said to himself. It seemed to him MSS could scare up fifteen operatives if they wanted something bad to happen to a CIA officer in HK. Perhaps whatever was going on here was off book, or MSS just didn't think they needed much muscle to do whatever it was they were about to do.

Court thought about Suzanne Brewer's assurances that MSS didn't get physical with CIA. Either these dudes weren't MSS, they didn't think he was CIA, or the rules had changed. There was an equation he'd have to solve to sort all this out, but that was a problem for down the road.

The man in the bathroom stood up slowly. He appeared calm, professional, and his English was accented but more than adequate. "Sit on chair by window." He motioned with the pistol for Court to enter the bedroom, and Court complied.

Across the ransacked space, a swivel chair pulled out from the desk sat positioned with its back just inches away from the twenty-fifth-floor window looking out over Victoria Harbor. On the desk to the right of the chair, a set of high-end steel handcuffs lay on a towel.

Court said, "If it's money . . . I have a little cash. My credit cards are in my—"

He felt the tip of the suppressor of the pistol jabbed against the back of his head. The man in the tracksuit spoke from behind. "You sit in chair!"

Court sighed now. "Okay, pal. I sit in chair."

Court crossed the room and sat down. The man in the business suit spun him around to face the window; Court couldn't help but look straight down, twenty stories, to the roof of an adjacent seven-story building below. Beyond that was a busy road, the headlights and taillights snaking in either direction in red and white. Court felt hands on his wrists, and then his arms were yanked behind him and the steel cuffs were clicked tightly in place.

His pockets were rummaged through. His wallet, his phone, and his hotel room key were tossed on the bed, and then he was swung back around to face the two men.

The men spoke to each other in Mandarin for a moment; neither seemed particularly worked up about what they were doing. Then the guy in the tracksuit disappeared into the bathroom.

While he was out of view, Court looked to the other man. "Do you speak English? Will you tell me what is going on?"

The man in the business suit made no reply. Instead he just went to the bed, laid his pistol down on it, and unzipped a black satchel. From it he pulled out two small blue items. In seconds he opened one up and Court recognized it for what it was.

A surgical mask.

Uh-oh.

CHAPTER

FOUR

Tracksuit returned from the bathroom with his suppressed pistol stuck inside his waistband. In his hands he held what appeared to be a Montblanc fountain pen. Business Suit placed a second surgical mask over Tracksuit's face, then pulled out his phone. Court noted that the man's pistol was still on the bed, which told him these guys were more than confident in their capabilities.

Tracksuit waved the pen in the air. "Do you know what this is?"

Court lied. He was pretty sure he knew, but his cover identity would not have a clue. "It's a pen."

"No. It is designed to look like pen. But, in fact, it's blowgun that uses compressed air to fire powerful powder that will alter your mind."

"Heroin? What are you going to do with—"

"Not heroin. Scopolamine hydrobromide. A truth drug. I blow this in your face and you will tell us what we want to know within minutes. Of course, you will be zombie for hours, but that is just side effect."

Court pushed a crack into his voice, the tenor of a man on the verge of panic. "Je-*Jesus*! I'll . . . I'll tell you *now*. No reason to use that shit! I'm just a businessman from Cleveland, here in town to . . . what are you doing?"

Business Suit stepped forward, raised his phone, and took a picture of Court's face, then stepped back to the far side of the bed, near the pistol lying there. Court watched while the man thumbed keys on his phone. He assumed the man was about to e-mail or text the photo to someone.

While Business Suit did this calmly, Tracksuit unscrewed the front of the pen. Like his partner, he was as relaxed as he could be. This was just another day at work for the two of them.

Court realized quickly he wasn't going to be able to talk his way out of this, to satisfy these two that they had the wrong man, or that the CIA plane he'd arrived in was something other than a CIA plane. And Court also knew there was absolutely no way to keep them from sending that picture to Chinese intelligence officials, something that would irrevocably ruin his mission here in Hong Kong.

Actually, there *was* a way. *One* way to save the mission. *One* way to stop this op from falling apart before it even began.

These two men had to die.

Behind the chair, Court's left hand reached over to his right hand, and he slipped the gold wedding band off his finger. He used his fingernails to pry free a thin stainless steel band that ran around the inside of the ring in a small recess. As he pulled the two-inch-long flexible piece of metal out, it straightened into a tiny metal shim.

The ring had been left for him in the backpack on the plane, along with several other common CIA gadgets from the Science and Technology Division. Court had left the majority of the gear on the aircraft, but he'd taken a few novelties, the wedding band included, because he'd worn such a device off and on for the past decade, depending on his mission and on his alias.

As Tracksuit moved closer, Court used his right thumb and forefinger to manipulate the shim. He'd practiced the move a thousand times, almost always behind his back, though this was the first time he'd done it in the field. He inserted the thin metal shim in front of the ratchet teeth on the cuff, pushing it into the cuff's main housing. He kept pushing, his thumb turning white with the pressure, until the entire steel shank had made its way in. This forced the teeth of the ratchet out of the pawl, a set of spring-loaded counter teeth inside the handcuff's steel housing.

With the teeth disengaged from the pawl, he quickly turned his wrist, popped open the cuff on his left hand, and moved the cuff over to his right hand, next to its mate.

The man with the scopolamine blowgun said something to the man thumbing keys on his phone, and both men chuckled.

Tracksuit switched to English. "You won't remember a thing after this. When we have all the information we need from you, I might get you to order room service for my colleague and me. I could go for a bottle of scotch and a lobster, paid for by the CIA."

Both Chinese men laughed again.

Tracksuit leaned forward now, just feet in front of Court, and he brought the blowgun up to Court's face. He only had to press the recessed button next to the clip and the powder would—

Court launched up and to the left, putting Tracksuit between himself and the man across the room. As he rose, his hands came out from behind the chair, and his right hand fired a jab towards the face of the surprised man in front of him. The momentum from Court's muscular legs and back all added to the power of the jab, and both steel cuffs were wrapped around his right fist like brass knuckles. He drove his punch through the blowgun on his way to the man's face, crushing the plastic device as well as the nose of the Chinese intelligence officer.

A cloud of white powder from the blowgun exploded into the air, all around Tracksuit's head as he recoiled with the impact of the punch. Court moved between Tracksuit and the desk on his left, well aware of the gun on the bed next to the other man. Court dove for the bed, right under the cloud of powder, holding his breath as he did so.

He slid across the bed, but Business Suit beat him to the pistol, snatched it up, and tried to get a step back to earn enough space to raise it towards the blur in front of him. He let his phone fall to the carpet as he stumbled backwards against the wall separating the bedroom from the bathroom.

Business Suit was just squeezing the pistol's trigger as Court rolled off the bed at speed and onto his feet, grabbed the suppressor of the handgun, and pushed it down. A subsonic 9-millimeter round left the pistol at 980 feet per second and scorched the air between Court's legs, puncturing the floor. Court swung a handcuff-encased right hook that slammed into Business Suit's temple and waylaid him, knocking him into the wall between the bedroom and the bathroom.

Court heard the sick crack of metal on bone, the man dropped straight down, and Court knew this man was out of the fight for now.

The unconscious man's hand let go of the pistol easily, and Court snatched it away by the hot suppressor.

Spinning around towards Tracksuit, he first saw the huge cloud of powder hanging in the air. The man was somehow still on his feet, his head in the middle of the gray haze, facing away.

Court shot the man twice between the shoulder blades. The Chinese intelligence officer tumbled over the swivel chair and hit hard against the floor-to-ceiling window, then crumpled down and to his left, out of Court's line of sight behind the bed.

Court heard the man cough, and it wasn't the weak, raspy sound of a man who'd just had his lungs ventilated by a pair of 9-millimeter bullets. Court realized the operative must have been wearing a Kevlar vest under his tracksuit. The two rounds had done nothing more than knock him down.

Court began moving around the bed to get another shot off, the pistol high in front of him. He stopped after only a step, though, as the expanding gray puff of toxic dust created a no-go zone in the middle of the room. He could hear persistent coughing and hacking from the man on the floor by the window, but Court didn't know if the man had his gun out and his wits about him.

Court realized the smart move was to find cover and then fire into the bed, hoping to get a round through and into the man's head or arms. He backed up quickly, still unable to see his target. He didn't want to get into a protracted trench-warfare-like gun battle here, and he thought about just retreating out into the hall and leaving the fight altogether, but he had other tasks to complete in the hotel room before he left. Both men were still alive, and there was a photo of Court's face on the phone of one of the men.

Just as Court made it near the bathroom, a hand with a suppressed Beretta pistol in it rose over the far side of the bed and began firing.

Court dropped low, out of the line of fire, just as the wall to his right shredded with the incoming rounds. Court crawled backwards to the bathroom, looked back out up the length of the bedroom, ahead and to his right, and his eyes locked on the large flat-screen TV on the wall. There he could see the reflection of the Chinese operative wearing the tracksuit. The man knelt low, leaning his back against the floor-to-ceiling window on the far side of the bed, his legs obviously unsteady, and he coughed and shook his head, fighting the heavy effects of the scopolamine hydrobromide. His face was almost completely smeared with blood, like something from a horror film. Court also saw that despite the man's struggle with the drugs, he kept his Beretta up and out in front of him and his eyes forward, looking for his target. Court knew if he just leaned inches to his right he'd get shot in the face by this blood-drenched and doped-up asshole.

Tracksuit turned and looked to his left, then locked eyes with Court in the reflection of the sixty-inch television there. He knew Court's exact location now; all he had to do was stand and shoot over the bed and through the far edge of the bathroom wall.

But Court wasn't worried about this. He might not have had an angle on the Chinese officer, but he *did* have a line of sight on the big window the man leaned back against.

Just as Tracksuit reached back with one hand to push his weight off the window to stand, Court pointed his stolen pistol at the portion of the window in front of him, just over the fallen swivel chair.

Court fired at the glass, over and over. The suppressed weapon popped and hot brass ejected, forming a continuous arc that flew through the air till the spent casings banged against the wall to Court's right.

He pressed the trigger over and over, emptying the pistol into the window.

The window glass pocked, then spiderwebbed, then shattered. Court watched through the reflection of the big television as the Chinese man in the black tracksuit tumbled backwards into the night behind a shower of crystalline shards.

It was twenty stories straight down to the roof of the adjacent building.

Tao shook his head slowly, wondering how long he'd been lying here unconscious. When he blinked to clear his mind, he realized the left side of his head dripped blood that ran down into his eyes. Smearing the blood away with the cuff of his jacket, he saw he was facedown next to the bed.

His head hurt like hell, and he knew he was still dazed.

He'd been out cold during the gunfight so he'd heard no shooting, but he smelled the burnt powder in the air now, and he had an immediate sensation that somewhere in the room a window had been opened.

He struggled up to his hands and knees and began reaching into his belt for a sheathed knife he kept there, but just as he got his fingers on the hilt he felt a pair of powerful hands grab him by the back of the neck.

He tried to draw the knife, but it lurched from his hands and fell to the floor as he was yanked up off the ground. His feet kicked in the air in front of him, and in seconds he was half carried and half dragged into the bathroom.

He tried to yell, to talk to the man, to say *anything*, but his necktie was cinched tight around his throat, his airway was blocked and the blood to his brain restricted, and all the flailing with his arms could not break the hold of the bigger man behind him. He heard grunts of effort but no words from his attacker, the CIA man whom he had so much wanted to kill for sport just moments before.

Tao was dropped to the floor in front of the toilet; he grabbed on to the porcelain bowl and began pushing himself up. He was more disoriented now than when he'd regained consciousness, his eyes completely unfixed after ten seconds of intense choking, but he was a highly skilled operative, well trained in hand-to-hand fighting, so he knew if he could just climb to his feet and spin around to face his attacker he would be able to—

Tao felt the rough hands again, now on the back of his head, forcing him forward and down, and the crown of his head slammed violently into the open toilet seat, just before his face was shoved down, splashing into the shallow bowl of toilet water.

Tao gagged a throatful of water instead of air, and only *then* did his brain cycle into panic.

Court would have let this man live, not out of sympathy but out of efficiency; it takes more time to kill someone than it does to leave him, and Court had no idea how much time he had before someone else entered the hotel room.

But this Chinese agent had seen his face, and Court knew the man could either report to his higher-ups or even run into Court again on Court's mission here in Hong Kong. The American had every intention of coming into contact with men like the man he now struggled to drown in the five inches of water in the toilet bowl, but those men he would come into contact with could not know he had deplaned from a CIA transport aircraft. The only way his mission here would be successful would be if he maintained his cover, and the only way Court knew to maintain his cover was to eliminate the compromise of the men here in the room with him.

There was little emotion in Court in the killing of this now-helpless man; there was only the work, the job. The man himself was a non-issue as an immediate threat, but he was a near-term threat to the mission, so Court killed him with all the sentiment of a file clerk operating a three-hole punch to fit documents into a binder.

This was, quite simply, what Courtland Gentry did for a living.

The small Chinese man went limp after nearly a minute. Court couldn't know if he was dead or just unconscious, so when the muscles in the man's neck went completely slack, the American lifted the head and drove it down hard, snapping cervical vertebrae against the cold, blood-smeared, and unyielding edge of the toilet bowl.

Court let the man wilt down to the tile floor, and then Court himself fell onto his ass, slipping on the splashed water from the toilet. He crawled back to his feet, quickly pulled off his soaked sport coat, wiped sweat from his face with it, and took a few calming breaths.

This done, he rushed back into the bedroom to pick up the man's phone off the floor. The screen had not yet locked, and Court's picture was there, attached to a text message. Business Suit had only had to push the send button and a close-up of Court's face with a beard and eyeglasses would have been transmitted to God knows where, and there would have been no chance he could continue on with his job here in the city.

But he deleted the image, pocketed the phone to dispose of somewhere else, and searched the gym bag to see if these men were carrying anything else that could help him understand how they knew about him. He found nothing of interest save for a second blowgun disguised as a pen containing the scopolamine, which he started to pocket, thinking it might come in handy later.

After a few seconds he thought better of this, realizing he couldn't take anything that would tie him to this incident. He slipped the pen into the man's jacket.

Court changed into dry clothing as fast as he could, and then, just three minutes after killing the second of two Chinese intelligence operatives, he began packing his own bag, rushing to get himself out of there as fast as possible.

CHAPTER

FIVE

C ourt Gentry walked along the promenade in front of Victoria Harbor at one a.m., his phone's wired earpiece in his ear. He'd destroyed the Chinese intelligence officer's cell phone and tossed it into the warm water seconds earlier, eliminating the chance that he could be located through the device, and now he rolled his wheeled luggage along next to him like a businessman who'd just arrived in the city on a late-evening flight.

After three rings his encrypted international call was answered on the other end.

"Brewer."

"It's me."

"Identity challenge, Racecar."

Court had a little trouble remembering his code schedule. Finally he cleared his mind of everything else, and it came to him. "Response, Requiem."

"Confirmed," Brewer said, and then she made a sarcastic comment about how quickly he was getting in touch with her after proclaiming just thirteen hours earlier he wouldn't be checking in for a while. "This is your idea of going dark?"

"Something's happened you need to know about."

"That doesn't sound good."

"It's not good," Court confirmed. "Two assholes just tried to kill me. And yes, I am sure."

It took Brewer a while to process the information. "How can you be so certain they were trying to kill you?"

"Fair question. It started with truth opioids, and when I resisted it went to bullets whizzing by my head, that sort of thing. Trust me, I'm a pretty fair judge of lethal intent."

He was being a smartass, and this was *not* the whole truth. Court had determined, on his own, to kill the men to protect his operation, but he didn't need his CIA handler second-guessing that decision.

"But you are okay?" she asked.

The right side of Court's rib cage screamed in agony, but only because he'd reaggravated an injury he'd picked up a few weeks ago. He wasn't dying, so he said, "I'm okay."

"And the two men?"

"They are not okay."

"I see." Court waited while she processed the information. "What is the situation now?"

"One man is in my room. He's DRT."

"DRT?"

"Dead right there. The other went out a twenty-fifth-floor window, fell a good twenty stories down, and is now lying on a rooftop. I'm no doctor, but I assume he's a goner, as well."

"Oh my God."

Court knew what would come next.

"Blowbacks on the Agency?"

"I got out clean, there is no tail on me, but the concern would be surveillance imagery inside the Peninsula hotel. They will tie the deaths to the room, obviously, and they'll look for stored recordings of the guest in the room."

"We can do something about that."

"Like what?"

"S&T techniques you aren't cleared for."

It felt surreal to Court to be talking about getting support from the CIA's Directorate of Science and Technology, chiefly because the CIA had spent a half decade trying to kill him. But everyone was on the same big happy team now, so he pushed any reticence about receiving help from the CIA out of his mind.

"Okay. Do you have cleaners here in Hong Kong?"

"Not our people, but I've arranged contingencies with the Brits and Australians over there. I knew there was a chance for something like this on your assignment, so all I have to do is make a call to get their teams moving."

Court gave Brewer the room number and the location of the building with the dead Chinese intelligence officer on the roof, and then Brewer told him she would call him back.

Court left the promenade, turning to the north and moving through the busy streets of Tsim Sha Tsui. He passed karaoke bars, fortune-tellers, twenty-four-hour bank branches, and so many stand-up fast-food restaurants that the smells from one mingled with the smells from the next just as all the neon seemed to turn into one multicolored ribbon of light.

One mile north and twenty-five minutes later, he answered his beeping phone. It was Brewer again, and they rushed through the challenge and response.

Brewer said, "A British cleanup crew is entering the Peninsula now, and NSA is in the process of altering relevant security camera images. The Aussies are sending a team to get that body off the roof next door. Asian men wearing clothing similar to that of the terminated intelligence officers will be seen and recorded leaving the building, and the men you killed will be dumped in the harbor. Our Hong Kong station will provide a case officer matching your description to enter your room tonight, then check out tomorrow. He'll come up with a story about the broken window."

Court was impressed with how much Suzanne Brewer had accomplished in less than half an hour.

"That sounds like a solid plan," he admitted. Working with the CIA had its perks, just as working *against* them had its drawbacks.

Brewer was cool, but still, she was more emotional about everything than he was. "Jesus, Violator, why did they go lethal? Could you have provoked them in some way?"

Court gritted his teeth. "*Provoked* them? They broke into my *fucking* hotel room."

"Couldn't you have kept your cover? Stuck to your story?"

"They tried to drug me with scopolamine. It's a drug made from a South American bush. The Colombians call it Devil's Breath. It's an old truth serum. Very nasty."

"Christ. Sounds like something from a bad movie."

"Welcome to my world."

Suzanne Brewer took command of her emotions and challenged her agent now. "Still . . . could you have taken it and fought off the effects? Aren't you trained in resistance to chemicals? It's in your file."

Court didn't answer.

After receiving no response, she softened. "Look, I get it. I'm not in the field; you are."

Court snapped back. "We can fix that easily enough. Why don't you fly out to Hong Kong? We can walk this op together. It would give you a feel for fieldwork."

"I'm your handler. It's my job to question your judgment." To that, she added, "But if you say you had no alternative to lethal means, I understand."

"I had no alternative to lethal means."

She let it go after a long pause. "Do you want to close down the operation? After this I can pull you. I *should* pull you."

Court shook his head as he responded. "No. You get this cleaned up, and I'll do my part to keep the Chinese from finding out I was involved."

Finally she said, "All right. But don't stay at the Peninsula tonight."

Court wanted to bark back, *No shit*, and tell her he was already a mile north of the hotel and off the main drag of the city, but he didn't have the inclination to explain himself any further.

Instead he said, "I'm back offline for now. I'll report in as needed."

He ended the call and slipped the phone back into his pocket.

Suzanne Brewer hung up her phone and immediately dialed an in-house extension. This was bad, she knew, and although she'd done everything she could think of to fix it from where she sat, she knew she still had one thing to take care of.

This wasn't about Violator; this wasn't about the operation in Hong Kong that had turned into a fiasco before her agent in the field had even arrived at the opening stage of the mission.

No. Suzanne Brewer wasn't thinking about Court Gentry. Suzanne Brewer was thinking about Suzanne Brewer. She wasn't about to swing in the wind alone with her agent in the field. Nope, she was going upstairs to pull someone else in with her.

Getting a meeting with the man in charge of all of CIA's intelligence operations would normally require a significant amount of work for a mid-level exec in the Agency's Programs and Plans department, but Brewer was handling Violator, so she knew she could get away with just walking right into Hanley's office or calling his mobile in the middle of the night. The current situation warranted giving Hanley an immediate update, but still, Brewer didn't want to look frazzled and out of her league, so she called Hanley's secretary and asked for ten minutes of D/NCS's time.

That Hanley himself came on the phone after a few seconds reasserted to Brewer the importance of Violator's op.

"Hey, Suzanne. Jill says you need a face-to-face?"

"Yes, please."

"How's the leg? I can run down to your office if you need me to."

Hanley's offer was a nice touch of chivalry, but there was no way she was going to look weak and needy.

"Very kind offer, Matt, but I am managing just fine."

"Then come on up," he said.

S uzanne Brewer had broken her leg just above her ankle in a savage car wreck weeks before, and it would be another week before the hard cast came off, and then only after six more weeks in a boot would her orthopedic surgeon allow her to walk normally again. In the interim she moved around with the aid of a knee scooter, a device that allowed her to step with her right leg while she kept her casted left leg bent to avoid bearing weight on it. With the bicycle-style handlebars used to steer her wounded appendage, she looked more than a little ridiculous kicking along the seventh-floor hallway, but she was still in the "sympathetic look" stage from her colleagues, and everyone got the hell out of her way, so she saw some additional benefit to the awkward contraption.

Just minutes after her call Suzanne Brewer struggled off her knee scooter and sat down in front of Hanley's desk. "This damn thing in HK is already going south."

Hanley raised a critical eyebrow Brewer's way. "He's on the ground fourteen hours and you're having problems?"

"Violator claims he was tailed from the airport. He doesn't know how he was compromised. I'm looking into the aircraft to see if it could have been exposed to the Chinese somehow. The surveillance team attacked him about an hour ago, he says, at his hotel in Tsim Sha Tsui." She paused. "He retaliated." After a sigh she added, "He killed both men, Matt."

Hanley seemed concerned but oddly unsurprised. "Does Gentry know who they were?"

"He thinks they were MSS operatives."

Hanley sat back in his chair now. Brewer knew he was thinking about the fallout, just as she was. About telling the head of the CIA that an Agency asset had killed two Chinese intelligence operatives in a five-star hotel in Hong Kong.

Brewer felt certain Hanley had more to worry about than Violator at this point, while she was in the middle, safe from both gunmen in Asia and politicians in Washington.

The only person she had to fear was Hanley, and from the expression on his face, he wasn't looking to throw her under the bus for this.

Not yet, anyway.

He said, "Shit. We knew he'd run into them. But we didn't know he would do it in the course of deplaning a CIA jet."

"No, sir."

Hanley rubbed his thick face, pressing red marks into his cheeks around his eyes. Brewer just looked on. She wondered if he was already thinking beyond Gentry, what he would do if his asset on the ground failed.

After a moment she said, "It's bad, no question, but if you look hard enough for good news, there is some. We've got facial recog spoofed at his hotel, he can't be ID'd from the cams, and he says no other MSS personnel could have made him. We've got cleaners from MI6, Australia's SIS, and our local station helping to maintain his cover, and he's clear of any other followers.

"Still," she added, a darkening tone to her voice, "there might be operational fallout for the men Violator killed. When he does come in contact with MSS, if they tie him to the Peninsula, which ties him to us . . . his secondary cover will be blown."

She added, "If I were him I'd be on the first commercial flight out of Asia."

Hanley replied, "But you're not him."

"No, sir. He wants to go forward."

Hanley thought it over a moment. "He is the best. If he took those men out, it was so he could stay on mission. I don't question his judgment in the field, and you shouldn't, either."

"Yes, sir," she said, but she didn't even try to make herself sound convincing.

Hanley leaned forward, propping his arms on his massive desk. "Suzanne, you know what success on this op means for us."

"Success could bring great advantages to the U.S., absolutely. But failure, *more* failure, could be extraordinarily damaging." She hesitated before saying, "Some might say doing nothing would be the prudent course of action."

Hanley leaned back in his chair. "It comes down to this, Suzanne. I have more confidence in Gentry than you do. You'll have to trust that my confidence comes from a long relationship and an understanding of his capabilities."

"Of course."

Hanley watched Suzanne roll out of his office on her leg scooter, then stop, turn, and struggle to shut the door behind her. He almost called out for her to leave it open, but he knew she was a proud woman, and she wanted to show her boss that her broken leg wasn't slowing her down one damn bit.

It was silly, but he just sat there and watched her struggle, until finally the door shut and he was alone again in his office.

Hanley found himself questioning his decision to put Suzanne Brewer in charge of the mission in Hong Kong. He realized from her comments that she would pull the plug on Gentry to save her own ass. As far as she was concerned, Gentry was a liability to her, even though he was an asset to Hanley. Still, she had a mind for this work, and while he didn't trust her, he knew that folding her into this operation would make her a better case officer, and it allied her that much closer to Hanley himself.

And while he didn't trust her, neither did he want her out of his control.

He saw Suzanne as the future of this agency. He had no doubt in his mind she might one day rule the entire building; shit, she had the moxie to be DNI, the Director of National Intelligence, the head of all sixteen U.S. intelligence agencies. If Matt Hanley was still around when that happened— through some luck or some curse, he didn't know which to bet on—then he'd need Brewer. And he'd need something to hold over her head. The Court Gentry operational relationship—or, as she seemed set on calling it, the Violator operational relationship—was off book and highly irregular. It was rife with opportunities for Brewer to get her hands dirty along the way, and Matt Hanley would know about it if she did. He wanted her as a friend, but he was hoping to solidify his place here by having a "special relationship" with a future top dog.

Hanley had been a field man, but he knew how to work this building, how to manage these halls and conference rooms. Langley wasn't as far removed from the sullied third-world streets in which he'd operated as it might look at first glance, and though you could pull Matt Hanley out of the field, you could never really pull the field out of Matt Hanley.

Brewer was the right person to run Gentry, of this Hanley was certain. But he did have to acknowledge he'd put Gentry in incredible danger on this operation, and Suzanne Brewer was the man's only lifeline.

He knew the opportunity awaiting the CIA in Hong Kong was huge; the potential benefit to the United States if Court succeeded was real and it was massive, and Hanley knew it was his job to risk an asset like Gentry. One of China's top government computer network experts was in the city and in the wind, everybody was after him, and Court was one of only a few with a real shot at laying hands on him. The risk to Gentry's life was worth it for a chance to gain the knowledge in Fan Jiang's head. Even if Gentry died in the process on this, winning in Hong Kong would be worth the sacrifice.

Hell, Hanley said to himself, *if we get Fan back to America and use him against the Chinese, this could damn well be one of the biggest intel coups of all time.*

But it was even bigger than that, because Hanley knew elements of the larger operation of which Gentry was just a part.

This whole op was a foul fucking mess; Brewer did not know the big picture, and Gentry sure as shit did not know the big picture.

Hanley thought he might bring Brewer into the fold at some point.

But Gentry? Hell no, Gentry would never find out the full scope of this, because if he had any clue what he was really in the middle of, he'd *fucking* run from it as fast as he could.

CHAPTER

SIX

Court walked the streets for hours on a surveillance detection route, which in most any other city in the world would have been a breeze at this time of night, because it's no great trick to detect surveillance when there are few people out and about. In Hong Kong, however, Court found himself constantly double-checking the faces of those around him, so thick were the sidewalks with pedestrians, even in the early-morning hours.

He stopped for a snack in a street stall, then wandered through a maze of kiosks selling cheap housewares and knock-off jewelry, still open at two a.m. He kept his eyes out for anyone who could have possibly followed him from the Peninsula hotel, but he saw no hint of a tail, and two hours before first light he found himself in the gritty Kowloon district of Mongkok, well north of Tsim Sha Tsui.

He stepped into an all-night market and pharmacy—it seemed just about every business down at street level stayed open twenty-four hours a day—and he bought two bags full of supplies, all of which he managed to cram into his backpack and roll-aboard.

Now that Court had picked up the items he needed and put some distance between himself and the crime scene he'd left to the south, he set off on the hunt for an out-of-the-way guesthouse. He realized Mongkok was the right neighborhood to find one, because there were, without exaggeration, tens of thousands of rooms for rent in the endless streets lined with skyscrapers.

The main drags here in Mongkok were still awash with the glow of neon, but this part of the city was nothing like down near the harbor where, even on the side streets and in the alleyways, the lights shone bright twenty-four hours a day. Once he got a couple of blocks off the major streets, he found less commercial glitz and more poverty-level residential buildings. Many of these structures were thirty, forty, even sixty stories tall, but still they had grungy unkempt facades and simple signs out front declaring what sorts of commercial and residential properties could be found inside.

On Ki Lung Street he found himself drawn to a gaudy glow of pink neon around a side door of an otherwise gray and poorly lit building. He stood in the dark across the quiet street and looked at the facade, noticing a small hand-painted sign under the neon promoting the "Pleasant Southeast Orchid Guesthouse." From the sign he learned the establishment occupied the first and third floors of the building, with a connecting business that offered "All-day, all-night foot massage" on the second floor. Even at this hour it was open and active, with an all-male clientele. He stood in the alcove of a building across the street and watched the place for a while longer, trying to decide if the guesthouse would suit his needs. Court didn't know if the foot massage locale was a legitimate business or if more was on offer, but from the steady flotsam and jetsam of men entering and exiting the front door of the building, he guessed there was something going on other than foot rubs.

This was about as far removed as one could possibly get from the five-star hotel he'd checked into the day before. The guesthouse wasn't low profile or secure, but he thought this place to be as off grid as he could possibly manage in the middle of an urban sprawl where he had no friends or contacts to draw from.

He assumed the rooms of the guesthouse would be seedy and nasty, but the low-rent nature of the place meant they wouldn't care about seeing a passport or doing anything to alert authorities to his presence, and above all he had a good deal of confidence that anyone looking for a man who had disappeared out of the Peninsula would not look here first.

He figured he might end up with contact dermatitis staying at the Pleasant Southeast Orchid, but he probably wouldn't get a bullet to the head by an MSS hitter, so he decided *this* looked like it had the potential to be his new home.

Court crossed the dark street, anxious for a few hours' sleep but ready to turn away if he saw anything he didn't like.

The check-in process to the guesthouse was a little more complicated than he'd anticipated, but only because the old guy behind the counter couldn't understand why the foreigner wanted a room here in the first place, why he was booking for two whole days, and why he hadn't brought a prostitute with him. There was suspicion in the man's eyes, disbelief that this guy was actually here seeking accommodations.

Court thought he could have walked in with a goat under his arm or a cavalcade of circus freaks in tow and gotten his room quicker and with fewer sideways glances.

He considered turning on his heels and going somewhere else, but the overall squalidness of the place made him feel confident that his secrets, despite whatever the old-timer behind the desk guessed they were, were probably safe here.

He paid in HK dollars that had been left by the CIA in a money belt in the backpack he'd found on the aircraft, then took the stairs out of the lobby and up to the first landing. Here he passed the door that simply read "Happy Foot Massage" with the outline of a foot in front of an outline of the sun, and he turned to take the staircase up to his floor. As he passed the door to the massage location, it opened and a pair of Asian men left together, heading down the stairs without even glancing at Court.

Nice, Court thought. He'd suspected the clientele here might avert their eyes from the other guests, and it was good to see he'd assessed the situation correctly.

If there was one thing in this world Court knew, it was shitty hotels.

He found his little room, and immediately it looked to him like the Pleasant Southeast Orchid Guesthouse had employed the same architect that designed cells in supermax prisons. There was no window in the eight-by-ten-foot box, and the ceiling was just six feet above the floor, which added to the claustrophobic feel. The walls were white-painted cinder block that had chipped and yellowed over time, and the ceiling was unpainted particleboard with black mold around the edges.

Court dropped his pack and his roll-aboard in the corner of the room next to the open plastic garbage can and sat down on the dirty bed. Facing forward, he found he could reach out and touch the rust-stained sink, even lean forward and wash his hands if he so desired, though he worried about the color and quality of the water he would find coming out of the faucet.

His gaze settled upon his own face in the little mirror above the basin. He looked exhausted and stressed. He'd killed two men hours earlier, and he'd come a hairsbreadth from dying himself. This had been a decidedly bad opening day, and his face showed the strain of every minute of it.

But Court was just getting started. He knew it was time to shake off the initial setbacks and to go on offense. He'd begin his operation here in Hong Kong, right here, and right now. He'd prep for tomorrow's action first; then he'd get a few hours' sleep.

He reached into his backpack, pulled out the plastic bag of items he'd purchased at the pharmacy, and got to work.

G entry left his low-rent guesthouse at nine a.m., slipping down the stairs and passing through the tiny lobby without the clerk noticing him at all. As he emerged from the dark and dank building out into the already hot morning air, he sported a completely new look. His beard was gone and he'd cut the hair on his head short. Gone, too, were his eyeglasses and his dress clothes, and instead this morning he wore lightweight cargo pants and an adventure-wear short-sleeve shirt designed for warm climates. He donned a burgundy ball cap and sunglasses and had another ball cap—this one faded and gray—folded in his pants between his waistband and his skin.

He didn't have a backpack or any other luggage with him; just a wallet, a cell phone, a money belt, and a few odds and ends in his pockets.

He descended into Hong Kong's impossibly clean and organized subway system, called the MTR. He climbed on and off four trains, switched out his ball cap, then finally reemerged at street level on Nathan Road, back in Tsim Sha Tsui, just a few blocks away from the Peninsula.

He didn't particularly want to come back here, but he had no choice, because his orders from CIA involved speaking with a man who lived in the neighborhood.

Chungking Mansions was one of the most famous buildings in Hong Kong. Virtually a city unto itself, it housed thousands of residences, over one hundred private businesses, and seventeen stories of accommodations ranging from budget at one end of the spectrum to very, *very* low budget at the other.

Court passed through the wide entrance of the building along with dozens of other people and immediately realized this place wasn't exactly what he was expecting. Though he'd never been here himself, he'd heard about the building over the years, and he knew it used to be something out of a dystopian novel. For decades criminal activity had run rampant in the filthy dark halls, gangs ruled individual floors, and an almost anarchist society had raged inside the various blocks of the sprawling structure.

But as he walked the halls now, he saw that the famous address was relatively clean, reasonably well organized and run, and, for Hong Kong anyway, quiet and even boring.

It was less like the house of horrors he'd expected and more like a large and run-down shopping mall.

Court had been told in his brief from the Agency that he could find a man in a little office at Chungking Mansions who, it was known by the local CIA shop, had his finger on the pulse of everything that happened here in HK. He'd been a police detective back when the city was a British protectorate, and then after independence he'd switched over to private investigations. His official job now was as the owner of a security consultancy, but the simple truth was that next to nothing went down in Hong Kong without Wu getting wind of it.

The place was full of commerce of all types; the hallways were crammed with impromptu markets and kiosks, many run by African and Middle Eastern businessmen who also rented rooms in the buildings. They were street salesmen back home, here in China to buy wares to restock their home operations. Enough of these travelers had set up kiosks to sell to one another here in the building that Court imagined some of their number never did make it back home; they just spent their time buying crap from low-end Chinese factories and selling crap to other street merchants from afar.

There was a prevalent smell in the building Court could not identify, but it wasn't pleasant. There was fry grease in the mix, to be sure, but competing incense burners and the body odor of thousands of residents packed tight in a can with limited plumbing options also led to the thick, stifling odor.

Court found all the elevators in this block to be out of order, a significant pain in the ass in a building seventeen stories tall, so he began climbing. Every few floors he looked out the glass door of the stairwell and into the halls of the floor, and he saw mostly residences, some no more than simple affairs separated from one another by curtains.

As was the case in many buildings around here, things got weirder as you went higher. He passed large restaurants and crowded markets and hookah bars, but he kept climbing, all the way to the sixteenth floor. Here he left the stairwell and began reading the little signs on the walls of the offices.

Many were printed in both English and Mandarin, and Court saw that there were a large number of attorneys, customs agents, and freight forwarders on this level. But down at the last door at the end of a long hallway he came to his destination. The English words on the door plaque read "Wu K. K. Consultancy."

He knocked on the door and was immediately buzzed in.

He explained to a seventy-something female secretary that he did not have an appointment but needed quick information from Mr. Wu. She asked the American for his business card, and he shrugged, said he would be paying for information but not giving much of any himself. When she inquired where he'd heard about Wu's consultancy, Court made up a name, saying the man was an attorney from London.

The secretary just nodded and stepped alone through a doorway.

A minute later she opened the door and showed the American in.

Wu appeared to be around eighty years old, but he seemed in reasonably good health. He sat behind his desk with a can of orange soda in front of him and a suspicious look in his eyes.

Wu spoke good English, a result of living in a British protectorate for the majority of his life. He asked Court what he wanted, and Court sat down in the one chair in front of the desk. "Same as anyone who comes through that door. A little information."

"The lawyer in London you mentioned does not exist. So . . . how do you *really* know about me?"

"I give *you* money, you tell *me* things. Isn't that the way it works?"

Wu smiled a little more. "You are American?"

Court lied; second nature. "Canadian."

Wu gave Court a wink. "Canadian. Very good. What do you want?"

"I want to know the whereabouts of someone here in the city. A prominent person from abroad, who arrived recently. How much will that cost me?"

"You give me the name. If I know nothing, it costs nothing. If I know something, it costs what it costs for what I know."

"Right," Court said, "I am looking for a British national who is visiting Hong Kong."

"Name?"

"His name is Sir Donald Fitzroy."

Wu did not hide his recognition of the name. "Sir Donald. Here? In Hong Kong? Why? Is there someone here who needs to die?"

Court heaved a big sigh and stood up. "Obviously I know more about this than you. Good-bye."

Wu held a hand up. "Five thousand Hong Kong dollars."

"For what?"

"I know Sir Donald is here, and I know where he is. Not exactly where, but what district. Maybe a little more about what is going on than this." He repeated his price. "Five thousand."

Court pulled a thick envelope of bills from his money belt, but he just held it up. "I pay for what I receive, not what you tell me I *will* receive. If I'm satisfied, *really* satisfied, I'll give you three thousand."

It was clear on Wu's face that he both had expected to bargain and felt pleased with his powers of negotiation. Whatever he had, he would have probably let it go for one thousand.

Wu said, "Okay. He's somewhere in the Peak."

Court knew this was a district on Hong Kong Island, up in the hills south of the harbor. "What's he doing there?"

"He is under the protection of the authorities."

"The . . . *protection*?"

Wu shrugged but didn't elaborate directly. He just said, "For what reason, I do not know. What I do know is Fitzroy's men came to me last week, and they wanted information about a crime gang here in HK."

Court wanted to ask more about Fitzroy's men, and he especially wanted to know what they were looking for. But he refrained. That would not be in keeping with his secondary cover, so he just pressed for information about Fitzroy's physical location.

"You said authorities. Are you talking about security officials?"

"Maybe you give me other two thousand, and I give you more information."

"Fine," Court said. It wasn't his money, anyway.

"These are men from the mainland. The Ministry of State Security. They are all over Hong Kong. Usually they are very quiet. A man here, a man there. Starting last week, they are everywhere. They even came to see Wu."

"What were they looking for?"

"One of the Triad groups. This is the same group Fitzroy's people were looking for. Days later I heard Fitzroy was taken from his hotel and up to the Peak by mainland security men. Maybe I can get you the address . . . for another five thousand. I'll need two thousand in advance."

Court wasn't surprised Wu was trying to put him on the hook for another two Gs, but he knew he wouldn't get, nor would he need, the address from Wu. Still, Court had a plan, and to see it through he agreed to the terms.

Court said, "I'm staying at the Pleasant Southeast Orchid Guesthouse at sixty-three Ki Lung Street. When you find out where Fitzroy is, you can reach me there. I'll give you the extra five thousand then. Nothing in advance."

Wu scrunched up his white eyebrows in confusion. Not many of his drop-in clients offered up their physical location—it wasn't the best move from a tradecraft standpoint—but the Chinese man only said, "I will try to find out more."

Court thanked the man and left the office, then made his way through the labyrinthine halls and stairwells of Chungking Mansions back down to street level.

He headed back in the direction of his windowless room in Mongkok, traveling directly, with no attempt at an SDR. His only side trip on the way home was stopping at a dim sum restaurant half a block from his building for lunch. It was the noon hour, the place was slammed, and Court ate his meal standing out front to avoid the congestion.

When he was finished with his lunch, he stepped over to a garbage can. Carefully he took the envelope in his money belt containing several thousand HK dollars, pulled a few bills out and crammed them in his pocket, then took the nearly full envelope, folded it up with the paper plate and napkins from his lunch, and shoved it in the can.

Court was just about broke now, but it was part of his plan for the next phase of his operation.

He returned to his guesthouse, climbing the stairs past men waiting in line for a lunchtime "foot massage."

Back in his hot cell of a room he took off his hat, but he kept his phone and his wallet in his pocket. He flipped on the overhead light, then lay down, fully clothed on the little bed, his body above the sheets. He was careful to keep his hands to his sides, away from his body. He felt this would present the most nonthreatening posture to the men who would soon kick in his door to kidnap him.

Court's entire objective at the office of Wu K. K. Consultancy today was to give China's Ministry of State Security the impression that a lone American had come to town looking for a British subject named Sir Donald Fitzroy. Fitzroy was Court Gentry's former employer, and the Chinese would know this, and even if they did not, they would have reason to be *very* interested in any strangers in town looking for Fitzroy.

He felt sure they would have been listening in to the goings-on in Wu's office, and that meant they'd probably come for him soon.

That had been the CIA's plan, anyway.

Of course this all would have been better if Court hadn't climbed out of a CIA aircraft yesterday and killed two MSS goons at the Peninsula hotel; because of this incident, MSS would already be aware that a new American who worked in the intelligence field was here in town, so Court had to somehow convince them he wasn't *that* guy.

It would be tough to pull off, but Court Gentry had developed into one hell of an actor over the years.

And he felt certain he'd have to deliver an Oscar-worthy performance in the next few hours to stay alive.

Yeah, Court knew what was coming and he wasn't looking forward to it one bit. He had a wound to his ribs from a recent mission that hurt when he moved in the wrong direction, and he was supremely confident that the jackasses who were about to kidnap him would move him in *all* the wrong directions.

This was going to suck, he told himself, and then he closed his eyes, hoping for a little sleep before it all went to hell.

Two hours later he woke to movement close to him. Rough hands grabbed him and rolled him onto his stomach. No one spoke, which meant these guys were pros.

Someone ripped his shoes off, and this pissed Court off greatly. He wasn't particularly mad at the man who did it; rather, he was angry at himself. He should have assumed they would take off his shoes, and he would have enjoyed his nap a little more comfortably if he'd been sleeping barefoot all along.

A bag was pushed over his head—there was always a bag with these things, and Court wondered if this bag had been washed since they'd bagged their last victim.

He told himself not to think about it.

He was yanked into a standing position, swiveled around towards the door, and guided forward with multiple pairs of strong hands holding his arms on his left and right. Still no one had spoken, and this continued to impress Court.

He was dealing with well-trained individuals. They were still goons, to be sure, but they'd clearly graduated with honors from a top-flight goon school.

They guided him down the stairs; he assumed he was moving past the massage parlor, but none of the men in line there spoke, nor did he hear anything from behind the counter in the lobby as he was pushed along at the bottom of the stairs.

Court hadn't seen uniforms on these men before they'd hooded him; he guessed either this crew was brandishing weapons or badges, or else they just carried themselves in that special way only secret police in a semi–police state carried themselves. While Hong Kong was supposed to be a separate entity of China still, the civilians in view of this spectacle would have no trouble guessing who was orchestrating this operation.

Either an organized crime group of some sort, or a government entity of some sort.

And either way, the civilians would do well to keep their mouths shut and their eyes averted.

Court was tossed flat in the back of a vehicle, which made the wound in his side ache. Three doors shut, almost all at once. Assuming the driver had already been at the wheel, this meant there were at least four in the vehicle with him now, although there could have been more than that.

Two pairs of feet settled on top of him: one on the back of his thighs, and another on the back of his head.

Court was utterly helpless. The men over him could stick a syringe in his butt or a knife in his spine or, at any moment, he might feel the cold steel of a silencer pressed against the back of his neck. They could take him out to a field and bury him alive, or they could torture him with battery acid to find out what he knew about their operation.

And there wasn't a damn thing Court could do about it.

Being the Gray Man didn't mean being in control at all times. Sometimes it meant relinquishing all control, playing the game, and dealing with fucking bullshit like some asshole standing on the back of your head.

Court told himself not to worry; he'd figure out his situation soon enough, and then he would adapt and overcome. In the meantime, he closed his eyes and did his best to enjoy the ride.

CHAPTER

SEVEN

He failed.

The drive lasted over an hour, and through it all Court was hot as hell on the floorboard, especially with his face hooded, and much of the drive took place in stop-and-go traffic, bringing the American with the two men resting their feet on him to the brink of nausea many times.

But at least they were heading in the right direction. A half hour into the drive Court could feel the vehicle begin to ascend as it took winding and steep roads, which told Court they were on Hong Kong Island, south of Court's hotel in Kowloon, and it also meant they were heading exactly where he wanted to go.

They were going to the Peak.

The air cooled as they ascended, but much less so under the hood, which was soaked with perspiration and stifling. Court felt a wave of nausea coming on, and he had a panicky vision of choking to death in his own vomit, but before he could either calm the fear or succumb to it, the vehicle lurched to a complete stop on a steep incline. Court was pulled out and onto his feet and led forward again. He had another brief moment's panic as the disembodied image of himself being walked off a cliff flashed in front of his eyes, but the image was dispelled when he heard a door open. His soaking-wet hood was slapped by icy air-conditioning as he was led forward, and then he was helped slowly down a spiral staircase.

He felt like he was being led through multiple doorways, and then he was pulled to a stop and pushed down into a comfortable leather chair. Here he sat quietly for a few seconds, listening to the sounds of men moving around him.

The bag came off his head abruptly, and he blinked because of the sweat, but not the light, because quickly he saw this room wasn't especially bright. He was in a small parlor, with a pair of chairs facing a sofa, and a wooden table between them. Court sat in one of the chairs, his back to the entrance of the room, and in front of him on the sofa sat another man, a steaming cup of tea on the side table next to his chair.

Court rubbed the sweat out of his eyes, focused on the man, and then faked surprise, because he *wasn't* surprised; he was pleased. He found himself exactly where he'd hoped to be, sitting in front of exactly *who* he'd hoped to be sitting in front of.

Sir Donald Fitzroy was in his early seventies, but at the moment he seemed older than that. He was drawn, tired-looking. Though he wore a suit and tie, his wispy gray hair was slightly askew, as if he'd been lying down.

Sir Donald looked at Court as if he were seeing a ghost. When the older man recovered enough to speak, his voice was even more gravelly than Court remembered it, though admittedly, it had been a couple of years since they had spoken. "Good lord, lad. I didn't know who they'd plopped in front of me, but I certainly did not expect *you*."

Court looked around a little more now. There was no one else in the room, and the door behind him was shut.

"Quite a taxi service you're running."

Fitzroy shook his head, waved a hand in the air. "You know the way the world turns, so I'm sure you sussed out the fact that those aren't my men that brought you here."

Court knew Fitzroy was a prisoner in this home, just as Court himself was. He knew much more about what was going on than he was letting on, but for operational reasons, he needed to play dumb.

"You look a little tired, Fitz, if you don't mind me saying."

Fitzroy shrugged; Court could tell the old man was still sizing up Court, trying to figure out himself just what was going on. He joked, "You know . . . it's Hong Kong. Twenty-four-seven nightlife and nonstop revelry for me."

Court made no reply.

"How long have you been in town?"

"Got here yesterday on a freighter from Singapore."

"Why?" The question was a challenge. Fitzroy seemed suspicious of Court turning up like this.

Court looked back over his shoulder at the door to the room, outside of which he was certain several of the men who kidnapped him still stood. "I came for the legendary hospitality."

Fitzroy turned his nose up at this. "Looking for me, were you?"

Court nodded. "Heard a rumor you were here."

"A *rumor*?"

"I was in London; I know a guy who knows a guy. I'd rather not say anything else about that, but I was told you moved your operation here."

"Temporarily," Fitzroy confirmed.

"How temporarily?"

The older man coughed. Court could see intense strain on Fitzroy's face. He glanced quickly to his right, towards an ornate cloisonné planter with a leafy bush growing in it. While looking at the planter, Fitz said, "That remains to be seen. Not up to me."

Court looked at the greenery himself while he replied, "You aren't running the show here, are you?"

"No. The gentlemen you just met are looking after me at present. They are treating me well, until an order comes from on high telling them to do otherwise."

Court leaned back. "And why would they get an order like that?"

Fitzroy hesitated again. He seemed reluctant to bring Court deeper into what was going on, and Court found this curious. He'd expected Fitz to be relieved by the Gray Man showing up on the scene, but instead, the older man was clearly wary.

Court waited the man out, though, and finally the Englishman explained. "I agreed to do a job, and I put some of my best men on it. The best since you, that is."

"You flatter."

"Anyway, the job didn't get done. The blokes you just met work for the holder of the contract, and they seem to have their collective panties in a twist about the fact that I've failed them."

Court took this in. "You know, Don . . . this isn't the first time in my life I've thought to myself how much easier things would be for everyone if you traveled with a fucking security detail."

Fitzroy smiled, but the expression just looked at once both tired and sad. "I learn from my mistakes, lad. I have had bodyguards for the past couple of years. Here I used a local company. They are top-notch, know the ins and outs."

Court said, "And they hit the bricks when these goons showed up."

Fitzroy said, "Just as well . . . it would have been a bloodbath. There are a lot more men here than I had watching my back."

Court said, "Not that I profess to be an expert or anything, but the men who bagged me looked like they could be from mainland China, and they *might* be intelligence officers."

Fitzroy bobbed his head to the left and right, as if trying to decide how to reply. He glanced again at the cloisonné urn filled with the large leafy green plant. With a shrug he seemed to settle on an answer. "I *am* an expert, and I can confirm your layman's intuition to be spot-on. You now find yourself in a building full of Guojia Anquan Bu."

"Which is great on lo mein," Court said.

"It means Ministry of State Security. There are some other departments involved with this. In fact, it's an MOD operation, at its core. But no matter, they are all members of the government of the People's Republic of China."

Court didn't bat an eyelash; it would have looked inauthentic to fake surprise at this information. Instead he said, "You took a contract from Chinese intelligence to assassinate someone. An organization that imposes its will with an iron fist. An organization that puts its own citizens in front of a firing squad for saying the wrong thing in public. You failed your mission for them, and now they are holding you personally responsible." Sarcastically Court added, "How could you have possibly guessed your employers would be such a bunch of dickheads?"

With his eyes flitting between Court and the planter, Sir Donald said, "I didn't know I was taking a job for Chinese intelligence. I satisfied myself this was a corporate intelligence mission, nothing too messy. A rogue computer hacker on the run with a firm's secrets, nothing more. These sorts of things happen with increasing regularity, and I've stepped in to help out on more than one occasion in the past."

Court knew Fitzroy was saying he'd sent assassins to kill people, but Court made no mention of this. Court knew this well; he had been a killer under Fitzroy's employ, after all. That Court always made certain his targets were worthy of the death he dealt made him feel better about what he did, but he didn't judge the old British ex-spymaster for his different moral compass.

After all, Court was pretty sure that, on the whole, he was more fucked-up than Don Fitzroy.

The American said, "Let me guess. Once your assassin failed to terminate his target, to kill this hacker you mentioned, all the cutouts melted away, and the MSS showed up to register their disapproval."

"Something along those lines. Actually, they allowed me a mulligan. A second chance to get it right."

"And the second mission failed, as well."

"That's it."

Court wiped the remainder of the perspiration off his face. "Backing up . . . what happened the first time?"

Fitzroy took off his eyeglasses and began cleaning them with a handkerchief. While he did this, he said, "Not sure, really. The two blokes I sent were found in a Dumpster in San Po Kong. Eastern part of Kowloon."

"Dead?"

"Quite."

"And the second operation?"

"The second team was three men; they came with me from London. My best chaps." He looked up from his work and put his glasses back on. "Best since you, without question. These chaps of mine went out into the field, with me to help them along the way with logistics and coordination with the Chinese . . . and then they promptly disappeared." Fitzroy sighed. "That was three days ago, now. No word." He turned back to the leafy plant in the corner and nodded towards it. "He showed up the next day and brought me here."

"You've been kidnapped by a philodendron?"

Despite his obvious stress, a low chuckle came from Don Fitzroy's belly. "I missed you, my boy." He hefted his teacup and took a sip. "No. The man in charge of it all. A chap named Dai."

"Who is he?"

"If he wants you to know that, I'm sure he'll tell you."

Court said, "I was asking around about you, and apparently he got word of my inquiries. He had me picked up and delivered straight to you. If he didn't want me working on this job, I doubt he'd bring me here and let you tell me this much."

Fitzroy's eyes narrowed. "You've got it all wrong, lad. He'll let you in on the particulars, and if he decides he doesn't want you knowing any more, or if he doesn't feel comfortable with you, he'll just put a pair of bullets in the back of your skull and be done with you." After a sly grin Fitzroy leaned closer to the planter. "I *do* hope he doesn't mind my saying all this."

Court changed gears, suddenly and dramatically. "Do you ever hear anything from your family?"

Court knew that Don's daughter and his twin granddaughters were his life, but he also knew Fitzroy was playing to the audio equipment in the room. If the English ex-spymaster was smart—and Court knew he was *very* smart—then he'd distance himself from any potential compromise.

Fitzroy sniffed. "Same as ever. They can all go to hell. Don't know about them. Don't care."

Court helped this ruse along. "You always were a selfish bastard when it came to family."

"You get nowhere in this world with personal relationships. You probably know that even better than I."

That sank in a moment; Court knew Fitz was just playing his part in this bit of theater, but the statement was true enough, and it stung. He saw the look in Fitz's eyes, a regret for going too far with his words, for not thinking them through.

"You are an old, sour prick, Fitz."

Fitz's eyes hardened, and he remained in character. "And you are a young, sour prick who won't make it to old age."

Now the two men were just in the moment, railing against each other and finding a little enjoyment in the freedom of it.

But Fitzroy dispelled the moment. "Now it's time for me to ask. Why are you looking for me?"

"You can guess. I need work. I'll take this job no one else seems to be able to pull off."

"You're quite sure about that?"

"I'd prefer something a little less high-speed for my first job in so long, but I'm going to go out on a limb and say you have all your other ops on the back burner while you deal with this one."

Another glance at the philodendron told Court that Fitzroy was about to speak for the benefit of the microphone. "I'd love to send you off on something else, but it is imperative I satisfy the contract here in Hong Kong before taking on other clients. You might have to be vetted by the employer first, but you have my blessing to get to work. Standard compensation package applies."

"Triple it."

Fitzroy shook his head. "Bollocks. Too much. And before you start prating on about how I am a cheap bastard, I'll tell you that's not *my* call, old boy. China is footing the bill, and China won't accept your terms."

"Then the extra two hundred percent will have to come out of your pocket, won't it? Looks like solving this little problem for you just might save your life, so I'd say that puts me in the driver's seat."

"Selfish prick," Fitzroy said.

Again, this talk was just for the mics. The two men had professional respect for each other. It used to be genuine affection, and Fitzroy still felt the same about Gentry. But Court had cooled to the relationship after Fitzroy had deceived him once before. Still . . . as far as Court was concerned, he did owe Fitzroy his life for an affair that took place after.

Court felt personally indebted to Fitzroy, but he wasn't going to reveal any compromise whatsoever to the Chinese listening in to the conversation.

Now Court asked, "Do we have a deal?"

"You and I have a deal, but as I said, you'll have to pass muster with the man who holds the keys to the door locks, and the leashes on the armed guards."

"So . . . when do I get to talk to this Mr. Dai?"

"Not for me to say." He looked past Court now, towards the entrance to the room. "But if I had to guess, I'd say you'll get to meet him right about now."

Two security men in trim black suits had entered the parlor behind Court. They walked straight to him, grabbed him by the shoulders, and pulled him to his feet.

As he was shuffled out, Fitzroy stood quickly. "Lad. Good luck. When you've done the job, I'll see that the funds are wired directly into your account. You and I can speak again when I'm back in London." A hesitation. "Don't come back here. There's really no need."

Court understood. Fitzroy was telling him to run. To forget about any foolish attempt to save Fitzroy when it was all through.

Court wondered if Fitz somehow understood the truth: that Court's successful fulfillment of his true mission here would probably lead to Fitzroy's death at the hands of Chinese intelligence.

And Fitz would rather he paid that price than have Court come back here to try to save him.

Court gave what he felt might be his last look at Donald Fitzroy, and then he turned and followed his minders as they led him out of the room.

CHAPTER

EIGHT

Fifteen minutes later Court sat in a modern home office space three flights of open stairs above where Fitzroy was kept. A massive projection television screen adorned one wall in front of a comfortable seating area, and beyond that sat a conference table for twelve. At the far end of the room from the entrance, an enormous black desk sat right in front of open sliding glass doors leading to a balcony that Court estimated to be larger than Fitzroy's entire quarters downstairs.

This residence surely cost tens of millions of U.S. dollars, so it was no surprise that the balcony and office sported jaw-dropping views of the skyscrapers of Hong Kong Island, Victoria Harbor, and, beyond that, the southern tip of the Kowloon Peninsula.

Court sat in a leather wingback chair in front of the desk and snuck glances out past the balcony. He imagined he could probably pick out the Peninsula hotel in the hazy distance if he looked long enough for it, but instead he focused on other buildings, trying to orient himself, to pinpoint his location for use later. He did not want to give away what he was doing, so he returned his gaze to the man seated behind the desk in front of him.

Dai was in his late forties, healthy-looking, and he wore a dark suit with a shiny gold necktie. A bit of his parted gray-black hair hung over his forehead, but otherwise he was perfectly composed, and Court detected the posture and bearing cues of a military man.

But the man's background was less important to him than the man's present disposition, and Dai's eyes told Court what he needed to know. The man had suspicious, almost paranoid eyes, and they had spent all of the previous two minutes scanning Court's face while both men sat in complete silence.

Court glanced out the balcony doors again at the skyline in the distance, waiting for Dai to speak. He did his best to give off a slight air of insolence. He would not show any fear, subservience, or deference, because Court didn't want to give this man any reason to think for a second he'd had anything to do with the disappearance of the two Chinese officers from the evening before.

No, Court was just a hired hit man looking for work, fresh off a boat from Singapore and now held against his will by a bunch of guys who were also holding his handler hostage.

He wasn't scared; he was pissed.

In addition to Dai, five more men occupied this sprawling office, either sitting on the sofa in front of the projection TV or standing at ease in the corners. They were Dai's bodyguards; that was clear to Court. He could see butts of pistols in shoulder holsters, and one of the men by the door had a submachine gun hanging under his right arm, but none of them were particularly on guard at the moment.

Finally the man behind the desk spoke, and Court fought any expression of relief that the examination was over. "I am Dai."

"Okay. I am Joe."

"No. You are Courtland Gentry. The one they call the Gray Man. We know who you are. We came to Fitzroy in the first place to secure your services, but he told us he fired you years ago."

"He's an asshole *and* a liar," Court said. "He didn't fire me; I quit."

Dai regarded this comment in silence. Court hoped the comment, along with Dai's listening in of the conversation between Gentry and Fitzroy, would convey a quagmire of complicated but ultimately irrelevant issues between the American and the Brit. It would help solidify the ruse that Gentry had come to Fitzroy just at this time out of need, nothing more.

Dai said, "Whatever reason you left his stable of contractors, when we found out you weren't with him any longer, he offered up two other teams of men to fulfill his contract. Both failed."

Dai's command of English was impressive, Court thought, even if his accent was strong.

Court said, "And now, like a rat to cheese, I've come back. Lucky you. I'll do the job. I'll start today."

Dai ignored the American's comment. "You are quite legendary. We have followed your exploits around the world. Most recently you were in Washington, D.C. Making yourself even more of an enemy of your countrymen, from the look of things."

"That was a misunderstanding. I went home to clear things up. Nobody wanted to listen. Now it's time I go back to work."

Dai nodded slowly, taking in Court's words, tone, mannerisms, and expressions like he was trying to solve a puzzle. He said, "When you went to Wu and inquired about Fitzroy, you gave him the address of your hotel. Did you not think it possible he would sell you out to us?"

Court doubted Wu had sold him out. It was much more likely that the MSS had been listening in to the conversation. Still, he said, "I was counting on it. Wu would sell me intelligence about Fitzroy, and then he would sell whoever had Fitzroy intelligence about the man looking for him. I figured whoever had Fitzroy would come to me to see who I was."

"And how did you know *anyone* had Fitzroy?"

"That's easy. Sir Donald doesn't take vacations. He came here for an urgent work matter; then his staff in London lost contact with him. It was a simple thing to guess he'd been snatched by the men who hired him."

Dai nodded slowly, apparently satisfied that Gentry's story made sense. He said, "I work for the Chinese government."

Court made no expression, but he said, "This is my shocked face."

Dai didn't understand the quip, but he let it go.

Court said, "Honestly, I kind of figured it was some local gang who picked up Fitz. I wasn't looking to get mixed up with government guys. When your boys grabbed me in my room and brought me here . . . I recognized them as pros. I took them immediately for MSS." Court shrugged. "Whatever. As long as your money's green, I guess."

Dai said, "I am not MSS. I am MOD. Defense. Some of these men are mine; some are borrowed from MSS."

Court acted like he didn't care. "You had the sense to leave your uniform home in the mainland. Like I said, you're a pro. You're a general?"

"A colonel."

"Hang in there."

The Chinese officer cocked his head a little, confused by the patter. Court was still playing a character, three times as smartass and annoying as he would normally be, and it appeared to him Dai was coming to terms with the fact that the legendary American hit man in front of him was a peculiar fellow.

Dai said, "I am sure Fitzroy told you this job had turned out to be difficult for his men."

"Yes, he told me. But I will not fail."

"We will see, Mr. Gentry. First I have to ask you about a recent incident."

Court felt tension in the pit of his stomach. "Incident?"

"Two men working for me here in HK were killed last night. Do you know anything about that?"

Court feigned a look of surprise. "Sounds like you are closer to your target than you are admitting."

"These men weren't pursuing the target. They were on a separate errand. They were to follow a man dropped off by a CIA plane. They tracked this man to the Peninsula hotel. Their bodies were found floating in the middle of the harbor by a passing ferry this morning."

Court stared blankly. "The Peninsula?"

"That's right."

"The nice hotel with the Rolls Phantoms out front?"

Dai raised an eyebrow. "You know it, then."

"I've been here before, back when I had money. I'm here in HK this time because I *need* money, remember?"

"Tell me . . . why is it you are so desperate for money?"

"Let's just say I made some arrangements with some people to get me out of my last jam. The deal stipulated I would get the money to pay them off."

"Or?"

"'Or' doesn't matter. I do what I tell people I'm going to do."

"These people, were they CIA?"

Court played his role to the hilt now, cocking his head as if he were wondering if the person asking the question might possibly be mentally deranged. "The CIA? You think I *bought* my way free of the Agency? I fucking *shot* my way out, pal." He rolled his eyes. "Pay off the CIA? They don't need me to pay them off. They are part of the U.S. federal government, the guys that print U.S. dollars, or didn't you know?"

Dai asked his next question in a flat, emotionless voice. "Did you arrive in a Dassault Falcon yesterday?"

Court furrowed his eyebrows. "No. I came in a freighter."

Dai took this without comment.

Court sighed now, feigning frustration. "You suspect me of being a CIA officer who stays in five-star hotels. If you knew as much about me as you pretend to, then you would know the CIA has done everything in its power to terminate me for the past five years. You'd also know I'm flat broke. I left the U.S. with the clothes on my back and no more than a thousand dollars. Is this a joke or are you really that incompetent?"

Dai's face reddened a little, but he didn't argue. Finally he said, "Very well. I'll find out who killed the two officers, and I'll deal with them. As for you, your target is now a man named Fan Jiang."

Court nodded, hiding his relief that, for now anyway, he seemed to have talked his way out of trouble. He said, "Fitz didn't tell me much about the target."

Dai reached into a drawer in his desk and pulled out an eight-by-ten photograph of a young soldier wearing the uniform of an enlisted man in the People's Liberation Army. He stared lifelessly into the camera through thick eyeglasses, his small frame swallowed by the camouflaged tunic he wore and the peaked hat on his head. Court couldn't imagine this kid weighing over 110 pounds, and he appeared to be in his early twenties.

"He is a defector from the mainland," Dai added.

Court cocked his head. "You are going to a hell of a lot of trouble to punish your defector."

Dai did not reply.

"Fair enough. This little fellow has taken down contract killers sent by Sir Donald Fitzroy. How did he manage that? Is he some sort of a trained commando?"

Dai laughed without smiling. "He is nothing. *Nothing.* An information technology specialist. A computer hacker. He is being helped by Wo Shing Wo."

"Who's he?"

The colonel did not hide a look of disappointment. "Not a 'he.' A *they.* They are Triads. A criminal organization. There are fifty different Triad groups operating in Hong Kong; this place is a cesspool of crime." His jaw flexed. "One of many nauseating, disgusting results of capitalism."

"Fitzroy says he sent two teams. One team is dead, the other team missing."

The man behind the desk just said, "They are dead, as well."

"Fitz didn't say that."

Dai swiveled his chair around and waved a hand at the massive sprawl of Hong Kong out past the open balcony door. "Look at this place. There are probably ten mobile phones for sale on every square meter of Hong Kong. You think Fitzroy's team wouldn't call in if they were still alive?"

It was a fair point, Court did have to concede. "And you think these Wu Tang guys did it?"

"Wo Shing Wo. We only assume so."

Court swept his hand around, a gesture to the armed men standing around the room behind him. "Why don't you get these guys to just go find Fan Jiang? Surely you don't need a dozen men here to watch over Sir Donald."

Dai looked annoyed. "I do have many teams of men in HK already, turning over all the rocks we know to turn over, and we haven't found our target. We assume Fitzroy's men got close to the objective, so we give them credit for that, but we also give credit to our adversaries, because clearly they have the ability to fight."

Dai leaned forward, his forearms on the big desk. "You have a reputation for always finding your prey. For Fitzroy's sake, you'd better be as good as your reputation."

Court turned serious. "This guy is that important to you? You'd *really* kill Fitzroy if Fan Jiang gets away?"

The other man did not blink. "Without so much as a moment's hesitation. You should keep that in mind."

Court just cocked his head again. "Why? I'm not doing this to keep Fitz alive. His troubles with you are *his* problem. I'm taking this gig because I need the money." Court leaned closer himself. "And maybe if I pull this off for you, you can slide more jobs my way. Maybe there are others out there you'd like dealt with."

"Not at this time. Let's concentrate on Fan Jiang."

Court was deep into his role now. "That's fine. I'm just saying . . . something comes up in the future, we don't need to involve Fitzroy. We can cut out the middleman."

Colonel Dai did not bat an eyelash. "Mr. Gentry, I can, quite literally, cut out the middleman right now."

Oops, Court thought. He'd just accidentally advanced the idea to Dai that he should kill Don Fitzroy.

Court masked his frustration and pretended to think over the idea a moment. Finally he shook his head. "I want Fitzroy alive. He's still my meal ticket. He gets the best contracts around the globe. Plus, I don't know you yet. You start killing men you are in business with, then I *will* know you. I'll know you can't be trusted. I will walk out the door here to go kill Jiang, and I will keep on walking.

"See your agreement with Fitzroy through. Show yourself to be a business-man, and *this* businessman *will* fulfill his contract. I kill Fan for you, and Fitzroy goes back to London."

Dai waved a hand in the air. "Fine. Frankly, I like Sir Donald's operation, in theory. If this situation is resolved, we will send him home safe and sound. Maybe he will work for us again someday. Maybe you will, too."

Fat chance on both counts, asshole. Court did not say it; in fact, he nodded in agreement. Glad he'd defused the situation, Court asked, "You know where I should start looking for your defector?"

Another photograph appeared from the desk, this one of three men. Two were white, tough-looking guys in their forties: one had short hair and a beard; the other was clean-shaven with a bald head. The third man was black, with a beard and mustache. He might have been a little younger than the others, but no less tough.

Dai said, "This is Fitzroy's second team. All from Great Britain, all former Special Air Service commandos. They called him three days ago from a bar in Po Toi. It is a small island south of central Hong Kong. They claimed to have tracked a group of Wo Shing Wo there, although they could not be certain Fan was with them. There were no other relevant details." He shrugged. "The team never made contact with Fitzroy again."

"You sent your men to this island to look for them, I assume?"

"Of course. No trace. Unfortunately, there are Triads operating on Po Toi, and they are able to identify police and security officers quite easily. But a *gweilo* like you should be able to appear nonthreatening."

"What is a *gweilo*?"

"It means 'ghost man.' A white person. You should be able to get close enough to the Triads to find out where they are hiding Fan Jiang, because they won't suspect you of being involved in the interests of the People's Republic of

China." He handed the photo and a notebook to Court. "In the notebook you will see a list of known Wo Shing Wo properties. Bars, restaurants, houses of ill propriety. Many *gweilo* businessmen frequent such places. It will help you find your way around or into the organization. You will also find all Fitzroy's notes about his communications with his men, before they disappeared. I had him write everything down to help us in our hunt."

Court took the notebook and slipped it into his cargo pants. "Okay. I can start with this. Can your boys give me a ride back to my hotel? Preferably *not* facedown on the floorboard?"

"You will need a weapon."

Court said, "Not yet. If I get eyes on the target, I'll have you provide me with something."

The PLA colonel cocked his head. "So . . . you just go out in the field with nothing but a phone?"

"I just need cash. I'll buy the equipment I require off the shelf, but like I told you, I'm broke."

"How much?"

"Twenty-five thousand U.S. For expenses."

Dai didn't seem happy about this, but he looked to one of his men and gave a quick nod. The man disappeared to get the money.

Dai then nodded to the men behind Court, and Court stood before he felt the hands on his shoulders that he knew would be coming.

Dai said, "Major Xi will take you wherever you want to go to begin your work. You do not have time to dawdle on your mission, and frankly, neither does Sir Donald. Keep me posted on your developments."

Court said, "If you want me to provide you with intelligence along the way, you have to assure me I'll still get paid and Fitzroy won't be harmed if your men get to Fan Jiang first." This was simply a ruse to establish his cover, and to stress that Court's assistance only came as long as Fitzroy was alive.

"You have my word. I am interested in the end result. That is all. Fan Jiang must not leave Hong Kong. The clock is ticking, Court Gentry."

CHAPTER

NINE

The Chinese intelligence officers hooded Court as they had when they brought him to the safe house, but on his return trip down the hills and through the tunnel under Victoria Harbor he was at least allowed to sit upright. A young man pressed against either side of him, and as Court sat quietly during the drive, he occupied a portion of his time by coming up with ways to take them down, relieve them of their weapons, and then hold the men in the front seat at gunpoint. It would have been no real trick for Court to pull this off; these MSS operatives were highly trained but they were not ready for him to make a move at all.

But the fact was they were correct to assume Court would come along compliantly. He wouldn't take these guys down; he wouldn't hold the driver and front passenger at gunpoint.

For the time being, anyhow, Court Gentry was Colonel Dai's bitch.

The men dropped him off once they were north of Tsim Sha Tsui; they just pulled over to the side of the road, yanked the hood from his head, and let him out of the SUV.

As the vehicle screeched off on the wet streets, Court saw that it was a BMW 2 Series Gran Tourer, a small minivan that looked like it had some power and cost a few bucks. Court watched it disappear, then turned and continued on to the north, back in the direction of his hotel.

Walking through Mongkok on a rainy late afternoon, Court realized he did have to agree with Colonel Dai on one thing. Hong Kong looked like capitalism had put its head between its knees over a big green beautiful island chain and vomited out its shinier, flashier, and baser elements. HK was New York on steroids. Vegas on acid. Virtually every square inch was a bright sign, an explosion of color and noise and scent, an assault on the senses thinly disguised as an offer to sell something, a product or service one absolutely could not afford to miss out on.

Or else it was a Dumpster, a garbage can, or a plastic bag full of the detritus of all this humanity squeezed together.

Court had been all over the world, and he'd seen all the other economic systems firsthand. They sucked more, to be sure, and he'd given the good years of his life fighting *for* the very system on display here, but he had to admit that this version of unadulterated capitalism was a mess to look at.

He believed in it, and he liked it better than any alternative; he sometimes just wished it would scrub itself up a little.

Court made his way through the orgy of noise, smell, and light, back to his guesthouse, where he passed through the lobby and endured the overt stares of the old man behind the counter. This was the same man who'd checked him in this morning, and he'd probably been here to watch the spectacle that had happened earlier in the day, when Court was frog-marched out by goons with a hood over his head.

The man behind the counter ended his condescending stare abruptly and turned away, surely curious about the business of the American but not wanting to make the American's business *his* business.

Back in his little room, Court immediately saw that it had been ransacked by Chinese intelligence. They'd done a fair job of it, and Court was instantly relieved he had not taken the Montblanc pen with the truth drug powder in it. That would have immediately tied him to the incident in the Peninsula, and had it been found in his room, he'd now probably be lying dead along the side of the road back up in the Peak.

He lay down on the bed and thought over his situation. There was no reason for him to leave the hotel for operational concerns; the men he'd run from at the Peninsula were on his side now, or as close to being on his side as they ever would be. But still, he didn't know who had seen him leave with the government goons, and the thought that there were eyes on him around here made him uncomfortable.

But he fought the urge to get up and go; as much as he loathed staying right where the bad guys knew he could be found, he recognized that leaving would just make Dai suspicious.

With his accommodations settled, he turned his thoughts to his larger operation. After a few moments' worry and the resultant pain in the pit of his stomach that indicated he understood the stakes of this assignment, he told himself to calm down. Other than the situation with the two attackers the evening before, everything was proceeding exactly according to plan.

The CIA had sent Court on this operation in the first place because they knew he could get close to Fitzroy, and Fitzroy would get him in with the Chinese. Brewer's orders to Gentry were to make contact with Fitzroy, act as if he were just an old employee looking for work, and get himself assigned to the Fan contract.

Court had done just as he'd been directed, and Dai had taken the bait. The colonel had given up little information about who, in fact, Jiang was, but Court knew why Dai wasn't in a chatty mood about the target. Simply put, the colonel was down here to fix an embarrassing mistake, and he wasn't going to reveal to a Westerner that such a mistake was even possible.

The Agency's brief to Court told him that forty-eight-year-old Colonel Dai Longhai was the new director of counterintelligence of the 2nd Bureau of the People's Liberation Army, General Staff Department (3rd Department). This meant he was army but served as the security chief of a very elite and secretive branch of soldiers tasked with creating advanced persistent threats into the classified intelligence systems of its adversaries. Unit 61398 was the Chinese name for the group, but the CIA referred to them by the code name they'd assigned to the unit—Byzantine Candor.

Unit 61398 was one of the chief cyber warfare arms of the PLA, and they had broken into many Western government secure networks, including those run by the Pentagon and the entire Department of Defense. As far as anyone knew, they had yet to get into JWICS, the U.S. intelligence community's most secure network, but it was not for lack of trying, and many in America's counter-cyberintelligence realm thought it was just a matter of time, because the men and women of Unit 61398 were exceptionally well financed, supremely well motivated, and, frankly, the best in the world at what they did.

And within the elite men and women working at Unit 61398, the CIA knew of an even more select, more exclusive group, and this was the outfit Fan Jiang belonged to. Though Fan and his colleagues in this handpicked detail worked and lived near the rest of the unit, they were sequestered from them because their job was something of the opposite of that of their colleagues. Fan was on a task force simply called Red Cell. They were charged with using the hacking techniques crafted by 61398 and then turning them around, retrofitting them for the purpose of attacking China's own secure intelligence networks to hunt for flaws in their counter-cyberwar systems.

Red Cell knew the West was doing just what Unit 61398 was doing, so they applied 61398's latest technology against their own classified systems. Day and night they sought to breach the most secure networks in their nation, to steal secrets from their own Ministry of State Security, their Ministry of Defense, even the Chinese Communist Party leadership.

The government of the People's Republic of China was not exactly the world's most trusting organization, so it vetted Red Cell members carefully, lest one or more of their number actually succeed in breaking into the systems and see something he or she should not see.

This made the members of Red Cell the most watched over and the most scrutinized of all the members of Unit 61398, who were themselves among the most highly vetted in the nation. Every single member of the team had undergone rigorous background and party loyalty checks just to get into the unit. They had been dosed with truth drugs and given lie detector tests; their families, friends, and neighbors were routinely subjected to intense and occasionally hostile interviews.

The Red Cell had been a successful unit in the four years of its existence. It had found weaknesses in the Chinese intelligence community's electronic communication practices by using the work of Unit 61398 to poke holes in what were thought to be secure networks. And they had done it all without one single security issue from any Red Cell member.

Until that night less than two weeks earlier—the night Fan Jiang ran from a hotel in Shenzhen and began his journey into the Special Administrative Region of Hong Kong.

The evening of the incident, Lieutenant Dai Longhai had been second-in-command of 2nd Bureau's counterintelligence department, which meant he was the number two man over security for Unit 61398, but he'd been called into work in the middle of the night and informed that, beginning that moment, he was now a colonel, and he was now in charge, and his *one* priority was finding a runner from Red Cell.

Dai was given unprecedented powers to call up forces from the military and intelligence services, to put the border guards on high alert, and then, when there were confirmed CCTV images of Fan Jiang in Hong Kong, Dai had been given authorization to go over the border himself with a small army of killers and spies, and even to call in Western contract killers to help him out, since Dai thought white faces might make it into certain areas where Fan might try to run—places where his Chinese military and intelligence officers could be easily identified.

Fitzroy was contacted to bring in the *gweilos*, but to date, Fitzroy had failed.

Court learned all of this in his CIA brief, although he was not told how the CIA obtained this information. This was an SAP operation—a Sensitive Access Program. Sources and methods had to be protected, after all. But the CIA freely admitted they did not have a clue why Fan Jiang decided to run in the first place.

Court understood how these sorts of things worked for security chiefs; if Colonel Dai Longhai returned to the mainland with Fan's head on a pike, his career would not benefit from this. He'd win nothing if he succeeded, but he would certainly lose everything if he failed.

The CIA did not want Fan Jiang dead, of course. They wanted him alive, which certainly complicated things for Court, but he understood how important it would be for him to succeed in his mission. Fan Jiang knew the Chinese secure networks inside and out, and Court couldn't imagine anyone on Earth the U.S. government would want to get their hooks into more. The Agency would offer Fan Jiang the moon and the stars to work with them, and if Fan turned the Agency down, then the dangling carrot would be replaced with a swinging stick.

American national security was at stake—Fan Jiang would not be given much of a choice in the matter.

Court wasn't sure if he was on a rescue mission or a kidnapping mission. It all depended on how Fan Jiang looked at his situation.

The only problem Court could see with the Agency's plan was that if brought to a successful conclusion, it would leave Sir Donald Fitzroy in a house filled with over two dozen Chinese military and intelligence operators who would all be extremely angry with him.

Dai would kill Fitzroy for Court's duplicity; of that Court had no doubt.

The CIA operation took this into account, at least on paper. Their plan was for Court to locate Fan Jiang, then for Special Activities Division Ground Branch paramilitary operatives to swoop in and snatch the Chinese soldier in such a way that made it look as if the Gray Man had executed his contract.

They would fake Fan's assassination, thus keeping the U.S.'s involvement secret and saving Sir Donald Fitzroy.

Hell of a plan, Court thought. How, exactly, this would all come to pass *was* a bit murky, since the Agency had no idea who was helping Fan, where he was being held, what his disposition was, and so forth. Court was simply to get the answers the Agency needed to go forward, involve himself in the ruse by being on scene when the man was taken in by U.S. operatives, and then report back to Dai that the job had been done. If Dai wanted pictures, DNA, witnesses, or even one of Fan's fingers to prove that Court had accomplished his mission, then the Agency could make that happen. If Colonel Dai wanted the body, then Court and CIA would devise a reason this was not possible. A sinking boat, a burning building, too many police to simply scoop up the body of an adult male and shuffle into a cab with him.

Yeah, when Court first read the op specs on the plane, he recognized that the details on how to placate the MSS were paper thin, but he noticed something else from the wording and the orders.

Saving Don Fitzroy was secondary to nabbing Fan. *Very* secondary. In fact, the CIA had put significantly more emphasis on Court Gentry's own personal security than on Fitzroy's life, which should have made Court feel better, but for some reason it did not.

Court lay there on his bed, analyzing his situation. Don Fitzroy had been a high-level officer in MI5, British intelligence, so Fitz must have seen the peril of his situation. He had to have known there was a huge chance he would be killed at the end of this operation, regardless of how it turned out. But he seemed to have done nothing to save himself.

Court understood. Fitzroy knew the Chinese had global reach, so he had to give them an easy target. Otherwise there was always the chance they would go after someone else.

Sir Donald Fitzroy's daughter and his twin granddaughters could have been used for leverage, and Fitzroy would die a thousand deaths before he let that happen. He'd sit there compliantly in Hong Kong, waiting for the day the colonel came downstairs with his gun in his hand, and by doing this, he'd protect those he loved.

In that moment Court felt nothing but respect for the old man held in the twenty-million-dollar house on the hill a few miles to the south of him. Fitzroy would fight and die for his family, but Fitzroy had no one fighting for him. The CIA, the Chinese, his own security detail. Everyone had, apparently, bailed on the Englishman.

But Fitzroy had saved Court's life once off the coast of Sudan. Court's own sense of honor told him he *could not* let Fitzroy die alone without a friend in his corner. Court would be Sir Donald's champion, and if CIA had a problem with that . . . then CIA could go fuck itself.

Court told himself there *had* to be a way to pull off the trifecta on this mission: nab Fan for CIA, get his own ass out of this in one piece, and get Fitz out of the clutches of the Chinese and back home safe.

It was doable, Court still told himself. Tough, to be sure, but doable.

To this end, Court's first objective would be to find the exact location where Fitzroy was being held. The only way he could be confident that he could help his former handler, especially if something went wrong during the extraction of the Chinese computer hacker by the CIA, was if Court knew he could always hit the big house up on the hill, guns blazing, and attempt to rescue Fitz himself. It was a last-ditch option, but if he did not know the location of the house, it was no option at all.

He knew how to solve his problem. He'd gotten a perfect look out the back window of the property, and he'd examined his view of the skyline of Hong Kong. With this information stored in his brain's memory, he could figure out the exact location of Dai's safe house.

So now he scanned the Peak on Google Maps, using the relative positions of several buildings he'd noticed from Dai's office as reference points. After a few minutes he recognized Dai's safe house, zoomed into Street View, and found it at 1 Pollack's Path Road. Typing this info into his search engine, he found the property on a real estate website and saw that it was available to rent for one month for sixty-five thousand U.S. dollars. Court wondered if Dai had paid this amount, or if the entire real estate concern was actually owned by mainland China's defense or intelligence services. It didn't really matter. What did matter was the fact that the real estate website had photos of the inside of the building.

Court had hit an operational-planning gold mine.

But only for his own personal operation. He would need this information if the CIA's plan to ensure Fitzroy's safety failed. If Dai and his people realized the Gray Man had deceived them and passed Fan Jiang off to the CIA, then he would need to engage in these desperate measures. He hoped like hell he wouldn't have to come back, but if the shit hit the fan, it might be necessary.

Court nodded off, hoping to sleep through the night to shake off the last vestiges of jet lag. Tomorrow morning he would go full tilt after Fan Jiang, knowing now he could finally focus on the reason he'd been sent here in the first place.

CHAPTER

TEN

I f Fan Jiang had known how hard this would be, if he had had any clue how many people would be put in danger by his actions, how many would lose their life because of him, there was no way he would have ever gone through with any of it.

Fan was not a violent man, not a hard man, and he was most definitely the wrong man to be in this place, enduring all this. But he was here now, far past the point of no return, and there was no turning back. He was on the run, and he would live or he would die, but pondering the wisdom of his decision was a ship that had long since sailed.

He had a birthday coming up, and he hoped he lived to see it. He'd be twenty-seven in a month, which meant he was young to die, but at the rate things were going, he felt the odds were stacked against his survival.

Fan Jiang was hot and cold at the same time. The hot, dank air in the little compartment all but cooked his lungs, but the cold metal floor he lay on stung the exposed skin on his arms. He'd spent almost four whole days in the bowels of this cargo ship, and for the last day he'd been rocking and rolling and vomiting as the ship had taken to the open sea.

He lay in a tiny dry storage room no larger than a hotel bathroom, just off the kitchen, with men looking in on him from time to time from a hallway outside. He wasn't a prisoner here—he'd readily agreed to come on this voyage, after all—but he got the impression he could not simply get up from the cold vibrating floor and walk up on deck whenever he wanted.

He'd eaten rice soaked in some chicken broth the ship's cook had brought to him in a bucket, and to relieve himself he'd been handed a second bucket—he *hoped* it was a second bucket—but otherwise he'd had little contact with the crew.

The rest of his human interactions—if you could call them that—were with the men in the hall: his bodyguards.

If you could call *them* that.

The five men in the hall were on his side, officially anyway, but they were also angry, and they were taking their anger out on him. Initially there had been eight of them, but three had died in the gunfight four days earlier, and one of the survivors now lay in Fan's sight on the cold rusty vibrating floor of the hallway, a bandaged bullet wound high on his thigh and a face that stared blankly ahead and turned whiter by the hour.

The man had been injured because of Fan Jiang, and others had died because of Fan Jiang, so Fan Jiang had no problem understanding their fury.

But Fan himself hadn't done it; he hadn't wanted *any* of this at all.

Fan spoke Mandarin and English, but both the crew on the boat and the other men here—his angry protectors—spoke only Vietnamese, so there was no way for Fan to tell anyone here how sorry he was for all the trouble, how much he regretted that there had been a fight, and how much he appreciated the fact that the five survivors had continued on with their operation despite the hardships and the loss of their friends.

Fan was worried about the future, to be certain, but he was so glad to be out of Hong Kong finally that he could hug the men in the hall. Not that he would try, because they would probably just pistol-whip him if he climbed to his feet and attempted to leave the storage compartment.

He guessed he was just ahead of his pursuers when he made it into Hong Kong proper, where he made contact with Wo Shing Wo, first by e-mail, and then in a bar in Tsim Sha Tsui. They agreed to take him in when he made them an offer they could not refuse: he'd give them a list of all members of their organization known to the Chinese government, as well as a complete rundown of all the surveillance measures being used against them.

This Fan did in an Internet café on Waterloo Road. Years earlier Unit 61398 had created a back door into mainland China's federal police network for the PLA, so it was no trick for him to pull up known Wo Shing Wo personalities and details on the police surveillance packages run against them. Once Fan had the info, he immediately raced out of the café with the Triads surrounding him for protection, because he had reason to believe the Chinese would be able to track the origin of his session in their network.

For the next week the Triads demanded more and more of Fan, especially as the heat on them grew and grew in HK. Clearly the MSS had been able to discern that Fan was working with Wo Shing Wo, so the cost of Fan's protection grew in relation to the cost the Triad group paid to keep him safe. He used other Internet cafés and coffee shops, a Starbucks on Argyle, an outdoor café with wireless access on Prince Edward Road, hotel rooms all around the Central and Western Districts—all to help Wo Shing Wo learn information from the Chinese mainland about rival Triads operating here in the city.

Fan's work had been helpful to Wo Shing Wo, but the heat from the mainland Chinese agents in the city grew, and soon it was too dangerous for both Fan and Wo Shing Wo to continue their relationship.

So the Vietnamese entered the picture.

The Vietnamese gang on the boat with him went by the name of Con Ho Hoang Da, the Wild Tigers. Boasting a membership of over one thousand, they paid bribes to communist leaders in Ho Chi Minh City and Hanoi to keep the police back and to let them move heroin, mainly from Laos, through Vietnam, and then on to small dry-goods haulers like the one Fan Jiang now traveled on, directly to Hong Kong, Singapore, and South Korea.

They weren't the biggest transnational criminal organization out there, not even the biggest in Vietnam, but Fan had done his homework while in HK, and he decided he would be safe with the Wild Tigers.

Fan made a deal with the Ho Chi Minh City–based gang to give them a month of his services in exchange for safe passage and refuge out of Hong Kong and into Vietnam; Fan promised to break into Vietnam's Interior Ministry's secure network and help the gang learn about measures against them, and for his work he only wanted a safe place to hide out for a month or so till the heat eased on the hunt for him, before finding his own way on to his next destination.

After the deal was made with the leader of the Wild Tigers, his Wo Shing Wo protectors took him in a high-speed boat to the southern Hong Kong island of Po Toi, a rocky and sparsely inhabited speck in the water accessible only via ferry, a few water taxis, and private boats. In a quiet bay, the Wo Shing Wo boat pulled alongside a seventy-five-meter-long and nine-meter-wide rust-covered dry-goods hauler called the *Tai Chin VI*.

Fan learned quickly that he could communicate with no one on board, other than to confirm that they would take him to Ho Chi Minh City.

Not long after the Triad boat disappeared around the northern tip of the bay, as the crew of the *Tai Chin VI* began pulling in the anchor, a trio of heavily armed men appeared on the deck—Fan only assumed later they had come from below the water's surface—and a vicious gun battle erupted and raged across the ship. Two white men and one black man fought like lions against the much larger force, but the Vietnamese protected Fan, rushing him to the very storage hold he now sat in. In the fighting, five Vietnamese boat crew and three Wild Tiger gangsters had been killed. All three Westerners died, as well; this was explained to Fan from hand gestures by the Vietnamese survivors, and the boat had to wait in the bay for two days before more crew could come up from Vietnam to sail the vessel back home.

Now Fan was on his fourth full day in this cargo ship, and just when he looked at his watch and realized night had fallen above deck on another day he'd not seen with his own eyes, the young Chinese man felt the change in the vibration in the floor, then heard the pitch alter in the cargo ship's engines.

They were slowing, and soon they came to a complete stop.

The Vietnamese gangsters led Fan out of the bowels of the ship on his unsteady legs and up a series of ladders, and he stepped into a humid night that felt amazing on his skin. He followed his protectors past the crane in the center of the deck and over the port-side ladder of the big cargo vessel, passing a large group of armed newcomers on the deck who appeared to be more Vietnamese gangsters. The men wore backpacks and looked like they were a new crew, already preparing for another mission.

At the bottom of the ladder, a large rigid-hull inflatable boat trolled in the black water alongside, and Fan climbed down into it. His protectors climbed in with him, the injured man was lowered on a litter, and then the RIB turned away and its pilot pushed the throttle to full power.

Fan sat in the middle of a group of young, quiet, and unhappy-looking men. Looking around in the distance for the first time, he saw the skyline of Ho Chi Minh City on both sides of him, and he realized he was no longer in the South China Sea at all. The *Tai Chin VI* had steamed up the Saigon River, which wound through the city like a partially coiled snake.

As they neared the water's edge in the boat, Fan looked back behind him; the *Tai Chin VI* had already turned around in the center of the river, and it was now heading back to sea.

Off the nose of the RIB, a dozen men waited on a poorly lit dock in front of a small motorcade of vehicles. Fan saw no weapons, but several of the men wore jackets in the warm night, so he assumed they were hiding pistols or folded-stock submachine guns. Despite his nerves, Fan climbed off onto the dock and approached the entourage.

A Vietnamese man in his forties stepped out from the group of men. He was well dressed, and he wore a wide grin. "Welcome," the smiling man said in English.

"Thank you," Fan Jiang replied, bowing low as he spoke.

With a handshake the man said, "I am Tu Van Duc. I am in charge."

"I am Fan."

"You will be well protected while you are with us."

The wounded Wild Tiger fighter from the boat was carried off the RIB next to the two men and into the back of an SUV. He looked like he could die at any moment. Tu looked him over, spoke authoritatively to his men, then returned his attention to Fan.

"I've been told you were attacked by a group of Westerners."

"Yes. I was on deck when it started, but your men protected me, some with their lives. I am sorry this happened."

Tu slapped Fan on the shoulder, knocking him back on his heels. "We have been fighting for one hundred years. It is in our blood. To die in battle is every man's dream."

Fan didn't know what to say. He was a soldier himself, in that he was a sergeant in the People's Liberation Army, but he'd never met anyone who much wanted to get shot in the leg and then slowly bleed to death in a rusty cargo ship.

Tu smiled now, as if a dying man had not just passed by. "You look like you could use some food, a beer, a shower."

Fan bowed again. "Thank you, sir."

"Tomorrow you will begin this computer magic you have promised us. Tonight you eat and rest."

"I will fulfill my end of our arrangement," Fan said as he was led into an SUV in the center of the motorcade.

Fan's ultimate goal was Taiwan, not Vietnam, but he had had to get out of Hong Kong, and this group had helped him do just that. Taiwan still felt like a long way off, but Vietnam would work for now, and he didn't think either the mainland Chinese or the unknown Westerners who had attacked the ship four days earlier just before they set sail from Po Toi Island would find him here.

He could not have understood the scope of the hunt for him, and he could not have been more wrong.

CHAPTER

ELEVEN

Court could have done without the four assholes trailing him from the hotel this morning.

Shortly after beginning the operation on his second day in Hong Kong he'd performed a quick SDR: entering and exiting a few electronics shops along the way, looking out into the street through the store windows. He bought a couple of items—Court was a kid in a candy store with all the low-cost and high-tech gadgetry on offer—but mainly he was in counter-surveillance mode.

He picked up the tail quickly, cussing under his breath as he made them.

The men tracking him up the road traveled in a pair of small four-door sedans, and he assumed they were MSS. With just a quick evaluation of their procedures he could tell they were cut from the same cloth as the two men he'd killed at the Peninsula, and a similar ilk to many he'd seen at Dai's safe house the day before.

Court stepped back out of an electronics shop with his purchases in his cargo pockets. In his hand he held a new mobile phone, and as he started walking north he dialed Dai's number.

The call was unencrypted, but Dai didn't seem to give a damn. "Yes?"

"It's me," Court replied.

"What is this phone you are calling me from?"

"Doesn't matter. It's a burner. I'll be using a different number each time we talk."

The PLA colonel answered, "Suit yourself. What have you learned so far?"

"Only that you are not a trusting guy."

"What does that mean?"

"Four guys on my tail. Two vehicles. Do you have more ready to follow me into the MTR, or will the passengers in these two cars have to bolt out and catch up if I go down an escalator?"

Dai did not reply to this.

Court said, "I work alone. I can shake these guys, or you can call them off. It's up to you."

Dai said, "I am impressed with your abilities. I will recall my surveillance team."

"If you send others, I'll see them, too. But if I see them, it might mean the people holding Fan see them, and I don't think that's what you want."

"No one wants that. Remember, Sir Donald's life depends on your success."

"I'm here for the payday, Dai. Not for the old British guy. I'll kill Fan Jiang for you, as long as I'm not the front end of a block-long parade of mainland Chinese gunmen."

Court hung up and kept walking towards the Prince Edward Metro station and then, as he began to take the stairs down, he turned and looked behind him. The two vehicles had peeled off somewhere in the past block, and he saw no one on foot who looked overly suspicious, although there were easily three hundred people moving along with him here on the wide sidewalks on Prince Edward Road, so it was impossible to be sure.

Satisfied he had done all he could do to ID any persistent surveillance on him, he descended into the MTR station, keeping his eyes peeled at all times for anyone who seemed interested in his movements.

After a thirty-minute transit across waters almost as crowded with maritime traffic as the sidewalks of Hong Kong had been with foot traffic, passengers on the Stanley–Po Toi ferry disembarked at the public pier on the southwestern side of the little island. Court Gentry moved down the boat ramp along with a mix of tourists, fishermen, and trinket merchants, then lagged back on the dock, letting everyone continue on ahead of him.

Court had spent some time looking over every cove of Po Toi on Google Earth, and to him it didn't appear like there was much of anything going on anywhere else on the scrub-covered rock other than here, in the little bay in view from the pier. His research convinced him he was right; the total population of this island was only two hundred.

He gazed out across the placid water of the bay as the other passengers kept walking. Ahead on his right was an open-air seafood restaurant with a wooden roof; in front of that, men who rented kayaks and boats sat in the sand next to their little vessels, looking expectantly but with noticeable frustration at the small number of tourists disembarking from the ferry and moving in their direction.

Court noticed a few buildings along a poorly maintained road that ran near the beach. On the far end of the bay, on the opposite side of the water from Court, a footpath ran along the waterline, past a smaller restaurant/bar that looked derelict and closed. It was open-air, as well, with a tin roof and a deck that hung out over the water's edge. Shacks ran up the steep hill above the bar, and the path continued to the left where, out of Court's sight at the end of the trail, he knew a Buddhist temple sat alone on a little cliff over the water's edge. He'd read that tourists visited the temple not because it was all that special in itself, but rather because of the nice pictures one could take of the ancient site in the foreground, and the turquoise water of the South China Sea in the background, along with tiny rocky islands jutting up in the distance.

Court pulled his binos out of his cargo shorts and focused them on the derelict building on the far side of the little bay from the public pier. The walls were open so he could look all the way into the dark dive, and he didn't see anyone at the tables inside. Panning up, he noticed the sign was in Hanzi, standard Chinese lettering. There was no attempt to draw tourists to the establishment, and it was half covered in scaffolding made of bamboo lashed together with rope. Initially it seemed like the place was closed, but now he noticed smoke from the kitchen rising out of the chimney and hanging over the shacks above it on the hill. The place looked like a dump; most anywhere else, even in Hong Kong proper, it would probably be condemned, but despite its outward appearance, it seemed to be open for business.

Court walked down the pier towards the beach road, trying to put himself inside the heads of Fitzroy's three men who had come here four days earlier. What were they looking for? And who would they go to in order to find it?

Fitz had written in his notes that his three operators reported following a speedboat full of Wo Shing Wo men here from the Kowloon Peninsula, but they didn't know if Fan was with them or what the Triads were doing here on the island. It had been eleven at night when Fitz got the call from them, so Court surmised Fitz's men hadn't taken the ferry, and this meant they must have had a boat of their own. The public pier was really the only place to dock on the island that he had seen from Google, although without knowing how large Fitzroy's men's boat was, it was hard to know if they'd just driven right up on some stretch of beach and landed themselves, or even anchored offshore somewhere.

The British ex-spymaster had relayed that it sounded like they were calling from a bar, so with little else to go on, Court decided he'd ask around at the bars here in the bay to see if anyone remembered the three Englishmen.

A few minutes later Court stepped up to the door to the Ming Kee Seafood Restaurant, right on the beach next to the kayak renters. Bright English signage welcomed tourists, and Court planned on entering right behind a group of Austrians from the ferry, but he stopped abruptly at the door when he noticed the hours of operation posted there. He saw that the place closed at nine p.m., just before the last tourist ferry left the island.

If Fitz's boys didn't make contact with him until eleven p.m., and they did so from a bar, this seemed like the wrong place to ask around about the three Englishmen.

Court decided to go to the more rustic establishment on the far side of the bay, thinking it might cater to anyone who lived in the shacks and any boaters anchored overnight nearby.

It was just a five-minute walk around the water to the footpath that led to the restaurant. The sun's heat scorched his arms and lower legs, but his ball cap shielded his face. He walked just behind a few tourists from the UK heading to the temple, and he listened in while they considered dropping into the restaurant ahead for a beer before continuing their walk.

As a group they decided against it as they got closer; the place really was a ramshackle and unwelcoming hole-in-the-wall.

Court saw no English-language writing anywhere on the small sign in front of the little establishment, but he did see from the hours posted on the door that the place was open till midnight each evening. If Fitz's men had been here following Triads, and if no other part of the island was built up, then it was quite possible, likely even, that Fitz's men had come to this bar.

As he entered the corrugated tin–roofed building, he expected to be the only Western face in the place, so he was surprised to see a pair of young Caucasian girls sitting at a table along the railing, looking over the side, down to the water ten feet below. Each of them had a bottle of Tsingtao beer resting on the railing in front of them. Other than the two young women, a man behind the bar sitting on a stool and playing a game on his phone, and a mature woman at a table reading a newspaper, the dark little establishment was empty.

Court scanned for security cameras as he moved along the chipboard-and-plastic-sheeting walls of the dive and towards the bar, and he decided quickly that the proprietors of this joint had spent the full measure of their technology budget on the three bug zappers hanging from the ceiling—certainly not on any sort of a CCTV security system.

Court sat quietly at a stool at the bar for thirty seconds, just feet from the bartender, but the young man remained huddled over his phone. Moving purposefully low profile around the world meant sometimes Court didn't get the best service, but he took advantage of the moment to continue checking out the facility: a couple dozen plastic tables surrounded by three or four dozen plastic chairs, some sturdier aluminum bar stools around the cheaply made wooden-topped bar with a warped surface that indicated it had seen a lot of spilled beers in its time, and likely some monsoon rains dripping down from the bad roof, as well.

Court was certain the builders of this place had violated every single building code known to man. There was some concrete-block construction in the corners here and there, but the overwhelming majority of this little dump seemed like it could have been built in a day by Boy Scouts rushing through the obligations of their woodworking badges. It looked to the American like a firetrap, a collapse risk, and a germ haven all in one.

Court eyed the two Caucasian women again, checking them as potential threats—not out of any real suspicion, rather simply a force of habit. One of the two was tall and thin, with white-blond hair in long braided pigtails and tattoos on both arms; her large backpack was on the floor next to her. She wore a cutoff Bob Marley T-shirt over a black tank top and worn-looking capri pants.

The other woman was of average height and had an athletic build, and she wore big black sunglasses. Her dirty brown hair was rolled into braids and wrapped in a simple leather headband, and she had a tie-dyed T-shirt and baggy pants rolled up to her shins. Her hemp sandals were cinched around her calves with leather ties.

Court put them in their late teens or early twenties, and Western European, for sure.

Neither girl had even glanced up at Court since he'd entered; they just gazed out at the water as they chatted and laughed, enjoying the view and their beers.

Court looked back to the bartender, a young Chinese man of no more than twenty-five, with a round face and thinning hair. The man noticed Court finally and put his phone down.

"Tsingtao, please." Court said it with a British accent.

When the man returned with the beer, Court kept up the ruse that he was a Brit. "Is it always so slow around here?"

The bartender chuckled, completely at ease. "Yeah, man. During the day it is. At night the boats in the marina and the bay come in, gets kind of busy. Usually it's just my mom here during the day." He nodded over to the middle-aged woman reading the paper at the table across the room.

Court hadn't seen much of a marina here, but he had seen a few slips near the pier, all of them empty.

The bartender started to turn back around to the cash register to ring up Court's beer, but Court spoke.

"Any chance you were here Sunday night?"

The man cocked his head, surprised at the question, then thought back. His expression seemed to darken somewhat. "Yeah. Till close. Why?"

Court pulled out five hundred Hong Kong dollars, the equivalent of a little more than sixty U.S. He said, "I had some mates here on Sunday, around eleven. Two white, one black. British. They would have been together. See anyone like that?"

The man looked at the money on the bar for several seconds, then back up at the American offering it. Court detected a slight twitch, a microexpression, on the man's face. "We don't get many Westerners here."

Court looked back to the white girls, then down at himself.

The bartender said, "At night, I mean. They all go back up to HK with the last ferry. Try the Ming Kee. You passed it coming from the ferry dock."

Court replied, "I tried the other place. But the Ming Kee was closed at eleven p.m."

The bartender nodded. "Yeah, that's right."

"I was supposed to meet my friends here, but I didn't make it. Having a hard time running them down since then."

The man shook his head and glanced up and to his right. "No, I don't remember them. Sorry."

Court affected nonchalance to the man's answers, but he was well trained to scan for clues of deception. While Court's easy smile did not waver, he noticed the fidgeting nature of the bartender; his hands played with the bottle opener now, turning it over and over, and he shifted a little from one foot to the other. Court had established a baseline for the man's mannerisms during their earlier conversation, just so he could pick out any changes when he began his interrogation. When he'd spoken about how slow the restaurant was and how it picked up at night, he'd not been fidgeting at all.

The Chinese man turned away quickly and rang up the beer, then put the tab in front of Court.

"Sorry I can't help you."

"Not so sure that you can't, mate. Anyone else working I can ask? Was your mom here then?"

Court saw the man glance a second time out to his right, not to his mother, who was sitting back over his shoulder, but to a point in the distance. Court knew eyes tended to flitter during deception, but it almost looked to Court as if the man was fixing his gaze to a specific point both times. A spot out in the bay? Court had seen a few fishing boats out there when he arrived on the ferry, but he hadn't paid much attention to them. Now he would have given anything to turn around and scan the exact area the man had looked off to.

But Court remained disciplined. He didn't want to let on that he'd picked up the subtle tell.

"No. She doesn't work at night. We get a rough crowd. Just booze. No food."

Court pulled out another five hundred HK dollars. "All right, mate, here's the deal. I was on holiday with these three blokes from London, renting a flat in the Mid-Levels. Two bloody weeks. The fuckers ran out on me a day before we had to pay the balance. They owe me a lot of money, and I'd quite like to have a chat with them about that."

The American had designed his explanation to calm the bartender, to give a credible reason why a man might offer up over a hundred U.S. dollars' worth of local currency to find three other men. But the bartender didn't seem to relax at all; if anything, Court felt like the man's defenses rose even more. He stopped squirming but became ramrod still. His body and his hands seemed to clench a little.

Court knew what this was. The man had told his lie, and now he realized his lie wasn't believed. Liars often go on guard to defend themselves, and sometimes they give out physical cues about this change in tactic.

But while the man's body remained still, his eyes flicked a third time out to the bay.

Court thought he understood now. A boat. The bartender was thinking back to Sunday night subconsciously. He had seen Fitzroy's men, and they'd had some involvement with a boat, right out there.

But if the bartender *had* watched the three Brits take a tender out to a boat, why wouldn't he just take the money and give up the information? What was he hiding?

The bartender showed his nerves now. "I told you, man. I didn't see anybody."

Just as Court was about to press once more, on his left one of the hippie girls from the table by the railing leaned against the bar and caught the bartender's eye. Court saw that the man was relieved to be rescued. While the girl with the big sunglasses and the headband ordered another beer for herself and her companion in Scottish-accented English, Court sat patiently, waiting for another crack at the bartender.

He took the opportunity to fake a slow neck roll, and to use the movement to look out to the spot the man kept eyeing. A few fishing boats lulled around in other areas in the calm water, but that part, out past the mouth of the bay, was empty. Whatever boat this man was picturing in his mind's eye was long gone now.

The girl returned to her table with her beers, and the bartender went out of his way to disappear from the American holding the two five-hundred-HK-dollar bills. He moved back into the little kitchen accessible from behind the bar, threw some noodles into a large fryer, and began turning them over and over with a strainer.

Court slipped the money back into his pocket and continued drinking his beer.

He decided he'd wait a few minutes, but then he'd take off. As far as Court was concerned, the bartender had told him plenty without saying much of anything. Fitzroy's men *had* been at this bar, they'd gone out to a boat in the bay, and there was some reason the bartender didn't want to talk about it.

Over Court's left shoulder the Scottish girl looked out at the water while her tablemate gulped her fresh beer and talked on and on in English, but in a heavy German accent. The brunette with the braids and the leather headband pretended to listen to the blonde from Hanover for a few minutes more while she glanced out to the bay, then back to the man at the bar who'd spoken with a British accent. She'd heard a slight twanging of his *a*'s when he said the words "have" and "that" to the bartender, and to her that sounded like American English. The girl knew languages, accents, and dialects, so she looked at the man again and decided after a time that he was, in fact, American.

Her head turned back to the water.

Now, the blond German began wondering aloud how hard it would be to score some Ecstasy back at her youth hostel, and the Scottish brunette across the little table just ignored her, shifting her eyes up to the green and brown hills of Po Toi Island.

What the hell is going on? she asked herself.

The Scottish brunette wasn't really Scottish, and the blonde wasn't really her friend. The blonde was just like the braids, the tie-dyed T-shirt, and the headband: part of the brunette's disguise. The two had met on the ferry when the brunette had sat down next to the blonde and introduced herself as Lilly, then struck up a conversation with Katrin from Hanover about the Buddhist temple on Po Toi. Since they both said they were vagabonding alone around Asia, they decided they'd go see the temple together once they got off the ferry.

But on the walk around the bay, Lilly offered to buy beers at the less expensive-looking of two bars on the path to the temple. Katrin had to make her money last for this trip, so just about any time *anyone* offered to buy her a drink she was up for it, and this was no exception. Plus, Lilly had cool hair and cool sandals so, Katrin figured, she was probably a cool chick.

Now Katrin talked recreational drugs while the Scottish girl who wasn't really Scottish looked back to the British man at the bar who wasn't really British, wondering how long he'd been sitting there before she'd noticed him and, even more importantly, how the *fuck* the Central Intelligence Agency had learned that the Triads had delivered Fan Jiang to the cargo ship here at Po Toi Island.

CHAPTER

TWELVE

The woman at the railing with her eyes on the man at the bar didn't think he looked much like a CIA officer, but he *was* American, he was here shaking down the bartender for information, and the bartender was having none of it. She knew this place was a Wo Shing Wo hangout, so either Fan Jiang had been here at the bar, or one of the Triad men who'd been involved with moving Fan Jiang had talked. Either way, the American *had* to be Agency; the coincidences were too many for any other explanation.

The woman calling herself Lilly and pretending to be Scottish struggled to maintain a calm countenance. She smiled and nodded at something Katrin said, but on the inside her guts were turning into knots.

The *last* thing she needed on this op was for the fucking CIA to start snooping around the target area on the very day of her hit.

Just as Lilly wasn't really Scottish, her name wasn't really Lilly; it was Zoya. Zoya Feodorova Zakharova was about as far from a hippie Scottish vagabond as she could be. She was an operative in the SVR—Russian foreign intelligence. She was in her early thirties but easily passed for ten years younger. She was here in HK operating with a clandestine SVR paramilitary unit. She and her task force had been ordered to bring Fan Jiang back alive to Moscow so that her intelligence service could learn everything possible about Unit 61398, including how to infiltrate both China's and America's most secure military and intelligence computer networks.

Zoya was the officer in charge of the task force, which meant in theory she shouldn't be out here like this, running low-level surveillance. But she found herself doing most of the footwork on this op herself because the men working with her were ex-soldiers first and foremost, and while they could shoot and scoot with the best of them, they weren't the slickest bunch when it came to blending into their surroundings. No, low profile was Zakharova's specialty, along with language, intelligence collection, surveillance, and countersurveillance, so she was here, playing a role that allowed her to sit in one of only two bars with a view of the bay, to attempt to get a tactical picture of the area so her direct-action team of snake eaters would be ready to board the ship when it returned this evening.

The Russians knew much of what was going on here in Hong Kong because of a highly placed source in the HK Triads. They'd even known that this particular hole-in-the-wall was frequented in the evenings by Wo Shing Wo men who smuggled heroin into the city from Vietnam, but Zoya had *not* known that the CIA was aware of Fan Jiang's existence, much less his escape from mainland China.

This was decidedly bad news.

The blonde from Hanover kept talking; now it was a story about buying bad pills in Korea the previous month, so Zoya looked up at her and smiled with an understanding nod. She realized the German girl had no idea the American had even entered the bar, and it occurred to Zoya she hadn't noticed the man enter herself, and this bothered her. She wondered how a man could have slipped into a nearly empty room without being picked up by someone with her skills of perception.

A few minutes ago she had been wondering if the time was right to slip away from the vapid blond German and probe the Chinese bartender for information. When she'd glanced up she'd seen the agitated, nervous look on the bartender's face. Only then had she noticed the man sitting at the bar talking to him.

It was as if the white man had just materialized on the bar stool.

Zoya then stepped up quietly to the bar, under the ruse of ordering another round, in an attempt to listen in, but she'd only heard that the man was looking for some "mates"; his British accent, while extremely good, didn't pass muster to a world-class linguist like herself.

She never really got a perfect look at the man. She thought about a little flirting, using her typical modus operandi and playing the female traveler engaging another tourist in idle conversation, but something held her back. She sensed a darkness there, a sense of danger to the man. She felt it without even looking into his eyes.

He was a serious player in this game; she knew this without a doubt.

She didn't want to engage, to risk blowing her cover, so she'd grabbed her beers from the bartender and returned to her table to think things over.

And now as she looked at the American from behind, only seeing flashes of the side of his face as he glanced around, she realized she wasn't certain she would recognize him if she saw him again.

This son of a bitch was *that* good.

Court Gentry decided the bartender was going to stand around in the back and fry noodles until the annoying customer at the bar left his establishment, so Court obliged. He threw a couple of bills on the bar top, leaving a tip for the asshole that he most assuredly did not deserve, because as bad as this man was as an intelligence source, he was even worse as a bartender.

Court then slipped off his stool and headed for the exit.

Zoya had not noticed the man when he entered, but she did watch him leave through the front door. She'd been careful to track him with her peripheral vision until the very last second he was in sight, and only when the door closed did she look back to her tablemate.

Katrin had noticed her new drinking partner looking towards the door, and she followed the gaze. Seeing nothing but a closing door, she turned back to the woman she knew only as Lilly.

"What?"

"Nothing."

Zoya Zakharova wouldn't attempt to follow the man. She wasn't here to tail CIA officers; she was here to nab Fan Jiang, and in this endeavor she would stay as far away from the Central Intelligence Agency as possible.

Katrin finished the last of her beer now, then spoke in her heavy accent. "Are you ready to visit the temple?"

Zoya sipped her own bottle. "You know, I think I've changed my mind. I like this island; I'm going to skip the temple and go find a hostel or a room for rent. I'll spend the night here, and check out the temple later."

Katrin took the comment with a look of shock on her face. "There is nothing going on here. I want to see the temple and then take the two p.m. ferry to get back to civilization. Discos, bars, the fun stuff. I thought you said you wanted to party."

"I'll catch up with you back in Kowloon tomorrow. I need a night of taking it easy to get ready."

Katrin smiled, proud that she was more of a party animal than the cool chick from Scotland.

The two girls hefted their backpacks and left the little pub, exchanged e-mails, and shook hands at the front door—even young Europeans tend to be more formal than Americans with casual or newly formed acquaintances—then walked off in opposite directions.

Katrin thought the two of them might become good friends, perhaps even travel together here in Southeast Asia.

Zoya, in contrast, didn't think anything about Katrin; her mind was on her mission, and it certainly didn't include ever laying eyes on the hippie stoner from Germany again.

Forty-five minutes later Zoya Zakharova stood at the top of a hill overlooking the bay. Directly below her was a steep decline that led down to a boulder-strewn beach at the water's edge; a hundred meters beyond that was the public pier, and two hundred meters farther was the far side of the bay and the little dive bar she'd just left.

She unslung her backpack and laid it on the dirt, sat on a flat granite rock next to her pack, and pulled out a water bottle. Two beers wasn't anything for her, but she knew enough about her body to know that two beers, followed by a fifteen-minute walk and then a half-hour steep climb on a rocky trail in direct sunlight and high heat and humidity, would dehydrate her if she didn't replenish soon.

As she took a few sips of the tepid water and looked off over the placid bay, she heard a voice behind her, close but muted, as if coming from deep in the waist-high foliage she'd passed before sitting down.

"You've got a fucking phone, *Koshka*." The language was Russian, the voice was male, and the tone was derisive. "Koshka" meant "female cat," and it wasn't Zoya's real code name, but the men she worked with had taken to calling her that a long time ago.

If there had ever been any real reason why, she'd forgotten it.

Zoya gulped more water down, ignoring the man a moment more. Then she said, "America is here. Just one man, but I think he's Agency."

After a significant pause, she heard another voice from the bushes. *"Der'mo." Shit.*

"*Da.* Couldn't get pictures or hear much conversation, but he's asking around, something about three British men. Sounds like they might be missing."

There was a rustling in the brush now; Zoya drank more water from her bottle and, after pulling her binos out of her bag, began scanning the buildings in sight around the bay, a futile attempt to see if she could get eyes on the American somewhere on one of the little roads down there.

Next to her a man appeared, head to toe in brown camouflage, his own binoculars in his hands. Zoya knew Ruslan had a suppressed sniper rifle, a VSS Vintorez, on a bipod somewhere back there in the brush. Through the high-powered optic on the rail of the weapon, and not through the binos in his hands, he'd been watching Zoya throughout her visit here to the island.

"I didn't see you talking to anyone but the blond girl and the bartender."

"I didn't talk to him; I heard him talking to the bartender."

"I never saw him."

"He's got skills."

"Who do you think the three British men are?"

"How the hell should I know?" Zoya asked, then lowered her binoculars and put them on top of her pack. She unscrewed the lid on the water bottle and drank some more.

Another man appeared from the brush behind. He was filthy. He'd been up here all night, Zoya knew, and he smelled like it. He said, "Satellite shows the *Tai Chin VI* passing to the east of Hainan Island. At present speed it will arrive here at twenty-one hundred hours tonight."

"And we'll be ready for it when it arrives?" she asked.

The filthy man said, "Don't know about you, Koshka, but me and the boys are ready for it *now*."

She thought about admonishing him for the nickname. They were in the field, and she had a code name. Her complete code name was Sirena Vozdushoy Trevogi, which meant "Banshee," but the task force operators were supposed to call her Sirena, not Koshka.

But she let it go, deciding to pick her battles. "We need survivors, Sasha," she said flatly. "This is an intelligence mission, and if there is no one left alive on that ship to tell us where Fan Jiang was taken, then we've all wasted a trip."

Sasha stood over her, blocking out the sun with his wide shoulders. "You will have your survivors to interrogate. We *have* done this before, you know."

She spun around on the granite rock and looked straight up at the man. "Oh yes, I know. I was there, in Kizlar, trying to interrogate that one survivor. You know, the man holding his intestines in with his shattered hands. He was rather distracted, barely heard me. Fucking useless endeavor."

Ruslan sighed audibly next to her. "You're never going to let us forget that night in Kizlar, are you?"

Now Zoya turned to him. "I'll make you a deal. You boys don't fuck it up tonight, and I'll try to forget the debacle in Dagestan."

"That would be good for all of us, yourself included," Ruslan said.

Zoya looked at her watch now. "It's twelve hundred hours. You both can go; I'll take watch on the hide. Have Vasily send another team up here by sixteen hundred so I can get back to the boat in time to prepare a brief for the task force before tonight's raid."

"*Ponial,*" Sasha replied. *Understood.*

Both men turned away from the woman sitting on the granite rock, and they headed back into the brown brush to collect their gear.

Zoya called back to them. "Leave the VSS."

She heard a low chuckle from Ruslan. "You gonna shoot the American if you get a chance?"

"Of course not. I'd just rather use that mounted scope than hold these binos up for the next four hours."

Ruslan said, "I'll leave the rifle behind, but you need to remember two things. One, keep your finger off the trigger. And two, there is no round in the chamber now, and I want to find it that way when I get it back."

Zoya was quick with her reply. "You need to remember two things yourself."

Sasha mumbled in the brush, "Oh shit, here she goes."

"One . . . I received advanced sniper instruction at Kavkazsky Dvorik, which, as you well know, is the premier FSB Spetsnaz training facility for long-distance shooting and sniper fieldcraft. And two . . . go fuck yourself."

Sasha cinched his heavy pack on his shoulders, laughed, and started walking down the hill to the northeast and out of sight of the bay. Ruslan hefted his own gear, minus his rifle. He then returned to Zoya on the rock. "I totally forgot that you were one of the boys, ma'am. I bet you were very popular at Kavkazsky Dvorik with your tits poking out of your little tie-dyed T-shirt."

He turned and followed Sasha down the trail without another word.

Softly Zoya said, *"Mu'dak."* *Asshole.* She looked down at herself. She was in "costume" for her cover alias: wig, big sunglasses, ridiculous clothing, and woven bracelets on her arm. Of course she wouldn't be taken seriously by the paramilitary unit working with her. They didn't live in a world that accounted for much art or personal expression.

She shook off the hostility from her male colleagues—it was nothing she hadn't heard ten thousand times before—lifted the binoculars back up to her eyes, and scanned out into the South China Sea. Tonight the cargo ship that had spirited Fan Jiang out of Hong Kong would appear from the southwest; it would be full of drug smugglers, but it would also contain answers to where Fan Jiang went and who was protecting him now. She and her black ops paramilitaries would board the boat not long after setting anchor; they would obtain those answers any way they could, and then they would go wherever in the world the intel directed them, so they could snatch Fan Jiang and take him to Moscow.

The men on the cargo ship would know where they delivered him and to whom, and they would talk; Zoya had no doubt in her mind.

It wasn't long before her binos swept back to the shore, and they scanned the streets slowly. She was thinking about the American again. Her mission tonight was going to be tough enough without worrying about mixing it up with the CIA. She didn't need this guy around here asking questions one damn bit.

She stood, grabbed her pack, and headed back into the brown brush. She'd climb behind the rifle and scan the bay with the scope for the next four hours, hoping like hell everything remained just as sleepy and peaceful as it appeared right now.

CHAPTER

THIRTEEN

C ourt took the half-empty ferry back to Kowloon at twelve thirty p.m., positioning himself in the center of a large cluster of empty seats near the bow on the bridge deck. Court surfed the Internet on his mobile during the ride back to the city, hoping to find a shop somewhere in Hong Kong that sold a particular niche item. He expected to find two or three stores at the most selling the goods he was looking for, assuming there couldn't have been that large a market for this type of equipment.

Instead his phone filled with listings, and at the bottom of the list was the option to go to the next page of results.

Hong Kong was a mecca for electronics, with no shortage of choices.

Court selected a store in Mongkok, not too far from his hotel, because the area was crowded and not so close to the Peninsula, which was damn important to the guy who'd killed two men there two nights earlier.

An hour and a half later he stepped into an electronics shop that specialized in high-end optical devices, surveillance equipment, and other wireless mobile security solutions of all kinds. He spent several minutes just reading tags and brochures, familiarizing himself with several items he'd never used before, and reacquainting himself with other items that were upgrades to equipment he'd known all his professional life.

First he bought a small handheld thermal monocular that would allow him to see heat registers in the dark, even from a great distance. He was very familiar with the technology, but the version he picked up here was a generation better than anything he'd used before.

Taking his time to look around at other items, he found something he'd never had access to during his time with the CIA. Clearly, technology for private users had moved beyond what a man in Court's line of work could field just five or six years earlier. It was a tiny wireless camera that linked with a smartphone and gave the operator the ability to view remotely in regular, low-light, and infrared views, as well as pan and zoom the camera. For just under three hundred bucks each Court thought they were a steal—if they worked as advertised—and it was Dai's money in his money belt, anyway. He bought three of the devices.

He also bought a radio scanner and another smartphone; Court told himself he'd pick up as many phones as he could reasonably carry around here in HK.

After leaving he took a cab to a scuba-diving shop on Sai Yeung Choi Street and bought a mask, fins, and a tank of "spare air"—a small pony bottle filled with oxygen, used as a supplemental emergency air source when diving. Court knew he might be swimming out to check over boats in the bay tonight, and if he had to do this in a low-profile manner, it would be nice to be able to swim under the surface. An entire scuba rig—a buoyancy control vest along with a full-sized tank, weights, and a regulator—would be ideal, but this would also mean carrying a bag back to the island the size of a full-sized suitcase and weighing over sixty pounds. Court much preferred cramming the fins, mask, and emergency air in a small backpack along with his other items, something he could drop and run away from if necessary.

At the dive shop he also purchased a small Kershaw fixed-blade knife with a sheath he could hang around his neck under his shirt. This was his only real weapon now, and it was strictly for defense, but Court had well-practiced edged-weapon skills, and he knew a small knife could be enough for him to "acquire" a firearm from an enemy along the way.

On his way back to his hotel room he slipped into a little tea shop attached to a grocery store, ordered a bottle of water, and jammed himself into an isolated corner, one of the more challenging things he'd pulled off all week considering the crowds here in the city. He popped an earbud into his ear and pulled out his smartphone. He downloaded a commercial app that let him make encrypted calls, then dialed Suzanne Brewer, all the while keeping his eye on the movements of those around him. He knew the ambient noise in the busy shop would work to his advantage, but if anyone decided they wanted to get close or linger too long, he'd have to go mobile.

The pedestrians on the sidewalk outside the window in front of him moved like cattle being pushed through a stockyard, so he really wasn't in the mood to negotiate the logistics of a clandestine conversation while shoulder-to-shoulder with foreign nationals.

As always, Court's handler was a pro. When he called, she answered, and quickly. "Brewer."

"It's me."

"Identity challenge, Apollo."

"Identity response, Anger."

There was a slight hesitation, and then she said, "That's a fail. You get one more chance."

Damn, thought Court. He was out of practice with this shit. Checking in wasn't really his bag. He thought back to his daily code changes. He'd memorized them on the plane over; he knew them all, but he'd forgotten the correct sequence. *What was this, day three? What was yesterday's code?*

He tried again. "Identity response, Angry."

"Identity confirmed."

For crying out loud, Court thought but did not say.

He did say, "I'm in play. I made contact with Colonel Dai yesterday. He is satisfied I had nothing to do with the MSS men killed at the Peninsula."

"That's a relief. And what about Fan Jiang? Did Dai hire you to terminate him?"

"Yes, I'm on the hunt, just as planned."

While he spoke to Brewer his eyes scanned, back and forth, searching for any surveillance. But to any untrained eyes gazing his way, he just looked bored.

"What have you learned about Fan's location?"

"Not enough. I have a lead to run down, but so far it hasn't turned into much."

"What's the lead?"

"Nothing confirmed. We were wrong about Dai and Fitzroy being able to point us right to the objective. This is going to take some detective work."

"Well . . . let me help you."

"I will . . . as soon as I need help."

Brewer adopted a more severe voice now. "I detect a certain sparseness with your intel, Violator. I understand your frustration with the compromise the other day, but I won't allow you to jeopardize the mission by keeping details from me. This isn't the way you are used to doing things, I understand, but you aren't running the show alone anymore."

"Yeah, I picked up on that when two jackasses followed me from the airport."

Brewer's voice stiffened even more now. "There was a mistake on our end, it's been acknowledged, so you've heard all the contrition you are going to hear from me on that. You are an agent. *My* agent. You managed to get this op back on track, and for that I am thankful. But now you need to do your job, and that means keeping me in the loop."

Court wanted to crush the phone with his hand. He told himself he didn't need an angry nanny.

But, in actuality, he did.

"All right. I'm looking for a boat that was at the mouth of the bay near the public ferry dock at Po Toi Island on Sunday night."

Court could hear typing in the background.

"What's the name of the vessel?" she asked.

"I don't know."

"Tonnage? Type? Registry?"

"Nope, nope, and nope."

"How do you even know that—"

"Because a nervous bartender looked out to a spot in the water."

"I'm sorry?"

"I told you what I had was thin."

After a moment to get her bearings, Brewer told Court to wait while she checked the Automatic Identification System vessel-tracking website, Marinetraffic.com, looking for any vessel that moored in or around the bay at Po Toi Island the previous Sunday night.

When the screen came up she told Court there were a few small fishing boats, but nothing larger than that.

But Court already knew the search would be a long shot. Most ships were not required to squawk an identity code if their gross weight was less than three hundred tons. And in the case of whatever vessel Fitzroy's men had boarded, it seemed clear it would be running black no matter the tonnage. If it was transporting Fan or providing the location of some sort of a meet for a group of Triads, he couldn't imagine they would squawk their identity and location.

When Brewer seemed to draw a blank, Court said, "Look, I need to get back to work. When I have a lead I think you can help with, I'll—"

Brewer interrupted him. "I've got it."

"You've got *what*?"

"Satellite images. Not from Sunday night, we weren't overhead then, but from thirteen hundred hours on Monday. There is a cargo ship in the mouth of the bay. Nothing else around the island even a fourth of the size. We have a shot from Tuesday, too. Yes, still there, in the same place."

Court just muttered, "Wow." He was impressed with the fast work of Brewer and CIA.

Brewer said, "I guess the Gray Man doesn't have his own satellite."

"It's in the shop."

She ignored the joke. "The ship was still there Wednesday, but after that it's gone."

"Can you see the name?"

"The angle is no good to read the bow. It's the same shot each day, more or less. I guess it didn't move around very much while it was there. I'll be able to ID the make of the ship in a second, running it through a scan. There are no goods on the deck, but there is a crane for loading items into the cargo holds. I see a couple of men here and there showing up in different locations, but other than these deckhands, no activity."

She then gave him the manufacturer information of the ship, and told him there were 343 known to be in operation around the world, and over 90 in Southeast Asia. "I can run down locations on all of these, but it will take a couple of hours. For those that aren't squawking their codes I can dig into ownership information, try to find out where they are, as well."

Court thanked her with a promise to check back later, then signed off. He bought some clothes and other items from nearby shops, went back to his hotel room for an hour and a half to open his new gadgets and test them out, then repacked them in his backpack. He dressed in a dark long-sleeve but breathable hemp shirt, dark brown linen drawstring pants, and black trail-running shoes. He would look like an adventure tourist inside an establishment or walking in the village, but he knew his earth-tone colors would allow him to move with some camouflage in the foliage of the island, if necessary.

C ourt returned to Po Toi on the ferry, arriving shortly after seven p.m. There were many more fishing boats out in the bay now as the sun began to set, but the bartender he'd caught looking out to the bay had been gazing out farther than any other vessel had moored or anchored, so Court didn't suspect that anything bobbing in the water now was related to Fan Jiang and the missing Fitzroy assets. He walked off the public pier with the rest of the light load of ferry passengers, then continued through the little village. There were a few Westerners and other tourists walking around, taking pictures, and drinking beer in simple cafés a few blocks inland.

Court imagined Po Toi couldn't have been on any travel publication's list of the top one hundred things to do in Hong Kong; there wasn't much to see here at all, but there was just enough tourist action around that he didn't look completely out of place walking the streets.

After strolling through just a few blocks in the village, he found himself climbing a winding trail that led up a wooded hill, past a few tin shacks, and then quickly into a steeply graded path that wound through granite boulders and thick brush.

After a ten-minute walk, he found himself at the summit, which offered an excellent vantage point on the bay below. Here he sat on a flat boulder and surveyed the entire area, from the beat-up little bar he'd visited earlier in the day in the distance below him on his right to the village and public pier directly below him, and then, to his left, a rocky beach in front of a higher hill devoid of any man-made structures. In the water directly in front of him he saw nothing but fishing boats and other small craft. He spent the remaining moments of daylight scanning them carefully with his high-power binoculars, until the sun set fully and darkness enveloped the island.

He called Brewer back and found out that of all the ships of the type she'd seen on sat images at Po Toi earlier in the week, eighty-one of the ninety-one known to be operating in Southeast Asia were displaying their AIS identification information. She listed the names and registry information of the ten that were not transmitting, but Court only wrote down the ones that were truly off grid, as four of the ten were known to be in shipyards at the moment.

She had one other piece of interesting information, although he didn't know exactly what to make of it. Checking older satellite images of the area, she determined that the cargo ship they were trying to identify had been showing up in Po Toi every five to ten days for the last several months. On all other occasions except for this week, it had remained only a few hours. Brewer had been trying to find it on other sat images to tell Court where it came from, but these were the most congested shipping lanes in the world, so this had proved tough going.

Court hung up with Brewer and then decided he'd spend the night right here, watching the area down below, trying to spot any evidence of interesting activity here in or around the bay. If one of the ships matching a name on his list showed up, he'd swim out to it if he felt he could do so in a low-profile manner; if not he'd just call it in to Brewer, have her look into the vessel if he could find anything for her to look into.

Other than this thin plan, he had no clear picture of what he was going to do here, but he knew what he was *not* going to do. He told himself he wasn't going to try to Sherlock Holmes his way through this. Fan Jiang could be getting farther and farther away from him, which would mean his op for the CIA would fail, and it would put his old handler Fitzroy in mortal peril. He was here to find a clue, and if he had to rush headlong into the situation to get the information he needed, that was just what he was going to do. He'd strong-arm, he'd break teeth, he'd do whatever was necessary to get answers.

At eight fifty p.m., a paramilitary operator working for Russian foreign intelligence lay in the overwatch position to the southeast of the bay, his eye in the scope of his suppressed sniper rifle. Slowly he moved his arm off the butt stock, then triggered his interteam radio headset with the push-to-talk button on his chest. He spoke without taking his eye out of the scope of his VSS rifle.

Softly, the Russian said, "Anna Seven for Sirena, over?"

It was quiet in the dark hide, other than a warm evening breeze rustling the dry scrub brush around the prostrate man, occasionally blowing enough to wave the wide brim of his dark green camo boonie hat. The hat, like the rest of his gear, had been purchased at a hunting supply store in HK, so there were no tags or brands that would associate him with Russia.

A reply came through Anna Seven's earpiece, delivered in Zoya Zakharova's unmistakable intelligent and sultry voice.

"Go for Sirena, Seven."

Anna Seven was a thirty-one-year-old operator named Mikhail. "She's right on time."

Through his scope Mikhail watched the *Tai Chin VI* approaching the island up the sea lane from the southwest. It was already slowing, heading towards its normal anchoring position at the mouth of the bay.

"*Ponial*," replied Zakharova. *Understood*. Then she said, "Alert me instantly if anyone leaves for shore."

"Yes, ma'am."

C ourt finished a bag of crackers, swatted at a fly, then stood to loosen his tight back muscles. He couldn't fully stretch out; his three-and-a-half-week-old gunshot graze to the right side of his rib cage, while fully closed and mostly healed, still stung like hell when he reached over his head with his right hand or did anything that involved twisting or rotating his torso. Still, Court Gentry was a man who had grown accustomed to dealing with pain in his life, to the point where it felt almost jarring for him to wake up in the morning without noticing an immediate ache somewhere on his body.

After he sat back down he reached for his binos to scan along the bay-side, but before he brought the optics to his eyes he noticed something new. In the dark distance, the lights of a cargo ship moved slowly and silently around the southwestern tip of the island.

This vessel was certainly no massive tanker, but it was much larger than anything else he'd seen around here.

It appeared to be the one from the image Brewer had sent him earlier.

Quickly he scanned the restaurant directly below him. It was closing down; the last of the patrons were leaving, and they began walking to the public pier to catch the last ferry of the night to Hong Kong proper.

Court then swept his binoculars to the right and pushed them up, where he found the derelict bar he'd dropped into before noon that day. It was nearly full now, with the opposite vibe he'd experienced when he'd sat at the bar.

He didn't know where all these patrons had come from. Some were certainly locals, and others would be fishermen staying on their boats; he could see the dinghy dock floating in the water ten feet below the railing of the establishment's deck. It was half-full with rubber dinghies and wooden tenders. But looking into the little open-air dive, he saw easily fifty people, all apparently men, sitting around at tables or at the bar. He didn't think they could *all* be from the village and these boats. He wondered if other boats were docked offshore at other points on the island.

He watched while the cargo hauler came to a stop, then dropped anchor in the same general spot the bartender at the dive bar had kept eyeing earlier in the day.

Slowly, excitement began to grow in Court.

Conclusive evidence? Not hardly, but he had a feeling he was onto something.

The ship had closed enough to where Court could read the lighted bow with the help of his binoculars. It was the *Tai Chin VI*, which, he saw to his excitement, was on Brewer's list of ships that had not run their transponders on Sunday. It was registered to a freight company out of Jakarta, and Brewer had noted that it never transmitted location information, even though its gross tonnage was 745, well over the 300-tons rule.

Interesting.

Court just sat there, watching through the night vision binoculars, occasionally switching to his infrared monocular to scan the deck of the vessel, then sweeping the device over different fishing boats in the area, before going back to his binos to look at the crowded bar at the southwestern end of the bay.

Less than thirty minutes after dropping anchor, one of two white tenders with outboard motors was lowered from the back of the *Tai Chin VI*. Several men climbed down a ladder and boarded. Court went back to his infrared device and used it to count the men on the tender. Five white-hot human forms, plus the heat from the little boat's outboard engine. As they got closer to the shore, he could see that a couple of the men wore backpacks, but otherwise they weren't carrying anything overtly on their bodies.

Their tender motored directly to the dinghy dock floating below the bar he'd visited earlier in the day, and they climbed up the narrow and steep stairs to the deck of the bar.

Court lowered his binos and drummed his fingers on them, trying to decide what to do.

It did not take him long.

He realized he'd accomplished as much as he could sitting on this hill. Now it was time to stir things up, to play the role of agitator.

He would go to the bar, where he would stand out like a sore thumb, but he would try to get close to someone from that boat, or any Wo Shing Wo Triads involved with Fan Jiang. He'd try to get bad actors to reveal themselves, using his own proximity as a lure. If they were tied to whatever happened to Fitzroy's men, well, then Fitzroy's *new* man would probably find some trouble, too.

And Court was looking for trouble tonight.

Before leaving his overwatch position, Court took a device out of his bag and turned it on. It was one of the wireless cameras he'd bought at the surveillance shop earlier in the day. Smaller than a deck of cards, it would run for eight hours on a single charge and send video directly to Court's mobile phone. The camera had a motor to pan left and right on a small disc, but Court just tied it to a branch on a nearby tree with pipe cleaners bought for the task, rendering it stationary. The wire in the pipe cleaners allowed him to adjust the angle of the camera somewhat, so he maxed out the ten-power zoom with the app on his phone, then physically adjusted the camera till he had it centered on the cargo ship anchored five hundred yards away. It wasn't the closest view of the ship, but with a single sweep of the mobile app, he could switch the low-light vision of the camera to infrared view, and using this he could see figures standing on the deck, represented as red hot spots.

With this camera he could keep an eye on the ship without yanking his binos or monocular out of his backpack in the middle of the bar, a tactic he couldn't imagine he could pull off while remaining covert.

At nine forty p.m., Court flicked his pack over his shoulder and began moving down the hill.

CHAPTER

FOURTEEN

There was another vessel in the water near Po Toi Island, but Court couldn't see it. It lay at anchor off the eastern shore, some two and a half miles east of the bay, and it was impressive to look at on the outside. But as luxury yachts went, the current occupants found it almost as cramped on the inside as living in military barracks. The yacht was a Numarine 68 Fly; it boasted a forty-seven-ton displacement and a cruising speed of twenty-five knots, and it had been rented out by the week from a service on Kowloon. Logistics personnel working at the SVR station in Hong Kong had acquired the vessel from the owners with an open-ended return date, stocked it for a week so it could house more than a dozen operatives and all their gear, then moored it in a slip at a large public docking facility.

Then the logistics personnel left it there.

And soon after they left, Zoya and the task force arrived and climbed aboard.

The boat was now crewed by Russian naval personnel brought down from Vladivostok, men who looked at this operation as a vacation from their normal daily grind on a coastal patrol boat, and they, as well as a team of security men brought in to secure the vessel, had no clue about the real mission of the main element of their small task force.

This yacht was designed to accommodate eight in luxurious comfort.

Now seventeen in all—sixteen men and one woman—lived in stifling proximity to one another, sleeping in shifts on every flat surface, their massive stocks of gear filling all the cargo holds as well as every possible nook and cranny belowdecks, even stowed under black tarps lashed to the main deck.

The yacht had been docked in a mooring field north of the Hong Kong airport for the past three days, but the previous evening they'd relocated to this spot off Po Toi. Zoya had ferreted out information from a rival Triad gang that a Chinese defector pursued by mainland intelligence in Hong Kong had been taken to Po Toi on a Wo Shing Wo speedboat several days ago. Here he was to be handed off to a cargo ship called the *Tai Chin VI* that ran heroin back and forth between Wo Shing Wo and some Southeast Asian drug concern. The information was thirdhand at best, but Zoya liked her chances, so she moved her task force here to set up shop off the island.

After confirming the presence of Wo Shing Wo on the island and after a Russian spy satellite had found the ship heading back to Po Toi, Zoya and her task force decided their best chance for finding Fan before anyone else was to hit hard and fast soon after the ship arrived this evening.

They didn't expect Fan to be on board, but they did expect the crew would know something of where the ship went last, and possibly even who had Fan now.

On the Russian yacht, a lone sentry armed with binoculars stood on the flying bridge and scanned the deserted shoreline to the west. On the main foredeck, two more crewmen readied diving gear, while inside the main-deck saloon, seven men pulled on neoprene suits. The operators were crowded, but they were accustomed to living and working in close proximity to one another. As members of the elite and secretive Zaslon (Shield) Unit of SVR, this very team of paramilitaries had helicoptered across eastern Ukraine and Dagestan on direct-action missions. They'd killed terrorists and kidnapped local rebel leaders in Chechnya after sitting huddled together in the back of armored vehicles for hours on end, and they'd parachuted into Syria to assist with the escape of a Syrian Army general from a position being overrun by rebels.

These men were all first-timers to Hong Kong, but tonight's mission was no different from others in their careers. They would raid a cargo ship from underwater, capture any on board who could be captured, and kill those who offered resistance.

Vasily was in charge of the Zaslon team, with Yevgeni serving as his second-in-command. They stood in the middle of the saloon talking over last-minute details of the mission while everyone geared up around them.

Just as the men began a final weapons and comms check in the tight room, the hatch to the lower deck rose, and Zoya Zakharova climbed up from below. She wore a black neoprene shorty wetsuit, her bare legs and arms exposed. Her chin-length dark hair was pulled back and banded tight against her head, obviously so she could pull on the neoprene diving hood she held in her hand. On her right thigh she wore a sheathed knife, and over her shoulder she lugged a black backpack.

She pulled a holstered Glock 26 pistol from the pack and dropped the bag and her hood on a chair in the saloon, then racked the slide of the weapon. As she slid the pistol into a holster on the utility belt and dropped it next to the pack, she checked the threads on the silencer, housed in a case on the belt. After doing this, she glanced up at the other men in the room.

All seven of the Zaslon operators just stood there, staring back at her.

"What?" she asked.

Vasily addressed the SVR officer. "Off for a nighttime swim?"

She looked back to her gear, then checked to make certain her three extra pistol magazines were in their pouches on the utility belt. "Don't start with me. I'm going with you."

"No, you're not. Someone will come back to get you when the *Tai Chin VI* is secure."

"It's ten minutes away. Twenty minutes round-trip. Plus, you might need me during the takedown."

"We'll have eight men. We *need* eight men. *Men.*"

Arseny and Pyotr both chuckled over by the navigation table.

Zoya asked, "What if that tender on shore returns to the boat? I can stay on the deck and watch the bay for any counterattack."

Vasily knelt down to load rifle magazines into a load-bearing vest propped against the wall. "Not necessary. Ruslan and Sasha will stay with us just long enough to clear B deck; then they will return to the main deck. They can keep watch for anyone returning to the boat during the operation."

"I can help them. I won't get in your way. I've been in combat multiple times."

Vasily snorted. "Really? Where?"

Zoya shrugged. "Classified."

"Right."

"You *know* I've trained at Yasenevo with FSB Spetsnaz forces."

Vasily snorted. "Like I give a shit. They probably gave you fluffy towels and massages."

"No, they did not."

"And we aren't FSB Spetsnaz, dear. We are Zaslon."

"Which means you belong to SVR. I am an SVR officer, I remind you, and this is my operation."

All the men looked at Vasily, but the paramilitary commander didn't budge. "I have tactical control of direct-action ops. And I say you stay here and wait for us to call you forward. End of conversation."

Vasily was technically correct. An SVR case officer had no authority to make herself part of the tactical team conducting a difficult "bottom up" raid on a ship full of potential hostiles. Still, they knew she'd passed all the Spetsnaz qualifications necessary to make her an asset to the op, not a detriment, so Zoya felt they should have had no problem with her trailing along.

But these guys were all ex-military, whereas Zoya was a civilian government employee and, of course, Zoya was a woman. These alpha males didn't want her fighting alongside them.

She wouldn't push it; she needed their help in this, and even though she thought these guys were assholes, she wanted them to remain focused on the mission at hand, not on her. Zoya said, "Very well. I'll go to the hide on the island when you stop to pick up Mikhail."

"Mikhail is breaking down the hide. We won't need it."

"Let me see you at work. I will give you overwatch during the raid, and I'll be closer than I am here." To that she added, "You can keep me off the boat, but you can't keep me off the damn island."

Vasily just shrugged, but before he could speak, Zoya's radio chirped. "Anna Seven to Sirena."

She grabbed her walkie-talkie out of her gear bag and brought it to her mouth, her eyes still locked on Vasily. "Go, Seven."

"I have another tender leaving the target vessel. Five men on board, just like last time. They look like they are heading to that same bar the other subjects went to."

This was good news for the Zaslon unit; they would have fewer hostiles on board the cargo ship. But Zoya didn't like it. She had no idea how many would be on the ship when they hit it. Could it be possible that all the men who knew what happened to Fan Jiang would be drinking in the bar she'd visited that morning? In that case, Vasily and his men would have to wait around for them to return.

Zoya looked to the Anna team commander. "That's ten off the boat you are hitting."

"I call that good news."

"Not if all ten come back at once."

Sasha broke into the conversation now. "Ten men on two fifteen-foot launches? A shooting gallery."

Zoya sighed, but Vasily acquiesced to her demand. He said, "You can go to the overwatch during the raid."

"Thank you. One more thing."

"What is it?" he growled.

"Survivors. Give me survivors. The more the better."

"Roger that, Koshka."

Zoya turned to go back downstairs to change out of her scuba gear and into clothing appropriate to return to the overwatch position. She stopped suddenly, then turned back around. "Oh, and I want the VSS up there with me. Just in case." She was speaking of the suppressed sniper rifle they had been using at the hide site all day for the reconnaissance powers of its scope.

Vasily showed his frustration with a heave of his big chest, then just waved a distracted thumbs-up her way before returning to his work.

Court Gentry approached the entrance of the raucous bayside bar and immediately caught long looks from many of the patrons standing around near the entrance. He acted like he didn't notice, and like he was perfectly comfortable, but in truth he was already wondering if he had just ambled into a bear trap.

When he'd passed through the door some eleven hours earlier, he'd been surprised to see other Western faces, but this time, there was no surprise.

He was the only *gweilo* in the joint.

He never felt relaxed standing out in any instance, but he'd known he wasn't coming in here to hide out in the corner. He was coming in here to provoke a reaction. The three British assassins missing for five days had been in this place—of that Court felt certain—something bad had happened to them, and people here knew about it. A new Western stranger was probably going to learn something about the fate of the others, Court surmised, although he knew his plan wasn't among his most subtle or nuanced.

He entered the dimly lit establishment, passed the edge of the bar on his left, then made his way through tough-looking Chinese men as he walked all the way down to the opposite end of the wooden wraparound bar. He was lucky to find a single metal stool around the turn at the end, farthest from the door. He sat down, taking off his backpack and sliding it in front of him, hooking his leg around a strap as a force of habit in case of thieves. On his right he had a wall to the kitchen, and behind him were a few empty tables in a darkened corner with concrete-block walls. The covered deck layout of the bar meant that just twenty feet off his left was the railing that looked down to the dinghy dock and the water of the bay.

While he'd garnered a lot of attention since he'd arrived, there was still a good bit of laughing and talking in the crowd; for every man looking his way now there were three or four more who either didn't know or didn't care that a new Western face was in the building.

The age range ran from early twenties to late forties, but most people he saw, regardless of their age, were dressed roughly the same. Some sort of undershirt, usually a tank top, under a short-sleeve shirt left completely unbuttoned. Baggy pants along with shoes or sandals. It was a common look in Hong Kong, but here it seemed to be a dress code.

It slowly occurred to Court that there was a possibility, perhaps a strong possibility, that everyone in the bar belonged to the same group.

He wondered if he'd wandered into a Triad meeting.

If that turned out to be the case, Court told himself he'd rip into Colonel Dai. Dai had given him a list of known Wo Shing Wo hangouts, and this wasn't on it.

Court noticed a big group of men in the middle of the room, taking up the largest portion of the dockside floor. They had pulled several small plastic tables together, and they sat around it drinking and talking. Court had just looked over at this group of men when another five men appeared up the stairs from the floating dock and began greeting the large group. These men were clearly not Chinese. Court thought they looked Vietnamese, Laotian, or Cambodian.

They shook hands and bowed to a group of Chinese at the near end of the row of tables, but on the far end, Court noticed several others who appeared to be of the same nationality as the newcomers. Since the five of them had just arrived from the water and he'd seen no new vessels in the bay for hours other than the *Tai Chin VI*, Court wondered if these ten or so men could be from the cargo ship.

Soon a good twenty men were seated together, Chinese and foreigners alike, drinking and smoking and talking, right in the middle of the dive bar.

Court took a full minute to scan his surroundings thoroughly. He decided that in any emergency, the galley kitchen, accessed from behind the bar, looked like the best possible avenue for escape, because he assumed it had a door to the outside. The only way to the kitchen from his side of the bar, however, was to go over the bar, so he'd have a damn hard time slipping away in any low-profile manner.

He watched while the bartender, the same man as earlier in the day, cleaned up a double shot of whiskey that had been knocked over by a man sitting at a stool and gesticulating to friends. The booze had been spilled over the warped wood bar top, and the man behind the bar sopped it up with a hand towel, then threw the towel on a shelf behind him, all the while grumbling at the patron for his clumsiness.

Court glanced down to his phone, held below the bar in his lap, and looked at the screen, which showed him a real-time view of the cargo ship from the camera placed on the hill. Using the infrared camera he saw a couple of men on deck but no other movement.

Court looked up just in time to see the bartender lighting a cigarette, tossing the lighter back on the bar, then stepping over to him. He looked at Court a long time, unease on full display as he recognized him as the man who had come earlier in the day and asked about the missing Brits.

Court was unaccustomed to being recognized, but he cut himself some slack. He'd made this guy nervous earlier, and he'd probably been the only Western male in the establishment since then.

Court smiled and faked his British accent. "Hi again. Can I get a Tsingtao?"

Without taking his eyes off Court, the man reached down in front of him, pulled a cold beer from a large metal ice bucket, then popped the top off the glass bottle and placed it down in front of his new customer.

Court smiled again. "Thanks very much, indeed."

The bartender didn't say a word; he just turned away and walked off with an expression that Court took for astonishment.

As Court drank his beer he kept his head low, but his eyes flicked up often enough to see that the bartender had moved down to the opposite end of the bar. He blatantly ignored one man reaching out asking for a drink and sought out a man in the crowd standing there near the entrance to the dive.

The bartender leaned into the group and began talking to the man there. The man listened intently, nodded, then glanced down the length of the bar at Court.

The man turned away from the bar and stepped over to a larger, younger individual, standing next to the group of men seated in the middle of the room.

Like a game of telephone, Court was able to watch the news of his arrival and the fact that he'd been asking about the three Brits from Sunday night make its way around the room.

Yep, Court realized, everybody in this place, other than himself, was part of one big group.

He was pretty sure he'd stumbled into a Wo Shing Wo get-together.

His plan to instigate a reaction from the patrons had worked, but he needed to learn something from their reaction, and so far he'd picked up nothing except that they didn't like strangers in their midst.

He took a long, slow, calming breath. He was here to gather intel, not to get into a bar fight. If something bad happened, he told himself, *he* sure as hell was not going to be the one to start it. He'd sit here, as cool and confident as possible, and if he was confronted, he'd talk his way through it.

Court feigned ignorance of the bad juju growing in the room around him, and he glanced back down to his phone one more time. He used controls on his touch screen to adjust the view on the camera, backing out some to look around at other fishing boats, then tightening back up on the cargo ship at the mouth of the bay.

But Court didn't keep his head down long. He had one foot on the floor and wrapped around his bag, the other tucked into the legs of the bar stool, ready to kick it out or hoist it up so he could use it to defend himself. He knew he needed to keep his own personal security in the forefront of his mind at all times.

He would have loved to leave the bar now, to just find a quiet copse of trees somewhere on the island and to sit there alone so he could concentrate on his camera, but he didn't have that luxury. He was very aware of the fact that men from that boat out there were sitting here with him in this bar, and he had more opportunity to glean intelligence from them here than to pick up something on the boat on his night vision equipment.

Just as he forcefully reminded himself to keep one eye up and on the room around him, both eyes instead locked on to the screen of his phone.

"What . . . the . . . hell?"

Quickly Court switched from his low-light vision to his infrared and zoomed in from three-power to ten-power.

White-hot dots moved on the water's surface, right against the hull of the cargo ship at the stern. They were human sized, clearly divers emerging from below the surface of the bay. He counted four close together, then two more up near the bow.

The figures at the bow grew, then rose from the water, seeming to float in midair away from the ship.

Court's mouth opened a little as he understood what he was looking at. Two men were climbing the anchor chain together, with four more at the stern, using a rope or a hooked ladder to ascend.

Right now, *right* out there in the darkness beyond the edge of the lights from the deck bar, just at the far edges of this little bay, the cargo hauler anchored right where he'd expected to find a ship related to the disappearance of Fitzroy's men searching for Fan Jiang was being boarded by some sort of raiding party.

Court looked up to check the men around him—they seemed to be more overtly looking in his direction now—while he quickly dialed a number on his phone. This meant he lost the image of the ship for a moment so he could use the number keys, but as soon as the line began to ring, he put his wired earpiece in his ear and switched back to his infrared screen.

Colonel Dai answered on the first ring. *"Way, ni hao?"* Yes, hello?

Court's voice was hurried and hushed. "Do you have an operation going on right now?"

"Of course. My men are all over Hong Kong looking for—"

Court interrupted. "I'm talking about a ship! Do you have men boarding a ship searching for Fan? Now. I mean . . . *right* now."

Dai seemed genuinely confused by the question. "No. No one has reported any sightings or investigations of that nature. What ship? Where *are* you? I hear talking in the background. What do you see?"

Court looked around him. Young men were definitely filling the space between him at the bar and the walkway along the bar towards the exit. No one had anything in their hands he could see, and they weren't staring him down, but they *were* closing in and their bodies were showing cues that told Court they were squaring off for trouble.

Shit.

He was still convinced he could talk his way out of it, but the groupthink of fifty drinking buddies confronting one man certainly affected the attitudes around, and not in a way that encouraged polite discourse.

Court said, "I'll check it out and call you back. Don't worry . . . This could be nothing. If it's something, I promise I'll—"

"Just tell me where you are and—"

Court hung up the phone, checked the ship again through the infrared cam, and saw that the two men on the anchor chain were now disappearing over the gunwale near the bow. Two of the men at the stern climbed together, one on top of the other, while two more held it steady at the water line. Court thought it possible more men would be hitting the ship on the far side, as well.

Quickly he thought about calling Brewer to ask her if he was, in fact, watching CIA paramilitaries in action. He knew local Agency assets here were looking for Fan, and a Special Activities Division Ground Branch team had been moved close, ready to support him as soon as Court made contact with the target. Could this possibly be the Agency conducting an operation without his knowledge?

His gut told him this wasn't SAD. He doubted Brewer would let a CIA hit take place without first making sure her asset in the area wasn't in a compromised position. She might go ahead with a hit without giving him a warning, Court acknowledged, but he told himself she seemed too worried about her op getting out of hand as it was; leaving him somewhere out in the field during a direct action didn't feel to him like the way she'd do business.

Plus, Court told himself, he didn't have time to call Brewer and deal with the challenge-response code. A half dozen men, all Chinese, had moved to within striking distance, and they squared off against him now.

CHAPTER

FIFTEEN

Court told himself it was time to leave, but he knew the truth; the real time to leave had been five minutes earlier, which was about the time he walked into the bar. These guys didn't want him around, and any hope he had of leaning on one guy in a corner to get intel about Fitzroy's missing men went down the toilet the second he realized everybody in the room was on the same team.

Plus, although he wasn't sure what was going on out in the water on the *Tai Chin VI*, he *was* certain he wasn't going to sit here drinking while some other group hit the cargo ship that *he* had discovered. He would do his best to clear out of here with apologies and then steal a boat.

After that . . . well, one thing at a time.

He fanned out a few HK dollars onto the bar, pulled his pack over a shoulder, turned to walk around the bar to head to the exit, and made it exactly five steps before the group of men moved directly between him and the exit. Court smiled and nodded, gave a little courteous bow, and then tried to manage his way through.

They just stood there, blocking the narrow pathway between the bar stools and the tables. A voice barked angrily from the group. "Who are you? What you want here?"

A man in his thirties stepped forward through the scrum. His hair was styled in short spikes, and he had the look of Triad lower-tier management.

He had a blue tank top tight on his fleshy frame, and he wore a black short-sleeve shirt with orange dragons on the chest. His right hand was jammed in his front pocket. Court knew he could be hiding a weapon there, but with the baggy shirt he could not be sure.

Court looked past this man, counting heads and gauging the eyes of the others around, trying to judge their fervency to this cause.

The entire establishment fell into complete silence now, all eyes on the Westerner.

"Why are you here?" The man in the dragon shirt shouted even louder now.

Court knew he needed to lay on the charm, and quick. In his British accent he said, "I'm a tourist, from the UK. Is there some sort of a problem?"

"You here earlier. Asking about other *gweilo* and black man."

Court smiled a little. "Right. Well, as I explained to that fellow right there behind the bar, I am looking for some mates who came by on Sunday night."

This appeared to be exactly the wrong answer, as more men stood up from tables and joined the half dozen. Several men behind Court formed into a group and stood close there.

He could make a run for the railing, twenty feet off his left shoulder, where he could then leap off the side, but he'd have to kick out far enough to miss the dinghies floating below, and he'd have to push his way around several men still sitting at tables to even get to the rail. He could also try his luck fighting his way forward or backwards, or he could move over the bar on his right, and then shoot out the back door that he assumed he'd find off the kitchen.

The man with the dragon shirt drew a knife now, flicked the blade open, and held it up in front of his face. "Show me identification. Hand over your backpack."

"Look, mate. Is that necessary? How about I just leave you gentlemen to your evening, head out the door, and go on—"

"Give me your bag!"

Court was *not* going to let them look in his backpack. His swim fins, mask, and small air tank and regulator device, along with his cameras and his scanner, weren't going to exactly get him off the hook with these guys.

Instead he decided his only reasonable course of action was to feign compliance, to start to hand over the bag . . . and then to bash this fucker on the head with it.

If there were fifty able-bodied guys here, he'd cut into that number with his opening move. Not by an appreciable amount, but this wasn't simply a game of numbers. No, there was another important factor at play.

Court had learned the power of applied aggression. Studies and papers had been written that were pored over in military and law enforcement circles, but it all boiled down to the concept that someone acting half-crazy and completely sure of himself, initiating a fight with disproportionate violence, could seriously degrade an opponent's will to fight. Even a much stronger or larger opposing force.

And if this guy was, as Court assumed, part of the organization's leadership, it might have even more of an effect.

Of course, Court put this all together in under a second. He'd undergone years of training and he had years more of application in the field. Now he compared the situation at hand to his knowledge base in an instant, and he chose his action.

Yes, the gangsters here were going to make him fight his way out of this shit hole, and the only way to do so successfully was to use shock and awe to slow down their reactions to his moves.

He'd crank it up to eleven and fight like a fucking madman.

With his left hand he slipped the pack off his shoulder and began extending it out in front of him while his right hand swept under the front of his black hemp shirt. The knife he'd bought in the dive shop hung in its scabbard there.

More men closed in on Court and he realized he wasn't going to win this fight if they all came at him, but he saw no choice but to hope he could winnow away attackers and pray that the others would decide they didn't think he was worth the trouble.

But from his evaluation of the men's will by the looks they gave him, this wasn't going to go his way. They looked like they *wanted* him to resist.

And then it happened. Just as he started to move his backpack around on his wrist to swing it, a five-round string of fully automatic gunfire rolled in from out in the bay. Court recognized it instantly as an AK-47 firing fully automatic.

The muffled blast of a shotgun followed close behind.

Court had been the only one in the establishment who had half expected to hear a battle rage on the cargo ship, so he was the only one who stayed on task when the firing started.

The other men's heads swiveled towards the bay in surprise, giving the American a second to begin his attack.

Zoya Zakharova had been lying prone, deep in the high brush of the overwatch hide site on the far side of the bay, looking through the ten-power scope of the sniper rifle at the *Tai Chin VI*. All eight of her men had disappeared moments before when they moved in teams of four off the main deck and into the superstructure of the seventy-five-meter-long ship. She knew from the briefing held on the yacht earlier that they would break into teams of two inside to clear cabins and the engine room, with another team climbing up to the bridge deck. She could listen in to their radio network through her own headset attached to her walkie-talkie, but there was nothing to hear. Anna team was maintaining strict radio silence, and they expected the same from her.

So she just lay up there alone, watching the scene.

Suddenly staccato reports of a burst of rifle fire pounded in the night, rolling across the bay from the ship. Zoya recognized it as the unmistakable sound of an AK rifle, firing 7.62-by-39-millimeter cartridges in fully automatic mode. All the Zaslon men had suppressors on their weapons that fired a different caliber, so she knew this had to be a hostile actor inside the ship engaging her commandos.

Der'mo. Shit, she said to herself. She'd hoped she wouldn't hear any noise out of the cargo ship at all.

The boom of a shotgun told her that another armed hostile was firing on the raiding party, and she started to worry that this operation was falling apart right in front of her.

Within one second of the shotgun blast, Court's backpack slammed straight down against the forehead of the man brandishing the knife, and the five-pound air tank inside acted like a hammer striking flesh and bone. The man dropped down unconscious in front of the crowd tight behind him, while Court brought his right hand out, swinging his Kershaw knife. He made contact with three men in this first swing, cutting two men in the arm and one deeply in his shoulder, opening his flesh to the bone. He brought the blade back around 180 degrees in the other direction, and this time he sliced across the hands of two more men, while all the others around him lurched back in surprise at the violence of the action that had just erupted from the *gweilo* who, two seconds before, had been meek as a field mouse and offering no hint of resistance.

Court couldn't bypass the dozen or more Triad men between him and the deck railing, so instead he leapt high, kicking his legs into the air. He landed on his back on the wooden bar, rolled off, and dropped behind it, pulling his backpack along with him. He ended up in a standing position and swung his pack at the astonished bartender, clocking him in the face with the air tank inside the bag, dropping the young man flat onto his back.

Nearly fifty men screamed in wild frenzy now; some made to leap upon the bar to climb over it, while others moved around to access it from the side closest to the entrance. Court saw knives everywhere in the scrum in front of him, but he saw no guns.

Bottles of alcohol rested in a well next to Court. He grabbed two full one-and-a-half-liter vodka bottles, then shattered their necks on the side of a waist-high refrigerator. He spun in a circle, flinging their contents all around the bar, soaking some of the men climbing onto it. He snatched up the lighter he'd seen behind the bar and lit the whiskey-soaked washrag, which immediately burst into flames.

He took a step back towards the doorway to the kitchen, then dropped the rag on the floor of the bar.

The flames began instantly; the alcohol vapor in the air around the three liters of spilled spirits caused a brilliant flash in the low-lit room, even flaring past Court himself for an instant. Several of the men on the bar found themselves engulfed in flame, and they scrambled frantically, crashing into others while trying to get away. Court shot straight back into the narrow galley kitchen, slammed the completely inadequate door there, and reached for the lock, but didn't waste his time with it when he realized it would just take a hard push to break the weak plywood door in, locked or not.

No one on the other side of that door was going to bother turning the knob; they'd come through hard and fast, and it would take no time before men began pouring at it, shattering it off its cheap hinges.

The fire behind the bar wouldn't last, nor would it stop anyone who really wanted at him; it would just slow them down for a few seconds.

Court's plan had been to dart through the back exit in the kitchen, but those hopes were dashed in an instant. He saw no exit that led back onto the footpath, only a closed door that, from its location at the southern end of the galley kitchen, meant it led out into the bar itself, very near the main entrance of the building.

Court reached as high as he could and grabbed onto the top of a metal shelving unit full of goods right next to the door he'd just entered, and he pulled with all his might. He thought it would be difficult to tip the tall, heavy structure, but he just had to give the old rusted unit a hard yank off center for its legs to bend and buckle, and then the eight-foot-high assembly crashed down in front of the doorway just as the door started to push in behind the weight of several men who'd made it through the fire. The shelving unit was full of cans of spices, bags of rice, boxes full of bagged grease, and other heavy items, so it held the door shut, for a moment anyway.

Court now sprinted for the other exit; it was only five steps away up the narrow galley, but after just three steps the door flew open and a pair of rough-looking young men appeared.

The first man lunged forward with his knife; Court continued his advance and sidestepped the thrust, pushing the man farther into the kitchen while the second attacker swung a switchblade towards him. The first man fell over the shelving unit while Court concentrated on the second. Court short-circuited this man's attack by blocking him at the forearm, then took hold of the hand with the knife and spun behind the man. He pulled the man's arm up high as he whirled behind him, and his own hands covered the man's hand clutching the hilt of the knife. Driving down hard, Court forced his attacker to stab himself in the neck.

While he did this he kicked his right foot back behind him and slammed the particleboard door into the face of a third attacker as he breached the door frame. This knocked the man back into the bar, crashing him into two others just behind him.

In front of Court, another crash against the plywood door broke it down and over the smashed shelving assembly and its contents. Men fell into the center of the galley kitchen on top of one another, just a dozen feet away from the American assassin.

Flames still licked high in the bar area; these men had just been too wild with the thrill of the hunt to care.

Court concentrated on the man in his grasp. He pulled him back a step, then spun him down to his knees against the door.

With strength and efficiency, he ripped the man's hands from the knife hilt deep in his neck, then rotated the blade across the kneeling man's throat, sending a spray of arterial blood against the wooden door and killing him almost instantly in the process.

The gangster's body crumpled against the door, holding it shut from men trying to open it.

Now Court turned back to the pile of undulating bodies lying in the doorway that led to the bar. The small fire from the bar area spread into the kitchen, fueled by frying grease and other items that had fallen from the crumpled shelving unit into the flames in the doorway. The pile of men—Court counted at least five so far, with more stumbling in through the dancing flames—kicked and scrambled to get up and away from the danger.

Court charged at them, reaching into his right front pocket as he did so.

Zoya Zakharova was pleased she hadn't heard any more shooting from the cargo ship, but now a new sound caused her to pull her eye out of the eyecup of the scope. The roar of shouts and screams of excitement came across the water, apparently from the only area of activity around the bay: the little dive bar.

Although she was 350 meters away here in her hide, the sound traveled easily in the night air over the still water.

She brought her binoculars up to her eyes to check it out and, to her surprise, she saw that some kind of a barroom brawl had erupted at the same moment as the raid. She knew it was possible the patrons had heard the gunfire from the cargo ship, but she doubted they'd be able to tell that was where it came from. If men on the *Tai Chin VI* had managed to contact their ten colleagues at the bar, they could have warned them, which might have brought the Vietnamese gangsters racing back to help their comrades, but she didn't see how it would have led to a fight there.

She didn't know what was going on, but any dustup might help slow the response from the Vietnamese and cover the actions on the cargo ship, so she was pleasantly surprised at this turn of events.

For a better look she shifted the entire sniper rifle so she could train its optic on the bar, and when she did so she saw the lighted covered deck, and a large mass of people moving around the poorly constructed building.

She squinted. *A fire?*

It appeared the bar area was ablaze, and smoke poured from the open-air building.

No one was down on the dinghy dock, which meant the Vietnamese weren't heading back to their ship to investigate the shooting there—at least not yet—so she began to lift the rifle back up so she could scan the deck of the *Tai Chin VI* again, but she stopped herself suddenly and lowered her eye back to the scope. The crack of a gunshot was unmistakable over the quiet bay, and this gunfire had come from the bar, not from the ship.

She couldn't see the shooter, she was too far away, but she felt like she should notify the Zaslon unit. She knew Vasily had called for radio silence and they were maintaining it, even though they were obviously engaging hostiles right now. Vasily had demanded she not transmit on the net unless absolutely necessary, but Zoya thought it prudent to tell them about shooting going on away from the cargo ship.

"All elements, this is Sirena. Be advised—there is gunfire coming from the bar on the northwestern shore of the bay. I can't see who is shooting. There is a fire there, as well. There seems to be an altercation that might be unrelated to our operation."

No one replied, but she hadn't expected a response.

More gunshots from the bar now; the reports sounded to Zoya to be coming from pistols, at least two different weapons firing in close succession. She had no idea what the hell was going on over there, but she decided she'd focus on the bar, watching the action in case this melee caused the ten men from the *Tai Chin VI* to head back to their ship, right in the middle of the raid.

CHAPTER

SIXTEEN

Court thought things couldn't get much worse; then some asshole out in the covered deck area started shooting blindly into the galley kitchen.

Awesome.

As Court sprinted towards the men falling in front of him, braving the flames, stumbling over one another and the destroyed shelving unit full of cooking supplies, he heard the shots and saw holes appear in the thin wall, not far away. Court ran on, launched into the air, and planted his left foot on the edge of a metal grill. In full leap he pushed off, vaulting high over the men in the pile, and grabbed on to the single hanging bulb lighting the kitchen area. He crushed the bulb, shattering it and sending the kitchen into darkness save for the flames licking in from the bar, the light of which did not reach into the far end of the galley. Still, he stuck his landing at the northern end of the kitchen because he'd calculated his trajectory before the light went out.

Court spun around, turning on the tactical flashlight he'd pulled from his pocket. The taclight sent nine hundred lumens of blinding white light back in the direction of the men climbing over the shelves, cans, and boxes. He laid the five-inch-long device on a shelf over a sink just to his right so the beam would remain constant up the galley and hide Court's actions.

Above the shelf he saw a stocked knife rack nailed into a wooden support beam. Court yanked a meat cleaver and a long carving fork off the rack, just as a man charged forward through the light, his eyes surely blinded, but either his adrenaline or his stupidity pushing him on. He held a stiletto in his hand.

Court dispatched the man with a parry of the knife with the carving fork and a brutal strike to the side of the neck with the meat cleaver. The man fell and writhed on the cement floor of the galley, and Court stepped back, nearly to the back wall, ready to take the next ten men to try their luck up the narrow aisle.

More Hong Kong Triads shielded their eyes and braved the danger of having no idea where the *gweilo* in front of them was.

Another crack of a gunshot caught Court's attention, but he didn't stop swinging as another man closed in the narrow space. He struck this man in the arm with the cleaver, causing the attacker to drop his blade and fall, clutching a long and deep slash.

The man just behind him stumbled over his fallen comrade and fell to the ground on his forearms and knees. Court drop-kicked this attacker in the face, spinning him 180 degrees before he fell in a heap.

Persistent gunfire cracked outside in the bar now. Court saw the holes in the walls getting closer to his position, and he knew he'd be hit in seconds if he waited around for the shooters to adjust their aim.

The walls!

Court had noticed earlier in the day that this dive looked like it had been put together with flypaper and baling wire. There was no way out of the corner he'd backed himself into . . . unless he made his *own* exit.

He heel-kicked at the wall behind him as hard as he could. It moved, shaking the entire kitchen, but the thin plywood held. As another man climbed off the pile and raced towards him with a blade, rushing out of the dazzling beam of light, Court kicked again, lower on the wall, trying to hit another of the weak boards at its least secure point.

This time he heard a crack, and the board separated from its fasteners.

The new man sprang on him, faked a kick that caused Court to commit to blocking, then barreled in with a jab of the knife. Court dropped fast to his knees, causing the blade to fire just inches above his upper back; then Court spun on his hands and kicked out hard, striking the man in the ankle on his weight-bearing leg. The appendage cracked and the man fell forward.

Court propped the carving fork on the floor, business end up. His attacker fell straight down onto it, killing him instantly.

On the ground now with men just feet away and surging forward like a flood, Court rolled out of his backpack, flipped onto his back, and kicked at the loose board in the back wall with the heels of both feet. After one hit it bent away and cracked again; a second try broke the board all the way through, sending it flying into a far corner of the bar's back deck.

Just then, Court saw the beam of his tactical light whip around the kitchen as someone knocked it to the floor.

Court rolled onto his belly and scooted backwards, pulling his backpack behind him.

He scraped his back as he did so, but he barely felt it in his overwhelming desire to get away from all the men trying to kill him.

Here he sprang to his feet, finding himself back in the bar, in the corner behind where he had been seated just a couple of minutes earlier. He was around the corner from the main part of the bar, but there was no way out from here, so he had to head in the direction of the gunfire and his Triad attackers.

He chanced a look around the corner, knowing this wooden wall wouldn't stop an air rifle from penetrating, much less a real pistol. He saw the near edge of the bar where he'd been sitting just a few feet away, and he knew there was a huge metal ice bin just on the other side.

He thought the ice bin would give him some cover from a handgun.

No one followed him out of the kitchen through the small hole because they knew there was a man on the other side with a blood-soaked meat cleaver in his hand, so by now men had begun flooding out of the kitchen doors, and word was surely getting out that the man pinned in the corner of the kitchen had managed to escape back into the open-decked bar.

As Court moved towards his cover behind the ice bin, he saw the man wearing the dragon shirt that he'd hit over the head with his pack to kick off the fight. He was sitting on the ground, bleeding from the head, and holding a silver automatic pistol in his right hand. He was only fifteen feet away from Court and facing away, and as Court watched, the man pointed his pistol over the bar and fired a round into the kitchen wall without seeing what he was shooting at.

He nearly hit one of his fellow Triads in the process.

Court sprang towards the man on the floor now, twisted the pistol out of his hand, and grabbed him by his spiked black hair. As men seemed to run around the entire dim establishment, some firing pistols themselves, Court began dragging the man backwards towards the relative cover of the ice bin.

He looked up as he did so, and it appeared that everyone in the room turned in his direction at the same time.

Twenty men charged, and Court found himself out in the open, pulling along a noncompliant hostage.

W ith her eye still in the scope, Zoya Zakharova pulled the charging handle back on the VSS rifle, chambering a 9-by-39-millimeter round.

She hadn't envisioned using the weapon this evening at all, and she hadn't fired a VSS since her sniper training four years earlier, but she had a target downrange now, and she was committed to killing him. She followed the man's head with the crosshairs of the rifle, holding just a touch high to account for the characteristics of this bullet at this distance.

The Russian operative blew out half the air in her lungs, hesitated a moment to catch her body between heartbeats, and then pressed the trigger.

The sound of the round firing through the integrally suppressed barrel was akin to a bicycle tire blowing out. A pop and an expression of gases made less noise than the action of the weapon itself as the semiautomatic rifle ejected the spent cartridge and then rechambered a round.

The large bullet left the muzzle of the rifle at a thousand feet per second, then raced from the top of the hill and over the full length of the bay.

Zoya kept her eyes on her target, the forehead of a man in motion, and when the bullet struck home there was no doubt, because she saw the head snap back, blood mist behind it, and then the body dropped like a stone.

The man landed flat on his back in the fifteen-foot-long boat.

There were two more men in the tender rushing towards the *Tai Chin VI*, but neither of them was aware that the man kneeling just behind them had been shot through the head. The roar of the outboard motor had covered the zing of the bullet as it flew overhead, its impact with its target, and the fall of the man to the floor of the small watercraft.

Mere seconds earlier, Zoya had watched these three men race down the stairs of the bar to their boat, one of them with a walkie-talkie held to his ear. She took it as a given they were in communication with someone on the cargo ship, and were now rushing away from the fight at the bar and back to the fight on the ship. The men then leapt into the closest of the two tenders and fired the engines, while Zoya reported the action to the Zaslon team.

She hadn't looked to see if Ruslan and Sasha, the two men Vasily had tasked with covering any counterattack, had made it back up to the deck of the cargo ship, out in the darkness off her left shoulder, and she wasn't going to move her rifle now to find out.

But when she received no response from Vasily after fifteen seconds, she knew what she had to do.

After her first shot and the elimination of the first of the three threats to her mission, she quickly centered her crosshairs on the man just behind the operator of the tender, but this time she held her sights true to aim, because the fast-moving vessel had moved closer to her position, eliminating the need for the holdover.

Thump!

Another round left her weapon, but just as it did, the operator of the boat steered hard to starboard, apparently to avoid a buoy in the water in front of him. Zoya worried for an instant her shot would miss, but she watched through the scope while the round slammed into the target's left collarbone, knocking the man backwards and flat in the tender.

Zoya's weapon loaded the chamber automatically and her finger remained taut on the trigger. She centered her sights on the man at the wheel now, piloting the vessel at full throttle past a small fishing boat moored for the evening. The tender continued towards the cargo ship, still 150 meters off its bow.

She fired again, striking the operator of the tender straight in the nose, knocking him off the boat and then into the black water with a splash.

The tender slowed to idle, then veered to its left a little and began sputtering towards the rocky shoreline, across the bay from the dive bar and just under Zoya's position on the hill.

She scanned for other targets, but the second tender of the *Tai Chin VI* remained tied up on the dinghy dock under the riotous fight in the bar.

Into her mic she said, "This is Sirena. Three hostiles are down."

She'd shot the men back to front, dropping all three with only three rounds. And although the weapon had flashed up here at the top of the hill, no one would have heard the gunshots from any distance, so she felt comfortable that she was in the clear. More importantly to her, this small rescue mission to the *Tai Chin VI* had failed, even if any of the three had somehow managed to survive.

She spoke into her microphone again after triggering her radio. "Anna One, how copy?"

There was no response from the Zaslon team, but a lightning-fast three-round volley of gunfire from the waterside bar diverted her attention.

From the speed of the fire, Zoya knew that someone new was shooting, and whoever it was, they sure as hell knew how to operate a handgun.

C ourt fired three rounds over the far end of the bar, striking three men charging his way.

The mass of approaching men recoiled like a single living organism, and the attackers began diving behind tables and chairs and against the bar itself. A few even leapt over the deck railing down into the water below next to the little dock.

With one hand still grabbing hard to the sticky hair of the Triad boss in the dragon shirt, Court fanned the pistol around behind him, checking his six to make sure no one was there. A waitress lay huddled behind a table in the corner, just in his view. Court yelled at her to stay where she was, because he was afraid if she got up to run she would get shot by one of the Chinese or Vietnamese men pointing guns in his direction.

The Triad on the dirty deck, now pinned there by Court's knee, looked up at him with blood all over his face. "Let me go! I'll kill you if you don't let me go!"

Court used his left hand to bang the man's face down hard against the deck, silencing him for the time being.

A shout came from the men holding their positions just thirty or so feet away. "Hey! *Gweilo!* You gonna die, motherfucker!"

Court pushed harder with his left knee to hold his captive down, and then he released his left hand from the man's hair. He dropped the magazine from the grip of the pistol, a Norinco Type 92, and saw he had eight rounds left. It wasn't a particularly powerful weapon, but Court knew his marksmanship would go a long way to make up for any shortcomings of the 5.8-by-21-millimeter round.

His mind assessed his situation quickly. There were still easily twenty-five or so potential threats here in this bar, but from the sound of the gunfire there weren't more than one or two pistols in the crowd other than the one in his hand. He wasn't terribly worried about the knives now that he had a standoff weapon; unless they all charged him at once, nobody was going to get into a knife fight with the Gray Man if he had a gun.

He heard a boat fire up downstairs at the dinghy dock, and he wondered if it was one of the tenders for the cargo ship. He thought he'd heard one a minute earlier, as well, but it was hard to tell with all the action going on.

With the revving of an outboard motor's throttle he was certain now he was listening to a tender racing away from the bar.

Another voice shouted out, startling Court and forcing his head down lower. This man spoke in Mandarin, and from the tone of his words it sounded to Court like he was barking out orders to underlings. A few other men replied, and it felt as if some kind of plan was being formed by the gang.

Not good.

Court didn't have a moment to spare. The longer he stayed here, the braver the men plotting against him would get, and the more organized their next attack would be.

Suddenly, several shots rang out in quick succession. Court heard glasses behind the bar shattering nearby, the sound of the ice bucket taking fire—he even saw splinters of wood kicked off the corner of the bar a foot from his face.

Christ, Court thought. These guys didn't have much concern about the well-being of the Triad boss on the floor under his knee.

Court reached the pistol around the side of the bar and fired two rounds without looking. The angle of the pistol was right to hit threats here in this target-rich environment, so even though he couldn't see what he was shooting at, he figured he was doing some damage.

The gunfire from the crowd stopped, but the shouting, the ordering, and the callbacks all continued.

Court assumed they were coordinating some sort of plan that included covering gunfire to pin Court down along with a movement forward by all the men with the edged weapons.

He felt around the body of the man underneath him, desperately searching for another magazine, but found nothing save for a wallet and a cell phone.

Court took a quick half peek around the corner. He saw dead bodies and wounded men around the tipped-over tables, then movement a little farther back on the deck. He heard the rushed voices of several men. He grabbed the Triad roughly by the neck and climbed off the man's back, staying low in a crouch, as if ready to launch.

The man Court held looked at him with a crazed grin now. "Stupid *gweilo*! They don't care if they kill me. You use me as a hostage? Are you fucking crazy, man? I no hostage. They shoot anyway."

Court looked to the railing of the deck, twenty feet across open ground. Upturned plastic chairs and tables lay in the way, but nothing he couldn't bull his way through in a desperate situation.

And he was pretty sure this predicament qualified.

Court pulled the Triad up to his feet but kept him in a low crouch. Leaning into the man's ear with his eyes on the railing, he said, "You aren't my hostage, buddy." Court looked straight into the man's eyes now. "You're my meat shield."

The Triad leader cocked his head in confusion, and then Court propelled himself up and out to the left, using his strong thighs to haul the man up with him. With his gun arm out in front of him he used the man in the dragon shirt for cover.

Court opened fire, simultaneously pulling the man along with him as he went for the railing.

Cracks of return pistol fire filled the night; the zing of a bullet burned the air inches from Court's ear. He pulled the Triad sideways as he moved. Three feet, five feet, ten feet. Straight towards the railing over the water, as fast as Court could go while yanking an unwilling man along with him.

The Triad boss lurched into Court as they shuffled quickly along like two men dancing badly; clearly he'd been shot. Then he lurched again a second later; another round in the back.

Court's pistol emptied and he dropped it, using both hands now to pull his meat shield along with him across the floor. The dying man took another shot, this time to the back of his head, and his legs gave out, but Court didn't let him drop.

Gunshots cracked across the room; Court both felt and heard a round scream by again, this time even closer to his own head, but he raced forward anyway, towards the edge of the deck.

Men with knives launched to their feet and gave chase now, getting in the way of the guns, and Court let the dead body in his arms fall, then turned and sprang onto the railing.

The closest blade was just two feet away and swinging fast as the Gray Man dove over the side, launching himself out past the dinghy dock.

He was going for a swan dive—it was the fastest and most efficient way to get himself in the water—but as he dropped, his legs rotated past ninety degrees and he hit the water with his outstretched hands, then his head, then his back and legs. It wasn't pretty, but the lights of the bar above didn't make it down to the water's surface, so once he broke through, his momentum sending him deep, he knew he was out of the line of sight and the line of fire.

As long as he didn't need to breathe.

CHAPTER

SEVENTEEN

Zoya's attention had been on a different part of the bay. She had just lined her rifle up on one of the four men in the second tender to launch from the bar in the past three minutes, when the man in her sights tumbled out of the boat and into the water.

She was confused for an instant, but when a second man dropped down in the boat a moment later, she understood; Ruslan and Sasha were firing their silenced rifles at the little boat from the deck of the cargo ship off to her left.

The SVR operative on the hill at the southeast edge of the bay flipped her weapon's fire selector switch up to the "safe" setting, then moved the rifle to her right, pointing it back at the bar. She was fascinated by what sounded like a full-on gun battle raging in there, and she wanted to see if she could get eyes on more of the action to determine what the hell was going on.

Just as she put her eye back in the cup of the scope, she focused quickly on movement. A man flew through the air, facedown and arms outstretched, swan-diving out of the bar and chased by what looked like two dozen or more frenzied men.

She saw nothing of the diver before he splashed awkwardly into the black surface other than the fact that he had dark clothing and he wore a backpack.

Men leaned over the railing now and held pistols at the water. Flashlight beams swept the bay, hunting for the man who'd disappeared there.

She put her crosshairs on one of the armed men on the deck, but she did not fire. He wasn't engaging her men and was no threat at all to her operation.

She watched the water through her scope for over a minute, waiting for the diver to resurface.

While she peered intently, half in disbelief at the diver's ability to hold his breath, Vasily came over the net for the first time since the raid began. "Anna One to all call signs. Objective secure. Report in."

Zoya listened carefully while all eight Zaslon men checked in over the radio. Only one, Pyotr, had been injured in the takedown, and he reported he was ambulatory and did not need any aid.

Satisfied and relieved, she pulled away from the rifle and sat up. She pressed her mic transmit button and jumped onto the net herself. "This is Sirena. How many survivors?"

There was a delay, to the point that Zoya called back into her radio. "Did you copy my last transmission, Anna One?"

Vasily replied curtly now. "One survivor."

Zoya fumed. She reached to key her mic when Vasily came back over the net.

"We're sending the RIB to pick you up now." A pause. "You probably should hurry up."

Zoya pressed the transmit key so hard her finger turned white. "Shit! Your *one* survivor is injured?"

"Affirmative. Anna One, out."

Zoya packed the rifle as quickly as possible, climbed to her feet, and headed towards the trail that led down the hill to the shoreline, cursing under her breath the entire way. As she started off, she gave one more glance over to the dive bar in the distance. She imagined she never would find out what the hell had just happened over there, but she couldn't help but think about the American she'd seen that morning.

Although for the life of her she couldn't picture him.

Court kicked with powerful strokes through the water, generating moderate speed as he swam through the black. He held the regulator of the spare-air bottle in his mouth and breathed slowly and calmly, and between his arms he held a fat rock he'd picked up from the surface of the bay to give him the ballast he needed to remain a steady ten feet down without additional effort.

He put his swim fins on when he'd made it forty or fifty yards away from his impact point, and he used the tritium compass on his watch to orient him back in the direction of the public pier.

It took him a few minutes to arrive at one of the coral-encrusted stanchions under the pier, and when he did arrive he simply dropped his rock and ascended slowly behind one of the vertical support beams, careful to make no bubbles or noise.

Holding on to the slimy wood to keep himself floating out of sight, he could see the well-lit bar in the distance. Someone had turned large overhead lights on, and it seemed as though the fire was under control. Men still looked over the railing into the water, and a half dozen dinghies churned circles around that part of the bay, waving flashlights around, looking for the white man who'd somehow managed to kill a number of their group and then escape under the surface.

Court was safe enough, and to his surprise he felt no new real pain, so he began to consider his next problem of the night. He had no weapon, and he had no boat. The only way Court could think of to get off the island was to find the captain of one of these vessels anchored around here, get him out of his bed with either the promise of money or the threat of a broken bottle in his face, and then demand a ride to Hong Kong Island or Kowloon.

Or else Court could just swim out to some small, unattended boat and pilot it himself. He knew how to sail, but he had a feeling the high-traffic shipping lanes between his origin point and his destination point would make sailing, even at this time of night, like being a student pilot landing solo at LaGuardia at night, or a student driver negotiating a rush-hour cloverleaf in a busy U.S. city. He'd have to avoid the Hong Kong coast guard and police, and he'd have to find a place to put the boat in where no one would immediately see him getting off.

Could he do it alone? Maybe.

Did he want to try? Not particularly.

Court pulled his night vision binoculars out of his backpack, doing his best to keep them from getting wet, and looked around the bay in the other directions now. He was surprised to see one of the two fifteen-foot tenders from the *Tai Chin VI* just forty yards behind him, beached in the rocks on the opposite side of the bay from the bar. The tender was two hundred yards away from the cargo ship itself, and Court saw no movement in or around the tender, other than light stirring as it rocked in the gentle waves of the bay.

None of the little boats looking for him were anywhere near the darkness on the far side of the public pier, so he decided he'd swim over and check out the tender to see if he could use it. He slipped his spare air back into his mouth and descended just below the surface, then pushed off from the support column of the pier and began swimming in the direction of the fifteen-foot-long boat.

Zoya Zakharova stood on the bridge of the *Tai Chin VI*, her arms crossed in front of her chest, her back leaning against the wall, and her eyes on the man lying on the floor.

The Vietnamese captain was alive, but Zoya didn't think he would remain so for long. A bullet had ripped through his gut above the navel; at first Zoya didn't think he had more than twenty minutes or so before he passed out and bled out, but when she saw the blood draining from the exit wound Yevgeni showed her when he rolled the man onto his stomach, she amended her prognosis to less than ten minutes.

Zoya gave Vasily a disapproving look when she saw the extent of the man's injuries, but he just turned away.

There were two more dead here on the bridge, and four more dead belowdecks. That made seventeen on board the ship in total when it arrived here in Po Toi tonight, with ten of the men going to the bar and seven remaining on the ship.

Other than Vasily and Sasha, the rest of the Zaslon unit was outside two decks below now, in covered and elevated positions, watching for anyone making a move out towards the cargo ship. Everyone expected a large response of police and firefighting forces on the way from Hong Kong proper because of the fire at the bar, but that was several hundred meters away. If any of the Vietnamese were still alive at the bar or in the water nearby, it wasn't impossible to imagine they would send police to their cargo ship to check out reports of an attack there, but Zoya felt confident she and her task force would be gone by then, and it was more likely the Vietnamese were either all dead or in no position to go to the local authorities for help, no matter the situation.

Zoya took a bottle of water out of her pack and knelt in front of the captain. She lifted the man's head, unscrewed the cap on the bottle, and poured a little water into his mouth, then more onto his forehead. This seemed to rouse him a bit, and he opened his eyes.

He blinked in surprise when he saw an attractive woman with short dark hair kneeling over him, cooling him off.

"Do you speak English?" she asked softly.

The man shook his head.

She switched to French. *"Français?"*

A slight nod.

In perfect French Zoya said, "The young Chinese man who boarded your boat Sunday night. You took him away. Where did you take him?"

The wounded captain closed his eyes and shook his head.

Zoya rubbed the water off the man's face, stroking her fingers through his long hair. Even more softly now she said, "It's okay. You can tell me."

For several seconds he told her nothing, but finally the man spoke, though his eyes remained closed. "Saigon."

Zoya nodded. "Saigon. Good. Who has him now?"

The captain's eyes opened. He looked to the ceiling. "I . . . I don't know."

"I think you do."

"Non," he replied. *"Je ne sais pas."*

Zoya smiled at the man a moment, still stroking his forehead gently. "It's okay. Just tell me."

He shook his head slowly.

Zoya sucked her lungs full of air, then blew out dramatically. Then she reached over onto the floor nearby and picked up an empty shell casing from one of the Vietnamese AK-47 rifles. She stopped petting the man, then calmly touched the steel shell against the open gunshot wound in the man's gut.

She pressed in and twisted.

The screams made their way two decks down to the commandos scanning the sea through their gun sights.

———————

Court swam between the shoreline rocks towards the tender, still not understanding why it was here and why it had apparently been left abandoned. Court closed on the boat, using his night vision binos to check it over from a distance and to look over the hillside nearby, searching for whoever had brought the boat here in the first place.

When he got to the boat he stepped onto the rocky shore and peered inside. To his surprise, two men lay on the deck, one facedown and the other faceup. Court leaned closer in the darkness, until he saw the bullet wound in the forehead of the man on his back. Suddenly Court realized there must be a sniper with eyes on the bay. He ducked back down into the low water alongside the boat.

But only for a moment; a groan from inside the tender caused him to move a few feet down the hull and chance a look over the gunwale, making sure to keep the little boat between him and the cargo ship, two hundred yards away.

The man lying facedown was clearly still breathing. He rolled slowly off his stomach and onto his right side, facing away from Court. Pushing himself up, the man now rose to his knees.

He grunted again with pain, and Court reached out and grabbed him by the collar of his shirt, yanked him over the gunwale of the little boat, and splashed back down in the shallow water with him.

They were both out of the line of fire from the cargo ship, although Court was only assuming that was where the sniper had been positioned when he'd fired on the tender.

The wounded man was in his late twenties; he had longish hair and a scraggly beard and mustache. He wore a plain T-shirt and dark pants. The man put up little resistance; Court saw he was severely wounded, with blood covering the entire front of his shirt and a gaping wound near his left shoulder.

Court searched the man quickly by pulling him up onto the rocks, then rolling him onto his stomach and frisking him. He found a pistol tucked into the man's belt and looked it over. It was a Type 54, an old Chinese knockoff of an older Russian model. In the dark here Court couldn't see the caliber, but he checked and saw it had a full magazine and a round in the chamber. He stuck it into the small of his own back.

A flashlight's wide, diffused beam from across the bay swept over Court's position, and he ducked low, pushing his captive down with him. When it passed Court decided he needed to get away from this boat next to him. With all the violence necessary considering the urgency of his situation, Court pulled the man up into a crouch and led him up the rocks and off the beach, then into deep scrub brush just ten yards away. The man groaned in a rhythm, almost sobbing as he walked, and Court had no idea if the man was reacting to his pain or his predicament.

They walked together for another minute, and then Court pushed the man down into the dirt in a thick grove of trees and knelt over him.

From his backpack Court pulled a small microfiber towel. It had gotten damp because it was in an outside pouch with only a pull cord closure, but Court nevertheless put it on the man's shoulder to stop the bleeding. The young man understood and held it there tightly himself.

He took the towel away after a moment and tried to look towards his ragged wound, but he could barely turn his head to see it on his collarbone. He applied hard pressure on his shoulder again to mute the pain and slow the blood loss, but Court still saw dark viscous blood oozing through the young man's hand and the towel.

Court asked, "Do you speak English?"

The man shook his head.

Court switched to French. *"Français?"*

Another shake of the head.

Court said, *"C'est des conneries!"* That's bullshit! And he pulled the Type 54 and pressed the barrel into the man's hand that held his shoulder together. Blood ran down into the dirt below him.

"Arrêtez!" Stop! The man's French improved dramatically. *"Je parle un peu."*

Court relieved the pressure on the man's wound by moving the barrel of the pistol from the hand over the shoulder to between the young man's eyes. He asked, "Where did you take Fan Jiang?"

"I don't know who that is."

"Look. If you tell me, *and* I believe you, then I will let you live. You get up and walk away right now. You don't tell me, or you lie, and you will die right here."

"I don't know anything. I am just a cook."

Court looked this guy over. He shook his head. *"Dommage, copain. Je ne te crois pas." Sorry, pal. I don't believe you.*

The barrel of the pistol went straight to the man's gunshot wound, digging deep into the hole.

Court used his other hand to stifle the man's scream.

CHAPTER

EIGHTEEN

The Vietnamese captain lying on the deck on his bridge cried out maniacally as the spent shell case dug deeper into his stomach wound, and his hands reached out to push Zoya Zakharova off him, but she easily batted them away. He began to kick and writhe, but she spun around and sat down on his legs to hold him in place.

Sasha stepped over from his position by the wheel, sliding his short-barreled rifle behind his back on its sling. He knelt and pinned the captain's arms down to the floor.

After nearly ten seconds of screaming and thrashing, Zoya pulled the casing out. The lower half of it was covered in blood.

The captain's heavy breathing was the only sound on the bridge for several seconds.

Zoya spoke matter-of-factly. "We can stabilize you. Not because we're nice, but because we want to take our time. I'll get what I need out of you, even if I have to take you back to my boat and work on you for days."

The man cried out in French, "I am just a ship's captain!"

"And a very good one, I am sure. But the men with you. Who are . . . who *were* they?"

The captain gave it up before the crazy woman tortured him again. "They are Con Ho Hoang Da."

"And what does that mean?"

"Les Tigres Sauvages."

Zoya translated from French. "The Wild Tigers?" She looked around to the two other men with her. Both Vasily and Sasha shrugged. "It's some sort of a criminal organization? A Vietnamese gang?"

The captain nodded.

"Very good," Zoya said, and she rolled off the man's legs, reached for her water bottle on the floor, and lifted his head once again. She poured water on his hairline and stroked his black hair back gently. "Please, Captain . . . tell me more."

C ourt subjected his wounded prisoner to twenty seconds of agonizing torture, the pistol's barrel jabbed into the broken collarbone now: twisting, pressing, digging.

Court yanked the gun away suddenly, then waited for the man to stop screaming before he pulled his hand off his mouth. Leaning close into his captive's face, he watched him pant hysterically for almost a minute. Finally the wounded man recovered enough to look Court's way.

Court spoke French. "Look at me, man. Do I look like I'm in a position to fuck around here? I'll do whatever I have to do to get what I need. Trust me, we're just getting started."

The wounded man spoke out between sobs. "Saigon."

Court rolled back onto his butt. "Saigon?"

"Oui. Je le jure." Yes. I swear it.

"Who has him there?"

The injured Vietnamese man looked at Court now. A confused expression. "We have him."

"Right. Who are you?"

The man seemed to puff his chest just a little, though it required considerable effort to do so. *"Les Tigres Sauvages."*

Court translated the words from French. "The Wild Tigers." He returned to French to speak to the young man on his back in front of him. "Cool." Then, "What the fuck is that?"

W hen Zoya had everything of intelligence value from the injured cargo ship captain that he could possibly give her, she brushed his hair back one more time, gave him a last sip of water, and lowered his head back to the floor. She rose and turned away with a final "*Merci beaucoup*" and began walking to the door. She switched to Russian and addressed Vasily, who was still standing there, waiting for her to hurry up. "He's terminal."

Vasily replied, "No shit."

"But he is not in pain now. Let's leave him to die in peace."

Vasily said nothing.

Zoya passed the Zaslon commander as she went through the open hatch and, as she stepped onto the ladder to descend down to the main deck, she heard a single suppressed gunshot from a rifle back on the bridge.

Vasily's rifle.

Asshole, she said to herself.

A minute later she was on the main deck, deftly kicking a leg over the gunwale to begin her descent down to the speedboat.

The rest of the Zaslon unit boarded the boat as well and lashed their scuba equipment to cleats along the sides, and the boat began slowly moving back in the direction of the yacht halfway around the island.

As they motored off to the east, Zoya leaned over to Ruslan. He had his binos up to his eyes, and they were focused on the lights from the dive bar in the distance.

Zoya tapped him on the arm. "See anything?"

"*Da.* Chaos." Still looking through the optics, he asked, "What do you suppose happened over there, Koshka?"

Zoya just shrugged. "Somebody didn't want to pay his bar tab, I guess."

When Court had extracted everything of intelligence value regarding the location of Fan Jiang from the injured Vietnamese gangster, he pressed him about the identity of the people who had attacked the ship. The young man knew nothing other than the fact that an attack was under way, and he just assumed the crazed man now torturing him was involved with that, as well. Court realized how confused he'd made the poor wounded guy by asking the question in the first place.

Court took the man's cell phone and identification out of his wallet, then helped the man stand and led him off in the direction of the bay, his blood-soaked T-shirt now off his body and used to stanch the blood flow along with the microfiber towel. Court thought the guy might make it; he was young and fit, though a lot of it had to do with how fast he could get to a hospital.

C ourt found his way off the island at one thirty in the morning. He swam out to a boat moored in the bay when he saw an older man sitting alone on the deck of his live-aboard thirty-foot fishing boat watching the fireboats and police boats near the wrecked dive bar. Court appeared on the deck and simply asked the man in English for a ride to Hong Kong. Court waved the Hong Kong dollar equivalent of a thousand U.S. in front of the man, and this made the Chinese fisherman an instant and utterly compliant co-conspirator.

Together they piloted out of the bay, past the dark and still cargo ship, past more police boats. Court knelt in the companionway, his hand hovering over the pistol tucked in the small of his back, ready to switch from the new best friend of the boat captain to his worst enemy if the old man tried anything funny.

But this captain was only too happy to make the money, and he made no problems for the suspicious *gweilo*.

Once back in the city, Court called Colonel Dai and updated him on the events of the evening. Dai said he'd dispatch his forces to look into the *Tai Chin VI*, and he reprimanded Court for not notifying him sooner, but Court gave the reasonable rejoinder that he'd gotten a lot more information in just his second night on the job than Dai and all his men had gotten since they'd arrived.

Court promised the colonel he'd call him when he woke up, and by then Dai said he would have a way to get Court into Vietnam to continue the hunt.

C ourt checked into a fleabag hotel in Wan Chai just before four a.m. The rest of his gear was back at his room in Mongkok, but it would have taken him another hour to get there, and he knew there was a good chance that Dai's men would have bugged the room.

With him here in his new digs, in addition to his backpack, he'd brought a plastic bag with four pony bottles of Jameson Irish Whiskey, some apples and pears, and a massive plastic container of cold rice pudding.

The combination was gross to think about, so Court didn't think about it. He drank a shot, then dug a spoon into the rice pudding.

After he'd eaten a few bites of the sweet dessert, he bit into both a pear and an apple. When he was finished with his odd little meal, he dialed a number on the sat phone, plugging in the phone to charge it while he waited for the call to go through.

"Brewer."

"It's me," Court said. He had more questions than information to give his handler right now, but she needed to know what the hell had happened. After they conducted their authentication sequence, he said, "Strap yourself in, because this op just got complicated."

"Sorry, Violator, but that happened the other day at the Peninsula hotel."

"As the SEALs say, the only easy day was yesterday." For the next ten minutes he filled her in on everything. He had no hidden agenda with the CIA other than the fact that he feared he might have to come back to Hong Kong, alone, to try to rescue Fitzroy if the CIA's master plan failed in any small detail along the way.

When he was finished, Brewer spoke softly, a hint of something in her voice Court couldn't identify. Perhaps exhaustion, perhaps disbelief. "So you just fought fifty guys at the same time?"

Court replied, "No. I just fought fifty guys, one at a time."

"Right. Are you somewhere you can get a drink? Because I'm pouring one now, having just heard all that shit, so I guess living it means you need one, too."

Court sipped his second airplane bottle of Jameson as he lay there on the tiny bed. "Brewer, I'm a drink and a half ahead of you."

"I'll have to catch up, then." Court heard the pouring of liquid, even over the satellite transmission. "You didn't mention any injuries."

"To me? No, surprisingly, I'm okay, although my back is starting to feel like it was attacked by a cheese grater."

"What happened?"

"Don't even remember. Just the typical knocks and rattles, I guess."

"And no idea who the force was who took down the *Tai Chin*?"

Court sighed into the phone now. "Remember all those times in the past ten minutes when you heard me say I didn't know who they were? That's still the case."

Brewer let the matter drop for now. "I guess we need to get you to Ho Chi Minh City."

"No," Court replied. "*Dai* needs to get me there. I called him already and reported. He's making travel arrangements now. I needed to show him that I'm straight with him, reporting in like the good soldier, ready to take this to the next stage. I couldn't be certain he didn't know anything about Po Toi, and if I'm going to Vietnam anyway, the last thing Fitzroy needs is for it to look like I'm running from the Chinese. That would be signing his death warrant."

"You're right," Suzanne Brewer said. And then she added, "Truthfully, I've never even heard of these Wild Tigers."

"Me neither. Vietnam drug smuggling isn't your regular beat, either, I guess."

Brewer seemed so overwhelmed with it all she just coughed out a laugh. He thought he heard ice rattling in a glass. She must have gotten control of her momentary lapse of authority, because her voice switched back into business mode.

"That said, I'll reach out to Director Hanley and have him pull in intel about this gang discreetly, from Southeast Asia assets and other sources. I'll be up to speed, and you'll be up to speed, well before you get there."

Court added, "I'll warn you now: if you blanket Saigon with CIA officers looking for Fan, or stir up any friendly assets at all there, these Wild Tigers might get word of it, or Dai might get word of it, and it will screw everything up. I just need you to get me all the intel on this group you can, and let me work the op."

Brewer answered back forcefully. "Look, you knew the stakes on this op from the beginning. You were our best chance of getting intel on Fan, but you aren't the only fish in the sea. That's not going to change just because the geographic focus of the hunt has moved." She paused a moment, and then her tone softened. "I know we need to keep all our activity low profile, not only to protect the activity itself but also to protect you and your mission. I will do my best to do just that."

Court knew that wasn't a promise. In fact, it was nothing he could hang his hat on at all.

He let it go. He had to. It depressed him a little to realize he was becoming a real team player.

CHAPTER

NINETEEN

Con Ho Hoang Da wasn't the biggest criminal organization in Vietnam, or even in Saigon. Their actual strength in terms of active members numbered less than 350, but their real might was not in their membership; it was in their influence.

The group had originated a decade earlier, when five former officers of the People's Army of Vietnam, members of an elite infantry jungle reconnaissance unit called the Tigers, were recruited to be high-profile bodyguards for a Saigon street gangster. For two years the five intelligent and capable ex-officers watched their uneducated boss oversee a stable of bandits who conducted nothing more than petty theft and pickpocketing. There was no real bodyguarding to do, but the gangster enjoyed the image of the team of polished ex–army officers shadowing him wherever he went. After a year of this work the five ex-Tigers decided their boss was small-time, and the only thing they had to protect him from was getting hit by a scooter as he staggered drunk out of a bar at night, so together the men devised a plan to have their employer arrested so they could take over his organization. They saw the potential for earning real money working in the underworld, but they couldn't do it with him.

They made deals with corrupt Saigon officials, and soon their leader was in Chi Hoa Prison, serving sixteen years for his crimes.

The five former bodyguards immediately expanded the organization from overseeing pickpocketing and snatch-and-grab petty theft to extortion, counterfeiting, and drug distribution.

The former Tigers infantry officers became the head of the Wild Tigers, Con Ho Hoang Da, and they trafficked heroin from the nearby Golden Triangle of Myanmar, Laos, and Thailand into Hong Kong and Singapore, produced and smuggled fake designer goods internationally, and illegally transported workers and immigrants across the border of Cambodia and into Thailand from Vietnam.

From the beginning they received protection from members of the local government, due to payoffs to police and party officials, and their ranks swelled as they sucked in other poorly organized and less disciplined gangs. As they grew from a few dozen to a few hundred members, the national government in Hanoi learned of their activity, and at first they reacted forcefully. But larger and larger payoffs, as well as the national government's realization that this was a criminal organization that would play ball with Hanoi on illegal international projects that helped the Socialist Republic of Vietnam, only strengthened the organization.

Chinese Triad groups operating in Vietnam were larger and more powerful on the streets, but when it came to raw influence, the Wild Tigers had become real players in the Southeast Asian underworld.

But all of this was in flux now. New leadership in the Ministry of Public Security in Hanoi had cracked down on all criminal organizations in the nation, including the Wild Tigers, and now of the original five leaders, one had been killed in a shoot-out with Triads in a restaurant in Saigon, a second was imprisoned in Cambodia, and two more had been detained in Hanoi.

One original member retained control of the organization. Tu Van Duc, a former army captain, now ran the Wild Tigers. The business hub of the organization was a medium-sized building on Nguyen Van Dau, in Saigon's Binh Thanh District, less than a mile from Tan Son Nhat International Airport. The building was lightly guarded by a few men with pistols under their shirts and AKs, shotguns, and a single RPK light automatic machine gun all stowed in lockers and under desks near the entrance. A pair of hired and armed uniformed security—off-duty local cops—manned the guardhouse in the front of the building, and another pair operated the gatehouse at the parking-garage entrance in the back.

The reason for the relatively lax security of the Wild Tigers was that they depended on the local government ties that still kept them operating more or less in the clear, despite Hanoi's pressure. They knew the police here wouldn't raid them, and even though there were larger Chinese gangs in the city, those gangs held on to their niches in the underworld—gun running, prostitution, meth—and they left the Wild Tigers alone, lest they be wiped off the playing field here in Vietnam.

But the Wild Tigers had other facilities and safe houses in the country, and none was more secure than a French Colonial villa on a farm ninety minutes west of the city, near the Cambodian border. The actual security setup at the villa there was just a few armed guards with dogs, but despite the perfunctory security measures, the Wild Tigers had a working relationship with the commander of the nearby military garrison, and it would only take one call by Tu Van Duc or any of his senior membership to bring out uniformed military troops to protect the compound.

Tu Van Duc was only forty-three, but he'd become a millionaire many times over. Since he'd received word about the attack on his ship by the three unknown Westerners, "Captain Tu" had lived in the French Colonial villa outside of town and beefed up his bodyguard force, but he still worked at the Wild Tigers building near the airport, so each day began with an early-morning commute to Saigon. This morning he arrived at the building in the back of his BMW 7 Series sedan, along with two armed bodyguards and a pair of police motorcycle "courtesy escorts" from the Ho Chi Minh City police department.

The sedan slowed in front of the steel barrier gates at the entrance to the underground parking garage at the rear of the facility, but only for an instant, because a uniformed guard in the rear gatehouse pressed a button and the cantilevered gate arm rose to let the vehicle pass.

Just minutes later Tu Van Duc marched down a third-floor hallway, flanked by two of his bodyguards. Perspiration hung on Tu's face; his head was tilted forward with intensity, and his footsteps matched the urgent look in his eyes.

A middle-aged man sat in a chair at the end of the hall, just outside a closed door. A snub-nosed revolver in a shoulder holster hung under his arm. As soon as he saw Captain Tu, he rose.

"*Chao buoi sang.*" *Good morning.*

Tu passed him by with only a distracted nod as he opened the door himself.

On the other side of the door, Chinese dissident Fan Jiang sat at a desk against a wall, his fingers tapping on a computer keyboard in a blur. The room around him had been a small office, but now it was set up like a bedroom in a college dorm. In front of him was a cup of tea and a bag of hard candy. He wore headphones and a white warm-up jacket with blue jeans, and he looked much more like a bored young college student working on a term paper than an escaped dissident on the run from the military and intelligence arms of a world power.

The only other person in the room was a young female interpreter, brought in to help him with translations on the Vietnamese government computer networks. When she saw Tu Van Duc, however, she stood, bowed, and left.

Fan himself bowed, but he did not get up.

Tu said, "I need to talk to you."

Fan clearly recognized the expression of concern on the man's face. "You were not happy with the progress I made last night? Those were the latest files from the Interior Ministry. I thought you would like the news that there are no imminent police operations in the works against your businesses in Hue."

"Your work product has been impressive. There is no problem there."

"Good," Fan replied with another subservient bow.

Tu said, "There has been a second attack on the ship that brought you here. Near the same place as before in Hong Kong."

Fan looked down to his hands. "I see. Is everyone okay?"

"No, they are not. Not at all. The ship was boarded and there was a battle on land, as well. Seven of my employees and all the ship's crew are dead. *Fourteen men!* Several Triads are dead, as well."

Fan spoke softly. A true sadness in his voice. "The attackers . . . they were from the mainland?"

"We do not know. A Westerner fought against my men at a bar at the same time as the attack, so we are assuming the attackers on the ship were Western, as well."

Fan slumped over and put his head in his hands. It took him a while to speak. "I don't know what is happening. I knew the PLA would hunt for me, but I didn't know they would come into Hong Kong in force. I thought they'd just order the Hong Kong police to look for me." He raised his head quickly. "This is terrible. I am so sorry."

Tu stepped over to Fan. "Everyone wants to know what you know. Everyone wants to get their hands on your skills." He patted the younger man on the back. "You are not safe here. It is no secret to many that this building is where the Wild Tigers operate. We are going to move you to a secret location out of town. The Internet works fine there, but the accommodations won't be as comfortable as living in the middle of Saigon."

"I will do whatever you ask. As I told you, I work for you for the next month, and then I will move on."

Tu Van Duc did not reply. Fan waited for some agreement to what he'd said, but instead the Vietnamese man turned and left the room without another word.

The interpreter returned and took her seat again next to Fan Jiang.

Fan stared at the screen in front of him. At first he was thinking about the loss of life that he had caused. Soon, however, his mind shifted to a new topic. He tried to figure out how he was going to get to Taiwan, because he was pretty sure the Wild Tigers weren't going to let him leave Vietnam for a very long time.

Court Gentry had begun his long day in Hong Kong at his overnight hotel in the Central District, waking at eight thirty in the morning after getting less than four hours of sleep. He called Dai as he left the building and walked to a bus stop, and argued with the Chinese colonel while on a bus heading north to his room in Mongkok. Dai's original plan had been to fly Court along with his own force of men into Vietnam on a private aircraft, but the American refused to travel with the Chinese, citing his need to operate alone to reduce chances for compromise. When Court told Dai he would just have to find his own way into the country, Dai balked, saying he didn't have time for Court to stow away on a container ship.

He told Court he'd come up with another plan, and to call him back in an hour.

Two hours after their first call, one of Dai's men met Court on a double-decker bus in Hong Kong's Wong Tai Sin District, and he passed him a small leather folio. Inside, Court found a Hong Kong Special Administrative Region Residency Identity smart card and an SAR passport to match, along with other ID, plus a thick wad of Vietnamese dong currency with a note telling him the total value was 1,439 U.S. dollars.

The name on the documents was Robert James, which sounded a bit lazy to Court, but the docs looked authentic enough. When Court looked at the picture used for both, however, he felt an icy chill run up his spine.

The photo was five years old, and it was authentic. This was the same picture the CIA had passed around the world in their hunt for him. A hunt now still officially in effect but unofficially suspended.

In the picture he wore wire-framed glasses and a blue blazer over a button-down shirt. He'd needed the shot for some Agency assignment when he'd had to fly commercial, unaware this would be the most recent shot of him available on the day he was burned by CIA and a termination order went out on him.

Court imagined all of the intelligence agencies of the world—from Sweden to Burkina Faso—had this picture, so it was no great surprise to see it in the hands of the Chinese. Still, the concept of using this same photo on a form of identification for an international flight almost made his head explode.

He called Dai angrily, demanding to know why they were setting him up for arrest in Vietnam, but Dai insisted the Vietnamese did not have the picture. Court had no idea for sure, and not a clue how Dai could know this, and he sure didn't like the tradecraft of walking around with this well-known and long-burned photo.

Still furious, he went himself to a pharmacy in Hong Kong and had his own passport photos shot. He was still the same person as in his official CIA photo, though five years older, but he knew the Vietnamese did not use sophisticated software in their customs process that would identify him, and this would decrease the chance his passport would raise any flags.

Dai's document people had to redo the papers, and the snafu with the photo added two and a half hours to his delay getting to Vietnam, but he used the time wisely. He picked up luggage and clothing for his cover, along with another remote camera, a new flashlight, and several other electronic gadgets, all of which he left in their original packaging. He then made his own way to Hong Kong International Airport, arriving just after two thirty.

His flight was so smooth that he slept through most of it, and he arrived at Tan Son Nhat International Airport at six thirty p.m. He deplaned with the rest of the passengers and then breezed through customs.

Traveling into Vietnam under dirty docs from the Chinese intelligence services might have been harder for Court if he looked in any way Chinese, but there were tens of thousands of white Westerners who had stayed in Hong Kong and accepted official SAR residency after the British officially relinquished governance, and Vietnam had no reason to believe any of them were working for the Chinese mainland intelligence services. No, they were bankers, businessmen, salesmen, and the like, and Court saw from his papers that he was entering Vietnam under the cover of a small-business services company.

With him in his bag he brought all of his surveillance equipment purchased in Hong Kong, which was something of a calculated risk, but even though his bag was opened and his electronics were poked at for a moment by a customs official, his several cameras, phones, binoculars, a tactical flashlight, and a monocular didn't raise any eyebrows, especially considering they were being carried by a well-dressed and well-to-do-looking person traveling from the electronics mecca of Hong Kong.

The fact that they were in their original boxes helped, too, Court imagined, because it didn't seem like a spook would smuggle in spy gear still in its shrink-wrapped packaging from the retailer.

On his taxi ride to the hotel, Court took in the city around him. Saigon was an amazingly vibrant and colorful place, with one-fifteenth the vertical sprawl of Hong Kong, and less than a fifth of the traffic on the roads and sidewalks, but to Court it somehow appeared every bit as lively. Court already knew he'd see twenty-five times the number of scooters and motorcycles here as compared to HK, but still the sea of two-wheeled traffic was an amazing sight to behold.

It was impossible for Court Gentry to be here without thinking of his father, who, Court knew, had spent a lot of time in Saigon long before Court was born. His dad had been a Marine Scout Sniper, and he'd fought combat missions north of here around Da Nang and in operations somewhere in the Mekong Delta to the west of Saigon. That was the extent of what Court knew about his dad's service, because although their small Florida home had been nearly covered in both Vietnamese and Marine Corps memorabilia, James Gentry didn't talk much about his service there.

By seven thirty p.m. Court had checked into his room at the Sheraton Saigon and, after just a few minutes to change into dark cotton slacks, a dark gray short-sleeve shirt, and black tennis shoes, he turned around and walked back out the door carrying everything he'd walked in with. He left the hotel and headed five blocks to a motorcycle rental shop, arriving shortly before closing time. Here he picked up a black 2009 Suzuki TU250X, a simple bike with enough power for city driving and a profile that wouldn't draw attention.

Court affixed a GPS unit onto his handlebars so he could type in his destination and then set out towards the Saigon HQ of the Wild Tigers.

The Russians arrived in Ho Chi Minh City at six p.m. after sailing in their sixty-eight-foot yacht directly from Hong Kong. They managed to bypass customs and immigration controls subjected to other ships and boats entering the nation by dropping the yacht's twenty-foot speedboat a few miles out of the shipping lane but inside Vietnamese international waters, filling it with Zoya and the Zaslon operators, and then linking up with a local cabin cruiser rented and crewed by Russian intelligence officers working at the SVR Residency in Ho Chi Minh City. The forty-footer then merged with the heavy maritime traffic heading up the Saigon River. The cabin cruiser offloaded its new passengers and their personal gear just outside the city, and the yacht simply went through the legal customs and visa process minus the passengers it had taken on from the speedboat.

Zoya Zakharova and the Zaslon force were picked up by the riverside in vans driven by Russian SVR non-official cover operatives working in HCMC, and then they were driven to a safe house in District One. Here Zoya and Vasily sat for a briefing on the Wild Tigers organization given by an SVR in-country analyst from the local SVR Residency, and then a second briefing about the local police and government counterintelligence structure. Zoya took information from both briefings—names, addresses, affiliations—and by late evening she felt like she knew enough about the organization to make her opening move.

At ten p.m. she leaned into the large upstairs bedroom where Vasily and

Yevgeni were just climbing into their bunks. To Vasily she said, "I need two of your men."

Zoya was dressed in blue jeans and a dark cotton pullover, with a zippered raincoat because the air outside smelled of an approaching storm. She wore a large messenger bag cross-body, and she held a black scooter helmet under her arm.

"For what?" Vasily asked.

"For about an hour. Maybe more."

Vasily frowned. "Why don't you call up those non-official cover guys who brought us here? My guys don't know Vietnamese. They don't know the area. Maybe you forgot, but we're the ones you send in when you already have a target fixed."

The good-looking brunette said, "I have a target."

Vasily cocked his head. "What the hell are you talking about?"

Zoya explained, and twenty minutes later she stood with Ruslan and Sasha out in the garage, picking through plastic containers full of used local clothing kept at the safe house for operations in the city.

She dressed both men herself, telling them they would need cell phones and headsets, but no sidearms or other equipment. When they were ready, she had both men dial into the same secure conference call number. She did the same, which put all three of them on an open conference on a secure network. The two paramilitaries climbed into a dark gray Toyota Innova minivan parked in the garage, and Zoya chose a black Honda Air Blade from the row of five scooters available. She put on her helmet and then hit the button on the wall for the garage door.

At five minutes before eleven, the two vehicles carrying the three Russians rolled out onto the tree-lined residential street and into the night.

CHAPTER

TWENTY

At nine forty-five p.m. Court arrived in the Binh Thanh District, in the neighborhood of the Nguyen Van Dau building of the Wild Tigers. He parked his motorcycle in a fenced-in parking lot and began walking the neighborhood, taking care to remain a street away from his actual target.

On his recon of the area he was happy to see quite a few guest housing options, and although there were no rooms for rent directly across the street from his target location, he considered this a benefit. If Con Ho Hoang Da were smart, they would have informants in the neighborhood, and any foreigner taking a room with an easy straight-shot view to the building on Nguyen Van Dau would be met with suspicion and further scrutiny.

Instead Court found a fourth-floor room that faced Le Quang Dinh, a major thoroughfare one block west of Nguyen Van Dau. The room was small and spartan but much cleaner than his place in Mongkok. There was no private bathroom, but a walk down a well-lit corridor led him to a public restroom with four stalls, each of which had a large window that opened to provide ventilation, though with the hot, sticky air and the large number of vehicles outside on the street, it almost made things worse. Court didn't need the ventilation, but with a little effort he found he could open one of these windows fully and pull his body through. From here he spent two minutes standing on the sill before he devised a way to pull himself up and climb onto the roof, careful to avoid both the electric wires hanging all around and the large swaths of pigeon shit here and there on the wall and the concrete eave that surrounded it.

Once on the flat portion of the roof he moved low behind a parapet until he arrived at the southeastern corner. Here, crawling forward carefully, he could see the Wild Tigers building some seventy-five yards away.

From the look of this roof, no one came up here regularly, and from a long, slow recon of the other roofs and balconies in the area through his night vision equipment, he didn't get the impression anyone would have eyes on him as long as he did not stand up and make a scene.

He found he could secure himself further by making a small lean-to structure using a five-by-three-foot square of corrugated steel sheet that had fallen off an awning of the next building over, balancing it on the parapet to enshroud himself in darkness and break up his outline from anyone looking his way from down the street.

Once he was satisfied with this hide site, Court began crawling and climbing to the south, from his building to the next. After dropping down onto an adjacent structure, he pulled a wireless camera out of his bag and positioned it on the ledge of a bank directly across the street from his target, standing it on the flat disc base that came with it and securing the base by tucking it under loose pieces of roofing tiles.

Lying flat on the cement roof just behind the camera, he used his phone to turn it on, then panned left and right, zooming in to the individual windows in the facility and then back out again. Employing this camera as well as his own overwatch to the north, he had the western side of the building covered, so he headed back to ground level to distribute his other remote cameras around the property.

A t ten thirty p.m. Court sat alone on a plastic bench, leaned over a plastic table in front of a sidewalk café, and ate a plate of *goi cuon*, rice paper rolls stuffed with noodles, vegetables, and pork. With this he downed a grilled chicken skewer and a bottle of beer, all the while taking in his new environment, trying to get a feel for the flotsam and jetsam of the neighborhood around him.

After his late dinner he continued walking this part of the district himself to learn the streets, alleys, buildings, and other features he might need to know during his operation here. He would have stood out if he were anyone else, as there were not a lot of Western faces around here at all, but he stayed out of the lights, in the deepest darkness he could find. Confidently but carefully he adjusted his gait and his route to cover ground without leaving any discernible trail.

Almost no one noticed a figure moving at all on the streets, and not a soul remembered him five seconds after he passed.

During his walk he put his second camera on a two-lane street that backed up to the Wild Tigers building, positioning it in some ivy about seven and a half feet off the ground. He stepped up onto a stoop to enter an apartment building, then held himself out to the side with one hand and formed his pipe cleaners around the device. He was still nearly one hundred yards away from the target, but with the ten-power zoom he was close enough to the back gate to ensure that he had a view without endangering himself or his operation.

The last cam went on the corner just forty yards to the southwest of the facility. This was wedged between a pair of signs outside a Pizza Hut delivery outlet and a small travel agency. The camera's body was well tucked away behind the wires that ran along the wall to provide electricity to the signs, but the lens itself was exposed. Anyone looking for it among the wires would have found this camera in moments, but Court knew he couldn't spend more than a few seconds standing here adjusting it to make certain it was low profile.

Back in his room he checked the function of all the cameras quickly. Their batteries would last only about twenty-four hours before he'd have to go back to all three locations, take them back to his room, charge them with the USB port of his laptop, and then return them to their hiding places around the Wild Tigers building.

But his cameras running out of juice was among the least of his worries. In fact, his concern was much the opposite: that Dai wouldn't give him twenty-four hours to prep before he hit the building himself, either killing

Fan in the process or scaring him away from the area, and leading to the utter failure of Court's assignment.

Court lay down on his bed and thought over his plan. He considered breaking into the headquarters early in the morning, then slipping into someplace where he could lie in wait, using the cameras he had stationed around to identify the area where Fan might be working, or even to see Fan himself through a window or arriving in a car.

But before he entered the facility he needed *some* confirmation that his target was even here, and *that* he did not have. Both Brewer and Dai had told him about this building and its relationship to the Wild Tigers, and neither of them knew of any other real HQs of the organization, although both of them had provided addresses of a few nightclubs, bars, and pool halls where gang members were known to hang out.

If Fan was somewhere else, Court getting himself wedged into a closet in this building would just waste time he did not have.

No, now he had to be prudent, to take it slow, despite the time pressures against him coming from all sides. For now it was all about holding Colonel Dai and his men at bay until Court had actionable intelligence.

Right, Court remembered with frustration. *And there was that other squad of assholes running around hunting for Fan Jiang.*

He needed to keep an eye out for the people who attacked the boat off Po Toi, too.

As a gentle rain began to fall outside his window, Court closed his eyes and tried to go to sleep on the lumpy little bed, knowing tomorrow was going to be one hell of a long day.

The rain had just begun to fall when Zoya Zakharova pulled into a narrow cobblestone alleyway lined on both sides with motorcycles and scooters. She found a spot for her Honda, parked it, and turned off the ignition, but she did not get up from the seat.

Instead she just looked around at her surroundings for a moment, making sure no one was close by and no open windows overlooked her location.

At five-seven and with her helmet on her head, her raincoat, and the messenger bag she wore instead of a purse, she might have looked like a man to anyone who glanced her way, but no one did. Instead she just sat there in the near darkness, in the rain, and she waited.

This was her third back alley of the evening, and the first two had been dry holes. The street in front of the nightclub on Pham Ngu Lau Street in District One had been too packed to operate there successfully, and a small dark bar on Nguyen Tat Thanh in District Four—while open and an easy mark from an operational standpoint—simply had none of the potential targets on Zoya's list.

Now she was trying her luck in District Three, on Dien Bien Phu, at a basement pool hall called the Gambler.

"In position," she said into her headset just as the back door of the pool hall opened and disgorged a group of young men. She watched as they lit cigarettes, pounded fists, and climbed aboard different bikes in the alley. She took in their faces but saw no one that spiked her interest.

"You receiving?" she said.

There was no response.

"Sirena for Anna element," she called a third time, and finally she received a reply from Ruslan.

"We hear you. Entering the front door now."

Zoya thought Ruslan and Sasha were par for the course for Zaslon men, meaning they were pricks. She had determined this the first time she worked with the team, and now it barely registered with her. She told herself it was only partly because she was a woman. The real problem was their dead-set belief that they were superior, both physically and mentally, to everyone they ever came in contact with in their life. Sure, if they were up with top brass in Moscow they would show deference, and certainly they'd all but groveled when called upon to do so during their military careers in GRU, Russian military intelligence. But now they were SVR Zaslon, out in the field, serving on a task force led by a woman with a civilian background; they probably had to swallow their tongues before every response so they didn't say something insubordinate, sexist, or both.

Zoya was so used to the back talk, the delays in response, and the downright insolence from this group as well as others just like them that it barely fazed her anymore, but it did have the effect of making her wish she were on another type of mission.

Her *favorite* type of mission . . . one where she worked alone.

The past week felt to her as if it were her job to manage a big group of overgrown teenage boys, although thinking back to her own teenage years, she realized her own father didn't have it so easy with her.

"*Tzarstvo emu nebesnoe.*" *God rest his soul*, she muttered softly.

She smiled a little now, thinking back to her childhood, and then she thought about the men with her here in Vietnam. Well, at least she didn't have to clean up after them on the boat or at the safe house; as rough as these guys were, as bad as they stank by the end of each day, at least they had military order in their lives that ensured each item in their possession remained zipped in the right pouch at all times. But still, these men, like most men, could be a mess. Zoya had lived in safe houses, team rooms, bunkhouses, and garrisons surrounded by men most all her adult life, so she knew how to keep her own personal space to her liking and mentally shut out the stench, clutter, and grime of large groups of men living in close proximity.

The Russian intelligence officer had just cleared her mind of her father and the jerks she worked with when she heard Sasha speak through her earpiece.

"Positive sighting on . . . break." She heard him mumble something to Ruslan, and she imagined the two men looking at the photos she'd texted them on their mobiles, right there in the middle of the pool hall. She closed her eyes, thinking about the shitty tradecraft, but then told herself these men had been given mere minutes to memorize the faces of thirty-five potential targets.

She'd cut Sasha some slack.

After twenty seconds, however, she spoke. "Who is it, Anna Five?"

The reply came after a little more whispering. "It's number thirteen."

Zoya's memory had been good her entire life, but it had been honed to a steel trap through years of training and practical application. "Bui something," she said without hesitation. "He's a local cop."

"Uh . . . affirmative. Bui Ton Tan. He's wearing blue jeans, a white shirt with a red track jacket over it. He's drinking at the bar alone. Do we approach?"

Zoya smiled a little in her helmet. "Just keep doing what you're doing."

She knew the two Zaslon men would not be operating in a low-profile manner. This guy would see them in seconds, if he hadn't seen them already.

A minute later she smiled again when Ruslan reported that the target appeared to be heading for the back door. "You want us to follow him out?" he asked.

Zoya replied, "*Nyet*. Just bring the car around."

CHAPTER

TWENTY-ONE

Lieutenant Bui Ton Tan was a thirty-three-year-old officer in the Vietnam People's Police, Ho Chi Minh City Public Security Office. He'd worked a full eight-hour shift today, getting off at eleven, and he'd been here in the bar less than fifteen minutes. He just wanted to get a couple of beers in him before going home for the evening.

He'd been halfway into his objective when he saw the two big foreigners in the bar and realized they were looking at him. It took a moment for him to be certain, not that the men were hiding it. On the contrary, they seemed to be going out of their way to stress the fact that they had taken an interest in him.

And this was deeply troubling in light of the news he'd received today.

He'd spent the day patrolling the Cat Lai Ward in District Two and hadn't had any direct contact with anyone in Con Ho Hoang Da, but he *had* received a text message this afternoon from one of his fellow cops who also moonlighted at the guard shack of the headquarters building. The message said all the guards had been warned about a potential attack from an unknown group of white foreigners, and everyone would be brought in for overtime to deal with the threat. Bui was confused by this; he'd heard about a threat in Hong Kong from a group of Tay, a Vietnamese word used to refer to non-Asians. But that had been earlier in the week and he'd heard nothing since. The Wild Tigers had next to no close connections to Tay in Ho Chi Minh City, so he immediately asked for more clarification, but his colleague had just said they'd need Bui to come in to the gatehouse tomorrow for a full shift on his day off from the police department.

He'd learned nothing else about the danger, but now a pair of big, mean-looking Tay were here.

Bui thought about calling out for help from men here in the pool hall, but the other Wild Tigers present were just young dealers and street thieves. He didn't know any of them—he worked security at the HQ, after all—and he wasn't sure enough of the nature of this threat to just assemble a quick posse of strangers. Anyway, as far as Bui was concerned he didn't need anyone else. Although these two guys were both six inches taller and forty kilos heavier than he was, Bui was carrying his police-issue Makarov pistol in a shoulder holster.

He wasn't worried about his personal security, but he was somewhat concerned about why the hell these two big Tay were consulting their mobile phones and then looking back up at him.

After quickly downing his second bottle of beer, he decided the prudent course of action would be to just walk out the back door, climb onto his bike, and get out of here. He'd text the security office at the Wild Tigers and report the incident as soon as he was clear.

Bui nonchalantly unzipped his jacket so he could grab his pistol in a hurry if he had to, then slid off the bar stool without looking at the two big men. He nodded to a couple of distant acquaintances on the way out the door and stepped into the alley.

A light but steady rain fell, which pissed Bui off, because he'd left his poncho at the station. He walked up to his Kawasaki bike and fished through his jeans pocket for his keys, keeping one eye on the back door of the pool hall in case the foreigners appeared.

"*Chao chu.*" *Hello, sir.* It was a woman's voice, close behind him in the dark, in the opposite direction from the back door. The voice surprised him because he hadn't seen anyone around when he came out the door, but the surprise did not scare him at all. He turned around. "Yeah?"

To his astonishment a Tay woman stood there in the dimly lit alley, holding a black bike helmet in her hand.

He didn't even have time to get a good look at her before she smashed him in the face with it.

Bui flipped backwards over the seat of his bike and then down onto the wet cobblestones. He saw nothing but stars for a moment; his lips and nose burned with pain, but he did not lose consciousness. He blinked hard, then reached into his jacket to pull his pistol, but just as the little weapon cleared the leather of his shoulder holster he felt strong hands on the wrist of his drawing hand, twisting it around, removing the weapon easily.

Bui looked up and saw that the woman had come around the bike and now she stood over him, the gun in one hand, the bike helmet high above her head.

"How about another?" She said it in English, and he understood only because of her tone and the context of the situation.

Bui shook his head to clear away the stars, spit blood, and then said one of the few phrases he knew in English, because it perfectly applied to his sentiment. "Fuck your mother, bitch!"

He had only a slight recognition of the helmet arcing down towards his face before the lights went out completely.

Zoya sat in the front room of the safe house, her legs crossed and her eyes on the lights of the car pulling up the drive. She looked at her watch and sighed.

Ruslan and Sasha had gone to bed as soon as they arrived and moved the blindfolded prisoner to a three-meter-square laundry room in the back of the house, tying his arms behind his back and his legs to his chair. Zoya watched them do this, thanked them for their help, and empathized with their obvious disappointment that they hadn't been the ones to bash the prisoner in the face.

In the vehicle on the way from the scene Sasha had reported to Zoya that her prisoner spoke neither English nor French. Zoya made a call while following the minivan on her scooter, and she requested that a Vietnamese interpreter from the SVR Residency be sent over immediately to interpret.

She'd woken her SVR contact from a deep sleep to do this, and was first told to come to the consulate on Ba Huyen Thanh Quan Street, sometime the following day after nine a.m.

"I don't do embassies," was Zoya's reply, and, after just a little pressure, her contact assured her he'd have an interpreter on the way within the hour.

Zoya sat and stewed the entire time she waited for the interpreter to arrive, but she recognized that there was a benefit in this. The guy in the back was doing exactly the same thing. If Zoya was lucky there would be plenty of time for her prisoner to think about his situation, to wonder about his fate, and to resolve to do something to help himself.

Like talk.

After the vehicle parked, Zoya led a young Russian woman into the safe house with a quick handshake and a check of the woman's credentials. Zoya offered no ID of her own. The new arrival was SVR, of course, but she was just an interpreter; Zoya saw this immediately. The woman was still in her midtwenties, and she seemed utterly bewildered to be called out into the night like this to work at some safe house she'd never heard of with a covert operative she'd never met. Zoya assumed this girl's whole world consisted of reading military or trade documents or translating recorded phone conversations and writing reports for her desk-riding superiors at the embassy.

The two women walked together towards the back of the house without any conversation, then arrived at the door to the laundry room, and here they stopped.

Zoya said, "Sorry, long night. What did you say your name was again, dear?"

"Svetlana. Call me Sveta."

"Okay, Sveta, did someone explain what we are about to do?"

"No, ma'am. I've been told nothing other than this address."

"Fine. I'll brief you now. We are going to obtain information from a man who is tied and blindfolded in a room here in the house."

"Oh. I see," Sveta said. The girl wore no makeup, so it was easy for Zoya to watch the color drain from her face.

But Zoya was all business; she had no time to bring little Sveta gently into her world. "We will do this by escalating means, beginning with simple questions, and then continuing to harder measures, if required."

The younger woman's eyebrows furrowed, then her eyes widened when Zoya leaned closer to her.

"Here's a prediction. They *will* be required."

Sveta's voice cracked. Compared to Zoya she sounded meek, mousy. *"Da. Ponial."* Yes, understood.

"You are to provide the man with a translation of what I say, and you will provide me with the translation of what he says. You and I will speak English, not Russian. Any delay, reticence, unease . . . *any* sense that you are bothered by *anything* that happens in that room cannot be tolerated. He will hear your discomfort and use it as an avenue to resistance. I can break through his resistance, but that takes time, and I do not have time for him."

Sveta looked like she would rather be anywhere else on planet Earth right now.

Zoya said, "Your background. I take it there is no military service?"

"No, ma'am. Moscow State University. Then I spent two years here working in the natural gas sector before coming in—"

Zoya cut her off. "Listen to me. We aren't going in there to hash out a gas shipment."

"I understand."

Zoya put her hand on the doorknob. "I hope so. Everything is on the table through this door. I don't think I'll have to gouge the man's eyes out . . . surely it won't come to that."

"No . . . no, ma'am." Sveta looked like she was about to break into tears.

Zoya closed her eyes. Took a couple of slow breaths. "Listen, if you cry right now, we can't go in there, and that will ruin my night. *Please* don't ruin my night."

"Of course not. I am . . . I am ready."

"Khorosho." Good.

Sveta saw Zoya push the handle on the door, and then her eyes lit up. "Wait. A guard."

"A *what?*"

"A guard. Shouldn't we take a guard in there with us? In case he—"

Other than a little roll of her eyes, Zoya ignored the comment. Instead she just opened the door and entered. After a moment's hesitance, Sveta followed her in and closed the door behind her.

The two women sat down across a little table in front of the blindfolded man. Bui heard the movement in the room and swung his head around. In Vietnamese he said, "Who is there? What the fuck do you want with me?"

Sveta stared at the man's busted lip, swollen nose, and blood-crusted nostrils, saying nothing until Zoya bumped her knee with her own.

Sveta translated his words into English.

Zoya did not answer; instead, she said, "You and I don't have to have a bad time tonight. We can take care of this quickly. We can come to an agreement, and you can be on your way."

Sveta did her job, but when Bui shouted something, Sveta looked reluctant to interpret.

Zoya bumped her knee harder this time.

The young SVR interpreter cleared her throat and turned to Zoya. She smiled apologetically, awkwardly, then said, "Are you that bitch who hit me? I will fuck you for that."

Zoya fought a smile of her own. "A tempting offer, but I'll have to pass." She shook her head. "No, don't translate that."

Sveta just nodded.

Zoya leaned forward on the table and spoke, and Sveta translated her words effortlessly now. "Your name is Bui Ton Tan. You are a lieutenant with the Ho Chi Minh City People's Police. You also work, illegally, as hired security for Con Ho Hoang Da. Once a week you drive a motorcycle in the motorcade of Captain Tu Van Duc, the head of the organization, and three times a week you work at the gatehouses on the perimeter of the office building in the Binh Thanh District. I would like to talk to you about this work."

The man still seemed utterly confused to be here. "Yeah? So? Who are you? Why do you care?"

"I ask questions. You answer questions," Zoya said.

When Sveta translated this, Bui began to stand, though his ankles were tied to the chair and his arms were cinched behind his back.

He screamed, "To hell with you, bitch!"

Sveta translated.

Zoya launched out of her chair and came around the table. She shoved him back down into his seat, took his arms, and wrenched them up high at the wrists. To alleviate the pain Bui had to bend forward, and when he did the female Russian operative slammed him in the back of his head, smashing his face into the table.

The Vietnamese police officer screamed in pain, and blood sprayed a few inches in all directions, spotting the table's white surface.

Sveta recoiled in horror, and Zoya, still leaning over the wailing man, shot daggers from her eyes at the young girl.

The young interpreter got control of her emotions, and she looked down to the floor.

Zoya twisted the man's hand until he dropped back to the chair. "Tell him he is not leaving till I have what I want, and if he doesn't tell me now, he will leave carrying one of his arms out of here in a plastic bag."

Sveta did this, keeping her voice calm. When Bui replied, still with his mouth pressed into the table, Sveta looked up at Zoya.

"What do you want to know?"

"I want to know where Fan Jiang is."

Sveta translated this, waited for the response, and then delivered it.

"I have no idea who that is," she said.

Zoya sat back down after patting the man on his back. She took a moment to adjust her shirt, to push a strand of her chin-length brunette hair back behind her ear, and then she nodded. "Okay, Mr. Tan. This, I believe. It is very likely you have no idea of the identity of the young Chinese male who appeared here earlier in the week and joined your organization. I will show you a photograph to help you."

Zoya stood again, pulling her smartphone out of her pocket. She tapped the screen, put the phone on the table in front of Bui, then stepped around him. She took his head, pushed it down inches from the image of Fan on her phone, and pulled off his blindfold.

The Vietnamese police lieutenant could see nothing in front of him other than the image. He looked at the picture for several seconds. Finally he nodded, and he spoke.

Sveta looked at Zoya, standing behind the prisoner. "Yeah. I've seen him. Came in yesterday morning. So what?"

Zoya smiled a little and winked at Sveta. "So . . . tell me more."

CHAPTER

TWENTY-TWO

Court climbed out of the communal bathroom in the predawn darkness, stood on the windowsill, and reached out to grab on to the eave of the four-story building's roof. Raindrops pelted his hand, and the surface felt damp. He hadn't planned on the rain continuing into the morning, but he was more than accustomed to things not going his way, so it didn't slow him down at all.

Pulling himself part of the way up on the eave, he used his feet to walk up the wall, then kicked away, swung out, and hoisted himself up onto the roof. He lay flat on his stomach to slip off his pack and then he rolled onto his back, taking a second to enjoy the cool rainfall on his face.

But only a second. Soon he began moving south on the roof to the corner of the building, and he crawled under the steel-sheeting tent he'd erected against the parapet there.

He settled into position and lay there, wet but out of the rain, curled up flat on a roof in a dark little hole. He felt like a rat, but again, he was accustomed to it, and he didn't find it unpleasant. On the contrary, the conditions weren't on his mind at all.

It was the clock that had him scared.

After using his binoculars to check the two sides of the building in view, he checked his phone to view the three cameras he'd positioned around the target the previous evening. He saw no activity at all, other than a couple of bored-looking guys in generic security uniforms sitting in the guard-house in the front, and one in the back.

He checked the time on the phone and saw it was almost seven a.m., and he wondered what time the workday started around here for the local mob.

He decided to call Dai to ease the desperate Chinese colonel's mind, to give him some calm, soothing words about how the Gray Man had everything under control. The truth was something different, of course, but Court felt like he needed to sell confidence to keep the Chinese from taking active measures themselves.

Court put his wired headset in his ear, accessed his encrypted voice-calling app, then dialed Colonel Dai's number. The international connection took a moment to go through and initiate, but when it finally did, Dai answered abruptly.

"My men have just notified me that they went to collect you at your hotel. They say you are not there."

"Got an early start."

Dai said, "You will tell me where you are and what you are doing."

Court replied, "I'm already in position watching the Wild Tigers building here in the city."

"What do you see?"

"So far, nothing, but I have the ability to get eyes on vehicles coming and going and into some of the windows, and I am developing an understanding of the security setup."

"What do the security protocols look like?"

Court said, "Nothing much, to tell you the truth. It's surprising."

"What do you mean?"

"I know there aren't a lot of all-out gang wars here in Vietnam, but this building doesn't even look well protected from local law enforcement."

Dai said, "That does not come as a great surprise. The local Saigon administration takes a cut of their operation. Beware of any patrolling police. They are probably on the payroll of the Wild Tigers."

"That wasn't in the material I read."

Dai just said, "Vietnam doesn't possess the purity of political thought we enjoy in the People's Republic of China. They have a large underworld, and some of their politicians benefit from it. It's disgusting, really. Hanoi is trying to rein it in, but quietly. They can't admit there is a problem."

Court had been around the block enough to know China bowed to no one when it came to top-down corruption and official cover-ups, but he wasn't going to get into a discussion of government malfeasance with Dai.

The colonel asked, "What is your plan?"

"Continued surveillance until I either see Fan himself or see security measures that make me believe he is here."

"We don't have time for that! I have sixteen well-armed and well-trained men in the city, and men from our consulate there are available to me, as well. We already know this location is where the Wild Tigers operate. We can raid the building today. If we don't find Fan Jiang there, we will find someone who knows where he is. Remember, whoever raided that ship two nights ago in Hong Kong has affected our operation. The Wild Tigers have to suspect that someone on their ship talked, so they will assume those attackers will go to Saigon next. We need to act before they arrive, or before the Wild Tigers move Fan. They might decide he is not worth the trouble, and they may wash their hands of him. If he gets away from them, we will lose our opportunity."

Court said, "The Wild Tigers have already paid a high price for Fan. They will get valuable information from him; I don't see them giving him up. Trust me, Colonel. When this place opens for business today, I will be able to tell if a well-protected person arrives."

"And how will you do that?"

"I assume there will be multiple vehicles, running in a motorcade. If not, the security setup will indicate this isn't the right location. We'll find him if he's here, but there is no reason to hit a four-story building if we don't know our target is inside."

Dai said, "You are not in command; I am! You are assisting my operation. If you are worried about our agreement regarding Fitzroy, I assure you it will be honored, even if my men terminate Fan Jiang."

Court watched the rainfall on the roof around him. The sky above was lightening as the morning broke. "That's not why I'm trying to keep your men back. I'm only thinking of the operation. Look, you brought me into this for a reason. We need a measured approach. I've been doing this sort of thing for a long time. I know when it's time to move on a target and when it's time to pull back and assess."

Dai pressed, as Court thought he might. "Every minute we wait is another minute our target can get farther away!"

Court put his forehead down on the gravel roof. He could feel Dai's urgency through the phone. This guy wasn't going to wait around for Court to find Fan on his own. Still, Court pressed. "We have a tactical advantage now. We know where the Wild Tigers are. Let me watch them to get more intelligence."

Dai was silent for several seconds. Finally he said, "I will give you more time. But not much. And I want results!"

"So do I," Court said, and he was about to hang up on Dai, but he heard the phone go dead before he got the chance.

B y early afternoon, Court's sense of foreboding grew, because although he had seen a significant number of HCMC police cars rolling by the Wild Tigers HQ, he didn't get any sense that there was a high-risk protectee anywhere inside the quiet building down the street.

At three p.m. he was still keeping one eye on his phone as he ducked into a garden restaurant and coffee shop a few blocks south of his target. He ordered from the counter and then found a table near a long line of scooters owned by the young patrons of the café who had rolled them past the vine-covered fences to keep them away from scooter thieves while they sat around the garden enjoying the food, the coffee, and the Wi-Fi.

Court's big bowl of noodles and bottle of water were brought to his table by a young girl, then delivered with a polite bow. Court made no eye contact, staying half hidden under a beige baseball cap and shades, and he dug into the hot bowl of noodles in pork broth with abandon while gulping the cool water.

The café was relatively busy, with most of the tables full and a decent line at the counter, but it was large enough that Court didn't feel like anyone would look at his phone if he checked his cameras. Though he was giving himself a little time for lunch, not much about his work here changed. He kept looking down to the feed every few seconds, swiping back and forth to get different angles of his target.

Court divided his time between his lunch, the views on his phone, and his immediate surroundings. He was supposed to call Dai again to report his progress, but he was worried his lack thereof would spur the Chinese colonel to do something stupid. In truth, at this point Court was starting to think Dai's idea about launching some sort of a raid on the facility was tactically sound, if only just to grab a senior officer in the group. Court had seen nothing from the outside to give him any indication the Vietnamese would put up much of a coordinated fight, and if the Chinese operators were careful, they could probably pull it off without the cops rolling in their vehicles up and down Nguyen Van Dau having any idea what was going on right next to them.

Yes, for the Chinese, this was the right play to make, Court had little doubt.

The only problem with this play was, of course, that Court wasn't here to help the Chinese. He was here to help the United States, and the Chinese having more intelligence about Fan's whereabouts than Court did would result in the failure of his real operation.

Just as he shook his worry off and dug his chopsticks back into his noodles, a young couple, both Western in appearance, entered the little eatery while holding hands. They surveyed the menu over the counter for a long time, then ordered, totally unaware that Court was checking them out from thirty feet away.

Court could hear bits of their conversation with the woman behind the counter. They were American.

The couple picked a table near the entrance, and they made soft small talk with occasional smiles. When their food came they chatted in halting Vietnamese with the young girl who delivered it, then ate their lunch, both of them occasionally looking to their phones while doing so.

The man said something and the woman chuckled, and then the man leaned over and kissed her before they both returned to their food and their phones.

While he was looking at them, Court kept his eyes flickering towards the street out front. Amid the scooters and pedestrians a man in a black hooded raincoat and sunglasses walked by. He was Asian, Han Chinese from the looks of it. He was taller than those around him, and his mannerisms told Court he wasn't just a foreign tourist or businessman passing by.

His head swiveled as he walked; his pace was a little slower than those around him.

He was one of Dai's men; Court even thought he recognized him from the mansion in the Peak neighborhood of Hong Kong.

Court finished his noodles, gulped the rest of his water, and wiped off the plastic table with a napkin. He got up, took his paper bowl and his empty water bottle and threw them in the garbage, then exited right next to the American couple and began walking up the street. As he did so he pulled his phone from his pocket and dialed Suzanne Brewer.

It was nearly four a.m. in Virginia. She answered quickly, but with a voice that told Court he'd woken her.

"Brewer."

Court said, "You need to pull Ken and Barbie. They are about two minutes away from getting made."

There was a delay, followed by a dry cough, then, "Identity challenge, Hermit."

"Dammit," Court muttered under his breath. "Response, Heathen. Did you hear what I just said?"

Brewer seemed to wake quickly. "Identity confirmed, and I *did* hear you, but I *don't* know what you are talking about."

"Two case officers, late twenties, doing the boyfriend-girlfriend thing a little too cutesy. I am pretty sure the woman thinks the guy is gross, and it's obvious the dude would rather have his tongue in her mouth than his eyes on his target."

"I . . . uh . . . Where is this?"

"You really don't know who I am talking about?"

"I hate to break it to you, but I'm not running all of Southeast Asia. I am running *you*."

"But these case officers are near the Wild Tigers HQ. They only know these guys have Fan because of *my* intel."

"So?"

"So, are you telling me that all Agency assets in Asia know about the product I generated?"

"Of course not. This went out codeword-classified. Only the necessary people know."

"And by 'the necessary people,' you mean a mismatched duo of B-team case officers right off the Farm?"

"I don't know what you thought you saw, but—"

Court was horrified at the prospect that this couple, and any other CIA surveillance in the area, might be noticed by the Chinese. If that happened Dai would start to worry even more, and perhaps he'd even make the reasonable association between the one American on his team and American intelligence. He said, "Trust me. I've been dodging people like those two for the last five years. They wouldn't see me if I walked up and slapped them in the face, but I can feel them under my skin."

Brewer did not press. "I'll talk to Matt. He'll know who they are."

"He needs to pull them off this target. I see them again, and I *will* burn them."

"You will do nothing of the sort!"

"Look, I've got a job to do. Things that are in my way, I will push out of my way. I swear to you, if they don't disappear now, I'm calling Dai and warning him American spooks are lurking in the streets. It's the only way I can save my op."

Brewer said, "I'll call Hanley and get them out of there."

Court ended the call and kept walking. He had no idea how many American assets were here in the area, but he immediately doubled his efforts to ID those who did not belong.

Just then, an HCMC police cruiser drove by; the two men in the front seat looked especially vigilant for wandering local patrol cops.

Shit, he thought. It was getting crowded around here.

As he turned the corner to return to his hotel, he saw a pair of young Asian men in a small white four-door, and instantly he knew they did not belong here any more than the American couple or Dai's operative walking the neighborhood. Court thought these guys looked like Han Chinese, as well; they were taller than the average Vietnamese and had a slightly lighter complexion.

And from their body language, their roaming eyes, and the alert head tilts, they were operational, just like the man on foot.

Court realized in seconds these guys were also Chinese intelligence officers, but he got the impression they were not Dai's men. They didn't have the edge of hardened killers. Court assumed they were from the local Chinese consulate or even the embassy in Hanoi.

Court wondered if the entire nation of Vietnam had been flooded by mainland Chinese government surveillance experts and hit men, all trying to find Fan Jiang.

By the time Court got back to the guesthouse, the clouds had rolled back over the city, and a warm rain had begun to fall. He knew if it got too dark and stormy his view from the roof would be severely limited.

He started to head for the bathroom to take a leak before climbing back out the window to retake his position, but the rumble of thunder made him rethink his plan. Instead, he used the bathroom, then went back to his room and sat on his little bed.

He plugged his phone in to charge it further, though he had two backup phone chargers in his backpack and one in his front pocket. He turned on his camera app and scrolled through the three views on the 4.7-inch screen.

The first view showed the southern side of the building; it was the same as ever, and there was nothing to see at the front gate, captured on the far left of the camera's view. The camera showing the east side of the building revealed the same picture as it had all day long other than the rain and a blue minivan pulling up to the rear gate. Court eyed it for just a moment and determined it was the work truck of an Internet service provider, and unlikely to be carrying one of the most wanted men in Southeast Asia.

He checked the front of the building on camera three and immediately cocked his head. This view showed a better angle on the front gatehouse than the cam on the southern side, and where there had been no vehicle at the gate seconds before, now there was a blue minivan, identical to the one in back, just rolling to a stop.

It didn't take him long to determine what was going on. "No," he muttered softly. "No."

Zooming in tight with the camera, he saw both guards in the gatehouse facing the driver's window of the minivan, standing perfectly still. Then, one after the other, they lifted their hands into the air.

He couldn't see inside of the van from the angle of his camera, but when one of the guards spun to the ground and a splatter of red covered the glass behind him, there was no doubt as to what was going on.

The other guard dropped right on top of the first.

"Shit!" Court stood, unplugged his phone, grabbed his motorcycle helmet, and slung his pack onto his back. He took just seconds to sanitize his little room, and then he shot out the door.

CHAPTER

TWENTY-THREE

As he began hurrying towards the stairs, Court called Colonel Dai. He could not know for certain whether these attackers were Dai's men or part of the mystery force who hit the cargo ship in Po Toi the day before yesterday, but either way, Court knew he was screwed. There was no way he could make entry to the building himself with whatever was happening in there. The state of alert for the Vietnamese gangsters inside would obviously be through the roof; there would likely be local cops on the way, and, it went without saying, the two vanloads of new actors on the scene showed no compunction in killing threats in their way.

And Court was armed with nothing save for a small folding knife.

All he could do was hope Fan Jiang wasn't in the building in the first place, or else that the Wild Tigers got him out of there before he was either killed by the Chinese or captured by the other unit after him.

He listened to his earpiece while Dai's phone rang and rang. Court ran down the stairs, through the narrow hallways of the guesthouse towards a back door that opened to a stoop in the back alley. Dai's phone still rang in his ear as he launched over the stoop and down into the alley, then sprinted to the gated lot on Le Quang Dinh where his motorcycle was parked.

Court gave up on the call before he got to the lot; he slipped the phone back into his pocket but left the earpiece in his ear as he put his helmet on his head. He climbed onto his Suzuki bike in the parking lot and fired it up, then waited for the attendant to raise the bar so he could pull out onto Le Quang Dinh.

He made a left into heavy scooter traffic, then another left onto a side street. This led him back in the direction of the Wild Tigers building, so Court slowed, then pulled his bike onto the sidewalk at the corner.

He quickly remounted his GPS unit on the handlebars of his bike, then stood there on the sidewalk, straddling the Suzuki, looking up the street through the steady rain. From his position here the Wild Tigers headquarters appeared to be as quiet as at any other time all day, so Court took the opportunity to pull his phone from his jacket pocket and check the camera feeds.

Just as he swiped to the rear camera, he saw movement on his screen. Two men leapt out of the front seats of the minivan as it sat parked in the back lot, facing the entrance to the underground parking garage. They dropped into combat crouches, pistols in their hands, both aiming at the dark entrance to the ramp down to the garage.

Court glanced around quickly at his own environment, then looked back at his phone.

As he watched, a black sedan launched out from the darkness of the underground ramp, so fast it appeared to Court to actually catch air for a moment before the vehicle bottomed out. It swerved hard to the right of the van, striking the shooter who'd jumped out of the driver's seat, knocking him into the air and over the hood of a car parked next to the minivan. The black sedan raced on, making a hard right to fire out the back gate, and then it took a ninety-degree left to head north.

Here it sideswiped a man pulling a food cart, knocking both him and his cart into the air, sending them crashing off Court's screen.

He watched it all on his phone, but he could hear tires screeching a hundred yards away on the far side of the building.

And then the sirens of approaching police vehicles began to wail.

Court couldn't see into the black sedan, but whoever was inside had to be important. Maybe Fan himself, maybe not, but certainly at least a major player in the organization.

With nothing else to go on, no desire to sit around here and wait for the cops to arrive in force, and no confidence that anyone important to him would be left alive inside the building across the street when this was all over, Court decided he *had* to go after the black sedan.

He revved the throttle on his bike and launched out into the rain and the traffic, leaned to the left, and whipped through the scooters, cars, and pedestrians.

It took Court a minute, but he did catch up to the fleeing vehicle, and it wasn't due to any high-speed daredevil feats on the street bike. Instead it was the lousy traffic that slowed the black sedan to a crawl just a few blocks north of the Wild Tigers building but nevertheless allowed a determined driver of a motorcycle to pick his way through.

Court found himself just a few car lengths behind the black sedan. From a quick look at the rear of the car through all the action on the street, he managed to ID it as a BMW 7 Series, and this convinced him even more that he was following someone who could help him with his mission. There were some luxury cars around Saigon, a significant number, in fact, but Court didn't imagine anyone short of top brass for the Wild Tigers would be escaping from their HQ in a ninety-thousand-dollar ride.

The black BMW 7 Series pushed its way through the congestion. The driver laid on his horn in an effort to coax vehicles out of his way. Court did the same some seventy-five yards back. Several times he stood up on the footrests of the Suzuki to try to pick out the sedan ahead in the heavy traffic, then immediately dropped down as soon as he did so in order to focus on something in his way.

He desperately wanted to check his phone to see what the hell was going on back at the building behind him, but the chaotic street ahead of him required all his attention. He whipped around the scooters and cars moving in the same direction but at slower speeds, fought his way through cross traffic at intersections, and narrowly avoided pedestrians who used the low speed of vehicles here to make their way across the street far away from any crosswalks.

He had just accelerated around a man with a pushcart when he saw a garbage man changing out a metal can on the side of the road right in front of him. Court couldn't believe this idiot was calmly standing in the far right traffic lane to do this, but he didn't mull it over for long, because he had to bounce his rented Suzuki up onto the sidewalk to avoid him.

Doing this put him right in the middle of an open-air market along the side of the street, and with the sedan continuing through the intersection, he had no alternative but to race through the milling crowd as he drove along the sidewalk.

Court found himself puttering along among the foot traffic, stuck on the sidewalk because of the long impenetrable wall of plastic-tarp-covered portable kiosks lining the side of the road. He shouted to move people out of his way, slowed down significantly when the elderly or those pushing strollers forced him to do so, then sped up to a dangerous pace when a pair of cops in loose-fitting green uniforms blew whistles and swung batons in the air as he passed.

He raced through a group of young locals, forcing them to dive to safety in all directions, then saw a tight opportunity on his left to squeeze back onto the road. He jacked the handlebars, began racing towards an intersection, then almost immediately saw the black BMW parked there, stuck in traffic, just on his left.

Court had no choice but to whip back to the right, almost flipping over his bike as he did so to avoid detection by his target, and then continue on down the sidewalk for another block before coming to a stop. Seventy-five feet behind him four local police ran through the crowd in his direction, voices shrieking and batons swinging in the air, but Court just waited, watching the intersection ahead, looking for the black BMW.

The traffic wasn't quite bumper-to-bumper, but it was moving along at only ten to fifteen miles an hour, so the wait for the vehicle he was tailing felt interminable.

When the cops were just twenty-five feet behind him the BMW rolled by, directly in front of a green and white city bus. As soon as he was flush with the rear of the bus he throttled hard, sending his bike out into the street and spraying the police with rainwater off his back tire.

For almost a minute as he drove, Court was blocked by the bus in front of him; he had no eyes on the BMW so all he could do was drive on and swivel his head to the left and right, checking the connecting roads to make sure his target had not turned off. Finally the bus turned to the right and

Court saw the 7 Series, five car lengths ahead, just as it made a left a few blocks short of the airport road.

Court followed suit, and soon his target merged onto an on-ramp for a six-lane street. Court stayed behind, and while he steered he carefully adjusted the screen on his GPS unit, backing out the scale so he could try to get some idea of where they were going.

As both vehicles sped up on the new road, Court's GPS unit on his handlebars indicated they were heading due west now, and it looked as if they were leaving the city altogether.

Court stayed farther back than he would have liked considering the congestion because he realized the person or persons in the vehicle ahead might be worried about being tailed right now, since they'd just raced away from an attack. He didn't want to lose them—he really had no fallback plan if he did—but he knew riding their bumper would mean immediate exposure.

Suddenly Court hit his brakes hard, shimmying a little on the wet pavement. Up ahead, three Ho Chi Minh City police motorcycles came out of a side street and seemed to link up with the BMW, which had moved into the right lane. The black car did not stop, but the driver rolled his window down and communicated with one of the cops; then the window went back up and the three motorcycles formed a triangle around the BMW, two in front and one behind. Court noticed the rear biker looking back over his shoulder a couple of times, but Court did nothing to stand out. He just rolled along with dozens and dozens of others heading northwest on the highway.

This was all good news to the American on the motorcycle fifty yards behind. The BMW would be easier to tail if it ran in a motorcade, and the possibility that someone important was inside the car, while already high, was now a sure bet.

For fifteen minutes they continued on, until the cement and bustle of the city began to give way to a configuration of leafy palm-lined suburban areas, broken up by some small cultivated plots of land.

Court had backed off further with the arrival of the cops, and he just managed to make out the black car and the three motorcycles surrounding it all taking a left across heavy traffic. From this distance the turn of the target vehicle would have been hard to detect on its own, but he was greatly helped out by the fact that the motorcycle policemen stopped the oncoming flow like they were running a legitimate motorcade, and the resulting jam wasn't hard to see, even from several hundred yards back.

Court immediately crossed traffic himself, bumped back onto the crowded sidewalk, and accelerated until he, too, made it to the intersection, and he steered to the left.

The BMW was ahead of him once again, still with People's Police motorcycles forming a triangle around it, and Court knew he had just dodged a bullet.

He could barely take his eyes off the four vehicles moving together because there were so many turnoff opportunities for them. It would take only one moment of reduced vigilance for Court to lose the entire entourage if they left this road and pulled into a parking garage or raced down a side street.

So Court kept his eyes on them, but as he did so, he carefully placed a call on his mobile and listened to the ringing in his headset.

Suzanne Brewer answered quickly; Court struggled through the challenge-response protocol, then said, "The Chinese hit the building. They didn't tell me they were coming."

"Shit! And Fan?"

"I'm tailing a vehicle that squirted." He added, "I don't know if Fan's in it. I don't know if Fan is back at the building. I don't know much of anything, but I'm making some educated guesses, and I think I'm doing the right thing here."

"What do you need from me?"

"I need you to tell me where I'm going."

"How the hell do *I* know where you are going?"

"I'm following what I believe to be senior Wild Tiger leadership to the west. We must be leaving the city because I can see rice paddies in front of me. I've had to back off several hundred yards, and I'll probably lose him if he turns off."

Brewer said, "I'll ask again. How am I going to know their destination? Do you think I have a satellite tracking you?"

"For once in my life that would be terrific."

"No sat, no drone." She added, "You were the one who demanded a low-profile approach to this, remember?"

Court said, "Last time I looked, this town was crawling with Agency hacks. Now I need some help and you're telling me I'm all by myself?"

Brewer replied, "Bet you wish we didn't call off the two case officers you ran into an hour ago."

Court said nothing. He didn't think Ken and Barbie would be any help to him now, but he'd sure made it easy for Brewer to use that against him.

"Whatever," he mumbled. "I'll just try to tail a car all the way across the country by myself."

She said, "Calm down. What do you want me to do?"

"Find out what's to the west of here, tap into cameras, look into what we know about the Wild Tigers, see if they have property or known contacts in this direction. I need to know something in the next few minutes."

Court read his GPS coordinates to Brewer, and she typed them into her computer.

"Jesus," she muttered, overwhelmed with the unspecific nature of his request and the timeline attached to it. "Anything else?"

"Yeah. I'm on a rented motorcycle. Can you find out if the government is working with the rental companies here to chip these things somehow so they can track them?"

To this Brewer was unequivocal. "You shouldn't have rented a vehicle. We could have provided you with something clean."

Court could hear typing over the connection to Langley. He assumed Brewer was already at work on his requests. "Thanks for the advice. I was in a rush last night, and I had to do this by the seat of my pants. Anyway, I wasn't worried about anyone tracking me in the city; there are enough ways to melt away."

"But now you're leaving the city."

"Right, and if I'm out here in the boonies and the police or intelligence services take an interest in me . . ."

Brewer interrupted. "I just instant-messaged our experts on HCMC, and they tell me we do not know if the rental companies are working with the government."

"Some experts."

Brewer did not respond to that, but she said, "I've got some information about your location. You are in the Mekong Delta, and the terrain around you is the same pretty much all the way to Cambodia. We know the Wild

Tigers aren't operating in Cambodia, so that puts a western endpoint on the search, but that doesn't mean the Wild Tigers don't have some property in the direction you are going. I've got analysts working on that right now."

Court drove along for a few minutes more, then spoke aloud into his headset.

"Brewer, you still there?"

"Still here, still working."

Court said, "Wanted to give you a heads-up. I'm dumping this bike."

"Just like that? How are you going to continue to follow the Wild Tigers vehicle?"

"Probably better you don't ask."

As Court raced along the flat two-lane road he watched a man on a dirt bike ahead, coming in his direction from the right along an intersecting muddy track that ran alongside a canal. Court would pass by on the paved road before the man arrived at the intersection, unless Court slowed down.

Court did slow down, and he came to a stop at the intersection with the unpaved road. He began waving his arms at the approaching biker.

"Hey!"

Brewer was still on the line; Court knew this because he could hear her furiously typing in his ear.

She said, "Hey, what?"

"Not you. Hang on a second." Court pulled the GPS unit off his handlebars and shoved it into his backpack.

The man on the dirt bike slowed and stopped, and the man turned off the engine, then removed his helmet. He appeared to be no more than eighteen, and he didn't show any defensiveness in his actions.

Court quickly looked up at the BMW sedan, now farther away than at any point since he'd started tailing it.

To the kid he asked, "Do you speak English?"

The man shook his head. *"Khong."* No.

Quickly Court reached into his shirt, then pulled a thousand U.S. dollars from his money belt. He held it up, then pointed to the man's bike.

The kid looked confused. Court reached out, and the man took the bills.

Now Court climbed off his Suzuki street bike, motioned to the dirt bike, and stole a quick glance at the BMW, a half mile down the road in the light rain. When the young man did not get off the bike, Court pushed him once in the chest. The kid was now both confused and angry. He started to yell something at Court, but the American pulled his knife.

The kid got the message instantly, and he climbed off his bike. Court said, "I'm sorry, dude. No time to negotiate." Almost as an afterthought he reached back into his money belt and grabbed a thick wad of Vietnamese currency. He shoved it into the young man's hand, as well as the dollars, while keeping his knife at the low ready.

In seconds Court was on the dirt bike, a Honda XR250. He fired up the engine, looked down at the fuel gauge, and saw, to his relief, the needle resting over the three-quarters mark.

Court took off his black helmet and handed it to the kid. He then pointed to the white helmet in the kid's hand. "I'll trade you."

Though he didn't speak English, the young man held at knifepoint understood what was being asked of him. He handed over his helmet.

Court fit it on his head and, with another "sorry," took off to the west with an open throttle, leaving the kid behind with the rented Suzuki and enough cash to buy himself a new motorcycle.

Court couldn't see the BMW and the three police bikes anymore; they were somewhere far in the distance. He just leaned into the wind, accelerating to a dangerous speed on the wet road, and concentrated on his objective ahead, trying to catch up.

Suzanne Brewer had listened to the entire exchange with the young man. She spoke into his ear. "You just mugged a guy. Stole his motorcycle."

"Not how I see it."

"How *do* you see it?"

"Colonel Dai just bought a used dirt bike in Vietnam. I was kind of the middleman."

"Tell yourself whatever works, Violator."

CHAPTER

TWENTY-FOUR

wenty minutes after opening the call with Brewer, Court was back behind the BMW and the three motorcycles. They were just three hundred yards ahead of him now, though Court strained to see them because of the light rain streaking across the visor of his helmet.

The good news was, for the moment anyway, there were few places for the motorcade to turn off and disappear. The terrain around this highway was predominantly fields and rice paddies, many of them flooded. Wide ponds covered in lily pads and canals filled with brown water were occasionally broken up by little villages and agricultural buildings. The traffic had decreased dramatically, and virtually all the roads leading away from the highway were unpaved.

As Court raced along through the rain he thought about calling Colonel Dai to find out what had happened in Saigon. Ultimately, however, he decided he'd wait. He didn't want to reveal anything about where he was and what he was doing, because the last thing he needed was a mainland China paramilitary force whizzing by over his head in a helicopter, hitting the BMW, and fucking everything up for Court's CIA operation.

No. Dai had hit the Wild Tigers HQ in Saigon against Court's advice, so as far as he was concerned, Dai could sit and stew.

For an instant Court conceded that there was always a chance Fan was now dead back in the building on Nguyen Van Dau, and his entire one-man pursuit of the Wild Tigers motorcade was nothing but a fool's errand.

But he told himself to trust his instincts, and he pressed on. Fan wasn't in Saigon at the HQ; he was in the car ahead, or else he was wherever the car was going now.

Fan Jiang sat at a table with his interpreter in an otherwise bare room with high ceilings, peeling wallpaper, and mold growing down the walls. A laptop computer sat in front of him along with a wireless router, various computer peripherals, and several notepads, all of which were covered in Hanzi characters, written Mandarin, as well as English translations.

Yes, his work was in front of him now, but he wasn't looking at it. Instead he looked at the door to the room.

He'd heard the vehicles pull up a few minutes earlier, and he'd gone to the third-floor window to look out, but he'd been surprised by a man walking by at ground level in the large field behind the villa. The man was armed with a submachine gun hanging from his shoulder, and when he saw Fan he motioned for him to step away from the window.

Fan did as he was told, but not before he saw the three motorcycles and the black BMW roll into view on his left and park on the grass near a canal that ran there. Tu Van Duc climbed out from the backseat of the black car, and he stormed towards the house, almost at a run.

Now Fan sat down and watched the door again because he could hear the banging footsteps up the staircase in the center of the house, and their speed and intensity matched those he'd seen from Captain Tu in the grass.

As he'd expected, the door to his room flew open and Tu Van Duc stood there in a brilliant white suit and tie, his hands on his hips. Two armed men stood with him, their rifles off their shoulders and in their hands, and for an instant Fan thought he was about to be taken out and shot.

But the leader of the Wild Tigers dispelled that notion immediately. "I made a good decision when I moved you here. We were attacked in Saigon. The building was raided by armed Chinese government agents."

"Chinese," Fan repeated. "Here in Vietnam."

"Yes. Someone in Wo Shing Wo must have talked. When this is all over

I'm going to go to Hong Kong and cut the throats of my business partners there, just so they know not to fuck around with Con Ho Hoang Da."

Fan didn't want Mr. Duc to do anything of the kind, but he was too intimidated to argue the point. Instead he just asked a question he was afraid to learn the answer to.

"The situation in Saigon? Were you able to repel the Chinese?"

Tu Van Duc just shrugged a little. "They killed some of our people. Took hostages. I just got off the phone with my secretary there. She said one of my lieutenants persuaded them you had been moved, and he didn't know where. That turns out to be the truth, which is good for us, but bad for him. Your countrymen used a power drill on his feet and knees, and then, when they didn't get anything from him, they shot him in the head. Killed four others."

Tu Van Duc surprised Fan now with a toothy smile. "We killed one of the bastards. My driver ran him down with my car."

Fan reached out to hold on to the desk. He thought he would either faint or vomit, and he did not know which would fill him with the most shame.

The Wild Tigers leader now said, "Don't worry. Keep working. You are safe here. This villa was a regional headquarters for the Vietcong during the war here. An hour and a half from Saigon and neither the French nor the Americans ever discovered what was going on here. It's built to keep the occupants safe, but if someone does come, I have a half dozen men here with guns and another half dozen at a checkpoint on the dirt road, and by tonight we will have a lot of new support coming to help us. Nobody can get to you here."

Fan nodded, hesitated, then asked, "Will you let me leave when I am ready to go? I mean, I told you one month. When my month is up, will you honor your agreement?"

Tu Van Duc smiled. "I only want you to be safe. As soon as it is safe for you, you will be able to do whatever you want. You are my guest, and you will remain so, as long as there is danger."

With that Mr. Duc turned on his heels, spoke roughly in Vietnamese with his bodyguards, and left the room.

Fan sat quietly alongside his equally silent translator, and together they listened to the stomping footsteps of angry and aggressive men that echoed through the old cavernous villa.

As Court reached the hour and a half mark of his pursuit, he began worrying about the rapidly diminishing fuel level on the dirt bike for the first time. He'd cut off the call with Brewer so she could work, but he called her back now to encourage her to work faster. As soon as she confirmed his identity, Brewer said, "Violator. I think I know where to vector you."

"Tell me."

"I've had a team looking into digital satellite images of everything west of your position, all the way to the Cambodian border. We've found a farm about four miles west and one mile north of that highway you are on, east of the Vam Co Tay River."

"What's so special about this compound?"

"A satellite image from six days ago shows a BMW 7 Series driving up the unpaved road to the farm, with a pair of motorcycles trailing behind. Police motorcycles. On another image, this one from eleven days ago, the BMW is parked next to the main building on the property along with several other vehicles, including a pair of local police cars. We looked into the location with local contacts at Hanoi station, and they checked property records. It's part of a small rice agricultural co-op, but the main building is a villa that was the center of a French rubber plantation back in the 1930s. Anyway, the current occupant of the compound did two years in prison in Saigon for smuggling heroin. We can't get hard confirmation that he's with the Wild Tigers, but we know they smuggle heroin via groups in Cambodia, and this place is less than a mile to the Cambodian border."

Court thought it over as he drove. "That's not all that solid, unless you consider the fact that I'm flying blind here. I sure as hell like it more than any intel I can create on my own."

"I agree. It's the only option I see." Brewer read off the coordinates of the property, and Court pulled to the side of the two-lane highway. He typed the location into his GPS as an old lady walked slowly by, swatting an ox onward with a little switch. She didn't even look up at the Tay on the motorcycle as she passed. To her Court was just one more Western tourist with nothing better to do than come to Vietnam to drive around on a bike and watch people work.

Looking at his GPS, he saw that his target location was just over one mile north-northeast from his position, and he started to feel relief, until he saw the ground he'd have to cover to get there. Into his mic he said, "Great. A mile on foot through flooded farmland."

Brewer said, "Well, there is an unpaved road leading to this place, and it cuts through the paddies, canals, and woodlands. But I don't recommend you take it. If this is a location where a senior member of the Wild Tigers fled after the Chinese attack, I'd say it's a near certainty they'd post security on the one easy way to their front door."

Court said, "I'm going to have to get wet for this one. There's a copse of trees right off the road here by a flooded paddy. I'll hide out there till dark, then I'll move out."

"Remember," Brewer said, "you are looking for positive ID of Fan Jiang, nothing more. If you determine this is the location where Fan is being held, then I will send Ground Branch assets in to grab him."

Court said, "If he's not standing in front of a window, I'm going to have to infiltrate the buildings there on the farm."

"Are you equipped to infiltrate a compound of armed gangsters?"

"I have a folding knife and some night vision and infrared equipment, and by the time I get to the compound, I'll have a very foul attitude. That's going to have to be enough."

Brewer said nothing for a moment. Then, "Maybe I should just move Ground Branch in now."

"No," Court said. "Don't worry about it. I can get in there."

"All right. What else do you need from me?"

"Can you have a pizza delivered?"

Court knew little about Suzanne Brewer, but he'd already determined she didn't have much of a sense of humor. After a few seconds she replied, "That would do nothing to help you maintain your cover."

Court just rolled his eyes as he looked around to make sure no one was anywhere close. The woman guiding the ox along was fifty yards on, facing the other direction, and the road was empty.

"Signing off for now," Court said.

"No unnecessary risks."

"Right."

Court walked the dirt bike off the shoulder and towards the trees near the edge of a rice paddy. He hid it there in tall grasses, not knowing if he might need it again later this evening.

A few minutes later he sat on a dry piece of ground in thick brush amid high trees lining the water of an irrigation canal and waited for darkness to fall. It was only five p.m.; he'd be here for a while, so he drank bottled water and pulled out two bags of snacks he'd bought the evening before. Looking over the bags, he realized he had a choice between prawn crackers and roasted cashews.

He slipped both bags back into his backpack. He decided he'd wait till just before setting out, and then use the nuts and crackers for the energy he'd need to make the arduous move to the compound.

But for now he'd just lie here, swat flies and mosquitoes, and check over his equipment.

He brought his night vision binoculars out of his backpack and pulled off his baseball cap. Looking both over, he got an idea.

It took him twenty minutes to get it right, but he used electric tape to affix the binos to the bottom of the bill of his cap. This gave him night vision goggles if he dialed back the zoom feature of the binos all the way. They were a little unwieldy like this, but it would be helpful to see in the dark with his hands free, and he found he could easily turn his cap around if he wanted to move the binos out of the way.

He made adjustments on other items in his bag, then secured all his zippers to ensure that everything inside would stay dry when he entered the rice fields. He knew the water would be chest deep or higher in some places, and it would be slow going with the mud and muck.

His dad had told him all about the paddies.

Court thought about his dad in the war now, over half a century ago. With a sly smile he wished more than anything in the world he had an M16 cradled in his arms and an entire Marine rifle platoon sitting here with him now.

No luck. It was just Court, a knife, and a mission that could go bad a lot more ways than it could go right.

He made himself close his eyes and try to rest up, just as light rain began falling again.

CHAPTER

TWENTY-FIVE

An old gray Mi-8 helicopter, bigger than a school bus and just about as aerodynamic, sat quietly in a gentle rain shower, alone in the middle of a parking lot. Around the hulking aircraft, four bearded men in their fifties and sixties stood with their hands on their hips, green flight suits dampening by the minute.

The pilot looked down at his watch after wiping water away from its face, then pulled a walkie-talkie from his pocket and checked the volume knob.

Tall grasses grew through the cracks in the asphalt parking lot between the helo and a row of derelict warehouses, just fifty meters away. On the other side of the rusty buildings lay the banks of the Bassac River, brown and slow in the warm afternoon.

Phnom Penh, Cambodia, languished under the same weather as Saigon, some hundred miles to the southeast. It wasn't officially monsoon season yet, but puffy gray rain clouds had hung intermittently over both capitals for the past few days, and more rain was forecast for tonight.

The pilot of the big helicopter had taken the bad weather into account, of course, but it would have little effect on his flight plan; on this evening's flight he planned on staying below the clouds and out of the mountains.

A rusty metal side door to one of the dockside warehouses creaked open, and a row of figures marched out into the weather. Each person in the line wore a large green backpack and a dark hooded rainproof jacket, most carried suppressed short-barreled rifles hanging from slings around their necks, and all of them wore radio headsets on their heads under olive drab, black, or green hats of various shapes and sizes.

The four crewmen of the Mi-8 looked to one another, then jumped into action. The pilot and copilot climbed aboard to start the engines, and both the crew chief and the door gunner helped the passengers load their equipment.

The eight SVR Zaslon commandos shook out of their heavy packs and threw them into the old civilian helicopter, and then they pulled themselves aboard after unslinging their rifles. They strapped themselves into the benches that ran along the fuselage as Zoya Zakharova, the last in the group, climbed into the helo.

Zoya wasn't encumbered with a rifle as were the men of the task force, so she had an easier time of it.

This Mi-8 was a Russian-made aircraft, and consequently Zoya had been in dozens of these fat birds in her life, but looking around at this particular Cambodian relic, she wondered if it would even start.

A minute later the engines coughed and shook, to the point where Zoya had doubts that this old bird would get off the ground. She kept her eyes away from the others and looked out the open door; the last thing in the world she wanted to do in front of these paramilitaries was to show any insecurity about flying in a fucking helicopter.

The Mi-8 did manage to fight its way up into the air, then it turned on its axis and tipped its nose. The pilot lifted his machine higher and picked up speed. He rose over the rusty warehouse, climbed over the Bassac River, then soared higher into the warm, wet air.

Soon the gray helicopter was racing along just below the gray clouds hanging low over the capital city of Cambodia.

Zoya looked down at the flat cityscape for a while, then decided to put her worries about the questionable transport out of her mind. She did this for two reasons, both of them logical—for one, there wasn't a damn thing she could do to prevent a helicopter crash from her seat on a bench here in the back. And two, she had a thousand other responsibilities now, and precious little time to prepare for what was to come.

The graceless aircraft shook and rattled as they flew out of the city, over green hills and muddy fields now, heading towards the border with Vietnam.

The Mi-8 was currently owned by Russian intelligence and kept at the airport in Phnom Penh, but it had seen service with the Cambodian military back in the Cambodian–Vietnamese War in the late seventies. The crew were Russian SVR pilots who'd been working an op in Indonesia and were flown in on a Russian military cargo plane for today's in extremis mission. This Mi-8 was not normally armed, but the crew brought two Chinese-made W85 machine guns along with them that they could hang from the sides and use as door guns by the crew chief and the gunner, but for now they kept the big weapons hidden in the cabin.

Zoya hoped like hell the machine guns wouldn't be needed, but she'd requested the extra firepower herself. She was meticulous in her planning, especially when working with others, and the uncomfortable truth was that the extraction phase of tonight's operation was a massive unknown. She had no idea what they'd find at the compound, and she wanted to be ready for as much that could go wrong as possible.

And, as Zoya had learned on dozens of operations in her career, sometimes big guns went a long way towards remedying big problems.

The primary intelligence about the location of the Wild Tigers secure compound came from the Ho Chi Minh City police officer Zoya had picked up the evening before. This man was still being held incommunicado in the laundry room of the safe house, and local NOCs had instructions to drop him off at some street corner when this was all over with a warning to keep his mouth shut unless he wanted it known he was the man who fucked over Con Ho Hoang Da. But he wasn't Zoya's only source. Since last night she'd communicated with the Russian embassies in Hanoi and Phnom Penh and checked into property records, police records, tax records, and other databases that helped her paint a picture with data about the people residing at the compound. By noon she felt certain the old rubber plantation facility near the Cambodian border was the current hiding place of Fan Jiang, and she immediately committed her entire task force to taking the location down this evening.

There were more subtle ways to be certain—satellite analysis, drones, human intelligence operations—but Zoya had no time for these measures.

If she could find Fan Jiang, she was certain the Chinese and the Americans could also find Fan Jiang, and they might not wait around for days building a target picture before they acted.

No. With what Fan Jiang knew about Chinese secure computer networks, she wouldn't have been surprised if the Chinese fired a cruise missile into Vietnam to kill the poor son of a bitch the second they discovered his location.

She felt good enough about her intel to go forward this afternoon, and she felt even more sure she was making the right call now. She'd received word from the SVR Residency in Hanoi just an hour ago about a shoot-out at the Con Ho Hoang Da compound in Saigon, and reports from police there that the culprits looked like Han Chinese.

China's Ministry of State Security and Ministry of Defense were getting closer to Fan, and they'd find this compound soon, so Zoya had to commit herself and her men tonight.

But while she wore a look of utter confidence in front of Vasily and the others, until she laid her eyes and her hands on the Chinese national she'd come all this way to snatch, she wouldn't take a single easy breath.

The Russian foreign intelligence operative studied her maps again for a few minutes, but then she took a break to look across the open cabin at Vasily. He was geared up in civilian dress like the rest of his unit and Zoya herself, and there was nothing to distinguish him as the team leader, other than the fact that he was a few years older than some of the others on his team.

And for his nature. In a group full of alpha males, Vasily was the boss.

Zoya knew Vasily wouldn't have allowed her along on the raid if he'd seen a way out of it, but the simple truth was he had no choice but to concede to her request to accompany the direct-action element on this mission. If she wasn't there with the rest of the task force, she wouldn't have the time she needed for the sensitive site exploration, the retrieval of intelligence there at the compound in the event Fan himself was not located.

But even though Zoya was on the mission to assault the compound, this did not mean she was on the team to hit the buildings themselves. Still, Zoya knew she'd be right there, just behind the action, and the only thing she would change by choice was that she'd rather be kicking in a door or two herself.

But while the Zaslon men had rifles, Zoya just carried a Glock pistol on her utility belt and some extra magazines in her cargo pants. She had a knife on her belt, as well, along with a second blade taped to the small of her back and a small Beretta Bobcat .22 caliber pistol in an ankle holster.

These were defensive weapons only, while Vasily and most of his men carried AKS-74U suppressed short-barreled variants of the AK-74, and Mikhail wielded the VSS sniper rifle.

Only twenty-five minutes after taking to the air, the pilot signaled they were approaching the landing zone. This wouldn't be a hot LZ; they would be setting down in a sparsely populated portion of eastern Cambodia, landing two miles inside the border so that they could approach the Wild Tigers compound silently and by using a network of irrigation canals for both cover and concealment.

The Mi-8 touched down on a gravel road alongside a creek, the helo shut down upon landing, and the four-man crew grabbed Kalashnikovs and set up a simple security cordon while the task force began donning their packs and stowing their weapons under their jackets. If they were seen around here on one of the established trails through the jungle or between the farms, they would appear to be just a group of Western hikers heading to the southeast. It would seem strange, maybe—this wasn't an area known for much tourism—but it wouldn't cause alarm.

The Mi-8 would wait here by the creek and remain in radio contact with the task force and then, when the call came from Vasily, it would race over the border either to an LZ closer to the target or, if the machine guns or a hasty extract were required, directly over the target itself.

The nine-member task force walked on roads, through fields, and even along a knee-high creek for over ninety minutes before they passed the invisible border between the two nations by stepping up onto a levee at the southern end of one rice paddy and then back down into the northern end of another paddy. Only their GPS devices told them they were in a new nation, because there wasn't a damn bit of difference to the mud squishing under their boots.

The Russians had timed their flight from the capital so they would cross the Cambodian border on foot right at the end of evening nautical twilight: the moment when the sun set twelve degrees below the western horizon, or the official beginning of nighttime.

Zoya checked her watch and was pleased to see they were right on schedule.

For the next half hour there was no conversation between the nine individuals moving single file, but just before eight p.m. Vasily spoke softly into his interteam radio and demanded full silence, because they were getting close enough to the compound to risk detection from any patrols out of the target location. No one really expected that the gangsters from Saigon would operate their rural safe house like a military installation, but Vasily hadn't made it this long in his dangerous career by taking chances.

At eight forty-five p.m. the nine Russians had all taken a knee in deep trees and thick brush that ran along the canal to the west of the compound. The rain had stopped and they took their time drinking from water bladders and eating rations. Ideally they would arrive late enough in the evening to dull the senses of any sentries at the location, but again, Zoya didn't want to wait for the middle of the night. They'd hit around ten p.m., use the darkness to their advantage, and use stealth as long as they could, and then they would just use surprise and violence to power their way to their target.

With a nod from Vasily, Mikhail pulled the second stage of a scuba regulator from his pack, adjusted the hose over his shoulder, and placed it in his mouth. He then climbed down into the canal. It was only five meters across and two meters deep in the center, but he'd use the air to stay under the brown water and remain undetected for much of his movement.

Zoya watched while the team's sniper crossed to the other side of the canal. There, with only the top of his head sticking out of the water, he began moving slowly in the reeds and brush towards the east. The progression through the three hundred meters of muddy canals was scheduled to take an hour.

She, along with the rest of the men, had small oxygen tanks and swim masks, as well, and they'd follow Mikhail ten minutes behind. But they wouldn't put their heads under the water until the last hundred meters or so, and from there they would each use their GPS wrist units to follow the canal. Mikhail would arrive minutes before the rest, set up on the far side of the canal, and use his VSS suppressed sniper rifle along with its infrared scope to identify any sentries outside the buildings.

A few minutes later, Zoya Zakharova and the rest of the task force slipped into the water, sank up to their necks, and dug their boots into the muddy surface below them. Together they began a slow, dreamlike push to the south.

CHAPTER

TWENTY-SIX

Court Gentry lay flat in the thick foliage by an irrigation canal, staring ahead through the head-mounted night observation device he'd made with his binos and his ball cap. He was tired and gross, covered in the slime of rotting foliage and mud, and he had no illusions that he would dry out any time before sunrise, which was eight hours away.

Through it all, however, he managed to look on the bright side. The moonless overcast night was sticky and warm, which meant he could survive being soaked to the bone here much better than he could in some colder climate.

He'd kept his gear inside his waterproof backpack for the two-and-a-half-hour hike through the flooded fields and thick bush, and he was glad he did, because he'd stumbled face-first in knee-high water at least a dozen times on his trek. Now he lay on semidry ground just south of the canal, and even though the hazy green image in front of him was narrow because of the optics he wore, he nevertheless had a perfect view of his target, because while his side of the canal was covered in trees and brush, the other bank had been cleared.

Just feet from the water's edge on the north side of the canal was an unpaved parking area. Court could see the black BMW he'd tailed earlier parked in the darkness there, along with a few other cars and trucks, and a few scooters and motorcycles, most of them covered with tarps. Beyond the vehicles was thirty yards of open ground, and then a large French Colonial villa in the center of the property that looked to Court like a slightly more ornate antebellum plantation home. Vines covered the walls of the three-story structure, weaving around the decorative architectural molding, much of which had chipped or cracked through the effects of weather and age. Old black shutters hung off half the windows, and the tiled roof appeared to be original, meaning it was probably a hundred years old, and it looked every single day of it.

Ahead to his left was a low wooden barn, and while there was substantial light coming from the big villa itself, the barn was dark and ramshackle and it appeared to be uninhabited.

Two sentries walked the three-acre property along individual routes; each moved alone in a predictable and lazy pattern, and they wielded flashlights. The long white beams moved up and down, not side to side, and this gave Court the impression they were just walking, not actively searching the grounds.

Through his NODs Court could see the shape of a human form appear from time to time in a southern window on the third floor of the big villa, and it looked to him like this person was probably guarding some room or a hallway in front of a room but had also been tasked with eyeing the waterlogged area to the south of the villa.

The front of the large building faced east; Court couldn't see the entrance from the south, so he had no idea if there were other guards at or near the front door. He could just see a bit of a porch at the back door on the western side, along with the closer portion of the western wall of the villa.

On his laborious sloshing walk here through the rice paddies he'd remained a couple hundred yards west of the one road to the villa, but through his night vision gear he had seen a pair of sedans set up as a checkpoint on the dirt road. Several men stood around each vehicle with shotguns, controlling access to the villa. Court imagined this roadblock had been put in place after the attack in Saigon today.

Yes, there was a decent security posture in place to warn of or even repel an attack up the road, but apparently the Wild Tigers here had no major concerns that a lone man just might splash, swim, and stagger overland through the slop for hours to get here on foot.

Not that it had been a cakewalk. Court now took his eye from his binos to pull yet another leech off his body, and he thought his feet would hurt for days where he'd rubbed sores into his waterlogged skin.

He'd been given a malaria shot on the CIA aircraft before he landed in Hong Kong, administered by the flight attendant, and he was glad for it now, because his arms and neck were covered in mosquito bites.

As he looked through his NODs he listened again to the night around him. It was full of the normal noises one might expect on most any farm anywhere in the world: dogs barked in the distance, a chicken clucked somewhere, and an airplane flew high overhead towards Ho Chi Minh City.

But there was one unnatural sound in the air; it wasn't loud but still it dominated the entire scene, and Court could not have been happier about that. A sixty-thousand-watt diesel generator the size of a car sat alongside the back wall at the southwestern corner of the villa. It was dead ahead of Court's layup position here, and it hummed along, covering the scene with a soft but prevalent white noise. This was the source of the lights inside the main building, obviously, and Court imagined that a generator of that size could power the entire house with ease, even providing electricity for televisions, radios, and computers.

Court scanned the corner of the house around the generator, then looked higher above the big rectangular device. Soon he decided this area would be his target. If he could cross the large parking area and make his way over a swath of open ground and then along the vine-covered wall of the old building, he could tuck himself between the generator and the building's wall and hide from sentries as they passed. Then he could shut off the device and wrap the entire location in darkness. A window two stories directly above the generator was open; Court could make his way up there by climbing on top of the generator, then using the architectural molding on the French Colonial building as hand- and footholds the rest of the way.

It would take time to make his way up; he was sure the wall would have weak or slippery handholds, but it looked like his best bet.

He felt certain once inside he could either find Fan or eliminate the possibility that he was even here.

This plan of his required an incredible amount of stealth, but Court had made it into and out of more secure locations populated by better-trained opposition, so while it was a definite risk, he had confidence in his abilities.

His confidence was blunted by only one hurdle. It was just now ten p.m.

He'd rather wait until much later, just an hour or two before dawn. But every fiber of his being told him he had no time to spare, and he had to move now. The Wild Tigers could relocate Fan at any time, or they could improve their security setup here. Or else Dai's men or even the other force out there involved in the hunt for Fan could find this location on their own and hit the place at any time.

Court was here now, he was here first, and he knew he needed to get his ass in gear and take advantage of it.

After stowing his equipment back in his slime-covered pack, he shimmied forward on his elbows through the brush and then pulled himself down into the canal, slowly and silently. Here he grabbed hold of a cluster of free-floating water hyacinth and used it for extra cover as he crossed to the other side.

Even though he'd made it the entire evening without encountering a single snake, Court had snakes on his mind now. *Of course* there would be snakes here, somewhere. This was their world, not his. Court's dad had talked about encountering pit vipers during his time in Nam, and he tried to picture his father swimming across this very canal forty-something years ago. Try as he might he couldn't see it, couldn't imagine his dad as a scared kid.

It took just moments to cross the canal, and when he made it to the other side he clawed into the mud and reeds at the water's edge to keep himself perfectly stationary so he didn't float off. Here he listened to the sounds around him, and he grew more confident in his ability to mask his own approach thanks to the humming diesel generator.

Court pulled his NODs out of his pack again, and with them he crawled up to the lip of the canal. He looked ahead, up to the window where he'd seen the lone sentry, and just caught the man as he moved out of view. Then Court waited a minute for a passing sentry to make his way across the open ground in front of the old villa.

When the slow-moving sentry and his lazy flashlight disappeared to the northwest, Court started a low crawl forward.

He entered the large grassy area used as a parking lot, then pulled himself under a pickup truck. From here he could see the black BMW parked closer to the main house. Court used the cover of the vehicles now to move quickly; he crawled under the work truck, then around a Toyota sedan, and he'd just made it between the cluster of covered motorcycles and scooters when he dropped flat and still. The other sentry passed by closer to the villa; he made no more of an effort than the last man, and he turned north along the western side of the main building. When he made the right to go back to the east he disappeared from Court's view, so Court rose, used his NODs to scan the villa again, checking in the window for the man who'd made a couple of appearances there, and decided now was the time to move.

The American stayed tucked low between the bikes as he advanced, then he raced over to the BMW. Squatting down low to move around it, he saw no one in the windows, and although the first sentry's flashlight beam shone on trees on the eastern portion of the property in Court's view, the sentry himself was still on the other side of the building.

Court stood up and raced through the darkness for the French Colonial building across forty yards of open ground.

After forty minutes pushing through the vegetation-covered canal, Mikhail finally made it into position across from the villa and climbed out of the water, up into the brush and trees on the southern side of the canal opposite the Wild Tigers compound. He pulled his rifle out of its drag bag, extended the bipod under the fore end, popped the rubber caps off the image-enhancing/thermal scope, and settled down behind the weapon.

He saw a few lighted windows ahead of him, and a swinging flashlight's beam coming from a source on the far side of the old French Colonial house, but otherwise he could see nothing through the scope itself. He reached up to flip it to the thermal setting to see if there were any heat registers indicating human forms moving around outside the property, and he began scanning from left to right.

Court made it around to the southwestern side of the villa, where the building's big diesel generator rested on a platform at the corner. He lay down next to the big noisy unit, only because it was directly below the third-floor window that he'd identified as his point of entry.

Now one of the sentries passed just twenty-five feet south of Court, crossing the open grassy area Court had just crossed himself. He tucked himself tighter under the bottom lip of the generator, the heat of the diesel device warming his wet clothing while he lay there.

Finally the sentry turned to his right and began walking along the rear western side of the villa's grounds.

Court scanned left and right with his NODs and saw nothing of interest. He was about to begin climbing onto the rumbling generator when he decided he would make another quick sweep of the area, this time with his thermal monocular, on the off chance someone was moving on the road without vehicles.

He pulled off the hat with his NODs and slipped them in his pack, grabbed the monocular from his cargo pocket, and removed its rubber cover. He turned it on and began scanning across the canal, across the rice paddies, and all the way out to the unpaved road, a hundred yards to his southeast.

Mikhail looked through his thermal rifle scope, sweeping the compound slowly. He saw a figure move into and then back out of a window on the third floor, and he saw a sentry with a flashlight moving off to the west towards the back of the location.

Quickly he realized that the largest heat register in his scope's view was not a threat at all. It was a big generator on the concrete pad on the southwestern corner of the main house. Mikhail couldn't see anything there in his thermal sight other than a large white-hot glow, so he didn't spend any time searching it. And when he detected no other threats, he determined the entire compound was secure on this side, other than the roving guards and the man peeking out of the third-floor window from time to time.

He touched the push-to-talk button on his chest and whispered, "Anna Seven to Anna One. In position at waypoint Omega. I have two mobile sentries patrolling the target grounds, and one static but intermittent subject on the third floor of the target location, south side. Suggest you continue your approach in the canal to the south and advise me when you are two minutes out. I'll talk you in."

The reply came after just seconds. "Anna One to Seven. Roger. Estimated arrival time, zero five minutes. Will advise when we are making the final turn before Omega."

Mikhail took his hand away from his PTT button, returned it to his rifle, and continued scanning with his thermal scope, looking for any more heat registers in the villa's windows.

Court wasn't sure what he was looking at, so he pressed a button on the top of his monocular, reversing his thermal's polarity from white hot, to black hot, and then back again.

There was something out there in the trees.

Court had barely moved a muscle while he scanned, but now he froze solid. A single, small thermal signal appeared on the far side of the canal, fifty yards or so from where he now lay, and just yards from where Court himself had lain prone minutes earlier as he surveilled the property from the far side of the canal. From the small size of the register he first thought it might have been an animal, but upon zooming in with his monocular on the small object, he realized he was looking at the head and shoulders of a man, the visible portion of a figure lying prone, facing Court and the villa. From the broken thermal outline Court thought the figure might be positioned behind a sniper rifle.

Court remained motionless for several seconds; he even slowed his blinking. He felt certain this person must have just arrived on the scene; otherwise he would have noticed Court crossing the canal, crawling through the vehicles, then racing across the open ground, all right in front of him.

And now Court lay directly in the line of sight of the sniper.

If the man had a rifle, then he definitely had a scope on it, and if he had come out here for a nighttime operation, Court felt sure the scope would have either night vision or thermal imaging capabilities. Court was rooting like hell for the latter, because although he might not be detected on a night vision scope if he didn't move, Court knew with thermal optics the warmth of the big generator above him would white out the sniper's scope when focused in his direction.

Either way, Court knew he couldn't move from his position as long as that sniper was there.

But who was he?

This guy *couldn't* have been with the Wild Tigers, the American surmised, since he seemed to be conducting surveillance *on* the Wild Tigers location.

Court thought over the possibilities. Was this man with Colonel Dai? Was he with the group who'd hit the ship in Po Toi? Could he even be one of the CIA Special Activities Division paramilitaries who were getting themselves in position to launch a raid on this location?

Court dismissed the latter as the most unlikely of all possibilities. Brewer had been clear that SAD were waiting on Gentry's signal to helo into the area. If she was telling the truth, it was highly doubtful they would put one man so close into an overwatch position.

But other than ruling out SAD, Court didn't have a clue who this guy was and what kind of a threat he posed. All the American knew for sure was that he was pinned down for as long as that sniper lay there facing his way.

Shit. He couldn't do a thing about the man fifty yards away with his folding knife, and it was getting hot here next to the diesel generator.

And then, just when he thought the prospect for the success of his mission was at its lowest point, he heard the sound of engines in the distance.

Big engines.

Slowly he shifted the monocular in his eye, directing his focus all the way out to the road far to his left. Some two hundred yards distant over the open ground of a flooded rice paddy, he saw the two vehicles parked at the checkpoint. As he watched them, the sedans rolled off to the side of the muddy road, just as they were bathed in the white lights of headlamps. Turning his monocular to the right to view the road farther to the south, he saw big heat registers. Quickly he reversed polarity to black hot and recognized the outline of two big canvas-covered military vehicles tearing up the dirt track as they neared the checkpoint.

The trucks rolled past the sedans without stopping, and the fact that the checkpoint let them pass indicated to Court that these big vehicles were on the same side as the Wild Tigers. This was bad news, because it probably indicated more security was about to show up here at the villa. It also almost certainly meant the trucks would be parking next to the other vehicles, which was to say, just twenty or thirty yards from where Court now lay, half under and half next to the diesel generator.

He thought about rising to his feet and running around the corner on his right towards the western side of the property, but the sniper with a perfect line of sight on his position caused him to remain still, to lie there and hope nobody who climbed out of those trucks decided to take a leak on the concrete slab holding the diesel generator at the corner of the villa.

The pair of olive drab, canvas-covered trucks rolled into view and stopped in the muddy grass. Court ID'd them immediately as old ZIL-131s, Soviet-era Russian trucks that had been used in the armed forces of most every nation that either bought or was gifted military equipment from Moscow.

Tailgates slammed down on both vehicles and armed men began leaping out of the back, down onto the wet grass. Court saw that these were regular army troops, all wearing the green camo uniforms of the People's Army of Vietnam.

As the trucks emptied, Court counted twenty-four men in all, each carrying an assault rifle, a backpack, and extra ammo on their chests. Most of the men then ran off around to the east, but a few ran to the west side of the building, passing Court's location on their way towards the back porch.

Court began to think he'd be stuck here until daylight, at which point his position would be obvious to anyone and everyone around him.

For an instant he thought about the burner phones stowed in his water-proof pack. One call to Colonel Dai and Chinese operators would descend on this location, although it might take them a couple of hours to make their move if they were still in Saigon.

But Court knew he couldn't grab his phone and make that call, and he didn't think even Colonel Dai would order an attack on front-line Vietnamese army troops.

No, the frenetic Chinese officer would likely just order Court to continue on his mission alone, to stage a one-man raid on this place to kill Fan, and use the life of Sir Donald Fitzroy as a bargaining chip to get him to do so.

Court closed his eyes in frustration. He found himself flat on his stomach, likely just feet away from his objective, with absolutely no idea what the hell he was supposed to do.

CHAPTER

TWENTY-SEVEN

Zoya Zakharova was on mission at the moment, but she couldn't help but harbor a quick fantasy.

In her imagination she was somewhere dry and sunbaked, with a drink in her hand and the smell of cut flowers close by, filling her with happiness and tranquility.

The dream faded as a blade of saw grass sliced her forearm just aft of her glove, bringing her back to the reality that she was wading through a god-awful-smelling canal full of snakes, leeches, and vermin. She'd spent almost an hour up to her neck in the slimy ditch, pushing a large clump of water hyacinth along with her to break up the outline of a human head. Her body felt like it would never dry out once she climbed out of this dank water, and even if it did, she was convinced she'd never be able to wash the smell of rotten vegetation off her skin.

Still, at least the op was going nominally. The Zaslon operators were in front of her, and she'd had no contact with them at all, but she'd listened in minutes earlier as Mikhail gave the all clear to the team to move on to the objective waypoint of tonight's action. The target location looked as it had on the satellite photos, the task force was on schedule, and the prospects of locating Fan were good.

But now, as she rubbed the pain on her forearm from the saw grass and just before the first members of the task force ahead of her approached the last gentle turn in the canal before arriving at the compound, she heard a new transmission from Mikhail. While his voice remained professional, this time she detected unmistakable urgency. "All call signs: hold, hold, hold."

Ahead of her Vasily raised his right arm into a fist, and the team stopped instantly in the shoulder-high water. The men tucked deep into the grasses alongside the canal, and Zoya did the same.

Vasily came over the net now. "Report when able, Seven."

Mikhail responded ten seconds later. "Anna Seven to all call signs. I have two PAVN trucks on scene. I count two-four uniformed dismounts, twenty-four, all armed with rifles. They are dispersing in squad-sized elements around the eastern side of the compound, a pair have remained at the trucks, and two more went around the western side, but I can't see around the vehicles there so I'm not sure if they went inside a back door or are still on the grounds."

It took Vasily a moment to respond to all this information; it was a surprising change in the equation, to say the least. "Is your position secure?"

"My position is secure, for now. I can't see the eastern entrance of the main house itself, but I think some of them might have headed inside. Most are moving on foot back over towards the road and the front of the property. None of them have come over here near the canal. It looks like they don't expect anyone to attack from the flooded fields, but they are setting up a defensive cordon close to the dirt road."

Vasily just said, "Roger that."

Zoya had listened to all of this, and she fully expected to next hear Vasily ordering his unit to stand down, to back out of the area without continuing the mission. They didn't know how many Wild Tigers were inside the villa, but now considering the fact that there were at least three times more armed opposition on the property than the total Zaslon force—in the form of regular army troops, no less—she knew it would be madness to continue on.

Vasily's next call left her momentarily dumbstruck. "Seven, this is One. We are approaching from the west now; notify us of any changes in the force distribution."

Zoya shook her head there in the darkness, then triggered her own radio. Whispering, she said, "Sirena for One. We need to retrograde out of the target area and reassess."

Vasily responded to this over the radio, not even bothering with the standard protocol of identifying himself. "Negative. We are at Omega. We proceed."

Zoya just stood there in the tall grasses. "We are not at the objective, One. We can exfiltrate. We *need* to exfiltrate."

"I'm assault commander, Koshka. We continue."

"*Nyet*, I am canceling the assault. I have authority to—"

Vasily came over the radio now, blocking Zoya's radio traffic with his whispering, angry voice. "We came for this target, we are *taking* this target. The PAVN infantry is a third-rate force. They do not have heavy weapons. We will not relinquish the advantage we have now. Stealth will get us close to the target, and our CQB tactics will get us the rest of the way. I will put Anna Eight on the far side of the canal along with Mikhail, and together the two of them can provide overwatch, engage and occupy the infantry on the east side of the compound if we lose the initiative while we hit the house." To all this Vasily added a warning. "We are going forward. Get off the net, Koshka."

The Zaslon unit began moving again. Zoya watched them for a moment, then muttered "*Der'mo*" under her breath. She pushed back out into the deeper part of the canal and followed the others as they began rounding the bend to the target. She felt confident this unit would be able to defeat the larger force in combat, but she had no interest in engaging in a protracted battle. Going loud was a last resort, but Vasily seemed ready to commit to it rather than risk losing the target.

In theory she could have pulled the plug on the entire hit, but the reality was Vasily controlled his men, which meant *he* controlled this operation, and this late in the decision-making process, Zoya was just along for the ride.

Court eyed the two PAVN soldiers standing next to the ZIL-131 trucks. They stood together talking, just twenty-five yards ahead of him and slightly on his right. They held their rifles in their arms but didn't act at all like they considered it possible they would be involved in any sort of fighting. From their relaxed demeanor Court got the idea these guys had been told to watch the trucks while the other men were sent to occupy security points in and around the villa.

These two young soldiers were the only people in view at the moment, other than the man lying on the far side of the canal, but he knew most of a Vietnamese army platoon was still close by, and he was still pinned into this position.

Court lay there next to the hot generator and marveled at what a complete and utter disaster this was turning into. The only good thing Court could see about this was that it all but confirmed his suspicions that Fan was indeed here on the property. There was no way this other paramilitary unit would show up, and the Vietnamese army would show up, unless there was something, or someone, *extremely* valuable in the big old house just off Court's left shoulder.

He kept his eye on the sniper through his thermal in the hopes the man would bug out now that the damn PAVN had arrived on the scene. But the sniper did not move at all.

And then, to Court's utter astonishment, a second man crawled out of the canal, slowly and with all the skill of a master of reconnaissance and sniper craft, just twenty feet or so to the west of the first man. Once on the other side of the canal, the new arrival turned to face the compound, and Court could see the telltale outline of a short-barreled rifle when the man brought it in front of his own body and obstructed his white-hot thermal image.

Now there were two assholes with eyes on Court's position.

It occurred to Court that it was possible these men were a support element for an assault on the compound, and that theory looked even more likely seconds later when several white-hot signatures began appearing over the lip of the canal.

One of the Wild Tiger sentries passed in front of Court with a flashlight again, and now the man swept it around with a noticeable increase in vigor. Court wondered if the man had been alerted to a new threat, or if he was just trying to look competent in front of the soldiers all around the villa.

The figures in the canal dipped down as the sentry passed, then rose again.

Court tried to do a head count and decided there were eight or nine in all, including the pair on the southern side of the canal.

He realized this force *had* to have known this place was crawling with Vietnamese regular army. In total there was a defensive unit here on the property at least four or five times the number of armed men in or by the canal. Either these attackers planned on doing this entire operation in a low-profile manner—something Court would like to see them try—or else this unit was just supremely confident in their abilities at large-scale ass kicking.

And this made Court think they might be Russian—Spetsnaz from the Russian military, or possibly even the vaunted Shield force from the Russian Foreign Intelligence Service; *Zaslon*, in Russian. Zaslon was known as the best of the best, akin to the CIA's Special Activities Division Ground Branch, the unit Court himself had worked in for years.

Zaslon guys weren't afraid to go loud, and they were often given rules of engagement that would allow just that.

Court wondered if this entire place was about to turn into a shooting gallery. If it did, he wondered if he would be able to just stay right here, tucked down and out of the fight, while chaos ensued all around.

He decided he didn't like his chances, but he thought he had a better shot of getting through the next few minutes than either the guys on the banks of the irrigation canal or the guys wandering around the big dark property unaware of the guys by the irrigation canal, so he decided he would just continue to lie there still and silent and be ready for an opportunity to make his way back to the flooded rice paddies as soon as possible so he could egress out of the kill zone.

Just as he decided to wait this one out, he saw a pair of flashes in the dark to the south, and then the two PAVN men standing at the back of the parked trucks fell to their knees. One man then crumpled straight down and slumped under the tailgate of one of the trucks, and the other rocked forward, slamming dead onto his face without making a sound.

The two Vietnamese infantrymen had been felled by suppressed rounds from the snipers in the trees on the far side of the canal.

Seconds later the white-hot images of seven figures appeared over the lip of the canal, and they began approaching the property. The team moved in perfect harmony; Court was immediately impressed with the craft by which they worked, and from their coordination and confidence he felt sure this was the same team he'd seen hit the cargo ship on Po Toi.

One pair of operators went to the west, towards the barn, moving behind the parking area and out of Court's view. The other five continued his way, through the grass lot where the vehicles were parked, just south of the trucks.

Court tried to identify their weapons and determined they were short-barreled Kalashnikovs of some type, and they all wore silencers. From this he thought it even more likely they were Russian operators, but he knew he couldn't make a determination from their firearms alone.

He also noticed that one member of the group wasn't carrying a rifle, just a pistol in his left hand. This man seemed a little smaller in frame than the others, and when he knelt down near the row of covered motorcycles, he seemed to Court to be separate from the other men moving through the lot.

While Court watched through his thermal, two of the operators slung their rifles, and then each of them took a dead Vietnamese soldier under his arms, then dragged him out of view between the two big trucks. Two of the other figures knelt down behind the BMW, and the one just carrying a pistol moved towards the BMW, putting his hand to his ear while he did so, as if listening to a radio call in his headset.

Court wished like hell he could hear that transmission.

Zoya Zakharova held her silenced Glock 19 in her left hand while she moved to the black sedan. As she progressed she used her right hand to adjust her headset to hear the transmission coming in from Yevgeni.

Yevgeni's voice came over the earpiece. "Anna Two to One. The barn is empty. We will advance on the villa from here across the southwestern side of the property, link up with you there."

Vasily was just feet from Zoya, tucked down behind a black BMW sedan. He keyed his mic and responded. "*Ponial*, Two. All remaining hostiles seem to be on the eastern side of the property, on the road, or possibly inside the villa. Both patrolling guards are out of view. We'll meet you on the southwestern corner of the villa by the generator and make entry around the back."

"Roger," said Yevgeni. "Anna Seven, are we clear to move?"

Mikhail still had the best overwatch on the scene. He responded from his position behind his sniper rifle. "All call signs: clear to move with caution."

Vasily and Sasha rose next to Zoya and started moving around the front of the BMW. Zoya herself began to rise, but Vasily grabbed her by the arm, jolting her back down. He just pointed at her angrily without speaking, then shouldered his rifle, looked around the front of the building with his night vision goggles, and took off in a steady but quick clip. Sasha followed right off his shoulder. They met up with Arseny and Pyotr at the trucks, and then all four advanced on the villa. They kept their weapons up, scanning in front of them, each moving in an arc to maintain overlapping fields of fire while they ran.

Zoya took a knee and looked over the hood of the sedan. She wished like hell she could hit the house; even armed with just a pistol she felt she could have benefited the team, plus if it went loud she could only help exfiltrate Fan under fire if she was somewhere near Fan when the firing began.

Here in the parking area all she could do was watch her task force advance on the villa and hope they got inside quickly and quietly, before the sentries returned or before anyone started looking for the two dead men dragged under the trucks.

She didn't like the decision to continue on with the raid, but she couldn't stop Vasily. She prayed he knew what he was doing.

Court Gentry saw a total of six men moving right towards him, two on his right from the barn, and four coming from dead ahead. They were forty yards out, but they'd be on him in seconds, so he *knew* he had to risk a move. It was perfectly dark in the shadows here, but he would be in plain view of anyone close by wearing night vision gear, and the gunmen heading his way approached as if they could see where they were going, so they *must* have been wearing NVGs.

Court remained low to the ground but began scooting back, using his feet and hands to move. The four operators covering the open ground were between him and the snipers, so he thought he would get out of the line of sight of the scopes of the long guns—for a few seconds, anyway.

He made it around to the back of the generator without getting shot, and once there he pulled his knife quickly. He couldn't be certain of the intentions of the men coming his way; for all he knew some of them were planning on hiding out here behind the generator, and if that happened, he'd have to try to fight them off with his small folding blade.

He'd die, of course, but he'd die fighting.

He was glad to see a row of three-foot-high bushes growing down the length of the west wall to the back porch, giving him some cover to the west if he tucked himself into a ball. This he did, and seconds later he heard the light beat of approaching boots over the hum of the big device in front of him. Staying as low as he could, he tried to widen his eyes to take in as much of the minimal light as possible, and he waited.

But he did not have to wait for long. In the back lawn off his right shoulder he heard motion as multiple sets of boots, still moving quietly, began passing his position. Court lowered as close to the ground as he could get, and as he did four dark-clad gunmen passed the generator heading around to the back of the villa. Just before they disappeared from view, the two who had been approaching from the barn met up with them, increasing their total strength to six operators.

Christ, Court thought. *Those guys are going to try to ninja their way into the villa to snatch Fan Jiang, while I just squat here and do my best impersonation of a fucking bush.*

But as much as the predicament he'd found himself in pissed him off, he didn't know what the hell he could do about it.

CHAPTER

TWENTY-EIGHT

Yevgeni took the lead in the tactical train as they moved along the rear wall of the villa, using shrubs that grew a few feet from the wall as cover. He took care to place each footstep as close to the wall as possible, knowing the men behind him would follow suit, and this would keep his team out of view of anyone at the back door until he was right on top of them.

When he reached the large rear porch, he stepped up onto it, still careful to move along the wall. He closed on the shallow alcove where the door stood, and upon taking one more step, through his NVGs he saw a PAVN soldier standing there, a rifle held around his neck by a two-point canvas sling.

Even though the light was bad, this sentry clearly sensed something in the dark, just a dozen feet away, and he began raising his weapon at the threat. As he did this he called out, and Yevgeni realized a second soldier stood there in the little alcove, as well.

Yevgeni danced fast to his left to make some room for his teammates, and he fired twice into the first man's chest, knocking him back against the door and spinning him to the porch before the Vietnamese soldier even thumbed off his weapon's safety.

Vasily was second in the stack, and he shot the other PAVN infantryman once in the forehead, splashing blood across the whitewashed wooden door.

Sasha and Pyotr raced past Vasily and Yevgeni and knelt over the bodies without saying a word. They grabbed the dead men's ankles and dragged them off the porch, one on each side, even jumping down themselves to move the men and their weapons silently out of view behind the shrubs.

Just then Mikhail came over the team's headsets. "Seven for all call signs. Sentry with a flashlight approaching southwest corner of target location in fifteen seconds."

Before the sniper finished his warning, Yevgeni already had a hand on the rear door latch. Sasha and Pyotr quickly retook their positions as the third and fourth men in the stack, and then Yevgeni waited for a squeeze on his shoulder, a sign from team leader Vasily to breach.

C ourt knelt in the bushes by the generator, seventy-five feet away from the back door, and watched the tactical train through his NODs as they disappeared silently inside the villa. They performed the breach competently and quietly, and Court wondered if six men really *could* make their way through the entire building, grab Fan Jiang, and get out of there without alerting the soldiers on the road and kicking off a raging gun battle. He still thought the prospects for this unlikely, but he had to give them credit for a nice set of opening moves. The nine-man unit killed four men right in front of him, and the remaining God-knows-how-many armed defenders of this property didn't seem to have a clue anything was going on.

Just then Court saw the beam of a sentry's flashlight as the man turned to walk up the western portion of the property. Court was out of the beam's light here behind the generator, and he knew the sentries had shown no interest in checking the bushes and trees for interlopers on their previous passes, so he would be safe if he stayed right here.

But he decided he would not stay safe, and he would not stay here. No, he had to act.

Court had been virtually paralyzed for the past ten minutes, caught in the line of fire of a sniper and then hidden in a ball while a team of commandos kept him pinned down.

But now he moved with purpose, because he had a plan, and he had a target in sight.

The sentry with the flashlight passed the generator fifteen feet from Court's shoulder and swept his light left and right idly, illuminating swaths of the low grass at the back of the big dilapidated villa.

As soon as he passed, Court rose to his feet but stayed low and began closing on the sentry at a forty-five-degree angle from the man's right. If his geometry was correct, Court would stay out of the scope of either of the two men lying prone at the canal to the south, as he would be covered by the southwestern corner of the villa and the big trucks parked in the parking area.

And if his geometry was wrong, Court was pretty sure he'd get shot in the back.

Court arrived within striking distance, and the sentry never heard a sound other than the humming diesel generator. Court took him from behind, closing off his windpipe with his left forearm, pulling up and tight, lifting the man violently off the ground. Simultaneously he shoved his four-inch blade hilt-deep into the sentry's ribs from behind, jerking it hard to the right as blood poured over Court's hand.

The man went limp, and Court let him drop to the ground.

Quickly he picked up the flashlight, turned it off, and dropped it into his pocket, then dragged the dead sentry backwards into the nearby shrubs.

Once down in the cover, Court took the rifle off the sentry's body and quickly inspected the weapon. It was a Galil ACE, an Israeli-made rifle that he wasn't trained on, but one he knew functioned much like the American M4, with which he was incredibly familiar.

He dropped the magazine and checked the bolt, finding the weapon was loaded with thirty rounds, and then he flipped off the safety and put the weapon in fully automatic mode. After a quick neck roll and a deep breath, he stood up to a crouch and began moving quickly through the shrubs along the wall towards the back door.

Just like that, the equation had changed, not just for Court Gentry, but for the Vietnamese, for this mystery team of paramilitaries, and even for Fan Jiang himself.

Everything was different now, because the Gray Man had a gun.

And as he neared the back door, he pointed his big unsuppressed weapon at the ground in front of him and placed his finger on the trigger.

The Zaslon force had successfully breached the three-story villa without making a sound, and now they moved in their train through a well-lit back hallway, closing on the sound of voices in a large room at the eastern end of the building. Vasily was fourth in line now; he and Sasha had cleared an empty storage room on their left, and now they all moved together, anticipating action ahead but careful to avoid any engagement until everyone was up close and had the room blanketed with complete fields of fire.

Vasily had hoped to find a staircase in the back of the house so he could begin a top-down clearing of the villa; experience had shown him that hostages and VIPs were normally protected vertically, meaning they were nearly always kept on or near the highest floor of a structure. But when the Russian officer found no way up at the rear of the villa, he realized he would not be able to clear this place without engaging the group of men talking to one another in the main front room. Still, with the Russians' suppressed weapons, their tactics, and a little good fortune, Vasily felt confident he and his team could eliminate the men directly in front of them quietly without alerting the entire property.

After that he would find a stairwell to lead them up to where, he assumed, Fan Jiang was being held.

He moved himself and the three men in front of him to the right-hand side of the wall, turned around to the members of his team behind him, and motioned for the last two in the stack to move to the left side of the wall to widen the coverage of the big room ahead when they made it to the doorway.

With hand signals he indicated he wanted a "wall flood," a room-clearing tactic that had half the team pushing into the room to the right, while the other half went left. By staying along the walls all the way to the corners, the six-man unit could bring a great amount of suppressed rifle fire on the room with speed, hopefully fast enough to squelch any hostile from firing back and alerting the men outside.

Vasily was still in the process of giving this silent order, and a portion of his team was still in the process of focusing on their commander instead of on the threats ahead, when the entire dynamic of the operation changed in the space of a single heartbeat.

Just outside the back door, only twenty-five feet from the rear man in the stack there in the well-lit hallway, someone opened fire with a fully automatic assault rifle.

Bam! Bam! Bam! Bam!

It was a short burst, but impossibly loud in the still of the night. Everyone within a half mile of the villa would have heard it and identified it for what it was, and virtually everyone within a half mile, Vasily felt certain, had a gun of their own.

Vasily had no idea what had happened; he didn't have anyone positioned back there. But all surprise was lost—any pretense of a covert entry just went out the window. The men in the rear of his formation spun around at the sound of gunfire, while the men in front began rushing up the hall, trying to close on the big room before the entire team was caught in the hallway, in the center of a "fatal funnel."

Vasily ran with Andrei on his left, just behind Sasha and Yevgeni. The group was momentarily divided in their reaction to the threat when two Vietnamese men in civilian clothing appeared from the main room. They both carried shotguns, holding them waist high, and their eyes widened when they saw the big, wet, dark-clad, *huge* men with guns, and beards, all wearing night vision equipment stowed high on their heads.

Sasha and Yevgeni opened up with their AKS-74Us, firing in full auto, dropping the first two men, though one fired a single shotgun blast as he fell. The buckshot went straight up into the ceiling, but more gunfire came out of the room at the end of the hall.

Three members of the Zaslon unit arrived in the doorway now. They found themselves face-to-face with a half dozen additional men, most of whom were dropping down behind chairs and couches in the center of a large, high-ceilinged room with peeling wallpaper and wooden flooring. Four of the remaining men were PAVN infantry, the other two were Wild Tigers, and everyone was armed with rifles and shotguns.

The Zaslon men had no time to scan for targets to try to identify Fan Jiang. They fired their suppressed weapons in fully automatic mode, pushing into the room over the dead men in the doorway so that their colleagues behind could aid in the fight, and they did their best to lay waste to all threats in front of them.

The Russians executed their wall flood; Vasily pushed to the right while Arseny and Sasha went left with Yevgeni. Behind them, Pyotr and Andrei took knees in the hall and covered the back door, ready to confront whoever was shooting out there if they came through.

Zoya Zakharova raced across the open ground with her pistol out in front of her, her night vision goggles restricting her peripheral vision but helping navigate her way forward in the moonless night. The fierce gunfight inside the building caused her to leave her cover to attempt entry herself, even though her run risked putting her in the sights of the nearly two dozen PAVN soldiers fifty meters off her right shoulder.

Mikhail and Ruslan were still prone, still behind her on the far side of the canal, and they were scanning the area to the east, ready to open fire on the soldiers as soon as they began moving towards the house. But the Russians wouldn't press their triggers until they had to. No sniper likes firing at night if he can avoid it, as the resultant flash from his weapon immediately announces his exact position to the enemy.

Zoya hit the southern wall of the villa and called over the tactical inter-team radio, begging for a report from the men inside. The gunfire she heard was from shotguns, unsuppressed assault rifles, and handguns, but she knew her task force's weapons wouldn't be audible here because of their advanced suppressors.

Suddenly the crackle of rifle fire kicked off from the east. This told her either she'd been spotted somehow in the darkness, or else the Vietnamese army was engaging her task force members through the windows of the house. Not wanting to take a chance that she was under fire, she dove around the corner, tucking herself between the generator and the western wall of the villa.

Behind her, Ruslan and Mikhail began firing their suppressed weapons; she looked back to the canal and could see the flashes from their muzzles as they engaged the numerically superior force by the road.

The battle raged on inside, as well. Even though she still couldn't hear the sounds of Anna team's rifles, it was obvious they were in the heat of a close-quarters war, and it was *also* obvious there was a huge chance they were going to kill Fan Jiang in the melee unless they watched what the fuck they were doing.

She worried that this op was disintegrating around her, and she wondered if there was some way she could get to Fan Jiang before the battle on the ground floor did.

She looked up at the wall above her. Through her NVGs she could see that the third-floor window, twenty feet above her head, was cracked open.

An idea came to her quickly. "Anna One, this is Sirena. Be advised. I'm going to make entry on a top-floor window in the southwest corner of the property. I'll keep you updated on my location as able."

She heard no response from the team inside the villa, but she knew they had their hands full. They were tier-one professionals; so long as they heard her she felt confident they wouldn't accidentally shoot her when they made it upstairs.

She holstered her weapon, silencer and all, leapt up off the generator, grabbed on to the thick vines just below a decorative edge a few feet below the second-story window, and yanked herself up using just her upper body. Her feet swung in the air below her as her hands let go of the vines; she flew upwards, grabbed on to the windowsill of the second-floor window, and heaved herself up again.

Zoya scaled the corner of the three-story villa as the gunfire increased, both inside the villa and on the other side of the property. She moved as fast as she could, racing against time to find Fan Jiang before it was too late.

Court sat in the bushes with his back to the western wall of the big villa and his right shoulder against the porch up to the back door. His head was low enough that no one coming out the door on his right would be able to see him, but if someone exited the building via the back—with Fan Jiang in tow, perhaps—Court would see them from behind as they stepped off the porch onto the ground.

A dead PAVN infantryman lay in the vegetation with him; the man's eyes were rolled all the way back, a bullet hole marred his forehead, and a massive wound hinged his skull open at the back of his head. It was a sickening sight but something Court was trained to ignore, so he concentrated his attention on the sound of the battle in the house behind him.

He'd wanted to make sure the attacking force got busted in the act of raiding the house, and his plan had worked, but now he wondered if this shoot-out just might get Fan Jiang killed. Court thought it was certainly possible, and if it happened it would be his fault, since he was the one who exposed the attackers as they were in the middle of their stealthy infiltration of the site.

But what the hell could he do about it except wait here and hope a couple of the assaulters rescued Jiang alive and came through this door while making their escape?

He looked left and right in his NODs, and then he scanned up to see if any light was coming from windows on the southern side of the villa. To his astonishment he saw a figure effortlessly scaling the wall above the generator. The operator was clearly going for the same window Court had planned on entering originally, but this guy was doing it faster than Court himself could have executed the climb.

Who the hell is that?

Court sat there in amazement for an instant, and then his head cleared; he swiveled the Galil rifle around quickly, lined up the iron front post sight on the head of the target, and put his finger on the trigger.

But he just kept it there.

Was this the right move? He'd drop a Russian Spetsnaz officer, assuming that's who this was, in a hot second if it meant grabbing the USA's biggest intelligence coup since the inception of the People's Republic of China.

But unlike the other guys in the villa, this one operator was not involved in the gun battle, and he was moving covertly towards his objective. Court realized slowly that he should be rooting for this little guy climbing the wall, hoping like hell he was the one who made it to Fan Jiang first instead of those gun monkeys shooting the hell out of the ground floor of the building.

If Court wanted his target to make it alive out the back door of the property, this spider monkey on his left was his best shot.

Court would then just shoot the spider monkey in the back when he and Jiang exited.

Court cocked his head now and rubbed his eyes, shoving his finger between his face and the eyecups of the night vision binos taped to his ball cap to do so. He only had a second or two to focus on the climber, but he saw the body shape of the operator. Slightly wider hips, a full chest under the raincoat.

In that brief moment he realized he was looking at a woman.

That was weird. Court knew of no tier-one paramilitary force in the world that employed women on their assault teams.

The climber slipped into the window on the third floor, and Court looked back to the western side of the property. He kept silent and still in his hiding spot, his rifle at his shoulder.

Woman or not, he still planned to shoot the operator if she left with Fan Jiang. The fact that she was female did not diminish the fact that she was in his way.

CHAPTER

TWENTY-NINE

Fan had been lying there frozen in his bed, afraid to move a muscle even though the gunfight below him had been raging for over a minute. For most of the shooting, starting with the crashing automatic fire right below his window, the fight seemed to be at ground level, but it was clear from the progression of the gunfire and the screaming that whoever was attacking this place was now just one floor below him on the stairwell that ran up the center of the villa.

As he squinted his eyes to will away the danger, Fan's door flew open suddenly and he turned to look. Tu Van Duc stood there wearing a white suit and tie and waving a silver .45 caliber automatic pistol around crazily.

He looked to Fan Jiang like a vision out of one of those Hong Kong action films he watched as a guilty pleasure on his computer.

Behind Tu, one of his men—Fan had been told the man's name was Cao—had a semiautomatic pistol in each hand, and he held them both up in front of him while he watched the long hallway.

Tu raced into the room and pulled Fan away from his bed and up to his feet.

"Come with me!" Tu screamed in English. His eyes were wild with terror.

Fan saw that the Vietnamese crime boss was nearly as terrified as he was, which only scared Fan more, but the young computer hacker did as he was told. Together the two of them followed Cao down the hall. Tu pulled Fan

Jiang by the sleeve of his black hoodie to keep him moving along as they ran past the stairs in the middle of the hall, all the way down to a large musty bathroom at the far end. Here Cao tucked one of his pistols in his underarm so he could open a small closet, pull out a plastic bag full of old towels, and then reach to the back wall. To Fan's surprise, a hidden panel in the closet opened, and he could see a dark narrow stairwell, with wooden steps leading steeply down. Cao knelt into the closet and immediately began descending while Tu pushed Fan, urging him onward. Fan stepped in and found himself fighting claustrophobia almost instantly, and when Tu pulled the wall closed behind him to hide the entrance, Fan realized he could not see at all. The leader of the Wild Tigers did not turn on a light; instead he just shoved and shoved from behind as Fan began descending, doing his best to fight his welling panic.

Fan realized he was in a spiral staircase when his head hit the wall. He descended with the winding stairs, and soon he was level with the second floor of the building.

The cracking of gunfire had dissipated somewhat, but as the men got down to the ground floor, Fan heard a fresh energy to the battle that was now being fought above him.

Fan realized this odd stairwell went all the way down into the basement without stopping at any other floor. He thought it must have been some sort of secret escape route built by, or at least used by, the Vietcong who operated here fifty years earlier.

The basement was a small dark space with little in it other than standing water, a foul stench, and the splashing and scratching sounds of rats in the corner.

Here Cao jabbed both his weapons into his belt, then knelt and slid three cinder blocks out of the wall. By doing this he created a hole only three feet high and a foot and a half wide.

Cao said something to Tu, who immediately translated for Fan Jiang.

Tu said, "Cao will go first. Fan, you are in the middle. Hurry!"

Cao crawled into the black hole.

Fan knelt down but hesitated. He turned back to Tu and shook his head. "I'm sorry. I can't do it. I am afraid of small spaces."

Tu snapped back, "And *I* am afraid of getting killed by the Americans! Hurry!"

"*Americans? How do you know?*"

"Because they aren't Chinese. They *must* be Americans."

Fan looked at the tunnel again, then back to the leader of the Wild Tigers. "Where does this lead?"

"There is a barn behind the house. It leads there. We can run into the rice paddies and hide in the trees until the Americans leave."

"Why don't we just wait here? They won't find the entrance above, and we can just—"

Tu Van Duc pointed his silver automatic in Fan Jiang's face. He said, "I *will* go, and I will not leave you behind alive so that you can reveal where I went."

Fan turned back to the darkness and began crawling, his breathing audible and labored as his chest tightened.

The Zaslon unit had been in near-constant enemy contact for the past minute and a half, but they'd cleared the ground floor and half of the second floor, and now were outside a door at the end of a hallway. Yevgeni, Sasha, and Pyotr stacked at the closed door, while Vasily, Andrei, and Arseny moved up the stairwell. The team was relying on their two-man overwatch outside to notify them of any hostiles breaching the villa below; just because they'd killed everything that moved on the ground floor didn't make things safe for them down there, since the soldiers outside near the road could always come in and reload the building with more hostiles.

Still, with only half a dozen men, Vasily knew he didn't have the personnel to leave men on the ground floor.

Vasily had heard the call that Sirena had entered through a window on the top floor, and for this reason only he waited before going up the stairs. He called her on the interteam radio, but she did not immediately answer, and he assumed she was probably moving silently.

As he waited a moment, he turned to watch Yevgeni lead his three-man team into the room up the hall. Anna Two gave a squeeze on the shoulder of Sasha, the breach man in the group, and he kicked in the door, then pushed in with his weapon high.

Four Vietnamese men lay in wait, kneeling behind upturned tables across the room. They held rifles and shotguns pointed at the door, and they opened fire on the breachers.

Sasha moved away from the doorway so his teammates could help him engage, and while doing so he fired at the gunmen in front of him. His burst caught one man in the shoulder, but just after this a shotgun blast hit him in the knee, buckling the appendage and sending Sasha sprawling to the floor.

Yevgeni and Pyotr both riddled all remaining Wild Tigers with bullet holes as they entered the room.

Sasha lay facedown on the wooden floor by the doorway. From his position by the stairs Vasily could tell Sasha's leg had been severed.

Just as Vasily started to move to help, another door on the opposite side of the hall flew open, and a Wild Tiger with a snub-nosed revolver appeared, the gun in his hand spitting smoke and fire.

The leader of the Russian SVR paramilitaries shot the man through the neck, sending him tumbling back into the room.

With constant gunfire below her, Zoya Zakharova stepped out of an empty bedroom on the third floor of the villa and looked out into a long hallway. Three lights in the ceiling ran down the length of the hall. She aimed at the one closest to her and pulled the trigger of her Glock. The weapon thumped as the suppressor absorbed much of the noise from the subsonic ammo, and the light blew out.

Quickly she shot out the other two lights in the hall, then pulled her NVGs back down over her eyes and stepped out, still covering her way forward with her weapon.

"Man down! Man down!" The call came from Vasily, spoken over the sound of close gunfire.

Things had clearly gone to hell below her, so all she could do now was hope that her target was safe, up here with her. She continued up the hall quietly but quickly, knowing time was not her ally.

Court heard shotgun and rifle fire one floor directly above where he sat next to the porch at the back door. Along with this, the chattering fire of multiple guns on the other side of the villa told him the snipers by the canal were probably having an incredibly busy and an incredibly bad evening.

He scanned around with his NODs while he sat there and was surprised to catch a hint of movement on the far side of the barn, fifty yards southwest of his position. He aimed the Galil at the motion but lowered it when he realized the action there was no threat to him.

Three figures ran from the back of the barn and over a large open field towards the line of trees that separated the compound's property from a large flooded rice paddy on the other side.

Court cranked up the magnification on the night vision binoculars attached to his ball cap. Through the ten-power magnification, he could see the three men as if they were only fifteen or twenty feet away.

Court squinted as he tried to make out faces in the dim green glow of the NODs. The man in front turned back around to wave the others onward. He was young and fit with a beard and mustache, and he carried two handguns. The man in the middle was the smallest; his hands were empty, and he faced away. And the man in back wore an ostentatious white suit and carried a shiny automatic pistol.

Court scanned back to the man in the center and tracked him for a moment. Suddenly the small figure stumbled, then turned back to look at the man right behind him.

The American sitting against the wall of the villa sixty yards away saw his face clearly.

Softly Court spoke aloud now. "I'll be damned. Fan *fucking* Jiang."

No doubt about it. Court Gentry had positive ID on his target. The Chinese man wore blue jeans and a black hoodie, and he was running for his life with the two men armed only with pistols. Fan didn't look like he had much experience running in a muddy field, or running at all, for that matter. And the men around him looked like Vietnamese gangsters. The guy in the back looked like he could be a serious player in the organization with his suit and tie and his shiny Colt .45.

Court looked around, quickly making sure there was no one else out here on the lawn, then he launched to his feet and took off across the property as fast as he could.

Zoya had cleared the entire third-floor hallway, save for the last room at the end. She used the tip of her silencer to push open the door, revealing a dark bathroom. She started to turn away but noticed a big bag full of old towels in the middle of the floor next to a small door. She opened this door, leveling her Glock in front of her. As she'd expected, it was a closet, but the items on the floor just outside caused her to reach around the area to check for a false wall or a false floor in the little space.

Just as she did so, Ruslan came over her headset. "Anna Eight to all call signs. I've got subjects fleeing the compound on foot to the west. Multiples . . . three—negative. Four subjects. They'll be out of my line of sight in five seconds."

Zoya raced across the bathroom to the back window, then looked outside. Through her NVGs she could see three men running together, and a fourth halfway between the villa and the men in the distance. The man in back was quickly gaining on them from behind.

She flipped up her NVGs, pulled a ten-power night vision monocular from her belt, and focused it on the group of three men in front.

She was certain in an instant.

Fan Jiang was in the middle of the three.

"All call signs, be advised. Target is in sight, one hundred meters west of Omega and running to the west."

Ruslan spoke next. "I've lost visual. They are out of my field of view."

Zoya knew she could run down the stairs and take off into the back, but the lower floor had not been cleared of hostiles. She could climb out this window and try to make her way down the wall, but by the time she hit the ground, Fan and the other three would have entered a tree line another fifty meters from where they now ran, and by the time she got to those trees, they'd be long gone.

She held the monocular to her eye with one hand and watched the men running away. With her other hand she keyed her transmit button, knowing the best thing she could do right now was to thin the herd, to remove Fan's protection.

"Anna One, I need every gun I can get pointed out the back windows in the next fifteen seconds. The subject is in a black hooded jacket and blue jeans. Second from the front of the group approaching the trees. Eliminate all other hostiles in sight before they get into the concealment of those trees."

Vasily responded quickly. "All Anna signs able. Engage targets to the west from the second-floor windows."

And then, to Zoya's astonishment, the man who had been running behind Fan and the other two stopped running suddenly, shouldered his rifle, and pointed it at the others. She had assumed he was one of the Wild Tigers protecting Fan, but before her eyes, his rifle flashed, and the first man in the trio in front of him fell to the ground.

The crack of a gunshot came just as a second flash came from the rifle.

The man in white running right behind Fan Jiang fell to the wet grass, the gunshot boomed back to the villa, and Zoya watched the man with the rifle run forward now and tackle Fan Jiang to the ground.

He was a much bigger man than the three figures with him.

She jabbed at her PTT button again. "All call signs! The target has been . . . he has been abducted! There is some other party here at the Omega, and they have the target in pocket. I just see one subject with the target at this time and they are heading west on foot towards the trees. The man with the rifle is now your primary. Shoot him!"

Vasily was confused by Zoya's call. "Confirm your last, Sirena."

Zoya shouted into her mic now. "All call signs at Omega! The smaller man is Fan Jiang! Do not shoot him! The larger man is a hostile. I repeat, the larger of the two is hostile. Drop him!"

On the second floor, while Andrei desperately tried to stop the bleeding on Sasha's leg, Vasily, Yevgeni, and Pyotr arrived at separate windows at the back of the villa at the same time. They broke out glass with the suppressors of their AKs, then raised them to look through their red dot holographic sights. Through their night vision goggles they could make out the two figures moving in the distance, and they distinguished their objective, Fan Jiang, from their target, the unknown subject who now had Fan Jiang by the arm and was pulling him farther away from the scene.

The sights on the short-barreled rifles were not enhanced, but rather simple holographic red dots: good for close-quarters battle, but less effective at distance. Still, the Zaslon men had the skill to hit a man-sized target on the move two hundred meters away.

All three operators looked through their night vision goggles, through the optics on the top rail of their weapons, and they lined up their red dots on the larger man, switched their weapons to fire a single round when the trigger was pulled, and began tracking their target to judge his speed so they could aim accordingly.

Just as the three men were preparing to fire, they saw the larger man stop abruptly, spin around, and drop to both knees. Next to him, Fan Jiang stumbled, looked at the man with the rifle, and then started to run away, taking advantage of the hostile's action.

The unknown subject raised his weapon now, but he did not point it at Fan Jiang. Instead he pointed it back in the direction of the villa, 185 meters away.

Pyotr said, "What the fuck does he think he's doing?"

Vasily shouted out, "I'm taking the shot!" He slipped his gloved finger onto the trigger of his weapon. As he started to put pressure on it he saw the flashes of gunfire coming from the rifle of the man on his knees in his sights. Vasily wasn't worried; he knew he was in no great danger. For this man to even see a man-sized target in one of the windows at this distance would be a hell of a feat. Hitting his target on his first try after running like that would take superhuman skill.

And Vasily knew the man wouldn't get a second try. He'd be dead in one second.

But as the Zaslon team leader began to fire his AK, a fireball erupted right in front of him in his window, and his night vision goggles whited out, blinding him.

To his left Vasily heard Pyotr and Yevgeni scream in surprise, and all three men lowered their weapons, dove for cover, and lifted their goggles so they could see.

An incredible explosion, louder than even the shotguns involved in the firefight, roared through the night, and the darkness outside turned to daylight. Inside the villa, those few lights still on went out completely, enshrouding the entire building in a blanket of darkness.

Vasily lay on the floor rubbing his eyes with a gloved hand in an attempt to clear them.

"What the *fuck* was that?"

Zoya's voice came over the net. "The son of a bitch shot the diesel generator at the back of the villa! He blew it up to blind our NVGs! I can't see a damn thing! We need to exfil Omega and go after the target, *now!*"

Mikhail's voice came next, transmitting from his sniper's hide south of the canal. "Anna Seven to One! We're blind over here with that explosion! Our night vision gear is toast. Can't see the PAVN units approaching the villa. Suggest you egress to the west, now! We'll lay down suppressive fire as long as we can, then we'll have to retreat!"

Vasily was up on his knees now. His goggles would be whited out for several more seconds, maybe up to a minute, and he didn't have time to wait, so he activated the flashlight on the rail of his rifle. As he began moving to the staircase with the other men he punched his transmit button. "Anna Two, call in the helo. Get them here in ten minutes."

"Roger that!"

Back in the hallway, he found Arseny kneeling over Sasha. He wasn't even rendering aid.

Vasily could see that the fallen operator had bled out from his catastrophic leg wound.

Vasily just said, "Get his weapon, but leave him. Move!"

CHAPTER

THIRTY

C ourt Gentry flipped his night observation device on his ball cap up and used his naked eyes to watch the huge fireball roll up higher than the roof of the villa, then fade to black in the moonless sky. He'd fired a dozen rounds from the levee into the diesel generator, hoping he'd get lucky, and the result was even greater than his highest expectations.

Diesel fuel was harder to burn than gasoline, but he knew a hot round puncturing the wall of the unit and sparking off metal in exactly the right part of the sixty-thousand-watt generator could ignite the pressurized fumes, and that explosion could lead to a catastrophic detonation of the entire two-ton device. He'd seen smaller diesel generators get hit by rifle fire in the field before, but he'd never seen anything like this explosion.

He was momentarily proud of himself and wished like hell somebody had been around to take a picture.

He hoped this move might slow down anyone chasing him out of the property and add to the chaos inside the villa, and since the paramilitaries who hit the house were all wearing night vision gear that would be sensitive to light, he knew that anyone near a back window when the big device blew would have to deal with annoying white-out conditions on their equipment for up to a minute or so.

Court's own night vision goggles were flamed out for the next minute, as well, but he considered this a small price to pay.

Of course he had no idea he had been a second away from taking multiple rounds from multiple weapons when he blew the generator, but he *did* know he was not out of the woods yet, either literally or figuratively. There were still a lot of foreign commandos, and a lot of Vietnamese soldiers and gangsters, and they all wanted what Court had: the Chinese cyber warfare specialist.

Court turned away from the villa, still illuminated by the fire pouring out of the wreckage of the generator, and looked across the dark levee. Fan Jiang was barely visible in the bad light, but Court could see that he had fallen to his knees in a mud puddle. Fan climbed back to his feet and ran on, but Court caught up to the small man right at the tree line and snatched him by the arm, then pulled him on in the same direction, pushing with him through the thick brush and trees, though neither man could see more than a couple of feet in front of them.

The Chinese national stumbled several times; he seemed terrified, exhausted, and unable to keep up the speed Court demanded.

Court encouraged him along with curses and shoves.

The six surviving Russians in the villa raced out the back door, their weapons high, sweeping for threats in all directions. Zoya was last through the door, her pistol at her side, but she was the first to see a man in civilian clothing leaning around the north side of the house with a shotgun in his hands. She fired three rounds, hitting the man once in the arm and once in the chest, crumpling him dead to the grass.

A second man tried to fire blindly around the corner next to where his partner fell, but Pyotr dropped to his knees and fired a long burst at the old stone masonry there, tearing it away with hot brass-jacketed lead. It took fewer than twenty rounds to expose the shooter behind the wall, and just one more round through his heart to end the threat.

The Zaslon team and their SVR task force leader continued sprinting to the west across the wet field.

The two Russians lying prone south of the canal had fired a total of over 150 rounds at the PAVN soldiers positioned in low ditches by the road, killing a few, wounding several, and preventing the rest from leaving cover for most of the firefight. Mikhail had the scoped sniper rifle, so while he took fewer shots he had more hits, but without Ruslan there to help him by firing short bursts with his fully automatic AK, then crawling a few yards to the left or to the right and firing again, the much larger force of Vietnamese soldiers would have targeted the pair of them and cut them to pieces in the opening moments of the skirmish.

Still, some of the Vietnamese had by now crossed the road bridge over the canal, and they were moving up the tree line closer to the two Russian paramilitaries, so after hurling a pair of fragmentation grenades to the east, Ruslan and Mikhail took off to the west as fast as they could while still maintaining some cover in the thick foliage.

Their escape was helped when Vasily sent Arseny and Pyotr to the barn with orders to each dump a pair of thirty-round magazines at the Vietnamese force to the east, less to kill the remaining dozen or so men and more to keep heads down and force the PAVN soldiers to second-guess the wisdom of a counterattack.

The ploy worked, and soon all eight surviving members of the task force made it to the two bodies at the tree line on the levee at the western edge of the property. They made a quick examination of the dead men, not wanting to dally here for long at all because they were less than two hundred meters from more than a dozen armed soldiers who very much wanted to kill them.

Zoya ignored the dead body lying facedown next to a pair of pistols, and instead rolled over the older man in the suit and tie. She flashed a red light on his face—choosing this color on her tactical flashlight because red did not carry as far in the dark.

She said, "Tu Van Duc. The leader of Con Ho Hoang Da."

Vasily grabbed her by the arm roughly and pulled her back up to her feet. "Nobody gives a fuck. The target isn't here. Let's move."

They took off again for the tree line, in pursuit of their target and the unknown subject who'd stolen Fan out from under them.

Court Gentry and Fan Jiang pushed out of the tree line, and by now Court's jerry-rigged NODs were operational again. Through them he could see the large flooded rice paddy to the west of the villa, a levee that ran west along the south of the paddy, and another tree line on the northern edge of the paddy, two hundred yards away to his right. Instead of jumping into the water and continuing west, Court jerked Fan Jiang's arm to the right and continued north at the edge of the trees, knowing that anyone who came after the two of them would be able to spot them in the waist-high water for the ten minutes or so it would take them to slosh through to the other side. If they continued north in these trees, they wouldn't get as far away from the villa as quickly as he would have liked, but at least they'd be able to move with some cover.

Fan Jiang had muttered some words in Mandarin, but more than anything he just seemed in shock and completely spent from the effort of the past few minutes.

Court finally spoke to him now, leaning into the smaller man's ear to do so quietly. "You are Fan Jiang, a Chief Sergeant Class Three in the PLA, Unit 61398. Your hacker name is Funky Monkey. I know you speak English. Listen very carefully. You are in a lot of danger, but not from me. I'm going to take you somewhere safe. Nothing bad will happen to you as long as you do what I say."

"But . . . who *are* you?"

"Well, I'm not the Chinese, and I'm not the Vietnamese."

"You are American, obviously."

"I'm the good guy. Let's just leave it there, for now."

"Where are you taking me?"

Court did not answer for a moment, because he didn't have much of a plan. He wanted to get himself and his "package" out of danger so he could call Brewer. She'd have to take care of their escape after that.

Fan repeated himself. "Sir? Where are you taking me?"

Court yanked the kid along, and as he did so, he said, "Cambodia."

"Cambodia is to the west. We are going north, aren't we?"

Court did not slow his hard march. "Right now, kid, west is a bullet in the back. We'll get there eventually; just do as I tell you."

Fan stopped talking as ordered, but his heavy labored breathing told the American holding him by the arm that this kid wasn't going to jog all the way into Cambodia.

Within a minute Fan confirmed this. "I can't keep moving like this! I'm tired!"

"Sure you can. You have no idea all the amazing things you are going to do tonight!"

"Amazing things? What amazing things?"

Court thought he heard a helicopter in the distance now. He couldn't see it, and by the faint thump of the rotors it was still a couple of minutes away, but he had no doubt it was heading in this direction.

"Like not getting shot," Court said. He pulled the man harder now. "*That* would be amazing."

Fan said nothing else as the two men struggled through the vines and bushes along the edge of the rice paddy. After reaching the northern tree line, they stayed deep within that cover, Court stopping occasionally so he could listen for the approaching helo.

When the Russians crossed through the first tree line they found themselves looking over a rice paddy that must have been half a square mile in size. Zoya scanned with her night vision, and then again with her thermal optic.

She said, "Nothing."

Pyotr said, "They entered these trees three minutes before us. How the hell did they cross this paddy so fast?"

Zoya looked around, again through her NVGs. "Impossible. They are either under the water or they stayed in the tree line. The canal is south. Maybe they went north."

Vasily said, "We aren't hanging out here, Koshka."

Zoya turned to him, but before she could speak the copilot of the Mi-8 came over the radio and announced he would be overhead in two minutes. Vasily ordered the helo to pick them up in a dry clearing at the edge of the paddy, and then Yevgeni flipped on an infrared beacon and threw it overhand to the middle of the landing zone.

While they waited on the helicopter, most of the team pulled security, keeping their guns and their attention back to the east in case they were being pursued by the Vietnamese. Fortunately for both parties, the PAVN officers who hadn't been killed inside the villa in the opening moments of the raid had the good sense to load their men into their trucks and bug out to the south, vowing to return with a company-sized force at first light to collect the dead. This would also give them time to come up with a story. The commander of the Ninth Military Region in Can Tho was on the payroll of the Wild Tigers, and this was his sector, but everyone here knew that if Hanoi found out the truth of what happened here—that a dozen uniformed military working security for a criminal organization had been killed or wounded at the hands of some foreign force—the implications, both foreign and domestic, would be massive.

C ourt could hear the approaching helicopter now, but he couldn't see it through the impossibly thick strip of jungle here north of the big rice paddy. It sounded like it was coming in for a landing somewhere just a hundred yards or so southeast of his position, and Court hoped like hell it would load up with those tier-one shooters and just fly away.

Fan had been compliant as they humped through the trees, and other than his heavy breathing and grunts of pain when he cracked his shins against roots or bumped his forehead on branches, he'd been relatively quiet. That all ended suddenly when he pulled to a halt and leaned over to put his hands on his knees. "This is impossible. Are we continuing in the jungle the entire way to Cambodia?"

"Negative. We'll have to get into the flooded paddies that lie between here and there. Trust me, you'll miss walking in the jungle about two minutes after you start sloshing through that shit."

Fan said, "We can't just walk through the rice paddies."

"Sure we can. I did it once tonight already."

"But . . . will there be swamp rats? I heard rats in the basement of the villa."

"Not too many in the paddies. The snakes killed them all."

"Snakes!" Fan said it so loud Court put the young man in a headlock.

"Shhhh," he said, holding the man in a vise grip. "Listen, Fan. I'm here to protect you, and I promise I won't let you get killed by a snake. But I can't promise you a Russian sniper or a Vietnamese mortar round won't kill you if you make too much noise."

Still in the headlock, Fan's head rotated up. "Russians?"

"Those guys at the villa that tried to grab you tonight were Russian. I'm positive."

"I don't understand. I thought that was you."

"No. We both came for you at the same time. I got lucky, and I got to you first."

"Are you going to tell me you saved my life?"

"Not really. Those other guys wanted you alive, too."

"If those people wanted me alive, it would be bad if they wanted me dead."

Court conceded the point with a nod, and the men started walking again.

Fan said, "But . . . you are a killer, like them. You shot Tu and Cao like they were nothing."

Court said, "If they were nothing, I wouldn't have shot them. They were a threat to my operation."

"It is so simple to kill?"

Court regarded the question while pushing through a thick portion of vines. "I don't kill people who aren't asking for it. Those guys were drug smugglers, and they were hiding one of the most powerful computer hackers to ever work against the interests of the United States."

Fan stopped walking again, and he looked up in the darkness. "Really? Who?"

Court just grabbed him by the arm and pulled him on. "*You*, asshole."

"You captured me because you think I have hurt the U.S.?"

"It's not a capture. It's a rescue."

"This doesn't feel like a rescue."

"You think the Wild Tigers were going to just say, 'Thanks for the help, and thanks for getting half our guys killed. You can go now'? No, that's not how criminal organizations work. They would have used you as long as you could be used, and then they would have killed you because you knew too much."

"I had to work with them. The PLA is looking for me."

"You're damn right he is. Colonel Dai sent a dozen men into the building in Ho Chi Minh City this afternoon."

"Dai? No . . . he is a *lieutenant* colonel. He is the deputy director of the security of Unit 61398. The colonel in charge is named—"

Court said, "Dai got a promotion, because the other guy was put in front of a firing squad after you ran." Court didn't know why he said that. It wasn't going to help this kid's morale to know he was getting people killed for his actions, although to Court it seemed perfectly obvious.

But clearly Fan was under no illusions about the trouble he'd started by running. "A lot of people are dead now. All because of me."

"Yeah," Court agreed. "And the night is still young."

The crew of the Russian Mi-8 racing in from Cambodia wore night vision gear, so they flew their helo straight to the LZ without lights, and they touched down without shutting off their engines. All members of the task force—save for Sasha, of course—quickly boarded the helo.

Just as the pilot lifted off and turned the aircraft back to Cambodia, Zoya Zakharova put a cabin headset on, and she spoke into the microphone. She ordered the pilot to run racetrack patterns over the massive rice paddy and trees that rimmed it.

Vasily put on a headset of his own.

"Three minutes! You have three minutes to look for the target, and then we are out of here."

The helo crossed back and forth once over the huge paddy, then flew lower, closer to the tree line on the north. Here it began slowly following along the length of the trees, just twenty meters above the ground, while Zoya, the pilot, and the machine gunner all used their night vision and thermal gear to try to find any hint of two men hiding there.

CHAPTER

THIRTY-ONE

C ourt Gentry lay under a narrow line of triple-canopy trees that divided
one rice paddy from the next, and he listened to the massive engines
of the big Russian helicopter as it neared his position. Under him was
Fan Jiang; the small man just lay there limp, panting, in pain both because
of the tight chest and leg cramps from the most intense cardiovascular
workout of his life, and due to the fact that a man who weighed fifty pounds
more than him was crushing him at the moment.

Court and Fan lay behind the rotting root ball of a felled broadleaf
mahogany tree. Court's plan was to keep their thermal signature broken
up by both the trunk and the few inches of standing water here in the
muddy hole left when the tree tipped over and ripped its roots from the
ground during the last monsoon season.

Other than his head Fan Jiang was completely covered by the muddy
water, but Court kept his torso and one arm out of the goo, because even
though he didn't want the helo to see any bit of him or his thermal signature, he wanted to keep his rifle pointed over the root ball in the general
direction of the Mi-8.

Court lined the rifle up on the helicopter above using its engine and
rotor noise to locate it, hoping he was aiming more or less at the cockpit.
He didn't really think he'd shoot it down, and he doubted he'd do much
more than announce his exact location by opening fire, but if it became

obvious the helo knew where he was, Court decided he'd rather go down with guns blazing.

Court's mood had deteriorated dramatically in the past five minutes. On the helo's first pass Fan had tried to race down the tree-covered levee and into the tall stalks of rice in the flooded field, thinking it could hide him better. Court understood the capabilities of thermal optics and knew Fan had made the wrong call, so he tackled Fan, but with more force than he'd intended, and the two of them rolled and slid down a muddy embankment. By the time Court righted himself and grabbed both his captive and his rifle, he realized his backpack had slipped off his shoulder in the tumble, and now it was somewhere either higher on the levee or down below the surface of the flooded rice paddy, and looking for it would put him in view of the approaching helicopter.

Now as Court lay there hiding in a little hole like an animal, he realized he had to come to terms with the fact that he no longer had a phone, money, papers, surveillance gear, food, or water.

He was so furious with himself he almost wanted to engage the big Russian helo with his stolen Galil rifle, if for no other reason than to expend some aggression.

But after some struggle, he kept his composure and did not fire, and the helicopter continued on to the east.

Minutes later he saw it pass back to the west, picking up speed and climbing away from the rice paddy as it did so, and Court felt sure it was flying away from the scene and back over the Cambodian border.

Court almost wished he could hitch a ride.

After a short while he stood back up, and then he yanked Fan Jiang roughly to his feet. He considered going back to look for his pack, but that would necessitate a climb up onto the high levee that would wear Fan out even more, and a fruitless search that would waste time they did not have.

He thought again about the Russians who'd hit the house, the woman on the team armed with only a pistol, and the Mi-8 that was now flying them back over the border.

After a moment he told himself it wasn't all bad, because even though he had a long way to go before he'd be somewhere safe and dry, he figured he had one thing those assholes in the helicopter did not have.

He had Fan Jiang.

Fan spoke up just as they began moving again to the west. "I am not an athletic person. I am too tired to continue." The last part was delivered in an unmistakable whine.

Court said, "Listen, Fan, if I have to sling you over my shoulder, I'm going to be even more pissed off."

"I am trying, sir. I am trying."

"Try harder."

After a minute more Fan said, "Sir . . . what do I call you?"

"I don't speak Chinese, and there is no one else here. If you say something in English, I will assume you are talking to me."

Fan nodded as he walked. "Yes. Of course."

A s soon as the Mi-8 dropped the Russian task force off at the Phnom Penh warehouse used by the SVR, Zoya climbed out of the helo without saying a word to any of the operators. She carried her own equipment and barged straight through the metal door, ignoring the small guard force protecting the building. Several vehicles took up the main floor of the large, well-lit room, but in the back by a kitchen a row of green cots and boxes of equipment was set up next to a row of tables used as a gun-cleaning station. Zoya passed these by as she headed to an open metal staircase that led up to a small office above the warehouse floor. Here she shut the door, locked it, and walked over to her own private sleeping area.

Still covered in the mud, grime, and crystallized sweat from tonight's operation, she pulled out her secure satellite phone and contacted her control officer in Moscow. She relayed the entire evening's events. As she did this, she was certain Vasily was downstairs doing exactly the same thing to his Zaslon leadership, but Zoya didn't give a damn.

She was in the right, not Anna One.

Yes, they'd lost a man tonight and they'd failed to secure their target, but Zoya had clearly ordered the team to stand down and egress before hitting the villa. It was Vasily who demanded they continue with the mission, and the results of that decision spoke for themselves.

As far as she was concerned, Vasily was the one who was going to take the heat for this fuckup.

Zoya explained to her control that she didn't know who had Fan Jiang now, but she didn't think it was the CIA. She'd seen only a single person involved in the Chinese computer hacker's capture, and that was most definitely *not* the way the CIA operated.

If the taking of Fan Jiang was, in fact, an American operation, it had been done by proxy. The kidnapper, Zoya maintained, was perhaps a foreign national who'd been watching the villa when the Russians arrived, and he'd then seen an opportunity to act when Fan, Tu, and the other armed Vietnamese gangster tried to flee the scene.

The "lone wolf who got lucky" scenario was the only one that made any sense to her.

She thought about the man she'd identified as a CIA officer several days earlier in Hong Kong. He'd been alone at the time, although that had been quite a different situation. He'd been drinking in a bar trying to get information about some men who disappeared, which was not exactly a tier-one commando raid on a building surrounded by fifty gunmen.

After she'd relayed all her intel to her control officer, she was told to wait by the phone for a return call. She hung up and went to the little bathroom off the office, and here she stripped out of her gear and clothing.

In the bathroom light she found leeches in her underarms and above where her belt had cinched her pants tight to her skin, and she sliced them away with a combat knife distractedly, with no great distress. After flushing the creatures down the toilet, she saw in the mirror that she'd picked up some bruising on her ribs, but she couldn't even remember how it happened.

She turned on the little shower; the pressure was that of a garden hose and there was no hot water. Still, she took a small bar of soap out of the backpack pocket where she kept her toiletries and stepped under the flow.

Five minutes later she was clean and dried off and dressed in jeans and a black cotton shirt, and she sat on her cot looking at the phone.

A minute later it rang.

"*Allo?*"

Her control officer talked for only two minutes, and when Zoya finally got a chance to reply, she was cut off, told the decision was final.

She hung up the phone and sat quietly on the cot in the little office.

But only for thirty seconds. Then she stood, opened the door, and descended the staircase.

There the seven surviving members of the Zaslon team all sat on their cots in the living area on the small warehouse floor; most of the men by now wore just their boxers or civilian tracksuits.

Sasha's bunk lay empty.

It was clear the men had been talking together, but everyone shut up as Zoya approached.

Anna One still wore his grimy clothing, and he still held his sat phone in his hand. She knew he'd been on a long call.

Zoya walked up to him and stopped, just looked him hard in the face.

Vasily said, "Look, Koshka. These things happen. You tried to bite off more than you could chew, you got in over your head, and then you—"

"You told them I ordered you into Omega."

"You *did* order us into Omega."

"Initially, yes, but when the PAVN trucks arrived, I told you to stand down. You know that, you son of a bitch."

The big commando shrugged. "By then it was too late. By then we were already taking accurate fire, and I determined the only way was forward."

"You lying piece of shit. There was no fire. That came after you hit the building." She looked around the room. "Every one of you heard my order."

No one spoke.

"Really? Are you all going to back up Vasily when you know *he* was the one who directed you to hit a building with two dozen PAVN around the perimeter?" She turned back to Vasily. "You had me removed from the task force. You had me recalled to Moscow. All to cover your ass and to make you feel better about *your* fuckup, the fuckup that got Sasha killed."

Vasily pointed a finger at her, got it right in her face, but before he could speak she snatched his arm and jerked it down with her right hand, yanking the unsuspecting paramilitary officer off balance.

She threw a hard left jab to his face, connecting perfectly with his jaw and mouth, compounding the magnitude of the punch by pulling him down and into it.

Vasily's head snapped back and he fell to the ground.

And then he got back up.

None of the other Zaslon operators moved while Vasily touched his hand to his mouth and then looked at his blood-covered fingertips.

Zoya stared him down. She didn't have the strength to defeat Vasily in hand-to-hand combat; objectively she knew that. But her fury had surpassed her judgment. She wasn't going to run, and she wasn't going to hit him again. Instead she waited for what she knew was coming.

"*Davai!*" she shouted. *Come on!*

The paramilitary operator slammed the back of his hand against her face, sending her spinning to the ground like a rag doll. He stood over her while she slowly rolled onto her knees.

"You are done, Koshka. You never were a team player. Go home."

She remained there on her hands and knees. Blood dripped from her nose, and the inside of her mouth began to swell. She spit on the floor. "We could have had him. We could have just sat back and watched the villa from a distance until the PAVN left. We could have taken Fan at a time of our choosing. The actor who took him couldn't have done it if we sat back and secured the area, and Sasha would still be here." She pointed to the empty cot. "Sasha would still be sitting right *fucking* there, with the rest of you idiots."

Vasily wiped his mouth with a dirty rag from the gun-cleaning table. He said, "Anna team doesn't sit back and watch. My men are not the guys you send in to run surveillance."

"Right," Zoya said, slowly climbing to her feet now. "Next time I'll do *everything* myself."

"The only thing you will be doing by yourself is flying home to Moscow. Me and my guys will take it from here."

Zoya gave one last look at the team, and then she stormed back up to the office. Five minutes later she returned with all her gear loaded into two backpacks. Her nose had tissue jammed in it, and the right side of her face was puffy from the blow she'd taken.

The SVR motor pool had allotted the team four vehicles, which were parked side by side on the warehouse floor: three Toyota Sienna minivans and a twenty-year-old Toyota Tundra pickup truck. Zoya opened the chain-operated garage door, climbed into the Tundra, and drove off without even a glance at the men standing around watching her go.

As soon as Zoya was out of the parking lot she fished in one of her packs for her satellite phone. Quickly she dialed a phone number as she drove through the darkened streets of Phnom Penh.

She knew that the local assistant resident of the SVR for Cambodia would be home asleep, and there was no way he would be aware of the decision Moscow had just made regarding her status on the task force. She didn't know the man well at all; they had just met for a few minutes the day before. He'd given her his mobile number and she knew his instructions had been to give her whatever she needed for her mission.

The man answered with a rough, sleepy voice. *"Allo?"*

Zoya said, "Ivan? I need help."

"Sirena?"

"Da. I need information . . . fast. Either I can come over to your place now, which will probably piss off your wife, or you can tell me over the phone."

The man coughed sleepily. "I'll meet you at the embassy. Give me an hour."

"I don't have an hour."

Ivan cleared his throat, and then she heard him moving around. She assumed he was leaving his bedroom.

Finally he said, "This is an open line."

Zoya ignored the comment and said, "Just tell me who we can send to help me find someone along the border to the east of the city."

"That's a little vague, isn't it?"

"I'm talking about a force. A persuasive force."

"I thought you *had* a force."

"Someone who knows the area. Who won't stick out. A proxy unit. I don't care if we never use them, have no relationship to them. I don't care if they are communists, drug dealers . . . fucking headhunters or cannibals. I don't care. I need them, and I need them *now.*"

"An open line, Sirena."

"Help me."

"Okay . . ." Ivan thought a moment. "What's in it for them?"

"The guy I'm looking for . . . He's valuable. *Very* valuable. If they can find him . . . they can have him."

"How does that help you? What the hell is going on?"

"This is an in extremis situation. I don't know the local underworld here in Cambodia, and neither do my guys . . . but you do. Right now I know where my target is, generally speaking. But if someone doesn't go get him right now, then he's in the wind, and we may never pick him back up. I want him caught by a known entity, so I can find him again."

This pause was even longer. Finally the assistant resident said, "The group you are looking for . . . they aren't Cambodian. The guys you want are Thai. They are well connected in that part of the country. But we don't work with them. We don't touch them. Ever."

"I need a phone number."

"Shit, Sirena, it's three a.m."

"And by four it will be too late!"

"Okay . . . I'll send it to you. They are based in Bangkok, but they smuggle over the border through Cambodia and into Vietnam all the time. The route they use is just east of the capital, the area you are talking about."

"Perfect," Zoya said. "Hook me up with them, and then you can go back to bed."

"I hope Moscow is okay with this."

"Moscow is interested in success. That is what I . . . that is what *we* will provide them."

CHAPTER

THIRTY-TWO

C ourt Gentry and Fan Jiang walked in the darkness for five hours, taking only short breaks when they found dry ground. The first portion of their hike, up to and including the border crossing into Cambodia, had been slow and arduous: a seemingly never-ending series of muddy fields and flooded rice paddies, broken every twenty minutes or so by thick, nearly impenetrable tree lines full of thorny underbrush and ankle-twisting root systems.

For the past hour and a half, however, they'd walked primarily along dirt or gravel roads as they continued to the west. They'd seen not another soul the entire time, which was good news for Court, because the batteries had gone dead in his night vision binos an hour earlier and he'd buried the device under thatch and fallen leaves, and without it he found it much harder to avoid dangers in their path.

Court had dumped the rifle, as well, although he felt sick about doing it. He knew there were a lot of threats in his path still; the Russians would have expected him to make a run into Cambodia, and the Mi-8 might come back looking for him.

But he couldn't just walk public roads with a carbine on his shoulder, so he disassembled it and threw it into a grove of thick jungle along the way, and hoped like hell he wasn't going to regret the decision.

Fan had been silent much of the way, other than occasional lamentations about his feet hurting and his legs cramping. Court had ignored him at first, then consented to his pleas for breaks every now and then. But now Court began to worry as the young man started limping noticeably.

The American realized they wouldn't be able to make it much farther.

They left a road when it turned to the north because Court wanted to keep going west towards the population center of Phnom Penh. He didn't have a map on him, but he'd studied the area knowing he might have to come this way and he remembered the route in a general sense, so they followed a dark narrow trail through rough jungle.

He thought he was saving time doing this: getting Fan to the west where he knew the farmland ended and there were more villages and even small towns. But after twenty minutes the dark wooded trail ended at a slow-moving river, with no way across anywhere he could see.

Court's heart sank. It was easily seventy-five yards across, and while there was a tiny boat dock and a dilapidated wooden shack here, there were no boats at the dock and no signs of life on either bank of the river.

When he saw the water in the low light, Court remembered from the map that this river wound around the southeastern part of the nation, and this told him he was farther south than he'd thought. He also remembered there were no bridges for miles in either direction, and he didn't think Fan would be able to walk nearly that far in his condition.

Court turned to the young computer expert. "Let me guess . . . you can't swim."

Fan replied defensively, "I *can* swim. But . . . but I am too tired. I will drown, I promise you."

Court nodded. He looked at the area around him and saw that the shack was missing part of its roof, but the broken concrete slab it was built upon was dry. The jungle and the riverbank looked like prime locations for snakes to hang out, so he told Fan they'd take a break right here on the slab.

Together they went into the shack and sat down on the hard concrete. Court knelt over Fan and helped him get his shoes off, then used the small penlight feature on his thermal monocular, basically the only item to survive sliding down the levee, to look over Fan's feet. They were blistered and bleeding, but only because they weren't callused to begin with. With a little bandaging Court decided Fan would be fine.

Court said, "Take off that hoodie, it's eighty degrees."

Fan did as Court instructed, and Court ripped the hood off, then cut it into two strips. The material was damp but not completely soaked, and Court tied them gently over Fan's blisters.

He said, "We can wait here until daylight, probably in another forty-five minutes or so. If someone comes with a boat, we get a ride out of here, and we get a phone. If nobody comes by in the next two hours, then we swim across, and we keep going."

"But . . . I can't walk any farther."

Court said, "That's why we're resting, and that's why I'm bandaging your feet."

Fan just nodded distractedly, then said, "This is crazy."

"What's crazy?" Court asked.

"Everything. This night. That, back there, with the shooting, the soldiers. You. This is not my life. My life is three computer terminals and access to the networks of the Strategic Support Force."

Court said nothing; he just worked on making himself comfortable. He had a good view up the trail, so if anyone came from that direction using flashlights, he'd see them long before they saw him.

Fan said, "But all this . . . everything that happened tonight. I guess this is what you do."

Court smiled a little, still looking up the trail. "What can I say? I'm not smart enough to be a computer hacker, so I get the shit work. Like this."

Fan gave out what sounded to the American to be a tired sob, then said, "I don't know what I'm doing here."

Court scanned the trees around him now, doing his best to absorb any light. While doing so he said, "Of course you do. You ran. They chased. If you hadn't jumped the border . . . we wouldn't be having so much fun right now."

"I did not want to run. It happened so fast."

Court kicked his own shoes off. They wouldn't dry out, but letting the skin of his feet get some air around it would help them heal. "Seems like an odd thing to do on the spur of the moment. C'mon, dude. When you escaped I'm sure you knew the Chinese would come after you, and I'm sure you knew any of the countries you'd worked against would be interested in you, too."

"You don't even know the work I did, do you?"

"Like I said, cyber warfare is a bit over my head."

"Well . . . I did *not* work against the United States. That's another portion of my unit. My job was to find access points into my own nation's secure networks by using the tactics of 61398. There is a big difference."

Court said, "Maybe to your conscience. Not to your desirability. Look, I just came because I was sent. I don't care what you did or to who. I wouldn't even understand it if you told me." Court lay down on the cement, facing Fan Jiang. "The only thing I am curious about is why you decided to make a break for it."

Fan did not respond for a long time. Court thought the kid wanted to say something but had decided against it. Finally the young man answered. "The security department kept watch on us at all times. But that was everyone in the unit. I worked with a team inside unit 61398 called Red Cell; there were five of us. They had another way to keep us in line. There was an official term for it, but most everyone called it 'family collateral.'"

"What's that?"

"Our relatives. Everyone on the team had a wife or a husband, children, other family members, who were kept at the compound in Shanghai. Treated well, full party benefits, but watched over, twenty-four hours a day by an escort . . . a member of the security unit."

"So they kept your wife and kids inside the military installation?"

"I was married when I was eighteen. The department encouraged it. She was a lieutenant in the PLA, which made it easy for us to prove our loyalty to the party. But six years ago she died . . . during childbirth."

Court looked up to the lightening sky. "Sorry."

"Yes. I was going to have a son."

"Damn."

Neither spoke for a full minute. Court was exhausted and he didn't know what this day would bring. He imagined he still had many miles to go before he'd find a way to pass Fan off to U.S. authorities.

But Fan wanted to talk. "When she died . . . when *they* died, I mean, security at 61398 brought my parents into the compound in Shanghai from their home in Beijing. Family collateral. My parents were my only relatives. I was told if I remarried they could return to Beijing, but I did not want to remarry so soon."

Court just said, "That must have been tough on your parents."

"It was the opposite. My father was a colonel in the PLA, and my mother had been a mathematician at the National Defense University. They were proud to support the work I did by living in the compound. They were assigned a guardian, Major Song Julong. He was charged with watching over them, and he had served under my father, so it was good for everyone. Me, my parents, and Song."

Court rolled up onto his arm now and looked at Fan. He understood, for the first time in this mission, what had started this entire situation. "But something happened, didn't it? Something that *forced* you to run."

Fan looked back to the American in the low light and nodded slowly. "Yes. Something happened."

TWO WEEKS EARLIER
SHENZHEN—PEOPLE'S REPUBLIC OF CHINA

Fan Jiang moved briskly, swinging his briefcase along with his stride, his tie loose and his parted hair hanging low and boyishly after a full day walking the exhibition floors of the China Information Technology Expo. The massive event was winding down for the evening; thousands of men and women filed out of doors, down escalators; they flagged cabs and stepped onto metro cars and buses. Fan was right along with the crowd, fitting in as an unremarkable young businessman, although one flanked by two much larger and much less talkative coworkers.

Fan was tired; most every day of his life involved twelve to fourteen hours sitting at a desk, so just participating in a trade show was real physical work to him. He was looking forward to getting back to his room so he could pig out on room service, then go to bed early. Tomorrow he and his guards would fly back to Shanghai, and by midafternoon he would be back in his uniform and back at his desk, and as novel as it was to come here to get intelligence on the work done by IT corporations around the world, he was ready to return to his normal and sedentary existence.

His bodyguards, Chen and Liu, were arguably more exhausted than their protectee, because while Fan had to talk to dozens of people and take pages of notes, the two security officers had to stay ultra vigilant at all times: tough to do considering the fact that the expo was a massive transitional space with thousands of people moving around.

The three men pushed through the revolving doors of the expo's lobby and out into the six p.m. heat, heading to the cabstand to catch a taxi back to the Sheraton. Before they made their way to the back of the long line, Sergeant Chen's cell phone trilled in the breast pocket of his gray suit coat. He pulled it out, looked down at the phone to identify the call, then held it out to his protectee without answering it. "Fan, it's your mother. We'll get in line; you sit on that bench right there by the door."

"*Xie xie*." *Thank you*, Fan said as he took the phone. Fan liked to be separated from the two sergeants while he spoke to his parents. Not because he had anything to hide; rather he was embarrassed to talk to his mother in earshot of the tough bodyguards.

As he sat on the bench he said, "*Ni hao, Mama*."

The voice on the other end of the line was not his mother. It was a male voice, but it was not his father.

Fan Jiang recognized the voice of his parents' government-issued escort, thirty-eight-year-old Major Song Julong.

"Jiang? It's me. It's Julong." Fan knew the man well; he'd become part of the family in the past six years since his parents were brought into the unit and moved to the compound in Shanghai. Song was with them virtually all the time, and Fan spent most of his free time at his parents' apartment, just a few buildings away from his own. When he did this, it was common for Song Julong to join them for dinner, watch television with them, or play games.

He'd become something of an adopted brother to Fan.

Fan said, "*Ni hao*, Song. Why are you calling from my mother's phone?"

The man spoke quickly. "Something terrible has happened."

Fan sat up quickly. "What's happened?"

Song's voice was serious, ominous. "You cannot react to what I am telling you. I did *not* call you. This is your mother calling. Do you understand me?"

Fan did not understand, but the man's tone made him nervous. "Put her on the phone. Or my father. They are both with you?"

"When the security department finds out . . . you know what they will do."

"Finds out *what*? What are you talking about?"

Song said, "Softly, Jiang. If Chen and Liu are there, do not let them hear you!"

Fan glanced up at the men in the taxi line. They were lighting cigarettes and talking to each other, not even looking his way. "They can't hear me. Tell me what is happening."

"Fan . . . there has been an accident. Just now. Not five minutes ago."

"Accident? Are my parents—"

"I was driving. It was me. A sand truck from the construction site on the Inner Ring Elevated Road backed up just as I was passing."

"*No* . . . Please tell me they are okay, Julong."

"Keep your voice down. You understand what this means for you, don't you?"

"For . . . for *me*? Where are my parents?"

Song shouted into the phone now. "They are dead, Jiang! They are both dead! Killed instantly. I am sorry. I am so, so sorry, but you can't react to what I am telling you."

Fan leaned forward suddenly, as if he'd been punched in the stomach.

Song said, "Your parents were good people. They were like my own parents, who I lost when I was young. You know that. You *know* I didn't want this."

Fan just stared at the sidewalk in front of the taxi stand now. Still in a state of shock, he tried to clear his head and think. "I'll tell the guys. They will get us on a flight tonight. I'll be home as soon as I can."

"No!" said Song. "You don't get it. You *still* don't get what I'm trying to tell you, do you? I am calling you now, before anyone in 61398 finds out, because of your participation in Red Cell. Ten minutes ago you had the highest security clearance in the nation. Now when the police get here and when MSS and MOD find out the identity of the dead, you will have no clearance. You will have all the secrets of the Strategic Support Force in your head, but you will be deemed untrustworthy by the government. You have no more family collateral, and when 61398 finds out . . . it will be all over for you."

Fan just looked at his two bodyguards. They were making their way closer to the front of the taxi line. Chen glanced his way and tapped his finger on his watch. Fan nodded, then turned away. "How much . . . how much time do I have?"

"You are in Shenzhen. We are in Shanghai. The car is burning; they won't find their IDs. I walked away from the accident; I'll tell them I hit my head and didn't know what happened."

"Why? What are you talking about?"

"You have ten, maybe twelve hours. By dawn tomorrow MSS will be in contact with MOD, and they will call Chen and Liu. MOD will order them to bring you straight into the security office of 61398. At that time they will take your credentials, and they will hold you. They will say it is for your own protection, because of your grief. But they will keep you for a day or two while the orders are signed."

Fan asked the next part with a lump in his throat. "Orders?"

"And then the security director himself, Colonel Le, or else his second-in-command, Lieutenant Colonel Dai, will order you shot. That's how it happens. *That's* how they remove the compromise to Red Cell."

Fan knew nothing of this; he found it so hard to believe. But Song had worked as a security escort for a dozen years. They were friends. There was no reason he'd say any of this if it weren't true.

Fan had seen two other men leave Red Cell when they lost family collateral. He'd been told they'd moved to other sectors. Now he wondered if they'd been executed.

He just said, "I served faithfully. I have done all that was asked."

Song sniffed; Fan could almost hear the tears running down the man's face. "They only believed in you because they controlled you. That control is gone." Song sniffed again. "You have to act tonight."

Fan shouted into the phone, loud enough that his two bodyguards looked towards him in surprise. "And do what?"

Song said, "You need to run."

Fan turned away from Chen and Liu. "I . . . That's *crazy*. I have no idea how to do that."

"It's okay, Jiang. I will tell you what to do. I will tell you what has worked in the past with defectors."

"De—"

"Don't say it! Just listen to me very carefully."

"But . . . What about you?"

"I'll be fine." Fan heard a slur in Song's speech now. Maybe it had been there the entire time.

"Why are you doing this for me?"

"I owe it to your parents."

Song tried to hide his drinking, but sometimes he showed up at Fan's parents' apartment drunk. Fan wondered if Song had been drinking today, if the story about the sand truck was not the complete story. But he did not press.

He just listened.

F ive minutes later Fan handed the phone back to Sergeant Chen without saying a word.

Chen was with Liu near the front of the taxi line and still thinking about the outburst he'd overheard. "Problems with Mommy, Fan? Did she buy you the wrong color underpants?"

Liu laughed next to him.

Fan just said, "No problems." And then, "Guys, I feel a head cold coming on. I've had to shake too many dirty hands this week."

Liu nodded. "We all have. Disgusting *gweilo*, mostly."

"Can we go to a market and get some cold medicine? Something that will help me sleep?"

It was a reasonable request, so Chen just shrugged. "There is a market around the corner from the Sheraton. We'll go there."

"*Wanshan,*" Fan said. *Perfect.*

PRESENT DAY
CAMBODIA

Court looked at the little man lying on the cement foundation by the river-bank, and he could hardly believe he'd had the guts to sneak across the border into Hong Kong while being pursued by the full military and intelligence apparatus of the People's Republic of China. That said, he understood the young sergeant had absolutely no choice at all.

He asked, "Did you ever find out what happened to Song?"

Fan nodded. The morning light had grown to where it was now possible for Court to see the pain and the fatigue on Fan Jiang's face. "I looked on the Internet when I was in Hong Kong. There was a single-car crash in Shanghai on the Inner Ring Elevated Road at the same time as Song's call. I looked at the video from the news report. It was the car Song drove, burning. It took an off-ramp too quickly and flipped. There was no construction site anywhere around. No sand truck involved, either."

"He was drunk."

Fan nodded. "And the guilt of killing my parents caused him to try to save me. The report said there were three victims of the crash."

Court blew out a long sigh now. "They terminated him."

Fan nodded, then concentrated on the American in front of him. "So . . . I told you all this. Now you must tell me the truth."

"Depends on the question."

"What is going to happen to me?"

"Don't worry. You're safe. First, I get you away from Colonel Dai and his men."

"And then?"

"And then I am to hand you over to some nice people who'd like a word with you."

Fan sat up. "Where?"

"I don't know."

"You are going to take me to the U.S. I know you are. I want to go to Taiwan."

Court didn't know why the kid wanted to go to Taiwan, and he didn't ask. He said, "The U.S. has good relations with Taiwan. I'm sure we'll work something out."

"You are lying. The CIA is going to demand I work for them. They will hold me for years, force me to work against my home country. And if I refuse . . . will they send you to kill me?"

Court chuckled. "It's the USA, not China. You might eat fatty food that gives you a heart attack and watch shitty TV that makes you want to kill yourself, but the CIA won't whack you."

Fan Jiang said, "I took nothing out of China when I left. No documents, no plans, no schematics for programs. I have nothing to turn over to anyone. I just want to go to Taiwan. Of course I know I will be debriefed, but I refuse to work against the People's Republic of China."

Court thought this kid was about to cry, but as far as he was concerned, Fan Jiang was hopelessly naïve.

Fan said, "I am from China. I am not against China. Not even after what happened. I am *for* Fan Jiang. Can't I just leave this all behind?"

I seriously doubt it, Court said to himself. Then he sighed a little. "I'll talk to some people when we get out of here."

It was bullshit, and Court got the distinct impression Fan saw through it, because he sprang to his bare feet and took off for the dirt trail through the jungle. Court reached for him but missed, then put his own shoes on and chased after him. The faint morning light kept Fan from running off the trail and into a low-hanging branch, but Court caught up with him in under a minute, grabbing him by his shirt and tackling him to the ground. The bigger American put a knee in the young Chinese man's chest. "Calm down, kid. It's not so bad. We're the good guys."

Fan Jiang struggled. "No, you are not."

Court realized he was crushing the kid while telling him he was a good guy. He pulled his knee back. "Well, we're the *better* guys. Dai will kill you for what you did. Those Vietnamese back there will kill you for causing that massacre, and if the Russians got hold of you . . ."

Court let that hang in the air for a moment.

Fan said, "I want to go to Taiwan."

"Right. Taiwan. Look, I'm going to hand you off to someone, and you can tell them that." Court pulled Fan to his feet. "You've had a lot of bad luck, and I really wish you all the best, but I have a job to do. And I *promise* you, if you run from me again, you will just make your bad luck even worse, because I *will* kick your ass.

"We're finished waiting around here. If you can run like that, you can damn well cross that river. I'll be there right with you. I'll keep you safe."

Fan started to protest, but Court took him by the arm and began walking him back down to the water. "C'mon, kid, let's go for a swim."

The light was even better when they returned to the little shack by the beach, but as soon as the two men had a view down to the little docking area, they both stopped in their tracks.

Three green powerboats, each some twenty feet in length, floated silently in the water just yards offshore, and in them some two dozen men, all armed with assault rifles and machetes, stared right back at Court and Fan with hard eyes.

Over a dozen muzzles pointed at the chests of the two foreigners.

"Well . . . *that's* not good," Court muttered.

"Who are these men?" Fan whispered.

Court sized up the men on the boats. They were sinewy, weathered, tan from living on the water and out in the elements. These guys knew the jungle.

"The kind of men you don't piss off. Raise your hands slowly."

"Should we run?" Fan asked.

Court raised his hands, and Fan followed suit. Yes, Court could have run. He could have dived off the trail, rolled down into a shallow ditch in the trees, and disappeared into the jungle.

But not with Fan.

Court said, "No, kid. We're going to do exactly what they say."

"Where will they take us?"

"Just a guess. Not to Taiwan."

CHAPTER

THIRTY-THREE

The powerboats were old and covered with rust and peeling paint, but each vessel had two huge and well-maintained engines, and the boats were each large enough to carry eight men. Half of the men waded ashore, their weapons pointed right at Fan and Court, and then one of the boats pulled up to the rotting wooden dock, while the other vessels just trolled in the river, the gunmen on board training their Kalashnikovs on the pair of new captives.

One of the men seemed to be in charge, simply because he began ordering the others around. He was of average size and build, and he appeared to be no older than twenty-five or so. He had a folded-stock AK-47 hanging off his shoulder and a simple assault vest on his chest, and he wore a red bandana that held back his long dark hair. His arms were covered in tats, like the others; also like the others, his skin was burnt orange and leathery.

His sunglasses and his wristwatch looked expensive to Court, but his gun and his gear looked third-rate.

Red Bandana looked carefully at Fan Jiang, even stepping up to him, pinching his face in his hand, and moving his head around, examining the Chinese man as if he were looking at a horse at auction. He appeared to be making sure he had the right guy. With a nod to the armed men around him, he reached into one of the magazine pouches in his vest, then pulled out a plastic Ziploc bag. He opened it up and retrieved a mobile phone. While he dialed a number he waved his free hand and shouted orders at the men standing around the two captives, and they all began moving.

Court's wrists were pulled behind his back and tied with a length of thick hemp, and the man who did it was clearly an expert at the task. Even though Court knew he couldn't undo his hands, Court was glad he was being bound, because he figured he was just the booby prize for these guys; Fan was the real catch.

Being tied up meant Court was going for a ride, and he found that much preferable to getting shot and left in the jungle for the bugs.

Court didn't imagine for a second this had been some sort of opportunistic kidnapping by river bandits who just happened by, so Court was glad that whoever was running the show on the other end of the phone didn't order them to just shoot the big American and be done with it.

Court asked them who they were and what they wanted, and although none of them seemed to speak any English, after a nod from Red Bandana, a large man wearing an assault vest adorned with a huge Rambo combat knife in a sheath came over and smacked Court in the side of the head with the butt of his rifle.

Court understood this language. Loosely translated, it meant *No more questions.*

Fan Jiang and Court Gentry were placed into the powerboat at the dock, and several gunmen climbed in with them. The prisoners were pushed down onto a bench in the middle of the boat, shoulder to shoulder, and while the commander continued his phone call on the bank, Fan leaned over and spoke into Court's ear.

He said, "They are Thai."

"How do you know?"

"I did some research on different organizations in Southeast Asia when I was in Hong Kong. The tattoos mean they are from a Thai Chao."

"What's that?"

"It just means they are an underworld group, from Bangkok. There are lots of different organizations, but the biggest and most dangerous is called Chamroon Syndicate. They are all over. Even in Hong Kong."

"Why didn't you work for them in Hong Kong?"

Fan just looked down at the deck of the boat. Softly, he said, "Because they are animals. Vicious animals. Very bad."

"Terrific," Court muttered.

Soon Red Bandana boarded the same boat and sat down behind the man at the helm, and then the big outboard engines roared to life.

F ive minutes later all three boats raced single file south on the river as the morning sun glared orange off the water. Court and Fan were seated among eight men, most of whom sat on the gunwales on the port and starboard sides and held their rifles out, as if there were real threats here on this river.

Court imagined there probably were, but he didn't think he could possibly be in deeper trouble than right here, in the middle of this boat.

Court looked at Red Bandana now. He sat on the bench facing inboard; he had a cigarette in one hand and the mobile phone in the other, and his elbows were back on the port-side gunwale behind him. He leaned back, relaxed and happy after making this catch so early in his day.

He hung up the phone a minute later and slid it back into the plastic bag, but instead of putting it back in his vest, he just tucked the phone under his leg on the bench. Court figured the phone was left out because Red Bandana was expecting another call.

Court eyed the man on his right, just past Fan. He was taller than the others, and his big Rambo knife stuck straight up from its sheath on the front of his assault vest. His rifle faced outboard, but he looked Court's way through cheap aviator sunglasses.

Scanning around the boat a little more, Court saw a space between two men sitting on the gunwale. It was on the starboard side, across from Red Bandana. The men looked out at the riverbank, with about three feet between them.

Court took everything in again: the cell phone in the plastic bag sticking out from under the right leg of the man ahead and on his left. The knife on the man's chest rig on Court's right. And the clear space over the side of the boat ahead and on Court's right.

Court gazed out of the boat now, across the brown water. On the starboard side the riverbank was only about fifty feet away. On the port side, however, it was a good forty or fifty yards to the shore. Court imagined there were some rocks or other obstacles in the river ahead that caused the pilot to hug the western bank.

One more quick scan around him and Court made his decision.

He leaned over to Fan and whispered, "Do everything they say; don't put yourself in danger. Sooner or later, probably sooner, they'll sit you down in front of a computer to do some work for them. When that happens, figure out a way to let America know where you are."

Fan shook his head now. "I'm not letting *America* know anything. The Taiwanese will save me. I just have to tell *them* where I am."

"Kid . . . you aren't getting saved by Taiwan. They don't even know you are on the run."

Fan turned to Court. "Yes, they do. They promised me a new life. A house. A job."

Court was confused. "When was this?"

"Right before they helped me get out of the mainland."

"What the *hell* are you talking about?"

"That's how I got away. Song told me to go to the Lo Wu border crossing and wait. I did this, and a man stepped up to me. He was from Taiwan. He gave me papers to cross into Hong Kong. He said I would be met on the other side and taken to Taipei, but when I crossed over, there was no one there. I realized I was followed over the border, so I ran."

None of this made a bit of sense to Court. If Taiwanese intelligence had spirited Fan out of the mainland, why wasn't Court told about it? Taipei had a good working relationship with CIA; there was no way CIA would not know of Taiwan's involvement in Fan's escape from the mainland.

Court said, "The papers you mentioned . . . they had your picture? They were already prepared?"

"Yes."

"So, Song must have contacted Taiwan on your behalf before he was killed? He was a double agent?"

Fan cocked his head a little, thinking about it. "No. Song was no Taiwan agent. The man at the border crossing said they had intercepted the phone call between Song and me and prepared everything. Then they just waited for me to arrive."

Bullshit, thought Court. If Song told Fan to go to that particular border crossing and wait, then Song set up Fan's escape with Taiwanese intelligence. Court saw no way that the CIA could be unaware of this, but he didn't know why the hell Taiwan helped Fan get out of the mainland only to leave him high and dry in Hong Kong. Something very wrong must have happened with the operation.

Slowly it dawned on him. Court had been told that the CIA got involved with this when they found out Fan was being hunted by Fitzroy, thereby creating a perfect opportunity to send in one of Fitzroy's old hit men in order to nab Fan.

But that story was a lie. No, this whole thing was some kind of a busted op—something involving Taiwan and the United States, perhaps—and CIA had sent Court in to help salvage it.

Court leaned back to Fan. "Wo Shing Wo . . . how did you get hooked up with them?"

"Desperation. I was walking the streets of Hong Kong for a day, afraid to even go to a hotel with the papers I had been given. I slept in an alley. Finally I went to an Internet café and called a number I found for the National Security Bureau, Taiwan's intelligence agency, but it was just some operator. I was put on hold. I got scared and left the café, but just after I left I saw men with guns race in."

Court mumbled, "Colonel Dai's men were already in Hong Kong looking for you."

"I went to another café and began looking for protection in Hong Kong. I knew I could work for some group, help them out, but it needed to be someone who wasn't afraid of mainland security."

Court had to admit Fan's plan had been solid and effective. He had surrounded himself with guns and a defensive infrastructure, and that got him out of Hong Kong and kept him from getting assassinated by Colonel Dai's men. But now, looking around at the wild river bandits surrounding them on the boat, Court thought Fan's run of relative fortune might have run out.

He said, "I'll find out what's going on. Don't do anything stupid, but find a way to reach out to us, and I'll come back for you. I promise."

Fan looked away and shook his head. "What are you talking about? You are in the same situation as me. You can't get away from these men."

"Yeah . . . you're probably right."

Court leaned over on the bench and looked down at the deck for several seconds, his head almost between his knees. He was the picture of compliance; not one of the eight men around him expected any movement out of him whatsoever.

While he looked like a man dejected, he was in fact already hard at work on his play. He slowly, quietly sucked in deep lungfuls of air, then blew them out through his mouth, careful to make no sound with either the inhalations or the exhalations.

In and out, he breathed so deep it hurt his chest, hurt the raw scar from his month-old gunshot wound to his ribs. Over and over.

The entire time he'd been perfectly still, but now he looked up and around slowly, calmly, still hiding his deep breaths. The positioning of all the important elements on the boat were exactly the same, and the rugged jungle terrain on the far bank looked identical here to the way it had during the entire time he'd been on the speedboat.

One more massive breath—he felt he'd stretched his lungs to capacity over the past minute—and one more long, slow exhalation.

And then he did it.

His right foot slid out in front of him. He swiveled his hips to his right, his butt left the seat, and he spun around, ninety degrees, and took one squatted step backwards across the tiny deck; his bound hands reached out behind him and he grabbed the hilt of the big knife on the man's chest rig before the man even turned his head towards the movement.

Court launched forward in the direction of Red Bandana, drawing the knife from the sheath behind his back as he moved, and as he flew across the width of the speedboat, he sucked in the biggest lungful of air he'd taken in his entire life. He landed on his knees next to Red Bandana, still sucking in, but as part of the movement of propelling himself forward, his head came down, and he held in his air and bit into the plastic bag holding the cell phone, right next to Red Bandana's leg.

The leader of the group shouted out, but he only pulled his leg away in an automatic reaction to the movement.

By now most everyone on board was shouting; some had begun swiveling their weapons inward to the blurring motion in their midst, and a small man at the stern launched himself up and started moving past Fan and towards the big American.

Court thrust his body up, going from his knees to his feet, and then he launched himself into a backflip off the boat, right through the open space between two men sitting on the starboard-side gunwale.

As he flew through the air he caught a last glimpse of Fan Jiang, still sitting on the bench, his eyes wide with astonishment.

Court crashed through the surface of the muddy river and disappeared below.

The men on the boat were standing now, rifles swinging in all directions. The man at the helm realized his captive had gone overboard, so he reduced the throttle and turned hard to starboard, in the direction the man had leapt.

The other powerboats approached the area, Red Bandana stood and screamed, and men on all three watercraft began firing their rifles at the place where the big American disappeared.

B elow the brown surface the first thing Court did, before he began cutting with the knife, was to reverse his direction. Everyone had seen him backflip off the boat towards the nearest shore, and it made more sense he would head that way because of both its proximity and the fact that he and Fan had been heading west when they'd been caught, so by swimming back under the wake of the speedboat and kicking back to the east, he knew he'd cause most everyone on the boats to look in the wrong direction.

Once he'd put twenty or thirty yards between himself and the spot in the river where he went under, he continued swimming, but slower now, while he carefully turned the sharp knife around with the fingers of his bound hands. He knew dropping the knife would probably mean he'd either get shot or drown, because without the use of his hands there was no way he'd be able to swim far enough away from the boats before surfacing to where he would not be seen.

He began cutting, concentrating on working as efficiently as possible, and also on keeping his teeth clenched on the plastic bag in his mouth.

Court could hold his breath for three and a half minutes without any trouble, but not when he was exerting himself like this. He figured he'd have to surface in less than a minute and a half, so he kept kicking while he worked, knowing every single yard he traveled would reduce the risk he'd be spotted when he finally did come up for air.

At the one-minute mark he still had a lot of cutting to do, but he kept sawing, kept kicking, kept holding his breath. His lungs screamed and he felt the muscles in his legs and hands hurt from the lack of fresh oxygen, but he just kicked harder, sawed faster, told himself his body could shake off the effects of another thirty seconds of oxygen deprivation so much better than it could shake off the effects of an AK-47 burst to the back of his head.

When he'd finally cut all the rope away, he slid the knife into his waistband at the small of his back, then took the bag with the phone in it out of his mouth and shoved it down the front of his pants, and now he began exhaling as he swam furiously, his mind dulling, his sense of direction beginning to fail him.

He surfaced slowly and silently forty yards away from where he went under, but the speedboats had moved closer to the western shoreline, so he was even farther from the men looking for him. He took in a quick three-second breath and then slipped back under the brown surface, feeling the ecstasy of oxygen in his exhausted body.

He made it another minute before surfacing once more, and soon he was eighty yards from the boats and in the thick river grasses. By the time he looked back around, the speedboats were turning back to the south and continuing on their voyage.

They had their main prize, so they'd press on.

Court couldn't see Fan Jiang but he knew he was still with the river pirates, and he knew the young man must have felt like he'd been abandoned by the man who told him he'd keep him safe.

And Fan Jiang was absolutely right about that.

C ourt crawled up into the jungle, waterlogged and exhausted, his muscles and his mind spent.

He pulled the knife out of his pants and stabbed it into the ground next to him before he took out the phone. After turning it on and figuring out how to use the old simple device, he tapped in Suzanne Brewer's phone number.

He sucked a few tired breaths, then looked down at the tiny screen.

No Signal.

He sighed, then dropped the back of his head into the mud. "Well, that fucking figures."

Court rolled over onto his knees, grabbed the knife, then half crawled and half staggered into the woods.

N inety minutes later he'd found a clearing at the edge of a sweet potato farm from where he could see a well-traveled highway in the distance. He sat down behind a large palm tree at the edge of the clearing, pulled out the phone, and tried it again.

It took forty seconds before he heard the phone ring on the other end.

He breathed a fresh sigh of relief when the call was answered on the second ring.

"Brewer."

"Hi, Mom."

"One second." Court sat there a moment, either while Suzanne Brewer tried to figure out how to proceed with the challenge-response protocol, or while she recovered from being called "Mom" by an agent roughly her age. "Hi . . . son. So nice to hear from you. I was just watching your favorite documentary about Venus."

This was his challenge code, delivered oddly, but effectively. Court just replied, "The one about Vesuvius is even better." His response was delivered in the same cryptic form as the challenge because of the open line.

"Right," Brewer said, confirming his response. "What's this number you're calling from? Are you in . . ."

Court said, "Yep. 'Fraid so. I borrowed it from a friend."

"I see. Are you somewhere safe?"

"Actually, I was hoping *you* could tell *me* where I am."

Brewer's voice displayed incredulity. "You don't know where you are?"

"Long night. You know how it is."

"Right. I can do that, wait just a second."

Court's reply dripped with sarcasm. "Nothing but time on my end, Mom."

Suzanne Brewer had been lying on her back on her sofa in her office when the call came through, and it had been some struggle to get back up onto her knee scooter and over to her desk to grab it.

She saw from her computer that the call was coming from a Cambodian cell phone carrier, and her agent was telling her he didn't know where the hell he was, which was confusing to her, but she knew what she had to do.

She pressed a button on her desk that went to the operations center.

A tired voice came over the phone seconds later. "OpsCom."

"I need you to geolocate the origin of the call I'm on right now. How long to do that?"

"Landline or cell phone?"

"Cell. Out of Cambodia."

"Forty seconds for the tower, another minute to a minute and a half for the GPS coordinates."

"Go."

"On it."

Suzanne hung up from Operations/Communications, then went back to the line from Cambodia. She said, "I'm working on getting you fixed up." Violator would know that by "fix" she meant they were ascertaining his location. "What else can you tell me about . . . about your vacation?"

"I'm hoping you can help me catch a ride right now, to get me out of here. I was traveling with a friend, but we got separated, so it's just me."

"Who was the friend?"

"The one you told me not to meet up with on my own."

Brewer kept her voice flat, knowing this was an open line. "Well, we can talk more about that later. I'm just glad you are safe, son." That wasn't true; Violator would know it, but Brewer didn't care. "Are you okay?"

"I'm fine, considering how hard we partied last night."

Brewer closed her eyes in frustration. "I'm disappointed in you, son."

"I know, Mom. I'm your wild child."

"Your friends from Hong Kong? Did they come with you?"

"No, but I'm sure they are wondering what's happened to me."

Just then an instant message popped up on her computer screen. She opened it and saw it was from Ops/Com. A satellite map of Cambodia was attached, and she clicked on it, enlarged it, and enlarged it again. A small red star showed her the position of the cell phone in Violator's hand, down to an exactitude of less than five feet.

"How the *hell* did you get there?"

"I've got stories for the slide show when I get home." And then he said, "And I also have some serious questions for you and Dad. I'm looking forward to a long conversation the next time we talk."

Brewer blew out a sigh, still looking at the blip in a clearing by a field alongside a winding brown river in the wilds of Cambodia. She knew what Violator was telling her, and she knew it wasn't good. "Let me get to work here, try to find some way out of there for you."

Violator replied, "I know where my friend is going. I'm heading there next."

Brewer shook her head, but she let on none of her disapproval. She just said, "One thing at a time, son. I'll send someone to pick you up; not sure when it will be, so just sit tight."

"It's that or start working on a dugout canoe."

"I'll get you home, Tom."

Tom? Court would realize that he needed to remember the name she just gave him.

He started to say something else, but Brewer hung up. She wasn't one to chat. She had to work on his extraction, and she had to figure out just what to tell him about CIA's involvement in the operation to extract Fan Jiang from China.

CHAPTER

THIRTY-FOUR

The helicopter was nothing but a tiny insect when he first noticed it: a speck of black hanging just over the endless green delta to the south. It seemed to flicker in the morning haze, still miles away.

It grew quickly, though, and Court caught himself hoping it would develop into the shape of a Huey. He had an affinity for the old helicopters; his dad had flown around in them in Vietnam, and Court himself trained in them almost exclusively with the CIA's Autonomous Asset Development Program, simply because they were smaller and cheaper to operate than the Black Hawks that all but replaced them, and since he trained alone and the U.S. government still had lots of old Hueys at their disposal, that had been his principal ride.

And now that he was here in Southeast Asia, looking to the sky for a savior, he thought it would be appropriate to have a Huey sweep in and pick him up.

He got his wish. Court recognized the UH-1Y, called the Yankee, though everyone in the U.S. military referred to it as a Skid if it carried a weapon or a Slick if it was unarmed.

He'd expected the aircraft to be unmarked; back when he was in the CIA as a paramilitary operations officer he sometimes worked with members of the military, but they were always black-side types: Delta Force, SEAL Team 6, special operations communications and electronic intelligence personnel, or deep-cover spooks from the Defense Intelligence Agency. He never flew on marked military aircraft.

But as the Huey got closer, Court saw the unmistakable markings of the United States Marine Corps. And as the aircraft hovered over the LZ he saw it was a Skid; a crew chief sat in the open door with a big .50 caliber machine gun poking out of the side.

It occurred to him that this meant the U.S. Marine Corps was conducting an armed invasion into Cambodia on his behalf.

Awkward, Court thought. How did Brewer manage this?

The Huey touched down on the grass of the clearing next to the sweet potato field; by now a few locals stood on a nearby levee and looked on. Court hoped these farmers didn't have a cell phone on them, but he had bigger things to worry about.

He ran under the spinning rotors and climbed aboard. The crew chief directed him to a bench along the bulkhead, strapped him in as if Court had never ridden in a helicopter in his life, and then put a headset microphone on Court's head.

The crew chief wore the rank of corporal on his flight suit. Under the big flight helmet and the blacked-out visor and the microphone covering his face, Court figured the Marine was no more than twenty-one years old. Still, Court let the kid run the show; this was his aircraft, and the filthy unshaved American hanging out in the flatlands of Cambodia was just a passenger.

The young man spoke into his mic, and it came through Court's earphones. He could hear the excitement in the Marine's voice about conducting such an odd operation. "Sir, can I have your name, please?"

Court followed the instructions given to him by Brewer just three hours earlier. "I'm Tom."

"Then we're your chariot, sir. We'll get you out of here and take you wherever you want to go." He added, "As long as we have the fuel."

The crew chief clearly knew nothing about what was going on other than his aircraft's orders to get to a particular grid and pick up a man named Tom, then to follow the man's subsequent orders.

"What are my options?" Court asked.

The aircraft took off immediately, rising straight up into the sky. "We've got fuel to get you to Phnom Penh or Saigon. Which do you prefer?"

"How did you work that out with the governments of Cambodia and Vietnam?"

The crew chief stared back at Court; he looked like a big insect with his black visor covering his eyes. "No idea, sir. I think something is arranged; we were told we could go wherever, but that's a little bit above my pay grade."

Court just nodded. He wondered if CIA had asked permission for this flight, or if they were going to just ask forgiveness after the fact. He decided it was above his pay grade, as well, so he didn't stress about it.

Court asked, "Did you guys come off a ship?"

A nod of the big helmet. "Yes, sir. We're on the *Boxer*. It's an LHD. Uh . . . that's an assault ship. We're just leaving exercises in the South China Sea."

"And where are you heading?"

The kid couldn't hide a little grin. "Bangkok. Forty-eight hours liberty."

Court nodded thoughtfully, looking down at the sweet potato farm rolling away below. "You think the navy would mind giving me a ride?"

"Don't see why not, sir. They give us Marines a ride, and we can be a handful. I doubt you'd be much trouble at all."

Court nodded. "Bangkok works for me."

"Roger that, sir." The crew chief switched channels on his radio and told the pilot to return to the ship. Back on Court's channel, he said, "About fifty mikes flying time. Make yourself comfortable. You look like you could do with some chow."

"You buying?"

"Sure am." The corporal handed Court a huge bottle of water and an MRE. Court drank half the bottle without stopping, then looked at the bag holding the prepackaged meal. Chicken stew. Court smiled, took a knife from the crew chief, cut the package open, and began wolfing it down cold.

The crew chief split his time between looking out the open door—close enough to the fifty cal to where he could slide over and operate it if trouble arose—and trying to steal glances at the man sitting across from him. Court let it go for a minute, then looked up at the young man and shook his head once.

The crew chief turned away and focused his attention completely on the river and jungle racing by below.

Court's mind went back to his mission. He'd been forced to leave Fan with the Thai river pirates because there was no way he was getting the young man off that boat without both of them getting killed. It had been a hard choice to make, but Fan himself had given him a lead as to what group had kidnapped him.

A Thai criminal organization had Fan now, and it was up to Brewer and Colonel Dai, each working alone, to figure out exactly where they would take Fan Jiang.

Court had gone nearly twenty-four hours without checking in with Dai. He'd have to call him after he got settled on the *Boxer,* so for now he just rode in the back of the Skid and tried to work on some story that Dai would believe.

He knew he'd have to spin one hell of an epic tale of bullshit to keep Dai from putting a bullet in Don Fitzroy's head.

And, speaking of tales of epic bullshit, there was Suzanne Brewer. He would call her first, and he would find out what the fuck was *really* going on. There was more to this mission than he understood, and he worried he wasn't going to like what he found out about it.

Suzanne Brewer had spent the evening hours moving mountains to arrange for an agent to be picked up in the wilds of Southeast Asia and ferried out to a passing U.S. Navy vessel. When everything was settled she'd lain down on the sofa in her office, elevated her leg to reduce the lingering pain in the weeks-old injury, and fallen quickly asleep.

The trilling of the phone on her desk woke her at four a.m., sending her rocking up slowly, where she grabbed her crutches, not bothering with her knee scooter to get across the room.

Ten minutes later she was halfway through Violator's after-action report of the events near the Cambodian border the evening before. He was on the USS *Boxer* in a secluded area and able to talk unrestricted over the secure line. He told his story chronologically; he seemed to include all the important details, and Brewer took notes on a pad while he spoke. She wanted him to jump ahead to tell her what the hell happened to Fan Jiang, but she knew better than to interrupt his train of thought as long as he was providing relevant information.

But when he said, matter-of-factly, "I feel sure the attacking paramilitary force was Russian," she interrupted, because *this* was an especially important development.

"How do you know that?"

"I've seen Russian special operations forces in the field before. GRU Spetsnaz, FSB Spetsnaz, and SVR Zaslon. This looked like the way they did things. I can't really say why, but I'm sure they were Russian. It wouldn't make sense for GRU to be involved because this isn't a military operation, and the FSB mostly works closer to Russia's borders. I'm guessing this was a Zaslon team."

"That's pretty thin," Brewer chastised.

"Yes," Gentry admitted. "Unless you put some credence in the intuition of a guy who's been working in this field for twenty years."

"Fair enough."

"Oh, and there was a woman with them."

"A *woman?*"

"In an operational role. She wasn't stacking up with the Zaslon guys, but she breached the target location alone at the same time they did."

Brewer spoke with authority. "Zaslon doesn't have females. None of the Spetsnaz groups do."

"I'm just telling you what I saw. My guess is she was not on the team even though she was jocked up like the boys. She might have had operational command on the scene."

"Could she have been an SVR case officer?"

"Maybe," admitted Court. "But she didn't come out of an embassy. She had a definite edge to her. A non-official cover operative of some sort, but one with a lot more direct-action training than they normally give Russian NOCs."

"Could you identify her from images we have of Russian female SVR operatives?"

"No. No way. Saw just part of her face for less than a second through NVGs."

Brewer changed course. "Okay, enough about the attackers. Tell me about Fan Jiang."

Court relayed everything Fan had told him about why he ran, the family collateral he lost, and his strong desire to be done with all this.

When he stopped talking, she said, "Okay . . . well, as I told you several times, your job was *not* to make contact with Fan. It was to get positive ID and then notify me so I could send in others."

Court said, "And now I know why you didn't want me in contact with Fan myself."

"Meaning?" she asked, though she knew the answer.

"Meaning I've been lied to from the beginning. I was not told that Major Song Julong, the man watching Fan's parents, was an agent for the West. I wasn't told that Fan only got out of the mainland with the help of a service friendly and intimate with the CIA. Why is that?"

Brewer said, "I did not have authorization to tell you. That's really all you need to know."

Court asked, "Was this a Taiwanese op that we jumped in to save, or was this a joint op, where we were involved with the fuckup from the start?"

Brewer remained silent.

"You have to tell me."

Now she spoke. "Yes . . . Major Song contacted someone at Taiwanese intelligence and told him Fan Jiang would try to cross the border with no papers. They threw something together, didn't reach out to us for help. Didn't reach out to anyone. They got him over the border, but Fan was followed over by some of Colonel Dai's men. The Taiwanese intelligence agents waiting for him had to call off the pickup, leaving Fan all alone. He panicked and left, and the Taiwanese weren't able to reconnect with him. They came to us, finally, and when Fitzroy was pulled into the operation on the Chinese side, we saw an opportunity to help find Fan Jiang by having you make contact with Fitzroy."

"And why wasn't I told all this from the beginning?"

"It wasn't relevant."

"Usually when someone withholds information from me, it's because they are hiding something bigger. What am I missing?"

"You aren't missing anything. We couldn't expose Taiwanese intelligence if you were captured when you went in to see Fitzroy. The knowledge that Taiwan helped with the defection could have started a shooting war between the two Chinas."

Court sighed, but he seemed to let the matter drop. "Look, Fan definitely does *not* want to go to the USA. He wants to go to Taiwan."

Brewer sniffed now. "You sound like you give a shit. It's not your job to give a shit. It was your job to find him so SAD can pick him up."

"It makes things tougher that he is unwilling. If this is a joint operation, he needs to go to Taipei. It shouldn't be that big a deal."

"No promises," Brewer said, and then she began railing at Violator about losing his means of communication during the op. "We could have picked Fan up hours before he was kidnapped by the Thais if you'd had your phone."

"I know that. Shit happens in the field, Brewer."

"That is what people say when they screw up. It becomes an excuse for their incompetence."

Court let it go. She was his handler and she was right. He'd fucked up, and he'd let her criticize him about it even though she was probably sitting there in a nice office with a cranberry muffin and a cup of coffee in front of her.

He said, "I'm going to Bangkok; I'll talk to Colonel Dai and get help from the Chinese. If you've got somebody better than me to nab Fan Jiang, you go ahead and get them on it."

"How can you go to Bangkok? The Thai gangsters who took Fan Jiang have seen you."

"The guys who saw me in Cambodia were smugglers. River rats. Fan will be handed over three more times before he makes it into Bangkok. Fan will be in Bangkok with senior management. I'm not worried about being compromised."

Brewer blew out a long sigh. "Violator, you probably don't need me telling you this, but this operation is not going well. I'm talking to Hanley as soon as he gets to the office."

"To tell him what?"

Brewer did not respond.

"To tell him *what*?"

"To tell him that we need to rethink our next steps."

"You can sit there and think about whatever the hell you want. I'm going after Fan Jiang."

"If you are told to stand down, you *will* stand down."

"Matt won't pull me off this. The stakes are too high."

"Exactly. They are too high to have one operator, one who is possibly exposed to the opposition, running around on a solo mission to grab this high-value target. Your initial job was to find out what the Chinese and

Fitzroy knew about the location of Fan Jiang. That intel is a week old and half a continent removed from where you are now. At this point, I consider your continued pursuit of the target an unnecessary compromise."

"I got damn close, Brewer. Hell, I had my hands on that kid's neck."

"And yet here we are." She let the comment hang in the air, the crackling phone line the only noise in Court's ear for a moment. Then she said, "Do you think it is a simple thing to order a Marine Corps helicopter to fly an in extremis exfiltration op into a nation like Cambodia? You think that was what I and the rest of the Agency needed to be focusing on last night?"

And with that, Violator hung up the phone.

Brewer looked across her desk at a sheet of paper lying there. On it was the direct line to the XO of the USS *Boxer*. With one call to him she could have a dozen Marines with M16s pull Violator off his bunk and throw him in the brig till the ship docked. The CIA SAD team in the area could then bring him back to the States and watch over him till the operation was concluded.

But she did not make the call. To do that she'd need the backing of Director Hanley, and she was not going to disturb him at home. It would make her appear weak and indecisive.

She grabbed her crutches and headed back to her sofa. She'd allow herself a few hours of sleep before she got back up, and as soon as Hanley came to work she'd talk to him and shut this entire operation down. With a little luck she'd be permanently free of Violator by midmorning, and her career would be back on track.

CHAPTER

THIRTY-FIVE

Court spent the entire afternoon in a small windowless compartment deep in the bowels of the USS *Boxer*. His door was shut and he never saw the captain, the XO, or the lieutenant colonel commanding the battalion of Marines on board. He barely even spoke to the Marine who led him down the ladderways and up the passageways to this little claustrophobic space.

He assumed Brewer had arranged everything. His compartment had a single bunk and an attached head, a small refrigerator with water, a coffin locker stocked with packaged food, civilian clothing, and medical equipment. A small desk attached to the wall was adorned with a laptop with Internet access, and two phones: a smartphone and a satellite phone. Accessories for the phones and computer lay on top of a small backpack.

Court wondered if someone on the *Boxer* had gotten all this equipment from sailors on board in exchange for cash from the CIA. Logistics and outfitting wasn't his department, but he was used to working alone, and he had to take into account the possibility for compromise in every face of the operation.

Court spent half the afternoon appreciating the fact that he was able to lay low here. The other half of the afternoon he questioned whether he was a prisoner. He wondered if Brewer had given orders to the Marines to watch over him and keep him, essentially, in a cell here on the amphibious assault ship till she found a way to get him shit-canned from his assignment.

He figured he'd only know the truth when it was time to leave. If he found himself on his own in Bangkok, then Brewer was leaving him in play. If a dozen young testosterone-filled bald-headed dudes in brown held guns on him and ordered him to stay on board till someone came to collect him . . . then he would know this was over.

That would mean Fan *might* be lost to the Thais, or to the Russians, or to the Chinese.

It would also mean, with absolute *certainty*, that Sir Donald Fitzroy was a dead man.

Court worried it might already be too late for Fitz. Going over a day without checking in with Dai might just send the Chinese colonel down to the basement of his big house on the Peak with a gun in his hand and Sir Donald's head in his sights.

By early evening, when they were just a few miles from port in Bangkok, Court was finally able to connect with a Thai cell network, and he locked himself into his small room and dialed a number on the smartphone using the unbreakable off-the-shelf encryption app he'd been using throughout this operation.

Court sat down on his bunk and waited, knowing he was initiating a very difficult and important conversation.

Dai answered immediately. *"Way, ni hao?"* Yes, hello?

Court decided he needed to go on offense from the outset to keep Dai focused on his operation. "Your boys did something stupid yesterday in Saigon. It's made my work a lot more difficult."

"Where are you?"

"I'm on a dry-goods hauler, heading for Bangkok."

"Why are you going to Bangkok?"

"Because I'm on Fan Jiang's heels. Let me guess. You don't even know he's in Thailand. Are your guys still running around Vietnam looking for him?"

"Fan is in Bangkok? With who?"

"I'll need your help for that. I chased him into Cambodia; then he got picked up on a river by a group of criminals run out of Bangkok. I think he was kidnapped. That's pretty much all I know."

Court worried Dai would want a play-by-play of last night's events, and he was right.

"Back up and tell me everything that happened."

Shit, thought Court. *Here goes nothing.*

Court knew how to lie; he used vast swaths of truth to sell the verisimilitude of the event, and only changed details that would have compromised him in the smallest manner possible.

Court explained that he had discovered the old colonial villa in the Mekong Delta after tailing the BMW sedan to the area, but he was caught inside the property and unable to move after the arrival of the People's Army infantry. This was true, more or less. Then he recounted the arrival of the Russians and relayed his concerns that they would try to kidnap Fan.

The only major changes to the facts began when Fan and the other two men left the barn of the villa. Court's new version had Fan escaping alone to the west, making it miles into Cambodia with Court close on his tail, where Fan was picked up by a group of Thai gangsters in powerboats.

He worried Dai would find it hard to believe Fan could accomplish so much by himself, and Court briefly considered telling Dai the Vietnamese men Fan escaped with had helped him for most of the way. But he wasn't sure Dai didn't have someone on the ground at the villa by now. If Court told the Chinese commander the two guys lying dead in the field behind the villa had helped Fan escape over the Cambodian border, Dai would know Court was full of shit.

There was one huge flaw in Court's story, of course. He could not reasonably explain why he did not contact Dai at any point to bring dozens of armed Chinese agents down upon the scene to kill everything that moved and eliminate the compromise.

No, he could not reasonably explain it, but he could *unreasonably* explain it. "My damn phone got wet in the rice paddies during the infiltration. I couldn't establish comms till I got a new one, which I stole from a sailor on this ship."

When the American finished his story and his explanation of why he'd been radio silent for a day, he waited quietly until Colonel Dai replied. And when Dai replied, it was instantly obvious that Court's powers of influence and persuasion weren't going to work on the colonel.

"I know everything there is to know about Fan Jiang, which means I know he could not possibly escape from Con Ho Hoang Da, the Russians, *and* you, then travel overland seven and a half miles, crossing a national border only to be picked up on a river by Thai criminals. I do not believe your story for an instant. I do not know what your game is, but I do know that your efforts have failed to date, and a price must be paid for that. I will encourage you to do what you said you would do, by showing you my willingness to do what *I* said *I* would do."

"What are you talking about?" Court asked, although he was afraid he knew *exactly* what Dai was talking about.

Dai did not answer, which gave Court an immediate feeling of disquiet. There was a shuffling over the phone, and then someone said something in Mandarin, but Court could not tell who was speaking.

Other voices now, their words indecipherable.

The sound of footsteps; Court sat up straighter on the bunk. "Dai? Dai? Talk to *me*. Don't forget, *I'm* the one you're pissed at. I'm also the one close to the target. I'm the one you have to keep on mission, and if you do anything—"

Court heard the first voice he recognized, the first words he understood. Sir Donald Fitzroy was far from the telephone, but he spoke loud enough for Court to hear him. "What's all this? What do you want?"

Court shouted now into the phone. "I swear to you, Colonel, if you do it, I will fucking walk from this job, and you will *never* get Fan! He'll end up in Moscow or D.C. before the week's out! You'll be shot, and your nation's secrets will go to your enemies."

Either Court was not persuasive, or Colonel Dai was not listening. Fitzroy shouted in alarm, and then he screamed. Court knew the sounds of a grown man in abject terror, and he knew the sounds of a grown man in hyperbolic, excruciating pain.

And over the next several seconds, Sir Donald Fitzroy made both sounds.

Court stopped yelling into the phone. He put his head down between his knees, still sitting on the little bunk. Still with his phone to his ear. The shrieks of pain and horror and pain continued for another half minute. Then it went quiet for a time, before Court could hear heavy, gruff breathing in the background.

He sat up quickly. Sir Donald was still alive.

"Don? Don?"

And after what seemed like an eternity, Fitzroy came on the line. His words were spoken in soft wheezes; Court could hear thick mucus in his throat, and the old man was obviously in agony. "I . . . I am here, Court."

Court squeezed the phone tighter. "What did they do?"

It took Fitzroy a long time to answer, and the stress in his voice made him hard to decipher. "Two fingers . . . sawed off with a straight razor. My fucking hand's bleeding like a headless chicken!"

Court's jaw clenched and his eyes stared across the room at nothing. "I'm sorry, Don. I'm trying."

"Sod the lot of them, Court! Just turn around and go, leave all this, this *shit* behind! Look . . . this is bigger than you know. This whole operation is worse than you can possibly understand. Just go. Walk away from this insanity while you still can."

"I can't do that."

Dai was back on the line now. "No . . . you can*not* do that. You are being paid for a job. If you complete the job you will also earn the bonus of retrieving Sir Donald . . . or most of him . . . or whatever is left of him. Whether you fly him first class out of Hong Kong on British Airways or have him shipped in refrigerated freight on a cargo plane . . . that is a question of how well, and how quickly, you fulfill your end of the transaction."

Court wished he could reach through the line and gouge the colonel's eyes out. Instead he just said, "I'll get Fan in Bangkok. Just calm the fuck down and give me some time."

"Time has always been the one precious commodity in this endeavor. Now there are two. Time . . . and the body parts of your friend here. You give me results, or you will soon run out of both."

Court sighed. "I've told you. He is my meal ticket, not my friend."

"Yes . . . you told me that. But you gave away your true motivation by your tone just now. If Fitzroy was just the man who could secure future contracts for you, the loss of two of his fingers would not be nearly as stressful for you."

"That's not—"

"Now . . . go to work." Colonel Dai disconnected the call. Court dropped the phone on the bunk next to him and leaned his head back against the wall of the little compartment.

CHAPTER

THIRTY-SIX

Director of the CIA's National Clandestine Service Matt Hanley had promised Suzanne Brewer a "direct feed" to him, meaning she could bypass everyone in the normal chain of command, report to Hanley directly, or come to him if she ever needed anything. She knew better than to abuse this privilege, but this morning when she found that Hanley was attending a daylong meeting in D.C. and would not be in the office till midday, she drove herself straight to the location and called Hanley's secretary to secure five minutes of face time with him.

Two of Hanley's men met Brewer in the parking lot of the Department of State; one parked her car while the other led her inside through a side entrance. She was on her crutches; the CIA officer offered to carry her purse but she declined, although she did allow him to hold open the door for her because there was no way she could have managed it on her own.

A female aide to the D/NCS joined them, and they went past a large conference room with guards posted outside and into a small, unoccupied anteroom.

A breakfast table had been set up with coffee, pastries, and bagels with butter, cream cheese, and jellies, and Suzanne was told to make herself as comfortable as possible. It was ten a.m. She had eaten breakfast from a snack machine at her desk three hours earlier and downed enough coffee since seven a.m. to make her twitchy, so instead she just sat at the table and ignored the food.

Matt Hanley lumbered in minutes later wearing a gray sport coat and dark slacks, his tie and collar cinched around his thick ruddy neck in a manner that Suzanne Brewer felt had to be painful.

"Hey, Suzanne. Don't get up." He headed straight to the breakfast setup, as she'd assumed he would.

Brewer said, "Sorry to pull you out of your meeting."

He poured himself a cup of coffee, grabbed a pastry, and took it over to her table. As he did so he said, "Not a problem. This is going to be a wasted day. I had no idea the amount of dumb shit I'd have to do in this job." He took a bite of the apple Danish and sipped the coffee. "What's up with our boy?"

Brewer blew out her air. "Where to start? Okay, Violator tracked senior leadership of Con Ho Hoang Da to a protected compound near the Cambodian border. He . . . I mean Violator, entered the compound, but shortly thereafter, some twenty-five or so Vietnamese military arrived, pinning him in position."

Hanley's eyebrows rose, but he did not interrupt.

"As he tried to make his escape, a group of nine paramilitaries hit the compound—"

"Chinks?"

He meant Chinese, Suzanne Brewer knew, but still she was taken aback. She hid it. "Negative. Violator thinks they might have been Russian."

"*Shi-it*. Same gang he saw in HK?"

"That is his assertion, yes."

Hanley blew out a chestful of air. "Fuckin' Russians. We knew they might show up. Okay. Chinks and Ivans. Go ahead."

"Uh . . . right. A protracted gunfight began, and in it, Violator somehow managed to make contact with the subject, Fan Jiang."

"Contact?"

"He escaped the compound with Fan Jiang during the confrontation between this undetermined group and the Vietnamese."

Hanley took another bite of the pastry. "Damn, he's good."

"Violator and Fan made it into Cambodia, where they encountered Thai criminals operating on a river. Violator feels sure this was not random; they had been sent there specifically to kidnap Fan. During this confrontation Fan was taken by the Thais, and Violator escaped."

"And what did Gentry learn from Fan?"

"Fan told him he was aided by a Taiwanese intelligence officer at the Hong Kong border, and then found himself alone in HK."

The director of NCS nodded slowly and thoughtfully. "We can work with that."

"Right," Suzanne said. "We dodged a bullet, clearly only because Fan doesn't understand what is going on. But Violator is suspicious. He doesn't get why Taiwan isn't still involved, and he doesn't get why we didn't tell him any of this. I told him what we agreed, and I think he bought it."

Hanley rubbed his face. "Where is Gentry now?"

"He's on a Marine landing craft heading into Bangkok. He has no papers, no local currency."

Hanley did not show the outrage over Violator's failures that Brewer had expected, even hoped for.

Instead he just shrugged and said, "We can get him set up."

"But . . . but *why*, Matt? We have assets all over Bangkok. Explain to me how any one of them isn't in a better position than Violator to locate and take possession of Fan Jiang. He's been seen by the Thais, and it's possible he's known to the Russians now. Violator was the key to getting us close to Fitzroy and the Chinese after Fan. That value has expired. Why don't we pull him out and you can send other assets after Fan?"

Hanley leaned forward on the table. Even though there was no one in the room, he was discussing a CIA Special Access Program, so he spoke softly. "We need to keep our actions deniable in this, remember? Taking Fan without the Chinese knowing we took Fan will exponentially increase the value of the product we get from him. Gentry can help with that. The Chinese don't know he's with us, the Russians don't know he's with us, and even if the Thai gangsters compromised him somehow . . . well, they're Thai gangsters. I like Court's chances against them."

Brewer pushed back on another front. "Matt . . . we knew from the beginning that bringing this asset into this program would help us keep our involvement hidden. But in light of what this agent has done in his past . . . I am concerned he might not be as reliable as you insinuate."

Hanley had finished his Danish. Now he gulped his hot coffee. "In what way?"

She hesitated, then said, "What if he's *too* successful? What if he uncovers the full truth about this operation?" She leaned forward herself. "There is a volatility to him. An unpredictability. What if he finds out he's being played . . . and he goes rogue?"

Hanley said, "Strictly speaking . . . he's *not* being played. He is on the operation we sent him on. His mission is Fan. Anything beyond his narrow mission parameters is not his problem. Yes, we lied to him, but only because his moral code would put the lives of good people in jeopardy. We need him; we're doing the right thing, so he was manipulated somewhat. Not knowing what he doesn't know doesn't make him more safe; it makes him more . . . comfortable with what he's doing."

Brewer said, "But if he learns certain things, certain things about the full scope of this operation, then—"

Hanley spoke over her. "He *will* rebel." He shrugged his huge shoulders. "But it's your responsibility to ensure he doesn't find out anything beyond his mission parameters." Hanley took another gulp. "Anything more than he's already figured out, that is."

"Yes, sir," she said, but her heart wasn't in it.

Hanley detected this. "Violator is unpredictable. You look at him as if he's a ticking time bomb, but I know he has to be the way he is in order to do the job we've given him. More than anyone I've ever seen, Court possesses the gift of aggression. And believe me, it *is* a gift. He'd be facedown dead long ago if he hesitated, if he wavered or thought his moves through. He's as smart and crafty a tactician as exists in this world, but when it comes time for it, he can act and act and kill and kill, no quarter given."

"No argument there. My concern is that his gift for aggression has been used against us in the past, and it might be directed towards us again if he learns about certain aspects of Operation Aces High."

Hanley raised a finger. "He won't *ever* hear *anyone* breathe a word of Aces High. Because if he did, you're absolutely right. He'd go off reservation, he'd become a satellite adrift, and he'd plunge back to Earth like a motherfucking missile."

Brewer cocked her head. "Help me with your metaphor. The CIA is Earth?"

Hanley shook his head. "No . . . you are." He winked. "You're the handler." Hanley looked to his watch. "Sorry, I've got to get back to that bullshit in the conference room. Outfit Gentry with whatever he needs. Help him locate the Thais who are holding the target. Keep our official cover assets the hell out of his way, and let him do his thing. He'll find us Fan Jiang. When he does, send in Ground Branch."

"Yes, sir."

He pointed again. He was a big man, and the gesture was intimidating. "But keep Court's blinders on. We don't want him to know how the fuck we fell into this whole mess in the first place."

"Right," Suzanne said. "Because if he knew that, he'd probably come back to D.C. and kill us all." The comment was sarcasm. Gentry had just left the D.C. area, and he had wreaked havoc trying to find answers to why the CIA turned on him years ago.

Hanley ignored the quip and turned for the door. "Do keep me updated."

Brewer stood herself and reached for her crutches. With unmasked discomfort she just said, "Sure thing."

CHAPTER

THIRTY-SEVEN

F an Jiang had arrived in the capital of Thailand from Cambodia in an old Partenavia twin-engine aircraft, surrounded on the flight by Thai men with guns who had nothing to say to him about where he was going and what plans they had for him when he got there. From the airport he'd been taken directly to a large commercial building somewhere in the heart of the city. There he was led to an elevator, then back out again on the fifth floor. He passed through a massive open room the size of a city block with literally hundreds of men and women working at computer terminals in little cubes. Fan assumed there were more rooms like it on other floors of the building, but he could not know for sure, because he wasn't given much of a tour. Instead he was simply led through this large room and then down a barren concrete hallway. A back room at the end of the hall was guarded by a pair of armed men in security guard uniforms sitting in plastic chairs. Fan Jiang was directed through the door.

That was three days ago, and he had not left this room since.

This windowless space that had become his home was set up like a cell, which Fan found appropriate, because he was, indeed, a prisoner. There was a sleeping mat on a cold tile floor, and a bucket for his waste, just as he'd had on the boat that took him from Hong Kong to Vietnam. But this room differed from the storage space on the cargo ship in that here he had a laptop computer on a desk that, it had been explained to him, was attached to the company's network.

Even though the portions of the building he had walked through appeared to be just any other technology-based business, there was one feature in this tiny room that reminded him that he was being held by a criminal organization: a large steel eyebolt cemented into the floor in the center of the room. Fan bumped his feet on it while he sat at the desk, and he surmised others had been kept here at the desk in chains.

It was a horrifying thought, but from what he knew about this place and the people who ran it, it was not surprising.

The group that held Fan Jiang now was the Chamroon Syndicate, and Fan's earlier research into criminal organizations had taught him this was both one of the most successful and most notorious transnational organizations in Southeast Asia. Not only were they in the business of computer hacking, identity fraud, and spear-phishing schemes; the syndicate was also heavily involved in heroin exportation and human trafficking, primarily bringing Eastern European women to serve as prostitutes for wealthy Asians, and Asian women to work as prostitutes in Central and Western Europe.

Fan knew enough about the group to understand they were horrible people, and this was before he'd even met any of their leadership.

Fan realized he was now involved with thugs many orders of magnitude more dangerous than the Vietnamese gang and the Hong Kong–based Triad organization who'd protected him before and, unlike those instances, where Fan was a willing participant to earn his safety and shelter, here he was a simple captive.

When he first arrived, a severe Mandarin-speaking woman told him what they wanted of him. His captors somehow knew exactly who he was and what value he could provide them. As his captors were in the business of, among other things, computer crime, it was no surprise they demanded he engage in criminal acts of fraud via the Internet.

For the first two days he'd given them nothing, and the woman had told him the men watching his work were getting frustrated with his lack of output.

He decided he did not want to test their patience, so today he decided he would show some progress.

At three p.m. Fan leaned back in his chair and rubbed the fatigue in his eyes. He had been working nonstop for nine hours, but his labors had borne fruit. He had just successfully breached a German-based mortgage company and pulled out all the personal data of over 134,000 individuals who had bought homes or condos in and around Berlin. With all the data on these German citizens, the men and women working in the massive boiler room down the hall could then open up credit cards, set up offshore shells in fictitious names, and purchase goods virtually using the fraudulent identities. The goods could be shipped and then sold, and the received funds wired into the offshore accounts in small increments that raised no suspicions.

An hour after he sent all the personnel data in a file to the men and women working in the boiler room, Fan Jiang shoveled stale rice into his mouth with his chopsticks. As he reached for a sip of tepid tea, he was surprised by the sound of the bolts sliding on the door to his room.

The door opened and a young man in a black suit, a tie, and a dark purple shirt entered, flanked by two other men, both wearing suits and ties themselves. Fan saw the butts of handguns sticking out of the belts of all three men.

They all eyed Fan up and down as if he were a caged animal, but he knew the one in the middle was in charge.

"My name is Kulap Chamroon," the man said in English. "You might know that my father started this organization thirty-five years ago. But you might not know he is just a figurehead now. My brother and I share ownership of the Chamroon Syndicate."

Fan thought the man seemed defensive, agitated, and a little jittery. He knew nothing about the man's father, nothing about the structure of the organization at all, for that matter.

Still, Fan bowed. "Yes, sir."

Kulap Chamroon said, "The records you stole from the company in Germany have my people working very hard. That is good. How long till you get into the other networks on the list you were given?"

Fan cocked his head. He *had* been given a file with desirable targets on the first day he arrived. But there were hundreds of companies listed. Surely this man didn't expect Fan to break into all of them. That would take years.

He said, "I can try the next on the list. But . . . may I ask how long I will be kept here?"

Kulap smiled, glanced to the two men with him, and then raised an eyebrow. "You don't like the accommodations?"

"It's just . . . I wish to go to Taiwan. I had an arrangement with two other organizations. I would provide them with help in my field, and then they would repay me by helping me get to Taipei."

Kulap Chamroon nodded dramatically. "An interesting proposition. You are saying you can work for me for a short time, and then I can help you be on your way. Is that it?"

"Yes, sir."

"Here's my counterproposal." The young man drew his pistol and stepped forward. He jammed it in Fan's left ear and pressed it hard, then took Fan's head with his other hand and pushed it in even deeper. The seated Chinese man let out a squeal of terror.

Chamroon said, "How about you work for me for as long as I tell you to, and in exchange for that I don't kill you? Does that seem like a fair deal?"

Fan just sat in front of his computer, his eyes shut tight and his hands squeezing the desk. "Yes. Thank you, sir."

Chamroon pulled the gun away, spun it on a finger, and jabbed it back into his pants. *"Di mak." Very good.* "Just remember. We don't fuck around here in Bangkok like they do in Saigon and Hong Kong. The Syndicate is the biggest and the best. We have the most money, the most guns, and the most power. You do what you are told, *when* you are told, or else you are a dead man. There is nothing else for you to worry about."

Fan just looked down to the floor.

Kulap Chamroon turned and left through the door without another word.

CHAPTER

THIRTY-EIGHT

The sleek black Mercedes sedan turned onto Royal City Avenue Alley, slowed to allow well-dressed pedestrians to pass at a crosswalk, then immediately found itself locked in bumper-to-bumper traffic. It was midnight, still just a little early for the real action in all the nightclubs on both sides of the street here, but the crowds seemed to be out in full force and the lines at the best clubs were already long and getting longer by the minute.

In the back of the Mercedes a white man in his thirties adjusted his cuff links and looked out at the mass of people all around him. It was a Thursday night, but the sheer number of partiers in the area cast a vibe that felt like New Year's Eve.

And all these civilians made Court Gentry a little nervous. He had a feeling about tonight, a sense that something could go wrong, and in Gentry's world, wrong usually involved danger to those in close proximity to him. So as he looked around from the back of the luxury sedan at the hundreds of people here in the flashy Royal City Avenue neighborhood of Bangkok, he did not see happy young partiers out for a good time.

He saw potential innocent bystanders. Would-be collateral damage.

He pushed away the thought; he had every intention of taking things slow and easy this evening, and anyway, how much trouble could he really start himself without a damn gun?

He'd asked for a piece when the Agency outfitted him for his work here in Bangkok, but Brewer had forbidden it. He was here for recon only; he wouldn't need a weapon, or so said the woman who Court imagined hadn't left the safety of Langley in years.

He let it go. He wasn't thinking about shooting up Bangkok. He was thinking about Fitzroy, about Fan, and once in a while he was even thinking about running from all this, but he knew that was more a fantasy than a plan. He had a deal with CIA and an obligation to Fitz, and he had a feeling that if he didn't get to Fan Jiang first, the Chinese or the Russians would, and either of those outcomes would be damaging to the interests of the United States.

As he rode in the back of the Mercedes, the stark change in Court's situation was not lost on him. Four nights ago he had been chest deep in muck in the Mekong Delta, tearing leeches from his waterlogged skin and swatting bugs on his face. Now he sat in a sleek black Mercedes S550 as it caught the eyes of many of the passersby. He wore a gray virgin wool Tom Ford suit and a black silk Forzieri necktie. His black leather Dolce & Gabbana derby shoes cost more than most people in Thailand made in four months, and the watch on his wrist shone gold, the face read Panerai, and it was a style that went for no less than twelve grand in the luxury shops around Bangkok.

But as was normally the case with the American in the back of the hired car, all was not as it seemed. The watch was a knockoff, the suit was off-the-rack and was to be handed back to CIA station before he left town, and the Mercedes, while expensive, was only here to drop him off. He planned on taking a rented four-door Toyota parked near his destination back to his hotel.

Court had been in Bangkok nearly four days, and in that time he'd accomplished little other than establishing his cover. He had a room at the five-star Okura Prestige; he had clothes and accessories from the upscale shops; he had a new haircut; and most of the visible bug bites, scrapes, and bruises from his time in Vietnam and Cambodia had disappeared from view.

But as late as this afternoon, he did not have any idea where to find Fan Jiang.

Then Suzanne Brewer came through. He called to check in, as he had done each day since he arrived, and she explained that Fan himself had slipped a cryptic identifier into a message received by the U.S. embassy in Taiwan.

Brewer explained, "We know he is being held by the Chamroon Syndicate, and we know he is trying to inform Taiwan of his situation. His correspondence must be monitored by the gangsters with him, because all he communicated was an encrypted SOS and the Chinese characters for 'Funky Monkey,' his handle."

Court asked, "Did the Taiwanese tell us this, or are we monitoring the Taiwanese covertly?"

Brewer hesitated. "That is something you don't need to know."

Court replied, "Actually, I do. If the Taiwanese told us directly, then maybe the Russians don't know about it. But if we gleaned that intel from Taiwan's secure comms, it's a fair bet the Russians have the same capability. I need to know if the Russians are coming for Fan in Bangkok. Trust me, that was news that would have been helpful in Hong Kong and in Vietnam."

Brewer replied, "I don't have the authority to answer your question. I'm sorry, Violator. It's as simple as that."

"Then connect me with someone who does. I want Hanley to tell me, or for him to allow you to do it."

Brewer snapped now, "I am your handler. You will *not* circumvent my authority."

Court didn't really have a way to contact Matt Hanley directly. He knew where the man lived, so theoretically he could have mailed him a letter, but he doubted he could just call some extension at Langley and ask to be put through to the director of the National Clandestine Service.

Brewer was right; she was his lifeline, and she was being stubborn. But Court let it go, because there was no time to waste. She had delivered time-sensitive information that Court had to act on immediately.

Namely, Court had to get himself to a particular nightclub this evening.

While the head of the Chamroon Syndicate was the seventy-five-year-old who started the group in the 1980s, all the operational leadership were young, wealthy, and ostentatious, including Nattapong and Kulap Chamroon, sons of the founder. They spent their days overseeing drug trafficking and computer crime and prostitution and extortion rackets, but their nights were spent blowing their money.

The Black Pearl nightclub was one of dozens of locations owned by the organization, but the local CIA station had pegged it as one of the main hangouts for the big shots in the group. Tonight, Brewer had explained to Court, a well-known European DJ was booked there for one night only, and Brewer's research into the group told her it was an absolute given that senior members of Chamroon's second generation of leadership would be in attendance.

She'd sent Court dossiers and digital images of the syndicate's main players, and then she told him to use whatever means he had at his disposal to locate Fan. She suggested he go in cover to the Black Pearl, get eyes on the leadership of the organization, and size up their entourage. If he could find a way to isolate a senior member from his security, then Court could press him for details about Fan's location.

It was clear to Court she was telling him to kidnap and possibly even torture, but as Court was an agent of the CIA and not a direct employee of the CIA, and since Brewer had not used either of the words "kidnap" or "torture," the CIA was in the clear, no matter what he did this evening.

But Brewer stressed again, as she had done at every single step of Court's operation, that SAD Ground Branch operatives were in the area and ready to act on Court's intel.

Getting a table or even gaining entrance to the Black Pearl was no simple affair, especially for a big event like the DJ's appearance tonight, but Court found a way. He was booked on the executive level of one of the most luxurious hotels in the city. Instead of having the local CIA station work to get him admittance to tonight's big event, Court simply walked down the hall to the concierge, explained he was a big fan of the Dutch DJ, and gave the woman working there a smile and a hundred dollars' worth of baht, the local currency. He told her the money was hers either way, but he would appreciate any help she could give him.

And, just like that, he received a call from the concierge an hour later letting him know he would have his name on a list at the front door and a private table for two inside.

Now Court walked to the entrance of the Black Pearl alone, passing the forward end of the block-long rope line of beautiful people waiting to get through the door. He spoke with a bouncer wearing a headset and holding a clipboard, passed the man one thousand baht, or thirty bucks, tucked into a friendly handshake along with a request for an out-of-the-way spot overlooking the action, and soon he was led by a beautiful hostess to a small table along a silk-curtained wall on a mezzanine overlooking the main dance floor and stage of the nightclub.

He flipped off the light at his table, ordered a Johnnie Walker Black on ice, and sat there in the low light.

The club was filling up quickly, the dance music was pumping, and the lights and fog were working in sync. Massive crystalline chandeliers hung over the entire floor, and the lights projected on them and through them pulsed with the beat.

Court looked around at the lavish establishment and wished he were instead sitting alone in a dockside Irish pub, a few stools down the bar from a couple of grumpy old men to listen in on for entertainment.

The Black Pearl wasn't his scene.

At one a.m. the DJ from Amsterdam took the stage and the crowd went insane. The music to Court wasn't quite as loud as an M249 machine gun firing cyclic, but it was damn close, and as far as Court was concerned, the noise of a gunfight was much more creative and interesting than this mindless and repetitive thumping and squawking.

Still, he pretended he enjoyed it and hoped like hell he was pulling it off despite the fact that he'd much rather listen to someone slaughter livestock.

The loud music and the crazed lighting effects inside the venue made surveillance difficult, to say the least, but Court had been eyeing a roped-off set of three crescent-shaped tables next to the dance floor and just to the left of the stage, expecting any Chamroon Syndicate players to head straight there if they came into the building.

At one thirty Court was moving his head with the thunderous music, nursing a scotch slowly, acting like one of the thousands of rich international businessmen he'd seen during his years traveling around the world. He'd brushed off several attempts by prostitutes to sit down and join him, and other tries by young local girls hoping to score bottles of champagne off a rich tourist almost old enough to be their father.

After one such rebuff, Court looked back to the roped-off tables, and then he looked away. A group of about twenty men and women were in the process of sitting down, and although Court realized he would not be able to ID faces from this distance and in these conditions, by the impeccable suits worn by the men and the obvious beauty and glamorous clothing of the women sitting with them, he felt confident the Chamroon Syndicate was in the house.

Several bodyguards stood at the VIP rope, and a couple more stood behind the tables, on either side of the entourage. The guards all faced out, hands clasped in front of them, and Court imagined they would be armed with handguns.

This didn't scare him . . . in fact, it pleased him, because Court knew where he could obtain a pistol if things started to go downhill around here.

He glanced sporadically towards the VIP area. As far as he could tell, all the men sitting at the tables behind the rope were Thai, and all the women European other than one lady in a sheer blue dress who appeared to be of African descent. There were fourteen females to five males, and six of the women seemed huddled especially close to one male who sat at the center of the middle table by the dance floor.

This screwed with the female-to-male ratio for the other men in the VIP lounge, but the guy getting the attention from the six girls didn't seem to care.

Court wondered if this guy could possibly be either Nattapong or Kulap Chamroon, who were brothers and the sons of Panit Chamroon, the man who'd founded the Syndicate thirty-five years earlier by bringing various disparate criminal enterprises in Thailand under one umbrella. He'd seen pictures of both brothers, but they looked so much alike Court couldn't tell who he was looking at across the smoky dance floor. Brewer's dossier on the group, which Court had just finished reading in his hotel room when he got the call that his car had arrived, told him Nattapong spent more time in Bangkok while Kulap traveled regularly on syndicate business, so odds were this was the former, but it didn't really matter to Court. He felt certain either one of the Chamroon brothers would know where Fan Jiang was being held.

Once Court established that he had eyes on people who could tell him what he wanted to know, he scanned the crowds both below him and up there with him on the mezzanine for any glimpse of others interested in this information. This was third-party awareness: the simple personal security act of realizing you and your target aren't alone in the world, that someone else might be watching them, or watching you. Court had been surprised twice in the past week by others moving on the same objective as he, and he didn't want it to happen again.

He looked in the best places in the bar to get eyes on the VIP section. Court himself had a good view, but he was relatively exposed in the center of the mezzanine above the dance floor. A better location to surveil the VIP area was up on the mezzanine but tucked into either corner where the lighting wasn't as good.

Court looked idly to his left and then to his right, his head still thumping along with the music.

And then his head stopped. *Well, that didn't take long.*

A Western-looking man in his forties, dressed not unlike Court himself, sat in the dark corner on Court's right, just beyond the staircase down to the dance floor. His eyes were on the VIP section below, just as Court's had been.

And also like Court, the man in the corner lifted his head and began scanning his surroundings.

Just then, a Thai girl who had tried and failed to get free drinks from Court a half hour earlier passed by with a girlfriend. Court reached out and took her by the arm, pulling her playfully towards him and down on his lap.

"Where have you been?" Court asked, suddenly interested in talking.

"Oh . . . hi," she replied, pleasantly surprised that she'd finally managed to get this rich-looking foreigner's attention.

Court said, "I seem to remember from our earlier conversation that you really like Cristal."

She smiled. "I do."

He looked at her friend now, who was already slipping into the seat across from him. "And how about you?"

She smiled herself. "Of course."

"You *both* enjoy expensive champagne? That's *crazy*! What are the chances?"

His new friend's name was Sky, or that was her story anyway, and her friend claimed that her name was Nicki.

Court saw their bullshit and raised them, telling them his name was Bob and he was a yacht salesman from Florida in the "U.S. of A." He ordered a bottle of 2006 Cristal Brut from a passing waitress, and while they waited they mostly listened to the music, because this wasn't exactly a venue where people could chat easily, even if they had something to talk about.

Court was glad that he didn't have to make too much idle banter. He was already thinking about the man in the corner, who, he felt certain, was here in an operational capacity. He had a slightly Slavic look to him, so Russian was his best guess, but he thought the man looked older and heavier than he would expect for a Zaslon operator, which meant he wouldn't have been one of the men he'd seen in Vietnam.

Still, he could have been SVR.

Either way, Court knew what he had to do. He needed to get closer to the VIP area to identify key personalities, and to decide how he would go about separating one of the top dogs of the Chamroon Syndicate from his bodyguards.

So for one of the first times in his operational life, Court decided he needed to get up and dance.

The Cristal came and Court and the two ladies each downed a flute of champagne, Court thinking all along about how he was glad he didn't have to turn in an expense report to Colonel Dai, because this five-hundred-dollar purchase of bubbly would probably result in Don Fitzroy getting one of his feet lopped off. When they finished with the drink, Nicki moved on to find a sucker of her own, and Court took Sky down to the dance floor, passing near the lone man in the corner by the stairs as they did so. Court snuck a glance in the man's direction when he reached the stairs and saw that the man's attention was fully fixed on the VIP section and the large contingent of Thai men and non-Thai women sitting there.

And, Court noticed, the man had a bottle of vodka on ice next to his table and a glass in his hand. This didn't necessarily mean he was Russian, but it didn't hurt the chances that Court had him pegged correctly.

On the floor Sky and Bob pressed in with hundreds of others, but within minutes, without Sky having any clue she was being used as cover in an intelligence operation for the United States, they found themselves near the roped-off VIP section.

Court noticed that several of the men and women had left the tables, presumably to dance themselves, but the floor was too tight for Court to see any of the known subjects of his surveillance. It didn't matter, though, because the one Thai man still sitting behind the rope was most definitely twenty-eight-year-old Nattapong Chamroon.

Chamroon still had the six women sitting close to him, pouring his drinks and leaning in close whenever he spoke. Court put five of them as Central or Eastern European, and the other as African, African-American, or perhaps even from the Caribbean because of her dark skin. In their stilettos the women were all probably taller than Nattapong when they stood up, and one brunette was a full head taller, but gauging by the cool grin on Chamroon's face he seemed fine with the height disparity.

The women appeared to all be in their twenties and they wore a lot of makeup, just like all the women in the nightclub, but even up close there wasn't one who was not breathtaking.

As Court and Sky got a little closer—now it was Sky who was pulling them in the direction of the VIP section because she wanted to see the exotic women and their flashy clothes—Court noticed all six ladies had dark and serious faces. Despite their bright and luminous clothing and outwardly poised mannerisms, Court read the eyes of a couple of the girls, and he determined in an instant they weren't here of their own volition.

As he and Sky made their way back towards the stairs up to the mezzanine, Court realized he'd seen expressions like these before in his career traveling through various terrible places.

These women were victims of human trafficking. Prostitutes, certainly working here in Bangkok for Chamroon's own organization. Brewer's notes on the syndicate had told him hundreds of young Central European women each year were offered good jobs in the hotel or hospitality industries in Asia, and when they arrived they were drugged, threatened, beaten, and forced into prostitution. Their passports were taken from them; local police were often in on the scheme, so the young girls had no one but one another to rely on. Soon, though, they would be moved around and administered huge quantities of drugs and alcohol, and they would give in totally to their situations.

Some would make their way back home after a time, but many would not.

Court didn't get a close look at all the girls around Nattapong Chamroon, but he saw enough in the compliant dead eyes of a couple of them to know the score. They wouldn't like Nattapong, but they'd be dependent on him, and this meant the girls could pose a problem if Court wanted to get him out of here, because they were all over him, and he wasn't sure they'd even leave his side if he went to the bathroom.

B ob and Sky returned to the table, and soon the bottle of Cristal came to an end. When he declined to order another, so did Bob's whirlwind relationship with Sky. She wandered off; to Court's pleasure her next mark was the guy in the corner with the vodka bottle and the shifty eyes, though this man sent her on her way gruffly and continued eyeing the nightclub.

The Dutch DJ took a smoke break a minute later, and though the pre-recorded music was still loud, the crowd wasn't as engaged, so Court took advantage of the relative calm to place a phone call.

Court called Brewer, established his identity, and quickly told her he wanted the SAD men in the area to create a distraction.

Brewer replied to Court's request instantly. "Negative. I'm not sending Ground Branch in until you have positive ID on Fan."

Court sighed. "Look, there is too much security here for me to do this myself."

"Do you have PID on Fan?"

"Negative, but I have an opportunity to get one of the brothers. I just need some help."

Brewer said, "If you want someone to help you get a prisoner out of that nightclub, you know who you can call."

Court understood what she meant, but he didn't like it. "There are five hundred civilians in this building. If Dai's men get involved, this could turn into a bloodbath."

"You'll just have to take care of everything inside the building, make it clear to him what you need. His men stay outside. Their job is to help you out of the area."

Court didn't hide his frustration. "Great idea, Brewer, but I don't have a gun. Remember?"

"You'll come up with something," Brewer said coldly. "I'm under orders myself, Violator. Ground Branch is a single-shot weapon. They swoop in for the snatch; they aren't a force that I can order around to flex muscle every time you want to question someone."

"But—"

Brewer said, "If you get PID on Fan, call me back. Otherwise, the Chinese can help you tonight."

Court hung up. As far as he was concerned, Brewer might have had her orders, but using Chinese intelligence operatives was just going to increase the chances something bad would happen tonight.

Still . . . it wasn't his call to make. He looked down at his phone and keyed another number. He put a finger into one of his ears and his phone tight against the other. He could barely hear the ringing of the phone, but Dai's voice came through loud and clear. "What is all that noise?"

Court said, "I am in a nightclub called the Black Pearl. It's a bar owned by the Chamroon Syndicate. I am going to make a move on a member of their leadership who is here, and I need your men to help."

Dai said, "I am glad to hear you are doing something proactive, finally, but why do you think Chamroon is the one holding Fan Jiang?"

"It is the biggest group around and it has the most reach. Chamroon Syndicate operatives smuggle through Cambodia and were likely the ones who picked Fan up there. And I've been asking around, and they are the only group around who can really employ a man with our target's skills. They have a large cybercrime operation run out of the city."

"That is all you are going on?"

Court faked a defensive tone. "Look . . . I don't know for sure, but I need to force a move. Nattapong Chamroon himself is here. If I can get him out of here and someplace where I can work on him, I'll find out where Fan is, or I'll find out who else might be holding him."

Dai said nothing. He clearly was not convinced.

Court played his trump card. "Did I mention that the Russians are here? They have eyes on Chamroon as we speak."

Now Dai spoke. "I have four men just minutes from you. I can have a dozen men there in less than a half hour."

"Thought that might get your attention. Tell them they are just here to back me up. I'll wait for an opportunity for Nattapong to—"

Court had been watching the VIP area below while he spoke. Now, right in front of him, Nattapong Chamroon and his group downed their full glasses of whiskey and began shuffling the girls with them towards a door at the rear of the VIP area. Three bodyguards moved along with them.

When the door opened, Court realized it led to a stairwell. Chamroon and his entourage were already on the ground floor, and he saw the body-guards leading them up the stairs, with the girls following behind. More men stood waiting on the stairs, and Court took them as security for Chamroon's entourage, as well. He hadn't seen these men in the nightclub and wondered what they had been doing up until now.

The VIP door closed before Court could get a head count or be sure everyone was going up, but he felt it was a safe bet. Brewer had told him that above the Black Pearl, a private club and spa entertained the rich of the city during the day, and it served as an occasional playground of the Chamroon Syndicate's leadership in the off-hours.

"Are you still there?" Dai asked.

Now Court waved at his waitress to bring the check. Into his phone he said, "I might have an opportunity to get closer to Chamroon. Keep your guys outside and ready to help me make it out of here with a captive. And hurry them up. I don't control the timetable with this . . . The bad guys do."

"I will do as you say."

"Remember, Dai. They stay outside. I will notify you if I need them."

"Of course."

Court hung up the phone, pulled out a wad of baht over a thousand U.S. in value, and began fanning bills. He was operating by the seat of his pants, but for the first time in the past four days, he had a hard-and-fast objective. Nattapong Chamroon was in his sights, and Court Gentry was supremely single-minded when he closed in on a target.

CHAPTER

THIRTY-NINE

Twenty feet to the right of where Court descended the circular staircase down to the dance floor, SVR operations officer Oleg Utkin took a slow sip of his iced vodka, then spoke into his hidden cuff mic.

"Anna One, this is Fantom. Subject has entered a rear door with three bodyguards and six prostitutes. I can't see if it's a stairwell, but the layout of the building suggests it is."

The reply came from Vasily seconds later. "Anna One copies. We will advise when we are in the building."

"*Ponial*," the SVR operative said, and he returned to his duty of keeping watch over the nightclub.

Oleg Utkin had been on another operation in Manila two days earlier when he'd received an emergency message from his control officer at the Lubyanka building in Moscow, letting him know he would be taking over an SVR task force whose previous commander had been recalled because of poor performance. He was ordered to fly directly to Bangkok and, as soon as he landed, he was picked up by the Zaslon operators.

In the safe house he'd read his complete orders and brief for the mission, and he'd been astonished by the overall scope of the operation, the incredible events of the past week and a half, and, most of all, the fact that the leader of the task force who'd been relieved of command was Sirena.

Utkin knew Zoya Zakharova, and while he couldn't stand that edgy bitch, he had *never* known her to fail in the field. She'd worked with Zaslon units much more than Oleg had; she was accustomed to guns and rope ladders and parachutes and all that other silliness, whereas Oleg was a "suit and tie" man, a different type of operative altogether.

He'd been warned by the Lubyanka that Sirena had not returned to Moscow as ordered, and although his control officer had asserted she'd probably just gone AWOL to drown herself in booze for a couple of days for being pulled off such an important operation, Oleg Utkin figured she was probably going it alone, still working some angle involving Fan Jiang, because he knew Zoya was a woman wholly unaccustomed to losing.

Vasily agreed with him; he insisted Sirena could turn up around any corner on this mission, and when she did turn up, she'd try to strong-arm her way back in somehow.

But neither Oleg nor Vasily thought Zoya would appear here in Bangkok. No, she was probably back in Cambodia, still wandering the jungles and swamps, which was exactly what the Anna team had done for an entire day, and it was exactly what they would *still* be doing if Russian intelligence had not intercepted an encoded message from Fan "Funky Monkey" Jiang, letting Taiwanese intelligence know he was in the hands of a Chao Pho known as the Chamroon Syndicate.

Moscow didn't know how the hell Fan had managed to escape Vietnam, or for that matter how he'd been picked up by the Thais, but that was not to say no one in SVR could have guessed how Fan ended up here . . . *if* they'd been read in on the op.

The assistant resident of the SVR office in Cambodia knew he'd put the SVR non-official cover operative called Sirena in touch with the Thai organization, but he knew nothing about Fan Jiang, and nothing about Russia's new interest in the Chamroon Syndicate. He was back in Cambodia and he'd been compartmentalized out of this, so he did not have a clue what he had started.

All he knew was that less than an hour after he'd set up the conversation between a Chamroon operative and Sirena, he'd received a call from the chief resident telling him Sirena was burned to the SVR, and providing her help was expressly forbidden.

When the assistant resident got this call, he just confirmed the order and hung up the phone, because he had been in government service long enough to know how this game was played. He couldn't very well admit he'd just connected Sirena with one of the largest transnational criminal syndicates in Southeast Asia. His completely legitimate explanation that he'd done so *before* he got the word that she was persona non grata would not serve as a valid excuse, because the man up the chain of command at fault for not passing on the information faster would simply change the timeline of events and throw his underling under the bus for his own failure.

The SVR assistant resident in Phnom Penh knew how bureaucracies like intelligence agencies operated.

Shit runs downhill.

Yes, the prudent course of action for him was to sit there with his mouth shut and hope his assistance to Sirena never came to light, pop antacids, and drink his worry away to help him along in this endeavor. Much better that than to immediately reveal the truth, because even though the truth would exonerate him, the truth was fungible, and he'd be sure to pay.

There was only one option that provided a pathway forward for the SVR man's career—quietly rooting for Sirena to die, to keep her mouth shut, or to weasel her way out of the bad graces of the SVR.

If the sexy operative who'd fallen out of Moscow's favor ever talked, the assistant resident would find himself just as fucked as Sirena.

The seven-man Zaslon unit was not inside the Black Pearl, but they were close enough to hear the music. Vasily and his team stood on the roof of the five-story condominium complex separated by a tree-lined alleyway from the four-story building holding the nightclub and a private spa above it.

Down below them in the alley there wasn't much light and there was even less activity, but a half block to their right, bouncers stood around the club's entrance, traffic cops sat on their bikes at the intersections, and the club's security cameras kept an unblinking eye on the scene.

But the dark roof of the target building was unguarded and unwatched.

After the SVR officer code named Fantom gave the word, Vasily nodded to Arseny and Andrei. Both men held thin cables, on the end of which were black grappling hooks. They spun the cables in circles, paying out a little more line with each revolution. When they let the hooks fly, they sailed over the alley and across to the lower rooftop. The hooks dropped among a tangle of HVAC piping a few feet off the ground. Then the men pulled their lines taut to hook them securely.

A minute later Andrei tightened the sling to his B&T APC9 submachine gun to bring the short-barreled, suppressed weapon tight against his chest, then hooked a carabiner affixed to the chest rig hidden under his civilian jacket to one of the cables strung over the alleyway. He hooked a second carabiner to the other line, then slowly and carefully leaned out over the alleyway, using his gloved hands on the cables to control his movement.

The lines had been attached to an iron beam on the roof of the condo building, and they were pulled taut, so Andrei knew this would be a quick ride if he lost hold—and that was only if at least one of the lines held. If both grappling hooks came loose at the termination above the nightclub and spa, then it would be an even quicker ride, but of course that journey would end with him dead in the alley five floors below.

But Andrei slid across in a safe and controlled fashion, and after removing the grappling hooks and securing the terminations of the cables, the rest of the team slid down even faster.

Six minutes after Fantom announced that tonight's target had gone up into the spa area of the nightclub, the entire Russian paramilitary team was stacked up at the rooftop door to the building.

Pyotr had already removed a blowtorch from his pack and was preparing to get to work on the lock when the door opened suddenly from the inside.

Standing in the doorway was a bodyguard. He'd already put a cigarette in his mouth and he held a lighter in his hand, but when he saw the group of men all wearing dark clothing right in front of him, he froze.

Pyotr dropped his blowtorch, grabbed the stunned man, and spun him out of the doorway, face-first onto the rooftop.

Court walked down a hallway on the ground floor of the nightclub on the opposite side of the stage from the VIP section. He found the bathrooms ahead on his left, and directly past them was a stairwell to the higher floors of the building. Court wanted to go up to look for Nattapong and his entourage, but he wouldn't be able to do so before he dealt with the headset-wearing bouncer who stood there on the lower step, so he made a left into the dimly lit men's room, passing a few men on their way out.

All four urinals were occupied and one of the two stalls' doors was shut. Court had planned on either lighting a fire in the garbage can or coming up with some other low-scale diversion to move the guard at the stairs away from his post, but before he'd had time to decide on his plan, the bathroom door opened and a young man in a suit entered.

A look at his clothing and his build suggested to Court that this guy was one of the bodyguards who'd arrived with the Chamroon leadership, but only when he saw the earpiece in the man's ear did he know for sure. The security man made a beeline for the unoccupied stall while Court turned to begin washing his own hands.

Court watched through the mirror while the four young men at the urinals headed back out the door, leaving Court, the bodyguard, and the individual enjoying the bathroom's ambiance from the comfort of the other stall.

The security man stood facing the toilet in the stall, leaving the door open. Ten feet behind him Court spun away from the mirror, crossed the tile floor quietly, then reached up and grabbed the header above the open stall door. He used this to hoist himself off the ground and arc back like a gymnast, and then he swung forward like a pendulum with his legs out in front of him. He kicked the man between his shoulder blades and knocked him face-first into the wall over the toilet.

The armed gangster slammed hard, then crumpled down to the floor of the stall, unconscious.

The man in the next stall called out in Thai, his voice filled with alarm.

Court knelt over the unconscious guard and ran his hands through the man's clothing. He pulled a Glock 17 pistol and two extra seventeen-round magazines, slipped the gun into his waistband at the small of his back, and dropped the mags into his pocket.

He also extracted the radio from the man's belt and pulled his wired earpiece. Court didn't speak a word of Thai, but he knew what it sounded like when people were freaking out about something, so he slipped the earpiece in his ear and the radio under his coat so he'd be alerted when word got out that this guy had been found.

The man in the next stall called out again, no doubt asking what the ruckus was three feet away from him.

Court went back to the sink and washed his hands. He heard the toilet flush in the stall next to his victim, and then the door to the hallway opened, and five young men with spiked hair entered, laughing and talking. Three of them stepped up to the urinals, and a fourth approached the stalls at the same moment the stall door opened. Court was already heading to the exit, but behind him he heard a quick and concerned exchange in Thai, and then a shout of surprise.

Court pushed quickly out of the bathroom as more men entered, and he pointed back inside, well within earshot of the bouncer, just ten feet away at the bottom of the stairwell.

And then Court said the one word all bouncers, all over the world, *love* to hear. "Fight!"

The man at the stairs quickly took a waist-high velvet rope barricade off a hook in the wall and brought it across the stairs, where he hooked it onto the banister. Then he took off into the bathroom in a run, transmitting in Thai on his headset mic as he moved.

Court looked back up the hall towards the front of the club, saw only a couple there making out and not facing his direction, then used the banister to vault the rope.

He shot up the stairs unnoticed.

CHAPTER

FORTY

As far as Nattapong Chamroon was concerned, he ruled the world. Well ... he and his brother did. He was twenty-eight years old and handsome; his father owned a transnational criminal enterprise that raked in over 240 million U.S. dollars a year, plenty of money to keep Nattapong and his older brother, Kulap, knee-deep in the best cars, clothes, houses, booze, and friends.

And women—*lots* of women, but Nattapong wouldn't count the girls in his life as expenses; in fact, he considered them revenue generators who just happened to provide additional benefits whenever he desired.

He was the cold and cruel son of a cold and cruel father, and he used the foreign girls in his stable as accessories in public and as toys in private. And tonight was nothing out of the ordinary for him. He'd had six of the nicest-looking women delivered to his house, and from there they had all traveled to the Black Pearl in a stretch SUV limo braced by a pair of SUVs filled with capos and bodyguards of the Chamroon Syndicate. The girls had spent the last hour sitting with him while he drank and got in the mood, and now he'd taken them up to the spa's wet area on the fourth floor: an ornate and massive marble-tiled pool and hot tub facility larger than a basketball court and designed to look like an opulent Roman bath.

Here Nattapong would *really* get this party started.

He lay shirtless on a lounge chair in front of the pool; large stone statues of lions and nude figures surrounded him, ornate marble columns lined the pool in front of him and ringed the hot tub behind him, and fountains shot streams of water in arcs from one side of the pool to the other in front of him. The lighting in the room was a moody dim blue haze, and a simulated starscape was projected on a ceiling above the pool.

The music piped into the room was ethereal and atmospheric, bouncing around the tile in the windowless space.

The six women sat or knelt on the marble floor in front of Nattapong in a semicircle. Some drank champagne, one snorted some coke, another popped pills. A couple of the ladies looked uncomfortable, but others appeared as relaxed as Nattapong himself.

He knew that the ones who'd not been drugged or demoralized into submission—the three new girls—would rather shoot themselves than have sex with him, but the eight bodyguards positioned around the Roman bath were always ordered to keep an eye on Nattapong's orgies: partially for Nattapong to get a few extra kicks by demonstrating his sexual prowess to his underlings, but primarily to make certain none of the girls tried to bite his manhood off. All his personal bodyguards were armed with Uzi Pros, a micro-sized 9-millimeter select-fire machine pistol that could dump 1,050 rounds per minute, but for the girls the guards rarely needed more than a hard look or the back of a hand.

Nattapong Chamroon regarded this evening's selection of entertainment appreciatively, and he knew this was indeed a special night. While he sometimes found some eights or even an occasional seven snuck into his orgies, this night every one of his girls was a ten.

It was clear to Nattapong that this group had been selected for both their beauty and their dissimilarity from one another. Tonight's potpourri included a short redhead from Poland with ample curves; an impossibly tall raven-haired Ukrainian with a runway-model body; an athletic platinum blonde from Hungary with muscle rippling from her tanned bare arms, shoulders, and legs, and dramatic eye makeup that made her look vaguely Middle Eastern. Next to her lay a spectacular ebony Namibian, a true rarity in Thailand and a top earner for Chamroon; then a brunette Moldovan with her hair in a short bob who looked no more than eighteen but might have been even younger. Lastly in the semicircle was an auburn-haired stunner from Russia whose distant dead eyes reminded Nattapong that she'd been working for him for a while, but he saw this as a plus, because that meant her skills had been properly developed.

The crime boss smiled at all the choices in front of him, then lifted a hand mirror off the floor and snorted two lines of coke from it. He rubbed his nose and his eyes, downed a shot of whiskey from a crystal shot glass, and called for his girls to come to him.

This was going to be one hell of a night.

C ourt slid open a second-floor window on the east side of the building and looked out to the fire escape. It had a retractable ladder so no one at ground level could reach up and grab it, but from here at the second floor he could ascend to the higher levels of the four-story building, or even the roof if he wanted to.

He passed the third floor after looking through the window and finding a single bodyguard walking down the hall, a headset over his shaved head. Court imagined the bodyguards were not on the same channel as the bouncers in the nightclub, which came as no surprise. Court flipped the dial on his stolen radio and found Chamroon's security channel.

Even without speaking Thai, he'd derived enough from the radio transmissions in the nightclub to figure out that the bouncers had found the unconscious man in the bathroom. Perhaps they could tell he'd gotten his lights knocked out by another patron, but either he hadn't come to yet or hadn't mentioned that someone had stolen his pistol, because the radio traffic didn't seem overly excited. Court felt certain he'd made it up the stairs without anyone alerting the bodyguards, because otherwise he was sure there would be a lot more agitation out on the net.

As soon as Court made it to the fourth-floor landing of the outdoor fire escape, he looked in the window and saw a dark hallway. A doorway across from him had a sign on it, so Court took a chance and shined his flashlight through the glass so he could see what it said.

Two words in Thai and then their English translation:

ROMAN BATHS

Court had no idea if Chamroon had decided to take his ladies for a swim, but he decided he'd have better luck picking a door lock on the roof than trying to get through this window quickly and silently, so he continued ascending.

Seconds later he arrived at the dark roof, took a look around, and found it unguarded. He moved across the flat roof to the door, only now drawing the Glock pistol he'd removed from the bodyguard, because he was certain he wouldn't be able to talk his way past anyone who found him skulking around up here.

As he arrived at the door to the stairwell, he saw a large form lying to the left of the closed door. He pointed his gun at it, thinking it to be roughly man sized and man shaped, but when he got close enough to get a good look, he lowered the gun.

A young man, clearly one of the Chamroon bodyguards, lay facedown with glistening blood surrounding a hole in the back of his head.

In an instant Court realized the SVR man downstairs had not been alone. The paramilitaries he'd run into in Hong Kong and Vietnam were here, as well.

He stepped to the door, found it locked, then went back over to the guard. He checked the man over and found a set of keys, then slipped his pistol in his belt and started trying the keys in the door, rushing through the process and cussing under his breath each time he failed to get in.

The first four Chinese arrived fewer than five minutes after Colonel Dai hung up his call with Gentry, because they had been close by in the Royal City Avenue neighborhood, staking out a bar owned by another group of Thai gangsters.

Despite Gentry's demand that the men stay outside the club, Dai ordered them to go straight in and perform recon for the larger force racing into the neighborhood, but when the four tried to get into the Black Pearl, they were confronted by a bouncer who demanded to frisk them. The men turned away before causing a scene, not wanting to endanger their cover before they had the guns in play to make a real stand. Instead, they backed off and took up positions around the large building, each covering a side of the building.

Three of the men were armed with pistols, but one carried an HK UMP submachine gun under his suit coat. He stepped into a poorly lit narrow alley on the west side of the building, tucked himself between a row of garbage cans near a kitchen entrance to the club, and squatted down in the dark.

The fourteenth key on the chain of fifteen unlocked the door to the stairwell. Court turned the latch and held it there, pocketed the keychain, and drew his Glock 17 again, then knelt down on one knee. He pulled the door open slowly, his gun in front of him, but on the other side he found only a well-lit and empty stairwell.

He considered whether he should descend or call this entire thing off, knowing now he was moving towards a team of well-trained killers and a group of less well-trained but numerically impressive armed Thai gangsters. He wasn't certain how far he was going to take this, but the fact that he knew of the existence of his opposition, while they had no idea he was even here, gave him the confidence to push on.

Nine additional plain-clothed employees of China's Ministry of Defense arrived on the streets around the Black Pearl in four different vehicles from three different locations around the city. Like the first four men to show up, these were not special operations paramilitaries; they didn't work as a tactical team and wear body armor and night vision equipment. Rather they were individual operators, accustomed to working with a small team on some missions, perhaps, although they didn't fight as a unit.

Some of the men carried CZ pistols, others had Walthers, and three more of this group had fully automatic submachine guns with folding stocks hanging inside their jackets.

They saw the huge crowd milling around the entrances and exits of the club, the substantial size of the building itself, and the large number of security at the entrances. Immediately Major Xi, the lead operative of all Dai's forces working on the Fan Jiang operation, put in a call to his control officer back in Hong Kong.

Colonel Dai Longhai stood on the balcony of his massive safe house in the Peak neighborhood of Hong Kong. He'd been up all night working with the Chinese embassy in Bangkok to try to find Fan Jiang, and when

Gentry called minutes earlier he knew he would not retire to bed until he knew the status of the in extremis operation currently under way nearly a thousand miles to the west.

When his phone rang he snatched it up from a patio table where it rested next to his cigarettes, and he answered the call.

"*Ni hao.*"

"Colonel, this is Major Xi."

"What is the situation?"

"We are outside the nightclub, but we won't be able to get in covertly. There is a lot of security here."

Dai growled. "Unacceptable."

"We can enter into combat with the security if you wish, but the building is four stories and an entire city block in size. Without knowing where our target is, it will be difficult to clear the building before local police arrive in numbers."

"Have you seen Gentry?"

"Negative, Colonel."

Dai looked out at Victoria Harbor, the lights still twinkling even though it was just a couple of hours before dawn. He said, "The Russians are there. They managed to get inside."

"Perhaps they are unarmed, sir."

"I doubt that." Dai thought a moment. "The building. Is it freestanding?"

"Yes."

"Then force everyone out."

A pause. "Fire alarm, sir?"

Dai did not hesitate. "No. A fire."

"You want us to start a fire?"

"Correct. Something to get the building evacuated. Leave men to watch all the exits, and make entry yourself. If the Russians get information on Fan's whereabouts first, then I will hold you personally responsible."

"*Xie de, lujon shangxiao.*" Yes, Colonel.

"If Fan is sighted, kill him. If any member of Chamroon's senior leadership tries to leave, take them. If no one important comes out . . . then you go in and find them."

"Yes, Colonel."

M ajor Xi and four other men walked briskly up the alley towards the western employee entrance of the nightclub, passing by their colleague with the UMP hiding between the garbage cans without even seeing him. A few men and women, employees of the club, were standing around on smoke breaks, a young man rolled garbage down a ramp towards the large bins in the alley, and an unarmed bouncer of the club sat on a little bench and played with his phone.

The Chinese drew their weapons when the man slid off the bench to confront them, and Major Xi slammed him in the side of his head with the butt of his CZ pistol, administering a severe concussion to the bouncer and knocking him out cold. Xi kept walking as the man fell to the ground, but a subordinate pulled off the man's headset while the others pointed their weapons at the other employees of the nightclub, all of whom just shriveled out of the path of the silent men in business suits waving guns.

Xi and his small team encountered their first armed security man in the kitchen. He worked for the club, but he was a Chamroon Syndicate henchman, so he carried a pistol in a shoulder holster. He leaned against a wall next to the door between the kitchen and the front of the house. He'd been hitting on a pretty cocktail waitress, but when he glanced away from her he found himself facing four armed men in dark suit coats. He reached into his own coat to pull his own gun, but he thought better of it when a silencer pressed hard against his left temple.

He was led into a walk-in cooler, then dropped onto the floor with a blow to the back of the head.

One of the four Chinese men stood guard while Major Xi and two others got to work. They pulled out three massive rolling laundry bins full of soiled tablecloths and doused them with cooking oil, then set them alight, all under the stunned gaze of a dozen kitchen employees. While one of Xi's men pushed the door to the nightclub open, Xi and the rest walked the bins through, shoving them hard through tables near the dance floor, catching several tablecloths on fire. One of the bins made it all the way to a wall curtain before it tipped over, and flames began licking up the curtain.

Men and women screamed, but their screams were drowned out by the loud music.

Only when a Chamroon Syndicate lieutenant in the VIP section pulled his Beretta and opened fire on one of the arsonists near the kitchen did others around the nightclub understand they were in danger.

The platinum blonde with the Middle Eastern eyes hadn't gotten into the action yet, nor had the black girl; Chamroon noticed this as he looked over the naked shoulder of the redhead from Poland. The Hungarian and the Namibian just drank champagne and looked on, sitting on the marble deck and dipping their hands into the shallow end of the pool while they did so. Nattapong almost called out to them angrily to demand their immediate attention, but the other four women were seeing to various portions of the Thai gangster's body and doing it well, and frankly, Nattapong wasn't sure where the other two would be able to push in.

So he decided he'd let the blonde and the African woman off the hook for now; they could drink and watch, and he'd save the best for last.

The sound of gunfire below did not make it up to the fourth floor, but the eight guards all had earpieces in, so when someone called into the radio, "Shots fired," Nattapong's bodyguards immediately launched into action. They began hustling around the pool and the hot tub in the direction of their boss.

This happened every now and then at the Black Pearl; some gang member would get pissed off at a bartender or the boyfriend of a mistress, and he would fire a round into the floor or the ceiling, or occasionally into another patron. A gunshot three floors down wasn't necessarily a massive threat to Nattapong Chamroon, but still they knew they had to surround their boss and get him somewhere secluded till the details of the situation could be worked out.

But as they raced into the orgy, a second call came over their headsets announcing that a fire had started, and to these men a fire in this building was worse than a gunshot three floors down, so they realized they had to get Nattapong the hell out of there now.

The bodyguards knew their boss would not want to be disturbed, but they knew their jobs, and they rushed around the pool, pulling young naked and nearly naked girls out of their way to get hands on their boss. They had just removed the Ukrainian and the Moldovan and started to shout over the spacey music and the moans of the Polish girl to tell Chamroon about the danger when the south-side double doors flew open, and a long shaft of light cut into the blue haze of the marble-tiled pool room.

The men and women turned to the disturbance on the far side of the pool and fountains, just as flashes of light came from the doorway.

Chamroon Syndicate security officers began dropping into the swimming pool, blood spurted over a headless statue, and marble tiles on the walls behind the orgy began cracking from bullet strikes and falling onto the floor.

Women screamed, Thai bodyguards returned fire, and Nattapong Chamroon struggled to yank up his pants, and then he grabbed the tall Ukrainian to use her for cover as he rushed to get behind something more solid.

Within seconds most of the women lay flat on the tile, trying to shield themselves with their hands, but the Hungarian blonde dove headfirst for cover around a marble column behind the hot tub, and the Russian with the auburn hair pulled a pool recliner onto its side and cowered behind it.

The young Moldovan with the bob haircut climbed to her feet and tried to run, but she was immediately caught in the cross fire. Her body spun and tumbled as she was hit by one of the Thai bodyguards' Uzis, and she fell dead next to the swimming pool.

A guard grabbed Chamroon under the arm and pulled him back to the door to the changing area, on the far side of the hot tub at the opposite end of the room from the gunfire, but as he pulled on the door latch he found it was locked from the inside. Gunfire stitched the door, and the guard pushed Chamroon out of the way, but in the process the security man took a round to the small of his back and fell facedown, paralyzed instantly.

Nattapong Chamroon grabbed the man's Uzi off the floor, then found cover behind one of the marble columns just four meters from the locked door. He saw the blond Hungarian girl had tucked herself behind the next column.

Nattapong reached around his column, and fired back in the direction of the attackers at the far side of the pool without looking.

Fifteen seconds after the door flew open, six of the eight armed Thai were dead or badly wounded, and the attacking force began bounding forward, closer and closer, using the columns, statues, and fountains as cover.

CHAPTER

FORTY-ONE

hree floors down, bedlam and panic erupted in the Black Pearl. Flames licked up the walls of the club, young men and women knocked into one another racing for the exits, and over a dozen Thai gangsters, some armed with pistols but many only with knives, were in desperate combat with a group of men who'd attacked simultaneously from both the front entrance and the kitchen.

When the Chamroon men began shooting, Major Xi called for five of his men waiting outside to come through the front door, not knowing if he was in combat with Russians or Thai. Xi and the three others who'd entered the kitchen to start the fire were still at the rear of the club, near the stage, and they shot across the open VIP section and through the door to the stairwell there. One of their number had been shot through the leg, but Xi and two others began racing up the back stairs, thinking it likely the Chamroon gangsters would try to ascend to get away from the gun battle.

A pair of Chamroon gangsters stood on the second-floor landing. These were just young men here at the Black Pearl to party tonight—not official security men guarding the top brass of the organization. Consequently, they were only armed with revolvers, and they just managed to graze one of the Chinese assassins on the side of his head before both Thai men fell dead, killed by Xi and his two associates.

After passing the fallen men, Xi felt confident he was heading in the right direction. He used his handheld walkie-talkie to order more of his men to find stairs or elevators and to get to the top of the building, and he called his man hiding out in the west-side alleyway, telling him to keep an eye on the fire escape there, because the raging fire at ground level was already filling the stairway with smoke, and this might force anyone upstairs to use the exterior to descend.

C ourt had made his way from the roof to an employee-only area on the fourth floor of the building, taking a different route down than the Russians who preceded him, obvious to Court because they had blow-torched a locked door that led to a main hallway.

Court continued through the employee-only area and into a large lab-yrinthine part of the spa, essentially an extended bathroom/locker room with moody orange lighting and a warren of showers, saunas, massage rooms, and storage areas for clothing and towels.

He made a careful turn towards the sound of cracking gunfire and found a changing area with marble tile floors and walls and teak benches. A door on the far side of this room had a sign on it that said Roman Baths, and Court could hear screams and gunfire on the other side.

The gunfire had slowed in the last few seconds, so Court advanced through the changing area towards the doorway to the action, hoping like hell he could find Nattapong in the middle of the mayhem and get him out of the line of fire.

V asily reloaded the magazine of his small submachine gun and leaned out from the stone fountain he crouched behind to search for a target. Through his night vision equipment he saw a few civilians at the far end of the pool; from their colorful and sparkling party dresses he assumed they were the hookers Fantom had mentioned over the radio a few minutes earlier. Most of them appeared to be alive, but one girl was facedown on the marble next to the pool.

Vasily did not have eyes on his target, and this worried him, because there seemed to be only a couple of shooters still alive downrange, and they both had small micro pistols. If one of these men was Nattapong Chamroon, it was going to be tough to take him alive.

Vasily was furious with that lazy fucker Oleg Utkin. When the Zaslon team came through the main door they'd expected to encounter three bodyguards in total, but by Vasily's count they'd already dropped six to eight men, and the gunfire continued. This should have been a quick door-kick-and-suppressed-fire snatch and grab, but it was quickly turning into the same shit they'd seen in Vietnam.

But while Vasily had lied and claimed Sirena screwed up in Vietnam so that he could cover his own ass, his anger at Fantom was real. No doubt the bastard had not even bothered to move from his table to see how many armed hostiles headed up to the spa, and now Vasily and his men were paying the price for it.

Still, they were getting the upper hand. Yevgeni was halfway down the length of the pool on the right with Ruslan just behind him, and Andrei and Pyotr had gotten nearly as far on the left-hand side. Soon they would have three angles on the remaining shooters, and the fight would be over.

Into his headset he repeated his order: "Watch your targets! Do *not* hit Chamroon."

Just as he finished his transmission he fired a long burst at the wall over the head of the man hiding behind a column, intending to keep him immobile so his operators could conduct their pincer movement. Marble tile broke off the wall. He was about to press the trigger again when he heard a transmission from Mikhail, just fifteen feet behind him, charged with covering the double doors in case anyone else came up the stairs.

"Contact rear!" Mikhail shouted, and his suppressed weapon began thumping in fully automatic mode.

Before Vasily could even turn to look at the threat, he felt an impact in the rear plate of his body armor, and it knocked him face-first into the deep end of the swimming pool.

Major Xi and his men were outgunned by the Russians around the pool, but they had them at a tactical disadvantage. The three Chinese shooters fired their pistols over and over into the dimly lit room, targeting the dark figures closest to them first. The return fire came almost instantly, showing Xi, himself a former special forces operative for the PLA, that the Russian unit had set up a rear guard even while in sustained contact from the far end of the pool.

He was impressed with their discipline, and it spoke to their training and skill, but while the Russians now scrambling for cover from both sides were certainly interested in bringing this fight to a close, Xi had one more sense of urgency they did not have. The Chinese operative was well aware that the building he stood in was burning to the ground.

One of the two men with Xi dropped dead in the hallway, and the other stepped out of the line of fire to reload his weapon. Xi himself knew he was down to the last couple of rounds in his pistol's magazine.

But just as his gun ran dry, four more Chinese operatives in black business suits came running up the hall from the elevators, and they took up the fight at the double doors. Xi stepped back and out of the way to reload quickly, while his men sent a wall of lead into the darkness.

As Court hugged the wall of the changing room, a new surge of fighting rocked the pool area next to him. He flipped off all the lights in the room, lowered to the ground, and crawled forward to the door to the pool. Keeping well to the side of the opening so he'd be out of the line of fire, Court pulled it open, and looked into the blue light of the pool area. He saw Nattapong cowering behind a column just a dozen feet from where Court lay. The twenty-eight-year-old held his right knee, and Court could see glistening blood on his hands. An Uzi machine pistol lay by his side, but Nattapong appeared uninterested in the weapon, so Court assumed its magazine was empty.

Just another dozen feet to Chamroon's right, the girl with the long blond hair and the muscular arms had her back to a column and her eyes on Court, and a few feet to her right and closer to the pool, four other women were hunkered down behind a pedestal holding a statue of a lion.

Court then saw the last of the six women who'd come up the stairs with Chamroon fifteen minutes earlier. The young-looking girl with the short hair was facedown by the pool, her body lying still.

Also lying about were at least half a dozen dead Thai bodyguards, and a couple of guards who seemed to be alive but out of the fight with grave wounds.

Court could see numerous muzzle flashes along both sides of the pool, down past the deep end, and out the double doors on the opposite end of the room from his position, and along with the sound of gunfire, the cracks of bullets impacting the marble and stonework at this end of the pool told him he, his target, and all these girls were downrange from the battle.

Court assessed the entire scene quickly. From the nature of the fighting on the far side of the pool he determined that the Russians were fighting it out with another group there—not Chamroon's bodyguards. He wondered if Dai's men had entered the building despite his begging that they wait outside.

Court's target for this evening, Nattapong Chamroon, was close by, injured, and unarmed, and he wasn't going anywhere, and neither the Russians nor the other group in the fight could make it down to this end of the pool without dealing with one another first.

Nattapong was so close Court decided to risk going for him. He ripped off his suit coat, rose to a crouch, and then sprinted out the doorway into the hazy blue light, taking just a few steps before he purposefully went down on his hip and slid along the marble all the way to the column behind which Chamroon hid.

Bullet strikes on the wall behind him knocked more tiles to the floor.

The young man next to him on the floor writhed in pain, still holding his bloody knee, and he did not even notice the American until he was on top of him. Court spun the young man around, grabbed him by the ankle of his pants because he wasn't wearing a shirt or shoes, and then stayed low while he dragged him the dozen feet back to the doorway to the changing area, while more supersonic rounds cracked above his head.

Court made it back with his prisoner, went down on his chest, and spun around on the floor to look back out the doorway. Just then a side door to the left of the big pool room opened, and several men in flashy suits filled the doorway, pointing pistols in front of them as they tried to figure out what was going on.

Christ, Court thought. These guys appeared to be more of Chamroon's men. Court raised his pistol to shoot at them, but he saw they had opened fire in the opposite direction. He decided the more guys who were fighting in other parts of the room, the easier it would be for him to get himself and Nattapong Chamroon back into the employee area behind the massage rooms, back to the hallway, and finally back to the employee-only stairwell in the rear of the building.

As he started to turn away to do just that, he again made eye contact with the blonde behind the column by the hot tub. She had taken off her high heels and risen to a crouch; it looked to Court as if she was about to try to make a run to the relative safety of the changing area.

Quickly he put a hand up, commanding her to stay where she was.

The gunfire was bad enough when Court made the dash to the column and back, but now the additional guns in the room meant even more rounds were pocking the walls. If any of the women tried to make a break for it, either to the doors to the left or the right of the pool, or back here to the changing room and the employee exit, Court felt certain they would be cut down from one side or the other.

Their best bet was to sit right where they were and wait out the battle.

Just as he motioned to the other women, imploring them to stay where they were, a long spray of automatic fire ripped hunks out of the pedestal on which the lion above them sat, sending marble chips all around the girls.

"Stay down!" he shouted.

And then he saw the smoke. From the air ducts here in the changing area, a few big puffs of black smoke belched into the room, and this told Court that there must be a sizable fire somewhere in the building.

Oh . . . fuck me.

The smoke began pouring in steady and thick, and Chamroon saw it now, too. He started to crawl away, but Court just rose and moved to him and put his foot in the back of the man's wounded knee, sending him into convulsions of pain.

Court chanced another look out into the pool area, saw flashes of suppressed gunfire, flashes accompanied by the sound of small arms, and determined that there had to be more than a dozen men ducked down in a dozen different locations in the big room in the middle of a protracted gun battle.

To his surprise the blonde who had been hiding behind the column had now turned in the other direction, and she ran under fire to the lion on the pedestal. This put her with the other four girls, and farther away from the changing area, but there was another door on the far side of the pool. Court didn't know if she was trying to get to that exit or if she just wanted to die with her friends. Either way, he thought her plan to be idiotic. Her friends were in much more danger than she had been, and there was no way in hell any of them were going to make it fifty feet to the side door, which was right at the epicenter of the fight.

All five women looked his way now, and he turned away. He had Chamroon. He had a brief window of opportunity where he could get to a back stairwell, down to the third floor, and out to the fire escape, then down to the street. He had his own car just two blocks away.

Success in this mission had seemed so improbable when he realized he was following the Russians to the target, just minutes earlier, but now mission success was all but assured.

But to succeed in his mission, he'd have to leave these five innocent and helpless women behind in the middle of a gun battle and at the center of an inferno.

Nope. He couldn't do it.

Court lay down flat, then reached out past the doorway and grabbed a twelve-inch square of marble that had fallen from the wall. It was chipped on one corner but otherwise intact. More importantly, it was a half inch thick. He knew it would stop most rounds from a handgun or a submachine gun, and it sounded to him as if everyone around here was firing one or the other.

Quickly he untucked his shirt and his undershirt, slid the cold marble under both and against his skin, and tucked everything back in. The tile would serve as a bulletproof vest to protect his chest cavity, but it wasn't much solace to him considering what he was about to do, and how many times he'd have to do it.

Court slid the Glock into his belt, knelt down, and ran for the lion.

CHAPTER

FORTY-TWO

Court Gentry slid like a baseball player stealing home, then up to his knees, and he put his back against the lion pedestal to shield himself from the three-way gun battle raging across the pool. He looked at the five women with him here behind the big statue. They all looked back at him, some with unrestrained terror in their eyes. He shouted over the gunfire, "English? Everybody speaks English?"

He saw looks of shock on some faces, and he was pretty sure a couple of the girls were high. The platinum blonde with the long bangs and the Middle Eastern eyes nodded first, and then some of the others said yes.

He drew his gun just as a Thai man rounded the shallow end of the swimming pool on his right, carrying a silver .45 caliber pistol in his hand. He was obviously looking for his boss, and he was braver and more loyal than he was competent.

Court shot him in the side of the head before he even noticed the group standing behind the statue next to the hot tub.

Some of the ladies screamed.

Court realized he couldn't shepherd all five of these women to safety at once. They would present a massive target, and everyone in the room would lock on to them during the forty-foot run to the changing area.

He shook the auburn-haired woman to stop her from screaming, and he spoke to the group over the gunfire. "Listen up! I'm taking you through that doorway over there, one at a time. When I get you there, run straight to the back. There is a stairwell. Find it. Don't wait on the others, just go!"

He heard an "okay," a "*da*," and a few other noises, maybe not a response from everyone, but they all seemed at least to understand he was trying to help them.

The girl with auburn hair sounded Russian. She looked up towards the ceiling, where the smoke poured into the dark room through the air ducts. Already the phony starscape on the ceiling was completely obscured. "There's a fire! There's smoke!"

Court looked around the side of the pedestal quickly, making sure no one else was approaching his position. While he did this he said, "We have to hurry. Go down one flight of stairs, then get into the hallway. There is a window that looks out on a fire escape. Take that down to the street."

A busty redhead wearing only a bra and panties cried openly. Court sized her up as the most unhinged of the group and decided he needed to move these women in ascending order of levelheadedness.

He took the busty redhead by the wrists. "You come first. Put your hands on me here." He turned away from her and put her behind him, placed her hands on his hips. "Move with me, understand?"

She sniffed and cried. Just then, a bullet snapped the tile floor just inches from where the group stood.

"Shit!" shouted Court in surprise, and this brought the redhead behind him to the edge of hysterics. "It's okay," he said, although it clearly was not.

"Just stay behind me and you'll be fine. Ready?"

And with that, Court moved across the open space, walking backwards and to his left, facing the threats of the room, covering the woman behind him.

It took just a few seconds to cross the forty feet, but it felt significantly longer.

When he got to the changing room, he saw that Chamroon was trying to stand. Court pointed his pistol at him. "I'll blow your other knee off if you try."

The young man stopped moving, and Court pushed the redhead on her way. He doubted she'd make it to the stairs before the next woman caught up to her.

Seconds later Court slid back behind the lion again. He stood back up, evaluated the remaining four, and took the auburn-haired Russian with him to the changing area, because she was clearly in shock. Still, she followed his commands, staying roughly behind him with her hands on his hips, and he traversed the area between the lion pedestal, passing behind the hot tub and the columns and finally through the door to the changing area. Here she ran off towards the back, and Court noticed that the smoke was now thick enough to affect his breathing, because the ceiling was lower here than in the pool area.

Chamroon was still there, still holding on to his bloody knee.

Court raced back to the lion again for the third time, but when he arrived he saw that the tall raven-haired girl had been hit by a piece of shrapnel across the back of her hand and forearm. It bled freely, and she screamed in pain and shock, but Court could tell it wasn't particularly serious, considering all the dangers close by.

Another man came around the pool now, again on Court's left, and Court shot him three times before he dropped his pistol and fell to his knees, finally crumpling onto his back just ten feet away.

Court reloaded, and got the tall injured woman to hold on to his hips like the first two, and again he launched himself out into the open, side-stepping back towards the doorway. He'd made it just halfway when the snap of a bullet cracked close on his right. "Get behind me!" he shouted, and the woman tucked tighter, and then Court felt the impact of a round high on his chest, slamming into the marble.

It rocked him back and he stumbled, but he kept his feet and the two of them made it into the changing area.

The woman looked at her bloody hand and arm; Court reminded her that she needed to run, and soon she did just that, disappearing through the thick gray smoke and down the labyrinth of halls towards the stairs.

Court did not hesitate; he ran back to the lion, exposing himself again to fire, and by now he saw that the smoke out here was obscuring his vision as well.

There were two women left: the black woman and the fit blonde with the Egyptian-looking eyes. Court sized up the black woman as being the more terrified of the two, so he told her it was her turn. She put her hands on his hips and they took off.

As they shot back the forty feet, Court could see a pair of dark figures in the smoke coming around the other side of the pool now, back to the right of the lion. He fired several times at the figures but missed, saw them dive behind a stone fountain and a marble bench.

Back in the changing area, the smoke continued rolling out of the vents and hung high in the room. The smell had gone from noticeable, to heavy, to now nearly overpowering, and visibility was dropping fast. But despite the worsening conditions and the insanity of the raging battle, Court was pleased to see the woman running off to the back without prompting, and Chamroon still lying in agony on the floor.

One more time, Court told himself, and he ran back to the lion through the smoky haze. This time he could feel the marble tile in his shirt shift and crumble where it had been struck by the bullet; it was almost useless now as a ballistic shield.

He dove feetfirst and slid the last ten feet to the lion pedestal, the marble cutting into his chest as he did so. As soon as he got there he raised his Glock 17 and fired back in the direction of the two figures he'd seen earlier, hoping to keep their heads down.

The blonde was still there, down on one knee with her back to the marble pedestal. She looked at Court through her heavy eye makeup with rapt fascination. She'd been the most "together" of the five women, so he'd left her for last, but now her odd expression had him wondering if she was finally going into shock herself.

"Your turn. You ready?" he said while he reloaded the Glock.

The woman spoke with a distinctive accent that he thought might have been Hungarian. "I am ready. Please, stay close to me."

"I will."

There was a fresh intensity to the gunfight at the deep end of the pool, and Court wanted to hurry up to take advantage of it. He turned away from the woman, she put her hands on his hips like she'd seen happen four times previously, and Court said, "Here we go!"

Court risked a peek around the corner where the figures had been, and then he moved quickly back to his left, scanning with his Glock in a wide arc as they moved together in perfect symmetry.

He used suppressive fire to keep heads down, because he could barely see ten feet in the smoke and poor light, but he somehow managed to make it a fifth time through the gauntlet. He kept moving deeper into the smoke-filled changing area. The girl with him kept her hands on his hips, and after he checked to make sure Nattapong Chamroon hadn't moved from the corner, he spoke to the blonde, still close behind him and holding on.

"It's okay, you're safe now. Follow your friends down the hall to the—"

Court started to look back over his shoulder when he felt the woman's hands leave his hips, slide up his body, then re-form in a grasp around his right wrist, just below his pistol. She spun her body around, pushed her back into him, then twisted his arm, all in a quarter second. She slammed her hips hard into his upper legs and yanked forward with a brute strength Court wouldn't have expected from most men.

The American felt his center of balance tip towards her; his feet rocked forward, and then the blonde swept her right leg back, kicking his legs out from under him. She threw him over her right hip, still holding his wrist so she could control the barrel of his weapon.

Court's feet went over his head, and he landed hard on his back. He felt the pistol pulled from his grasp at the same time that the air was knocked from his lungs.

The blonde dropped down on him, placing a knee hard in his chest. He didn't see the gun, but he was certain she had it now. Instead, he just looked up at her, her face inches from him.

"I'm taking Chamroon," she said.

She stood quickly now, holding the black Glock pistol on Court as she moved over to Nattapong Chamroon. She grabbed him by his arm, pulled him up to his feet, and half dragged him towards the back hallway. Chamroon coughed in the smoke and grunted in pain each time his right foot came down and his wrecked knee took his body weight, but he followed along.

Court rose to his knees, still watching the blonde, still trying to take a breath.

At the door she glanced out into the hall for an instant, then turned back in Court's direction. Just as he managed to suck in some smoky air, he saw her raise the weapon towards him.

She fired once into the wall, just a foot to Court's right.

Court looked at the bullet hole, then back at the blonde.

In English she said, "If anyone ever asks, I missed. Is that cool?"

Court just stood there, utterly transfixed by the woman. He said nothing.

The blonde repeated herself as she struggled to muscle Chamroon all the way up against her body so she could move with him. "Is that cool?"

Now Court replied softly, "*Very* cool."

She shoved Chamroon into the hallway, and they disappeared in the smoke, leaving Court alone in the room.

He spoke to himself now. "What the fuck just happened?"

At the far end of the pool, nearly thirty meters away from the changing room, a soaking wet Vasily decided to give the order to retreat. He would throw away any chance he and his team had to capture Nattapong Chamroon, but he made the decision because this gunfight had turned into a stalemate, and smoke in the room had gotten thick enough that he felt the attackers had no more chance to achieve their objective than he did.

The men at the double doors were Chinese; this Vasily had worked out quickly. A group of Thais had stormed into the single door halfway down the pool on the right side after the Chinese arrived, but Vasily and his men had killed all but one or two of them relatively quickly. Not so with the Chinese, who had the sense and the skill to remain in the cover of the doorway and just fire into the large open room.

Vasily had climbed out of the swimming pool by pulling off his jacket, his body armor, and his chest rig, and now he knelt behind a marble nude at the deep end. Mikhail lay dead right in front of him, faceup with a bullet wound in the side of his mouth. Yevgeni was seriously injured, hemorrhaging from his thigh, and only a self-administered tourniquet had prevented him from bleeding out in the past minute. Ruslan had been shot through the arm, but he was engaging a Thai gunman with his pistol now.

Over one third of Vasily's force had been decimated by the Thais and the Chinese . . . and the motherfucking building seemed to be on fire.

He'd lost his headset somewhere in the pool, but his waterproof handheld walkie-talkie had survived. Into it he said, "Anna One, all signs! We are leaving via the fire escape on the west side. Exfil together. Keep your shape!"

His men rose from cover and began bounding back in retreat, engaging both the Chinese and the smattering of Chamroon men while they attempted to disengage from the fight.

Zoya Zakharova shoved Nattapong Chamroon hard over a stack of tables on the second floor of the building. The wounded man crashed down onto the floor, grabbed at his back and his leg simultaneously, and wailed in pain.

Zoya knelt over him with the gun pointed at his face. "I won't ask you again!"

"I told you! I don't know what you're talking about!"

"Then you and me are going to sit here until you figure it out, or until you burn!"

The two of them were closed off in a large storage closet for the nightclub two floors below the pool, and even though there were no air ducts in this room at all, the gray smoke swirling about made it hard to breathe. Zoya rubbed her eyes hard, smearing eye makeup, and the dark color only made her look more dangerous to her prisoner.

Nattapong screamed now. "My brother! My brother handles the computers! I just handle the girls!"

Zoya said, "*Da*, you *handled* me with your nasty fingers right between my legs as we walked up the stairs to the pool, didn't you?"

"I'm . . . I'm sorry! It was just a touch!"

Zoya slammed her heel into the man's bloody knee, and he screamed. "Where is your brother?"

"I . . . don't know."

"After this. After tonight? Where will he go? Where will he hide?"

Nattapong Chamroon cocked his head, thinking over the question. "I . . . I don't know for sure."

Zoya placed the barrel of the gun over Chamroon's crotch now, and she pulled his mobile phone out of his front pocket. "Why don't we get him on the phone right now. You will tell him you have been attacked by the Chinese, who are looking for Fan Jiang, and you will tell him they are coming for him next. That will force him to make a move from where he is, and he will take Fan with him as a bargaining chip."

She handed him the phone, and then she said, *"Di chan poot tai dai."* I can speak Thai. It wasn't true; she'd studied Thai for a grand total of two days, but she was a polyglot with skill and technique at picking up the important components of a new language quickly. And she knew if Natta-pong thought she could speak his language, he'd be less likely to try to trick her when talking to his brother.

He cocked his head. *"Khoen kauwtsjaaj phom maaj?"* He was testing her, asking her if she understood him.

She did not, but she played a hunch on what she thought he was saying. *"Ka,"* *Yes,* she said, "but speak English to me."

Chamroon looked at the smoke filling the room. "The building is burning down! There is no time for this."

"Then let's not wait any longer. Call your brother. Find out where he is, where he is going, and no fucking tricks. *Khao jai mai?" Do you understand?*

CHAPTER

FORTY-THREE

Vasily moved down a dark and smoke-filled hallway, his team around him. With one hand he held a pistol out in front of him, and with the other he held his walkie-talkie to his mouth. He spoke between coughs. "Anna One for Fantom, how copy?"

Oleg Utkin was standing in front of the Black Pearl in a crowd two hundred strong watching the activity as fire trucks pulled into position and men and women covered with soot continued staggering out the door.

"Loud and clear, Anna One. What is your status?"

"We're *fucked*, Fantom! I've got one dead, one injured that we are carrying, and two walking wounded. We need to make a hasty exfil down the fire escape, but we can't see down to ground level from our position. Get to the west side of the building and make sure the alleyway is clear of hostiles!"

"Roger that," Utkin said, then he crossed the street to the west and peered down the dark alley. In the distance, out of the lights of the intersection, a few attractive young women staggered arm in arm out of the alleyway. He thought they might have been the hookers he saw with Chamroon earlier. Behind them the fire escape was clear, and he saw no one else in the alley.

"Anna One . . . confirm you are clear to the west."

Utkin couldn't be certain, but he wasn't going any deeper in that alleyway to check it out. No, he'd been here waiting for a report from Zaslon, and now that he had it, he knew he needed to get clear of the area before the cops started pulling people out of the crowd to ask what they'd seen. There was an emergency rally point for the Russian task force just two blocks away, and he'd go there.

Vasily came back over the radio. "How the hell could you have checked the alley that fast?"

Fantom snapped back at the macho asshole on the radio. "I said it's clear. I'll meet you at rally point Boris. I'll get the van ready to roll. Out."

The Chinese asset kneeling between the garbage cans in the alley on the west side of the building had been watching the fire escape for the past fifteen minutes, but other than a group of four half-naked soot-covered women in bare feet, no one had come down. He found this surprising because smoke poured out of the windows of the building, and he'd heard the transmissions from the men fighting on the top floor. There, a wounded but still-in-command Major Xi had announced that the Russians had egressed out of the battle, but the man between the garbage cans had not seen a trace of them.

Suddenly he heard the noise of squeaking metal, several stories above him. Seconds later, he detected movement up there in the darkness. One big dark form, moving very slowly down. It wasn't until they passed the third-floor landing and started down to the second that he was able to see individual shapes in the mass. Still, he wasn't exactly sure what he was looking at.

Finally he realized the men above him were big and Western-looking, he could see weapons among them, and they were carrying one of their number by his shoulders and legs.

The man squatting in the alley pressed the button on his radio.

"This is Yisheng, west side. I have six *gweilo* descending the fire escape. One is injured."

The call came quickly. "Yisheng, this is Major Xi. Engage them. You will have to do it alone; we are escaping through the nightclub and still engaging the Thais."

Yisheng was a Ministry of Defense operative and a former PLA special forces sergeant, and this, plus the fact he had a tactical advantage over the men descending the fire escape, made him confident in taking on the superior number.

But it didn't matter if he was confident or not. Major Xi worked for Colonel Dai, which meant failure to comply with Xi's order would mean certain death.

Yisheng sighted his fully automatic weapon on the head of the first man in the line, tracked it for an instant, and wondered if he was about to press a trigger for the last time in his life.

Yisheng opened fire.

Pyotr carried Yevgeni by the legs and was just looking back to make the turn at the landing that would take him to the ladder. The plan was to lower the injured man on Ruslan's back, which would probably mean both would fall several feet into the alley.

But it was a hell of a lot better than staying in the burning building.

Just as Pyotr turned back and adjusted his grip on Yevgeni's ankles, his head snapped to the side and he tumbled the half flight down, crashing onto the wounded man and pulling Ruslan over with him.

An automatic weapon boomed in the alleyway. Arseny took rounds to both legs, then fell off the side of the stairs, down two flights, landing on his shoulder, snapping his neck instantly.

Vasily saw the origin of fire below, down between the garbage cans, and he turned his B&T submachine gun to engage it, but before he could press his trigger he felt a hammer blow to his right hip. A second strike to his right thigh sent him tumbling forward on the staircase, tumbling over the top of Yevgeni and barreling down through Ruslan, who was just trying to get his gun up to fire after falling down where Pyotr had crashed into him.

In seconds the five Russian operatives fell into one massive heap on the first-floor landing. Every last one of them was dead or injured, but those with any life in them at all struggled frantically to get their weapons pointed at the source of the gunfire.

Oleg Utkin heard the shooting from the alley he'd just left. A single weapon firing automatically and unsuppressed indicated to his trained ear that his team had just been ambushed.

"*Der'mo,*" he mumbled to himself, then he picked up the pace. He'd get to the RP and he'd wait for the men, and if they didn't show up he'd drive out of here, keep on driving till daylight, and get himself over the border.

This shit wasn't his doing. He'd been ordered into a fucked-up operation in progress, so he wasn't going to take the blame when it fell apart around him.

C ourt Gentry followed the blood trail of Nattapong Chamroon all the way from the changing area on the fourth floor down to the second floor. This would have been tough enough in any conditions, considering he was looking for individual drops of blood sometimes separated by ten or more feet. But compounding the difficulty was the fact that he had to keep a head up for hostiles, and the rooms and halls were roiling with noxious gray smoke.

In a hall on the second floor, which served as offices and storage for the nightclub below, he found the body of a gunman who appeared to Court to be Chinese. Rolling him over quickly, Court saw that the man had a pair of bullet holes center mass in his chest. Court also found the holster for a revolver under his jacket, but there was no sign of the weapon itself. In the man's pocket Court found a speed-loader with five .38 Special cartridges.

Court assumed the woman who'd just stolen his Glock had also picked herself up a backup gun.

Court searched the body a moment more, passing on the man's phone and wallet, but when his hands grasped hold of a black Montblanc pen, he pulled it out and looked it over quickly.

Yes, it was the same kind of scopolamine hydrobromide blowgun that the Chinese operatives had tried to use on him back in Hong Kong. He hadn't taken one before when he had the chance, but now he slipped the device into his pocket, thinking it was possible it could come in handy as he tried to track down Fan Jiang.

Court continued following a blood trail, and it led him to the body of Nattapong Chamroon in a room full of tables and chairs. By turning on the overhead light in the smoky room he could see that the twenty-eight-year-old had been shot right between the eyes.

The American knew instantly the blonde had been after information from the man, and it seemed clear enough that she got what she needed.

And with this, Court knew what he had to do now. He had to find the blonde, because he was certain she'd been looking for Fan, and she now knew more than he did.

Court went back out into the hallway and started for the main stairs, but in seconds he was met by a group of firemen coming in his direction. One of the firemen placed a gas mask on Court's face, and he sucked in the air greedily. While the other firefighters continued on through the second floor, Court and his rescuer moved down the hallway to a window on the eastern side of the building, where Court saw a red ladder truck. He crawled down the ladder, leaving the firefighter behind in the building.

Once Court was on the ground, a Thai police officer rushed up to him and frisked him perfunctorily. He felt the pen in his pocket but ignored it, and in seconds Court was being patted on the back by a sympathetic cop and directed to an ambulance that had just set up on the corner.

Court thanked the policeman and walked towards the ambulance, but when the cop turned away Court bypassed the vehicle.

Three minutes later he was climbing into his rented Toyota four-door up the street, wiping sweat and soot off his face, and drinking a bottle of water to clear his throat. He gave himself only forty-five seconds to rest, then he fired up the engine and headed back towards the Black Pearl.

Zoya Zakharova had made it all the way down into the nightclub carrying two pistols in her hands, but when she saw a purse left unattended on the floor by someone who'd raced out of the building, she scooped it up to hide her weapons. She then joined up with a group of civilian stragglers. Most had been hiding in a women's restroom, and a few had taken cover behind one of the bars on the mezzanine. But firefighters and police had arrived, and Zoya blended in with the mixed crowd of both Thai and foreign clubbers, and the police cordoning off the building outside didn't even glance at the blonde in the skimpy teal dress as she began walking barefoot down the street and away from the action.

She had no intention of leaving the scene, however. She knew from her intuition and experience that Vasily's team would take the fire escape down to ground level if they felt they could do it covertly, or else they would try to use grappling hooks to cross the alleyway to the nearby roof. As soon as she noticed that the buildings on both sides were higher than the one that held the Black Pearl and therefore their roofs would be harder to reach, she felt sure they'd risk the fire escape.

She turned into the alleyway on the west side and found it dark and empty-looking, and she saw the metal stairs attached to the building some forty meters ahead. Smoke poured out of the windows on several floors, obstructing her view. As she looked on, a window exploded out on the second floor, showering part of the alley with broken glass.

She moved closer, waiting for a break in the smoke, and wondered if perhaps Vasily and his team were still caught inside.

Then she saw it; on the second-floor landing, she noticed a massive form lying there. Even from forty meters away she could tell she was looking at a pile of bodies.

Zoya slipped around a tape line erected by the fire department and sprinted barefoot into the alley.

By the time she made it around the broken glass and to the fire escape, she could see that three of the men from the Zaslon team were lying on the asphalt below the ladder, and three more were piled in a heap above her. Nearby, a Chinese man in a business suit lay against the wall of the building opposite the Black Pearl, between two garbage cans. He appeared dead, and an HK lay by his side.

Zoya looked back over her shoulder quickly, making sure no one on the street behind her had entered the alley. When she saw the coast was clear, she lifted a suppressed Brügger and Thomet subgun from Arseny's still form and shot the Chinese body twice in the head at a range of fifteen feet.

Dropping the weapon, she knelt over Arseny. The Russian operator was dead with gunshot wounds and a broken neck. She moved quickly to Ruslan and found him alive but unconscious. She saw that he had been shot on the right side of his pelvis, and his left arm was badly broken. Zoya wondered if he had fallen or dropped intentionally from the landing above.

Vasily was the third man lying in the alley. His legs and lower torso had been shot several times, and he was conscious, but barely.

As she leaned over him, he looked at her with confusion.

"Koshka?"

She pulled the medical kit from Ruslan's tactical vest under his jacket and yanked out a tourniquet. With it she began cinching Vasily's right leg, and while she worked she asked, "The others?"

Vasily looked up at the fire escape landing above him. He shook his head.

"You are *certain* they are all dead?"

He nodded now. Then he said, "What are you doing here?"

Zoya did not answer. She wrapped the tourniquet around his upper leg, tightened it just below his crotch, and then yanked as hard as she could to completely cut off the blood flow. Vasily yelled out while she tied it off, but she covered his mouth with a free hand.

When he recovered, the Zaslon commander said, "Fantom. Where's Fantom?"

Zoya knew another officer from the SVR would have replaced her, but she was surprised to hear Vasily use the code name of Oleg Utkin. Utkin was known as a competent officer, but she'd personally never thought much of him as a leader. He was the guy SVR sent in to wine and dine foreign turncoats, not to run a task force of Zaslon snake eaters. She assumed he must have just been the closest, most senior operative at the time Zoya was relieved of command, so Moscow had sent him here to pick up the operation where she left it.

Fucking fools, she thought. Fan Jiang was too important a mission to hand over to Oleg Utkin.

She grabbed Vasily's walkie-talkie off his belt and depressed the talk key. "Fantom, this is Sirena. How do you copy?"

She put down the radio and kept working on Vasily, then checked on Ruslan again. Finally Utkin replied through the little speaker. "What are you doing on this net?"

Zoya picked up the radio again. "I'm on Anna One's radio. Where the fuck are you?"

"I'm at the RP."

"You have a vehicle?"

"Of course we have vehicles. We have two here. The Anna team has a minibus, and I have a two-door Audi."

Zoya replied coldly, "Well, you'll only need the car. There are two survivors. Get to the alleyway west of the Black Pearl, now. Hurry!"

CHAPTER

FORTY-FOUR

C ourt sat parked seventy-five yards away from the blond woman in the skimpy teal dress. Through the binoculars he'd pulled from his go-pack on the front seat next to him, he could see the woman on her bare knees in the narrow alley, treating one of two men lying there.

He wondered if she still had the Glock and the .38 on her. Her teal mini-dress was formfitting, with a high-rise waistline, so it certainly didn't lend itself to hiding two pounds of steel, polymer, and ammo, but Court couldn't see well enough into the dark alley from here, and for all he knew she could have taped or tied the weapons to her thighs if she had to, or she might have had a purse she'd laid next to the men that he couldn't see from here.

While she continued to work alone in the dark below the fire escape, flames and smoke poured out of the windows of the building right next to her. Everyone else—civilians, police, firefighters—were all staying out of the alley because of the danger there, but Court knew the blonde wasn't going to remain undetected for long, because she was just forty or fifty yards from the intersection on the opposite side of the block from Court, and there a Bangkok fire department truck and a crowd of onlookers were in plain view, and she was in plain view of them if they took the time to shine a light up the alley.

As Court focused again on the woman performing immediate-action first aid on the two prostrate figures, a black Audi coupe rolled up to the mouth of the alleyway between Court and the blonde, just half a block from the American's Toyota four-door. The Audi turned into the alley but stopped abruptly, likely because of the fire and the narrowness of the channel between the buildings.

A man climbed out of the driver-side door, then knelt and pulled his seat forward to access the backseats in the coupe. He left his door open as he jogged off up the alley.

Court realized instantly this was the man he'd pegged as an SVR operative in the nightclub earlier. Clearly he'd left the car door open because he planned on carrying the injured men to his car.

Court looked at the open back door on the far side of the man's vehicle, then quickly pulled one of his phones out of his pack along with the Bluetooth earpiece he'd bought with it, and he climbed out of his Toyota. He took off in a sprint for the Audi.

As he ran he dialed the number of his other phone—he'd written it on a piece of tape affixed to the back of the device—and then he paired that phone with the Bluetooth earpiece. As soon as he got to the car he ducked down behind it and looked up the alley, and there he saw that the man in the suit and the blonde were both kneeling over one of the men lying on his back.

Court reached into the Audi and crammed the cell phone under the driver's seat, then took the tiny Bluetooth earpiece and wedged it between the driver's headrest and the seat back, careful to position the device so only the microphone tip was visible, and then only to someone really looking for it.

Court spun back out of the Audi, then ran back for his own car in a crouch.

O leg Utkin knelt down over Vasily and Ruslan, but he did not render first aid. Instead he looked up at the bright intersection ahead, which was crowded with firefighters.

He slowly surveyed the alley around him. A dead Chinese man in a black suit was crumpled against the wall between some metal garbage cans. He asked, "Where is the rest of Anna?"

Zoya pointed up, and Utkin looked to the fire escape. There, just a few meters over his head, Pyotr, Yevgeni, and Andrei all lay in a heap, their bodies a twisted mass. Blood dripped down from multiple locations, missing Oleg by no more than a couple of feet.

Zoya said, "Before he passed out, Vasily said Mikhail was killed on the fourth floor."

"*Der'mo.* How bad are they?" he asked, referring to the two survivors.

"They'll survive if we get them to a hospital." She had removed their guns and gear and radios, Ruslan's body armor, and the extra magazines she found in Vasily's pockets. She threw the equipment over by the dead Chinese operative.

Oleg knelt down and started to lift Vasily.

Zoya said, "What are you doing?"

"Taking him to the car. Get his legs."

"I just told you they need a hospital." She stood up, waved to the firefighters forty meters away on the well-lit street, and shouted for them to help.

Oleg said, "No! These men can't be interviewed by police!" He started to heave Vasily up alone, but Zoya grabbed Utkin by the arm and spun him to face her.

"They'll die!"

Utkin said, "Then they'll die! I have my orders. No compromise."

But Bangkok firefighters had heard Zoya, and they were already running over. Zoya found one who spoke some English, and she showed the man the wounds on the two men. He immediately spoke into his radio, while other firemen grabbed the victims to pull them farther away from the burning building, closer to the dead Chinese gunman.

The firemen stared in astonishment at all the weapons and bullet holes in the four men, and Zoya realized they hadn't even seen the dead men on the fire escape's landing.

Zoya walked over to Ruslan and Vasily and said some soft soothing words in English while she appeared to hug them, one after the other, in plain view of the firemen, but in truth she was fishing around for their mobile phones, both of which she pulled off of them.

Utkin just stood there in the dark, fuming.

Zoya stood and walked over to him and spoke softly in Russian. "Where's your car?"

"Right there." He pointed up to the corner, behind the building where the Audi sat with its back door open.

Zoya said, "Let's go."

"Where?"

But she was already heading to the car. "Away from here."

A minute later the Audi raced through the nearly empty streets, heading north. Hundreds of yards behind them, Court followed along with his earpiece in his ear and his mobile phone broadcasting anything said inside the vehicle, though the sound wasn't great and Court's Russian was far from perfect.

He also had the screen of his mobile in his lap displaying an application that showed him the location of the other phone, a feature he'd taken pains to set up the day before, knowing that with this app the phone could be used as both a surveillance device and a tracking device.

The conversation in the Audi had involved a good bit of shouting, mostly from the man behind the wheel. Court could tell the man was driving because his voice was much closer to the microphone.

It was hard for Court to understand them at first, but as he tuned into their voices his comprehension improved. The argument hinged on whether it was the right call to hand the survivors of their group over to the Thai authorities. The blonde insisted she had no choice, and the big man chastised her, saying this was his operation and she had no authority to do what she had done.

The two Russians went a full minute without speaking, and then the man said, "I was warned you might show up. You were ordered to return to Moscow. You have no business here."

The woman did not reply to this.

"And what the hell are you wearing? You infiltrated the Chamroon Syndicate dressed as a whore? Your father would be so proud of you."

"Fuck you, Oleg."

"Seriously. Your presence here has compromised—"

"Why are we talking about me? Your whole team was just wiped out, while under your command."

"And that's *my* fault? I reported what I saw, and they went in. Where were you when Vasily's team took fire?"

"I was upstairs in the middle of the firefight." A pause. "Where the hell were *you*?"

"I don't answer to you, Sirena."

"*Da*, you're right. You answer to Lubyanka. In fact, why don't we just call them right now?"

There was another significant pause. Court could tell the man was looking to deflect blame onto the girl, who was clearly an SVR operative herself, and one who was already in trouble with her masters.

The driver then asked, "What did you learn in there?"

The woman answered, "Nattapong Chamroon is dead in the nightclub. His brother, Kulap, is the one with Fan. He is on the move with him now. I know where they are going."

"Where did you learn this?"

"Nattapong told me."

"You just said he was . . . oh . . . I see. Where is Kulap taking Fan?"

Court cocked his head in the trailing vehicle when the woman called Sirena didn't answer.

The man behind the wheel said, "Listen, Sirena. I came here for intel, and I'm going to get it!"

"Is that some sort of a threat?" she asked.

"This has been a costly evening already. I'm just suggesting you don't make it worse."

Court listened in as he drove, concentrating on every word to understand. He could not see the vehicle ahead of him, but on his phone he could tell they'd just turned left on Rama IX Road. Court was a minute behind them, at least, but he didn't want or need to get any closer.

The woman replied, "I'll talk to Lubyanka after you drop me off."

"The hell you will." The man said a woman's name now, but Court couldn't pick it up. He thought it might have been Stoya. "I can blame you and put this entire affair behind me."

"Ha," she said, clearly not taking him as seriously as Court took the threat. "Too bad for you Ruslan and Vasily are still alive."

"They'll cover for me," Oleg said coldly.

"You're insane," Sirena said. "I'll make a deal with you, though."

"I'm listening."

"You know how important it is to get Fan back. You also know that the minute Lubyanka finds out what happened tonight, on top of what happened in Vietnam, they will pull us out of the field."

The man said, "Have you forgotten they did that to you already?"

The woman ignored Oleg, and Court listened to the passion in her voice. "Dammit, Oleg Petrovich! I am just asking for you to come help me now. I know where Fan is going, and we can get him. *Then* we can contact Moscow. Otherwise all this has been for nothing."

Court liked the intensity of this woman, even if she worked for the wrong team. He caught himself rooting for her to win her argument.

But when Oleg did not reply, Court started to worry.

And when he saw on his GPS phone tracker that the car was pulling off the road and stopping, his concern only grew.

The woman spoke in confusion, now, but not in alarm. *"Ti choto?"* *What the hell?*

He heard a struggle, banging and grunting, and then the woman screamed. *"Podozhdi! Nyet! Ne nado!"* *Wait! No! Don't do it!*

A gunshot cracked in Court's earpiece, and he floored the gas pedal, racing towards the blip on his tracking app, a half mile ahead.

CHAPTER

FORTY-FIVE

Whatever had taken place inside the Audi between the two Russian spies, it was over by the time Court arrived. He pulled up behind the vehicle a minute later with his headlights off, and he stayed fifty yards back, though he wanted to drive right up to the rear bumper. But since he was unarmed, and since he didn't know what the situation was inside the black coupe ahead, he decided he could not get any closer.

He'd heard a total of three gunshots over the speakerphone, and sounds of a brutal struggle, but in the last twenty seconds all had been perfectly silent. He wondered if both Russians had been shot, but as he peered into the dark car parked next to the sidewalk on the two-lane residential street, he saw the driver-side door open. First a pistol fell out the door, clanked on the asphalt, and lay still. Then it seemed as if the man called Oleg was going to climb out; Court saw his head and left shoulder emerge from the car, but then his entire body just tipped sideways and rolled out, and he fell headfirst on top of the gun. His lower torso was pushed or kicked until his entire body was out of the car and lying still on the street.

Court heard the woman's voice in his earpiece now. *"Mu'dak."* Asshole. And then the car door closed and the Audi raced off on squealing tires.

Court waited for the Audi's taillights to disappear in the darkness, and then he drove on, keeping an eye on the GPS phone.

He was surprised by her voice again in his ear, just five minutes later.

She'd made a phone call, obviously, but Court would have to concentrate on her half of the conversation to work out who she was speaking with.

"It's Sirena." A pause. "Identity code . . ." She said a long string of numbers, but Court couldn't follow them, and wouldn't remember them five seconds later, anyway. He followed the blip on his mobile app, careful to keep his speed down and his eyes on the road.

A moment later the woman said, "That doesn't matter. I am in Bangkok, as I'm sure you will work out quickly. Anna One and Anna Eight have been taken to a hospital. All the rest . . . *all* the rest, are dead. Yes . . . Fantom included."

Court knew that for Russians, "Anna" was akin to "Alpha" in the NATO phonetic alphabet. He presumed the dead gunfighters were all part of "Team A" of whatever unit they belonged to. After a brief pause she entered into a back-and-forth with the other caller where she refused to give any information about herself, why she was there, or how she knew the status of the Anna team.

After this, she regained control of the conversation. "Listen carefully. I know where Fan is going. Don't ask me how, just know that I will go, get positive ID, and contact you. Have another team prepped to travel."

After a moment's pause, she said, "You aren't listening to me! This operation is too important. We have to do *something* to blunt China's rise. Beijing will swallow up all of Asia in a couple of years. Russia can't stop them, and America *won't*. If we can get to Fan before the Chinese kill him, get him to work for us . . . then it could have incredible implications. China's secure intelligence and defense networks exposed? Their classified operations and personnel revealed? Forget Russia, this is the best opportunity the West will ever get to tip the balance in our favor."

The woman was silent for the next minute, other than a couple of unsuccessful attempts to interrupt the person on the other line. Finally she said, "You are making a mistake. The Americans were there tonight. Not in force, but they are in a better position to take Fan than we are, unless you sanction me to continue the operation."

After another pause, Court heard a sound that told him she'd hung up her phone and dropped it on the seat next to her. Another sound, he guessed, was the Russian woman pounding the steering wheel in frustration.

A minute later the blip on his mobile tracking app stopped moving.

Zoya Zakharova knew it was a compromise bringing Oleg Utkin's vehicle and gear to her room here at the big youth hostel in the Bang Rak neighborhood, but she wasn't terribly worried, because she also knew how the SVR task force had been operating. Utkin might have tracking devices on his gear or in his rental car, but the Lubyanka would just now be looking for his vehicle. Once they did pinpoint the GPS coordinates of his car, it would still take security officers from the local residency an hour at a minimum to muster up a team to go to the location in force.

And Zoya only planned on being in her room here at the hostel for ten minutes to shower and change and grab her gear.

She entered the building with a master key given to each of the hostel's guests, and then she walked down to her room at the end of a long hallway. She entered with another key, flipped on the light, and then stepped into the bathroom to turn on the shower.

While she waited for the water to warm she removed her blond wig with the long bangs, slipped off her torn and bloodstained teal dress and her sweat-soaked underwear, and tore off her fake eyelashes.

She looked in the bathroom mirror now and saw blood splatter across her face from where she'd turned Oleg Utkin's pistol against him during the fight. She was still coming to grips with the fact that the prick had tried to kill her, but she knew she had to push that out of her mind so she could figure out the other aspects of the night that still did not make sense.

She took the stolen Glock 17 out of the stolen purse and put it on the sink within easy reach of her in the shower, and she pulled the five-shot .38 revolver and brought it with her into the shower, placing it on a tiny soap ledge.

She washed herself as quickly as possible, using a copious amount of cheap industrial liquid soap out of a pump bottle attached to the wall, and while she did so she thought back to what she could not help feeling was the most confusing part of the night.

The American.

The man who'd risked his life to come back for her and the other girls, with no possible benefit to his objective. In fact, the stranger had completely sacrificed his mission by returning to Zoya and the others, although he hadn't known that was what he was doing at the time.

But why?

The man seemed to be operating completely alone, and this was not the modus operandi of the U.S. intelligence services. Zoya had spent over a decade on foreign jobs where knowledge of the CIA's operating protocol was necessary to her completion of the mission. And this man's actions didn't look like a CIA job *at all.*

Some non-official cover operatives working with the Agency might function in a singleton capacity, but they sure as hell wouldn't hit a nightclub with dozens of armed men while flying solo.

But what this American did . . . *that* took balls. She thought about him racing into the gunfire several times to rescue the girls, and she thought about how she'd left him there in the changing area, stealing both his gun and his captive.

She felt like shit about what she'd done, and this was a strange feeling for her.

She wondered what had happened to him, and then, at the moment she realized she couldn't really remember what he looked like, she realized this was probably the same American she saw sitting at the bar on Po Toi Island, a week and a half earlier. He had been in the middle of Wo Shing Wo there, he was in the middle of the Chamroon Syndicate here . . . so it was only natural to wonder if he'd been the mysterious man who had absconded with Fan in Vietnam.

Why not? He certainly seemed crazy enough to do that on his own, as well.

Zoya had spared his life tonight because he'd helped the other women. She had spent two full days with victimized African and European human traffic victims, and while the first day she had wanted to wring some of their stupid necks herself, over time she had developed an odd bond with them.

Still, she didn't know if she would run through gunfire multiple times to save them.

Zoya turned off the shower after just a minute and a half, and then she reached out to grab the towel. She started drying herself off, pushed the plastic curtain out of the way to climb out . . .

. . . and then dropped straight down to the floor of the shower onto her knees, grabbing the revolver off the ledge as she went down.

She extended the pistol in a combat crouch out in front of her, pointed it back towards her room, and held her breath.

The Glock 17 was gone from the sink, and the bathroom door was now closed.

After a few seconds a voice came from outside the door, speaking English. "If you toss the .38 out, I'll throw in your clothes."

Zoya recognized the American's voice, and she knew he was in her room now, along with the pistol she'd stolen from him.

She didn't know what to do. There was no good place for her to get behind cover in this tiny bathroom. Sure, she could open fire into her room, blast through the flimsy wooden door, but he had more room to maneuver for cover than she did, less space to fire into, and more bullets in his weapon, so he would have all the advantages in that fight.

With the presence of mind to use her Hungarian-accented English, she called out to him. "What do you want?"

"I just told you what I wanted. Shall I repeat it?"

Zoya cocked her head. There was a surprising composure in the man's voice considering the two of them now held each other at gunpoint at a distance of three meters.

The door opened a foot, but the lights in her room were off, and the light from the bathroom didn't reveal anyone out there.

"Toss it out, and I throw in some clothes."

"No deal," she said. "I can fight naked. I *can't* fight without a gun."

The American's response came quickly. It was loud enough to be heard, but soft enough so that she was unable to pinpoint just where in the room the man was standing. "I'm trying to *avoid* a fight. Trust me, Sirena, this is the best deal you're gonna get from me."

How the hell does he know my code name?

After a few seconds her shoulders dropped, and she lowered the handgun. She opened the cylinder of the .38 Special and let the five rounds fall to the floor in the shower. They made a clinking sound that would have been obvious to anyone out in the bedroom. Then she put the revolver on the floor in front of her and slid it out through the opening in the door and into the room.

"Thank you," came the voice. And then, "Are you ready?"

"*What?*"

The door opened a little further, and a few seconds later a black V-neck T-shirt and a pair of jeans tumbled through the air. Zoya caught the items, noticed there was no underwear, and just as she was about to say something about that, she heard the disembodied voice again.

"Oh . . . sorry."

Folded underwear out of her backpack came sailing in.

The door was then pulled shut. Zoya wondered if the man had tied a string to the latch, because she'd neither seen nor heard anyone move inside the room. "No rush," said the American, and she detected sarcasm in the statement.

Zoya thought this had to be one of the strangest things she'd ever experienced in the field.

A minute later she was dressed, though her feet were bare, and her chin-length dark hair was still wet and tousled, half tucked behind her ears and half drooping in her face. She opened the door slowly and saw that the lights had been turned back on.

"Come out slowly, hands high."

She raised her hands, stepped out, and looked into the eyes of the American she'd seen earlier in the night. He stood in front of the door to the hall; the big Glock pistol was low in his hands, but when he saw that her hands were empty he slid the pistol into his waistband at the small of his back.

She lowered her own hands and looked the man over.

He was in his thirties, perhaps thirty-one, perhaps thirty-nine; he had brown hair cut short but not severely so, an athletic build, and eyes that might have been brown, hazel, or amber. He wasn't particularly tall, his clean-shaven face was pleasant enough but in no way descript, and his expression was impossibly calm, considering all that had happened tonight, and everything she had put him through. There was a little dark soot on the man's face, but he'd changed clothes into a gray T-shirt and black cotton pants.

Zoya still used the Hungarian accent she'd been employing the past few days. "Who are you?" She felt sure her nervousness was obvious in her voice.

"You know who I am because I'm the one who *wasn't* wearing a blond wig and ten layers of makeup tonight. I want to talk to you."

She shook her head. "I have nothing to say."

The man now asked, "Maybe I'll just hang out here till you change your mind. How much time before someone comes here looking for you?"

"Other than yourself, you mean?"

"You know what I mean. From the residency."

"I don't know what you—"

"I placed a bug in Oleg's car." Then he switched into English-accented Russian. *"Ya govoryu po russky." I speak Russian.*

And with that, she muttered, *"Der'mo."*

"I'll ask you again. How long do you have before they come for you?"

She sighed a little, sure she shouldn't be talking, but unable to see what it mattered at this point. He was here, and he knew who she was and what had happened. She let her Hungarian accent drift off, and her very light Russian accent appeared. "I need to leave. Now."

"I wouldn't take the Audi."

"No kidding."

The man smiled a little, but he did not move.

Zoya said, "Well . . . If you came looking for Nattapong, as you can see, I'm not hiding him anywhere."

The American replied, "I found Nattapong where you left him. I'm no doctor, but I don't think he's going to be much help to me."

Zoya swallowed. Yes . . . now she understood the American's plan here. He had come to torture her for the intel she picked up from Chamroon so he could get his hands on Fan Jiang. She wondered if he'd kill her when he was done.

She gauged the distance between herself and the door, and the distance between herself and the man with the gun in the small of his back. She thought she could get to him before he got the weapon out, but she found herself unwilling to try. He wasn't particularly big, and he had not threatened her overtly, except by his presence here. But Zoya knew what this man had done tonight—part of it, anyway—and he'd certainly be wired to suspect some sort of resistance on her part.

And he'd be ready for it.

To her surprise he said, "I'm here to ask for your help."

With suspicion in her voice, she asked, "What kind of help?"

"First, let's take my car and get out of here. We'll go somewhere safe. Then we can talk."

The Russian girl with the wet dark hair looked down to the floor, bit her lip, and then shrugged a little. "You have the gun. So I will agree to your terms."

"Good."

"But I have to pack first."

The American lifted her bag off the bed and onto his shoulder without taking his eyes from her. He said, "I took the liberty of packing for you while you were in the shower. And since I'm a gentleman, I'll go ahead and carry this bag that has two folding knives and a switchblade in the outer pockets."

"How very nice of you," Zoya said, and she realized she was now a prisoner of the Central Intelligence Agency.

CHAPTER

FORTY-SIX

Court drove a Toyota Vios, essentially a newer Tercel made for and marketed to the Southeast Asian market. He moved his own big pack into the backseat and threw the Russian woman's bag in next to it. He moved his pistol from the small of his back to his left side, then climbed behind the wheel while she got into the passenger side.

Court said, "I'm not going to tie you up, and I'm not going to hold a gun on you. I need to earn your trust, so I'm just going to ask you very nicely not to jump out of the car until you hear what I have to say. After we talk, if you want me to drop you off somewhere . . . I will do as you ask."

The woman said, "Right."

Court could tell she didn't believe him.

As he pulled away from the youth hostel she looked around at the little gray four-door. "I would have expected the Agency to give you a nicer car."

"The agency? You mean the car rental agency?"

The Russian just stared at the American for a moment, then asked, "Where are we going?"

"It will be dawn soon. I'll get us a hotel room, someplace near the airport where it won't look strange to show up so early. We will get checked in, and then we'll sit and talk. Are you hungry? We can find some food first, but I don't want to talk in public."

The woman shook her head. "No. I am not hungry."

Court said, "Well, I'm starving and, like you said, I've got the gun."

"I could eat something, I guess."

Thirty minutes later they were checked in at the Novotel Suvarnabhumi, within sight of the airport runways at Bangkok's Suvarnabhumi International Airport. Before they even took their bags to their room they sat in the restaurant, their plates full of items from the breakfast buffet.

Around them a few businessmen and businesswomen started their day in small groups, many already talking about work.

But Court and Zoya ate mostly in silence, and they drank copious amounts of coffee.

Even while Zoya ate her eggs and bit into her toast, she never took her eyes from Court. She was mistrustful, confused about the entire situation, but on top of that she was trying to commit his face to memory.

Court ate a bite of oatmeal, then, apropos of nothing, said, "Your . . . colleagues. Did any of them make it?"

Zoya looked down to her plate. "Two. They are injured, but they should survive."

"Friends of yours?"

"No. I wasn't even working with them tonight."

"How many did you lose?"

The woman seemed hesitant to answer. Then she gave a little shrug. "Five men died."

"I'm sorry. I heard Oleg mention that you were recalled to Moscow, but you didn't go back. Is that true?"

The Russian woman snapped back now. "If you heard him say that, then you have your answer, don't you?"

She chewed her toast slowly, still looking hard across the table. When Court said nothing to this, she said, "I was down here on my own, trying to help. Obviously, I failed."

Court sipped his coffee. "That's not obvious to me. Your team walked into a buzz saw tonight. There was a unit of well-trained operatives from the Chinese mainland hitting at the same time your countrymen did. And the Chamroon Syndicate hires its security officers from only two places: Arintharat 26, which is the Royal Thai Police Federal SWAT team, and—"

The Russian woman interrupted him. "And the Underwater Demolition Assault Unit of the Royal Thai Navy. SEALs, basically."

Court said, "Sounds like you did your homework. Your friends shouldn't have hit that fortified location."

"I'll tell them if they ever get out of surgery. Of course, that will be difficult because they'll be in a Thai prison."

Court called for the check and got two full cups of coffee to go, and then the two of them went upstairs to the room. It was a small suite with a living room with a sofa and chairs divided by a door to the bedroom and the bathroom. Court tossed the packs against the wall, then sat down across from the Russian in the little sitting area.

She asked, "Do you want to clean up first? I can still see the soot from the fire on your face."

Court shook his head. "I'm pretty sure you will walk out if I turn my back."

"Why would I do that? You have some amazing proposal to offer me, and I'm free to leave at any time." She said it with obvious skepticism.

Court smiled a little. "Oleg called you by name, but I couldn't understand it."

"Just call me Sirena."

"That's a shitty code name." Zoya did not respond to this, and Court thought a moment. "Sirena Vozdushnoy Trevogi. Your code name is Banshee."

She neither confirmed nor denied, but Court didn't wait for her to do either.

"That's better than Sirena."

"What is your name?" she asked.

"I'm Bob."

"Right. I'm Jane."

"I like Banshee," Court said. "You told Oleg, and you told your handler, that you found out where Fan is being held."

Zoya said, "I just told them that to get them to help me. The truth is, Nattapong didn't talk."

"So you just gave up and shot him?"

"That's right."

"You don't strike me as a quitter."

Zoya looked right at Court but said nothing.

He switched gears. "I saw you at the Wild Tigers safe house in Vietnam, climbing the wall of the villa."

Without blinking, Zoya said, "If you saw me, why didn't you shoot me?"

"I couldn't. I was lying low, impersonating a plant."

"I'm sure you were very convincing." She lifted her chin a little. "And I saw you on Po Toi Island. You sat at the bar, pretended to be British, and you asked the bartender something about some men you were looking for. It made him nervous, and it made me curious."

Court's eyes narrowed. "I don't . . ." With a slow nod, Court just stared at her, dumbfounded. "You wore a leather headband?"

The woman nodded.

"I thought you were about nineteen."

"Who says I'm not?"

"Who was the other woman?"

"From Germany, I think she said. I met her on the ferry and attached myself to her. Thought I'd look less suspicious that way."

"It worked," confirmed Court.

"It usually does. My 'hippie girl traveling with others' is my best third-world cover."

"Better than the Hungarian hooker?"

"They both have their place." With a challenging tone she said, "How about you, Bob? What's *your* best alias?"

"Quiet guy who asks a lot of questions but doesn't answer many."

She gave him a quizzical look but said, "And you are in character now."

"Actually, this is the real me. I want to know where Fan Jiang is being held."

Zoya looked out the window.

Court said, "You seem nervous being here with me. If I posed a real threat to you, do you really think I'd take you from your hotel, bring you here, and buy you breakfast? You are in danger, sure, but not from me. I wish you would relax a little so we could talk freely."

Zoya thought about what the man had said, but she did not let her guard down. "Obviously you saved my life tonight, and obviously I took advantage of your kindness, stole your gun and your prisoner."

"And you threw me over your hip. Don't forget that."

"Yes, I did. I have no right to expect anything else from you after what I did."

Court said, "I understand the job. You had an objective. I was in the way."

"If you understand the job, as you say, then why did you risk rescuing the five of us?"

"Just because I know what my job is, it doesn't mean I always do it."

"Your employer must get very frustrated with you."

"You have no idea."

Zoya waved a hand in front of her. "But you seem to be back on mission now, because you are here, with me, and you are asking about Fan. Why am I not in some CIA rendition facility getting water poured up my nose?"

Court chuckled. "I don't work for the CIA."

"Right."

He leaned forward. "I saw what happened tonight, and I know that whatever happens to you, you aren't going back to Russia with Fan Jiang to receive a hero's welcome. Any decent investigation by the SVR is going to show that you killed Oleg. The circumstances of why will be irrelevant. I hate to break it to you, but you are no longer an operative with Russian intelligence."

She nodded. "No . . . I am not. But why do you care?"

"The question is, why should you care about my operation? And I'll tell you. I heard what you said to your handler, and you are absolutely correct. China is a great danger to both of our nations. The USA sees it. Clearly Russia sees it, too. We're going to need intelligence from the Chinese intelligence networks, and that kid Fan can do that for us."

"We?"

"I mean the West. China has plans for the world. What you and I do now can help us slow down their dominance, maybe knock them down a few steps."

"What do you mean, 'what you and I do'?"

"You tell me where Kulap Chamroon is hiding Fan Jiang. I go and rescue him. I'll get him away from the Thais and save him from the Chinese before they assassinate him."

Zoya cocked her head. "Why on earth would I help America?"

"Maybe I'm wrong, but I don't believe you are my enemy. You were thrown off this mission, but you came back on your own, despite the danger. Despite what you knew it would do to your career to defy the Lubyanka.

Well . . . you still have a chance to succeed now. Not for Moscow, but for the West."

"How do I know you won't just kill me when I tell you?"

Court sighed. "Would it help if I handed you my gun now? Would that demonstrate to you I was no threat?"

Zoya nodded slowly. "That would help a great deal."

Court made no movement towards the pistol tucked under his T-shirt.

"Well?" Zoya asked.

"You aren't getting a gun. Jesus, lady, I'm a nice guy, but I'm not fucking crazy."

"No, I don't believe you are. But I also don't believe you are as heroic as you make yourself out to be. I think you are . . . What do you guys say in America? I think you are playing me."

"You mean you think you are being played?"

"Yes. That's it."

"I just want Fan, and you know where he is. It's as simple as that."

Zoya said, "The truth is, I don't know Fan Jiang's location. Nattapong did not know exactly where Fan was being taken, only that Kulap would move Fan and get out of Bangkok because of what was going on at the Black Pearl. He was going someplace where he'd be protected."

Court said, "But you know where."

"Nattapong told me where he *thought* his brother would go. Still . . . I only have the guess of a Thai gangster to go on."

Court said, "It's more than I've got. Will you tell me?"

Zoya looked at him a long time. "Where is everyone else on your team?"

He shrugged. "It's just me."

"You are a liar."

"I'll rephrase that . . . it's just me on the hunt. I have been told I can call in some help on the ground for the actual rescue, but for now, everyone else is somewhere safer."

"Then your colleagues aren't much better than mine."

"At least they haven't tried to kill me." It was a bald-faced lie. The CIA had spent years trying to do just that, but since he was back in their good graces, sort of, and since he was only speaking about this particular mission, he felt he was being honest enough.

"Yet," Zoya said.

"Right. Yet," Court allowed.

Finally, she said, "I was given a job, and my job is not completed. I want to go with you. I want to see this operation through to the end."

Court stared at her a long time. Finally he said, "Agreed. Where do we go to look for him?"

Zoya hesitated a moment; she was afraid to play her one card. But finally she said, "Phuket, Thailand."

CHAPTER

FORTY-SEVEN

For the next hour Zoya and Court sat in the hotel room and pored over Court's computer looking at maps of Phuket, a few hundred miles south of Bangkok along the ocean. Zoya explained that Nattapong's father, Panit, owned a large jungle property that ran along the coast. Panit was abroad, and Kulap had told his brother he would lay low in Bangkok for a day or two, and then he would go to the Phuket estate.

Zoya also explained that Kulap had a helicopter, and if he was, in fact, at the estate, then the helo would be there, as well.

The two operatives used Google Earth to zoom in to the walled property, just inland from the coast. In the center was a large ornate home in the traditional Thai style, surrounded by tropical gardens, rimmed by thick jungle on all sides.

Less than a half mile west of the property was a large five-star resort. Court and Zoya agreed they would go to the resort, check in under the cover of an American couple, and begin their reconnaissance.

It looked like the journey by car from Bangkok to Phuket would take twelve hours if they split up the driving duties, which they agreed to do. They were both dead tired already, but Zoya offered to drive the first leg while Court slept.

Court agreed to this, as well, but he said he needed to go for a quick walk and make a phone call before they left.

"You are calling your handler, obviously," Zoya said. "Why can't I listen to you? Obviously you will tell him about me, you will tell him about Fan, and you will tell him about our plan to find him."

Court shook his head. "In this instance I truly believe that less is more. My handler would be very upset if I revealed I am working with an SVR asset."

"You could tell him I was fired."

Court stood and headed to the door. "We are a team, you and me, but you'll have to trust me that I know what I'm doing. My handler is—"

"Your handler is a woman, I take it."

Court cocked his head. "How did you—"

"You keep saying 'my handler,' so as not to give the gender away. You wouldn't do that if your handler were male."

Court was at once pissed at himself for the tell and stunned by her powers of intuition.

"Yes. My handler is a woman."

Zoya said, "Most men I know would have just lied." She shrugged. "It's a bad sign that my new partner gives away his secrets so easily, but maybe it's a good sign that my new partner is, at least, a *little* honest with me."

Five minutes later Court stood in the open parking lot of the Novotel, watching an Airbus A320 take off from the airport just a half mile away. In his hand he held his mobile, and while he waited for Brewer to come on the line he thought about the woman upstairs.

He wondered if she'd run, now that he wasn't watching her. Of course he knew he couldn't trust her to stay, and he couldn't be sure she wouldn't call someone. He'd taken her mobile phone from her, but right now as he stood here she could have been on the hotel phone calling the police, the Russian embassy, or some other group. There were all sorts of people who could come in and ruin Court's day, and he'd done nothing to prevent Banshee from contacting any of them.

But he trusted his instincts. And while his instincts did not tell him to trust her fully, they also told him she wanted the same thing he did, and she was practical enough to realize she needed help to get it.

Suzanne Brewer answered the phone with unmasked concern in her voice. It was ten p.m. on the East Coast, but at this point in the operation he took it as a given that Brewer would be in her office when he called.

"Identity challenge, Dastardly."

"My response is Denver."

"Confirmed. What's your status? Everything I've heard about the Black Pearl has been disconcerting. I was wondering if your body was going to be found in that smoldering building."

"I'm okay, but I have to tell you, your idea about calling the Chinese in to help last night really sucked."

"The Chinese went into the building?"

"The Chinese *and* the Russians. And God knows how many Thai. Don't worry, I kept a low profile. There are no comebacks on the Agency, and I managed to get some intel. From what I learned, Kulap has an estate in Phuket, and he might bring Fan immediately, or else it could take him a couple of days to get there. There is a helo that will be on site if Kulap Chamroon is on the property."

Brewer pulled up satellite data of the area immediately. Looking it over, she said, "No helicopter on the ground, but the most recent image I have was four p.m. yesterday. As soon as I get updated imagery I'll check again."

Court said, "I'll be on the ground there by late this evening."

Brewer said, "Tell me how you got your intel."

Court said, "Not prepared to do that. Trust that I'm working, and trust that I'll check in as soon as I have something actionable for the team."

And with that he hung up the phone. He knew he'd just pissed Brewer off, but he had to be careful with what he said. He was calling an audible working with the SVR operative, and he was certain Brewer would disagree with this decision.

Next he dialed Colonel Dai, and he told himself he had to keep his rage with the man under control.

Dai opened the conversation with, "What happened last night?"

"From where I was sitting, it looked like your men burned down a building full of innocent people, killed a dozen or more Thai gangsters and a team of Russian paramilitaries, and still managed to fail to accomplish anything."

Colonel Dai said, "I lost seven men in that nightclub."

"Then I guess you should have listened to me when I told you to keep them outside."

"If my men had not gone in, the Russians would have captured Chamroon, and by now they would probably have Fan Jiang on a jet to Moscow."

Court rubbed his temples. "No. If your men had not gone in, *I* would have captured Chamroon, and by now Fan Jiang would be dead."

"I could not take that chance."

Court said, "It doesn't matter. I have a new lead on where Fan is located."

"Tell me."

Court hesitated. "It might not bother you that everywhere your people go there is a massacre, but I'm not going to be a contributor to it. I'm going after Fan on my own. I'll kill him, and then I will contact you. It should have been this way from the start. Your people are only good at slaughtering. They lack the precision they need for this job."

"You are forgetting that Sir Donald Fitzroy is with me. What if I decide your insubordinate attitude will cost your old boss a few more of his appendages?"

Court said, "Then I won't know about it, because I'm hanging up now. I will call you back when I have taken care of Fan."

"Gentry!" Dai shouted into the phone, but Court heard nothing else, because he did as he said he'd do and hung up the phone.

He wasn't certain this was the right move. The colonel was crazy enough to kill on principle. But by not giving him an audience, Court deprived him of any real benefit he would get from killing or injuring Fitzroy.

Now Court just had to put that out of his mind and get back to his operation.

Zoya Zakharova had spent the last ten minutes going through the backpack of the American who called himself Bob. Along with the knives she had with her pack, he'd taken both guns with him to make his call, so she wasn't looking for weapons, but she wanted to get any intel she could from the equipment he carried.

The bag was stuffed with phones, basic surveillance and first-aid gear, and clothing.

Eventually she pulled out a black Montblanc pen and looked it over, because it was different from the other items in the pack. It looked authentic on the outside, but it didn't match with the other items the man carried with him. His watch was an obvious fake. His pack, his belt, his shoes; they were all just average, nothing she would ever notice.

So why was he walking around with such a fancy writing instrument? As she suspected, it wasn't just a pen. While it had a nib with ink in it, when she took the cap off and turned the base, the nib slid out of the way, exposing a hollow-looking tube. At the end of this was a CO_2 cartridge and a small clear vial of dark gray powder. There was some tiny writing on the side of the tube, and Zoya had to move it into the bright lights of the bathroom to even see it. When she could finally make it out she realized she couldn't read it.

It appeared to be in Chinese.

It had been well disguised, but Zoya wasn't fooled. She knew exactly what it was.

She'd seen scopolamine hydrobromide blowguns before in books, but never in real life, and never housed in a Montblanc pen.

Russian intelligence had used scopolamine hydrobromide back in the KGB days; she remembered studying it in her training at SVR, and while the Russians had moved on to other truth serums, she knew the Chinese still used "Devil's Breath" as a relatively effective interrogation enhancement.

The Chinese? Where did the American get this?

She almost slipped the pen in her pocket to use as a defensive weapon if it came down to it, but she decided the American was too smart to allow her to be up here with his gear all this time without taking an inventory when he returned.

She put everything back in the pack exactly the way she'd found it, and then she lay back on the bed and closed her eyes.

The American still might have been playing her, she hadn't worked that out yet, but she certainly could not argue with his logic. Zoya couldn't take Fan back to Russia without getting herself thrown in prison—or worse—for the killing of Oleg Utkin. She'd no doubt take the fall for the destruction of the Zaslon team, as well, regardless of whether Vasily and Ruslan survived and spoke up in her defense.

No . . . she wasn't going back to Russia. And while the American seemed to be reticent about some information—clearly he was keeping pertinent details of his operation from her—he also seemed to be one of the most sincere people she'd ever met. His willingness to partner with her based on a gut feeling was something she was completely unaccustomed to.

But still . . . this man must have some angle here, some ulterior motive she hadn't yet worked out.

Zoya had the clarity to realize that her mistrust of the American was not based on him at all. No, it was based on her, on her experiences, on her relationships in the past, both professional and personal. Other than her older brother, Feodor, she'd never in her life known a man who had earned both her trust and her love. She had loved her father; he had done his best, but she had known most of her childhood that she could only trust her father to live for his work.

Her father had done just that, and then he had died.

Her brother Feodor had been the *one* man different from all the others . . . and Feodor was dead, as well.

This calm but dangerous American had done everything humanly possible in the past few hours to prove himself to her—he'd saved her life, jeopardizing his mission; he'd asked for her help instead of taking the information from her that he needed; and he'd told her the truth when he could easily have lied. If he had ulterior motives in all this, at least related to her, she was unable to identify them so far, and she prided herself on her skill at sniffing out the schemes of others.

Still . . . she'd keep an eye on this man, fully expecting the other shoe to drop.

And just as she told herself this, she heard the key card in the door.

Court Gentry returned to the suite and entered as quietly as he could, expecting that the Russian woman might have nodded off to sleep. As he stepped lightly into the bedroom he found her on the bed, but her eyes were open, looking back at him. "Everything go okay with your conversation?"

"Fine. I thought you'd be sleeping."

"I wasn't sure if you'd come back. Now that I've given you my intel, I wondered if you would just leave your pack behind and drive to Phuket."

Court shook his head. "I want you right where I can see you. If I left you behind I expect I'd bump into you in Phuket anyway. We have the same objective, and if there's one thing we've learned in the past couple of weeks, it's that working against each other doesn't seem to turn out so great for either of us. I beat you in Vietnam; you beat me here."

She said, "Okay, Bob. I guess now it will be you and me against the world."

There was sarcasm dripping off the comment, but Court just smiled and hefted his pack. Zoya climbed to her feet and grabbed her own bag, and soon they were heading for the car.

CHAPTER

FORTY-EIGHT

Zoya and Court drove through a perfectly sunny day along Phetkasem Road, which ran north to south from the capital all the way to the Malaysian border. They took turns resting and driving, but for large swaths of the trip they were both awake. The conversation was stilted; both of them were tired despite catching a little rest, but the main impediment to their new relationship was the fact that neither was very experienced in opening up to others, especially others affiliated with foreign intelligence services.

Six hours into the drive, Court was behind the wheel, and he decided he'd try to probe a little, if only just to help him stay awake. Zoya sat with her knees to her chest and her chin resting on them; she looked out the window, bored.

Court said, "I know I'm not going to get too much out of you regarding your past, but I have to ask. Your English is the best I've ever heard from a Russian. Where did you learn?"

"In school," Zoya replied, and she left it there.

"You say phrases that are uniquely American. A lot of Europeans are trained in British English, but not you."

"I watched TV. We had a lot of shows from America."

Court didn't believe her, and he sighed in frustration.

Upon hearing this, Zoya said, "Tell me about your Russian. Where did you learn that?"

Court had learned in the CIA, mostly on the job, and he sure as hell wasn't going to say that even though he figured she'd be able to guess. After a few seconds he said, "You made your point." They drove along in silence for a few more seconds, and then he tried something else. "I saw you climb the side of that villa the other night. That was pretty impressive. Were you in the circus when you were a kid?"

"As a matter of fact, I was."

"Seriously, you were like a damn spider monkey."

"Thanks, I guess."

Court waited for the real story, but it never came. She'd had some sort of advanced training, perhaps even paramilitary training, and she'd maintained her skill, through either more training or real-world ops.

He didn't call her out, and he didn't push her.

He just said, "It's going to be a long drive, isn't it?"

She turned to him. "What kind of music do you like?"

Court shrugged. "Stuff you won't find on the radio in the backcountry of Thailand."

Zoya nodded. "Then yes, it's going to be a long drive."

Delayed by a flat tire and a traffic accident that backed up the two-lane highway for miles, the Toyota Vios finally crossed the bridge that brought them onto Phuket Island at ten p.m. local time. Court and Zoya stopped for dinner at the first restaurant they found. Court chose *khao neow moo ping*, pork skewers in rice, while Zoya proved herself to be the braver of the pair by ordering *tom luad moo*, a soup made from pork intestines and lungs and flavored with Thai chilies.

They then drove to the Trisara Phuket, a five-star resort in the Thalang District on the northern side of the island with a view of the Andaman Sea, part of the Indian Ocean. They checked in for three nights, and Court used the passport delivered to him in Bangkok by the CIA station that claimed his name was Chad Waverly.

When the man at hotel reception asked for Zoya's passport, she rolled her eyes, leaned onto the desk, and gave a tired smile. She told the hotel employee her name was Whitney Waverly, she was Chad's wife, and in what Court thought was an incredibly convincing Chicago accent she explained that her purse had been stolen in Bangkok and, so far, the U.S. embassy had been "absolutely freakin' worthless" in helping her get a replacement passport.

Court couldn't help but stare in awe at her Oscar-worthy performance; Zoya sold her legend completely, and soon they were on their way to their ocean-view suite.

As they walked Court said, "You grew up in the States." It wasn't a question.

"No," she said; her Chicago accent was gone, again replaced by just the faintest Russian accent.

"You're gonna tell me you learned that watching TV back on the collective farm?"

"Collective farm? I grew up in a house, same as you, I guess. Running water, indoor plumbing. Almost like a real person."

Court was egging her on, trying to get information. "Yeah, well, I hope my Russian sounds half as convincing as your English does."

"Say something in Russian and I'll let you know."

Court switched to Russian and made up a quick story that mirrored hers, claiming his name to be Ivan Ivanovic, saying he was from St. Petersburg, and he'd accidentally spilled caviar on his passport.

Zoya just rolled her eyes, and when he was finished she said, "You want the truth or do you want me to be nice?"

"I'm tired. I'll take nice."

"You sound like a Russian with a head injury and a speech impediment."

"Jesus. What if I said I wanted the truth?"

"Then I would have said you sounded like an American with a head injury and a speech impediment speaking bad Russian."

Court knew his Russian was better than that. He couldn't pass as a native speaker, but he could carry on conversations without too much trouble. Still, with her skill in languages, it was no surprise she was a tough critic.

"Why did I ever marry you, Whitney?" he joked.

Zoya did not miss a beat. "Must have been the head injury, Chad."

C ourt and Zoya toured around their well-appointed ocean-view suite, then went out on the patio off the bedroom and looked past the private infinity pool to the beach and the Andaman Sea. To the east, the lights of several large private villas owned by the resort lay sprawled along a green hillside, and beyond them the hills turned into thick jungle.

The Chamroon property was out there, just off to the east. And the resort afforded two Westerners the perfect reason to be here in the first place. This was one of the most luxurious and romantic destinations in Thailand, after all, so no one would doubt that a young couple of means from the States might be walking around here, swimming in the ocean, or hiking the nearby jungle trails.

They'd have to do everything as a couple, but they were both pros, and they could adopt their aliases easily.

Court surveyed the opulent grounds with his binoculars from his patio, and he knew that right about now Suzanne Brewer would be sitting in her office looking at an American Express charge that would make her blood boil.

Back inside he found the woman who now called herself Whitney adjusting the stereo, finding a new age station and turning the volume up on some atmospheric music that made Court think the Russian woman was about to start doing yoga on the floor.

She then went into the bathroom and turned on the water in the tub, then returned to Court and took him by the arm out to the patio.

He'd expected her tradecraft to be as practiced as his own, but he was fascinated to watch her. She did things much as he did, and as a singleton operative, he found it strange to see someone else virtually mimicking his way of functioning in the field.

She said, "We can see Chamroon's property from the beach to the east of here."

Court said, "We have to allow for the fact that Chamroon has informants at this resort. If he is running a criminal organization the size and scope of this syndicate, it would be foolish to leave this hotel next to his estate as a blind spot in his security setup."

"I agree," Zoya said. "And if anyone here at the hotel has their eyes on us, our going up the beach with binoculars right now, just after arriving, is going to look suspicious." She added, "Our clothes will look strange, too. I don't have anything for a beach vacation, but there's a boutique off the lobby I saw on the way in."

The image of Suzanne Brewer looking at more of Chad Waverly's Amex charges, especially charges that included women's beachwear, gave Court a brief moment's pleasure.

He said, "First thing tomorrow morning we'll get some suitable clothes, and we'll do some exploring. For now, we get some sleep."

Zoya said, "Okay."

She looked uncomfortable for a moment, and Court thought he understood.

He said, "You take the bed. This will seem strange, but when I am operational, I usually sleep in the closet."

"I sleep in the closet, too," she said.

Court continued to be amazed her tradecraft so closely matched his own.

Zoya added, "But . . . there is just the one closet."

"No problem," Court said. "I'll take the floor on the far side of the bed. And the pistols. That will make me feel a little safer."

"You won't give me one of the guns?"

Court shook his head. "Not even one of the knives. Sorry, Banshee. I like you, but I'm a shitty judge of character. I've liked people in the past who've tried to kill me."

They both slept hard and woke up early the next morning, and after breakfast they went for a walk along the beach to the east that took them to the area below the Chamroon estate high on the cliffs. The helipad was just south of the home, which meant if there was a helicopter there they should have been able to see it from where they walked, but they saw nothing but a mansion surrounded by a low wall.

They returned to the hotel lobby and the boutique there and, fortunately for both of them, they were able to outfit themselves with clothes that would help them fit in on the beach or hiking through the jungle. Zoya made a joke about Chad's company paying for their trip, the insinuation being that she knew the CIA was footing the bill, but Court didn't go for the bait and say anything more about his relationship with the Agency.

By the early afternoon they'd hiked all over the area around the resort to get their bearings. The Chamroon estate was massive and walled but just guarded with a couple of gatehouses, a few patrolling guards, and a couple of Jeeps with young men sitting in them. Also, as had been the case in Vietnam, the local police presence seemed to be watching over the estate, as both Court and Zoya had noticed the occasional patrol car rolling by.

They rented kayaks in the late afternoon and looked at the area from a few hundred yards offshore, and while Zoya and Court agreed that the facility seemed well protected, neither of them had a baseline on the guard setup to compare against, so they couldn't say whether Fan Jiang and Kulap Chamroon were inside. It might have just been the case that the hearty security situation was common for the property, or that the boss was expected in the next day or two.

They agreed they would not breach the property until Kulap's helicopter arrived or they had some other indicator of an increased security profile around the area. They decided they'd rent a boat and diving equipment the following morning, then take a picnic lunch to a small island just offshore of the estate. There they would be able to use their optics to get a decent look around the area, and possibly even inside windows of the building.

Court and Zoya had worked well together all day, and Court found that Zoya's earlier reluctance to open up to him was slowly giving way. She'd mentioned she'd enjoyed boating as a child, and she talked about some of the upper-body exercises she did to keep in shape. She also gave Court some insights into her ability to disguise herself with wigs, changes to her eyes, and foreign accents.

It wasn't much, and it was positively wooden for two people who were supposed to be married, but Court found himself hanging on every word Banshee said that didn't have to do with the operation.

Moving around the resort all day meant they attracted the notice of the hotel staff, so they decided that for their second evening here they would need to do something in keeping with their legends. They both agreed dinner and drinks out among the other guests would help bolster their cover for status.

They went to the bar for a drink at sunset, dressed casually but neatly, just like everyone else here at the stylish lounge with the views of the sea. There were several other couples and even a few families sitting around, and the two intelligence officers made small talk with others around the bar when spoken to. A South African family regaled them about their travels, and a British couple in their fifties enjoying a second honeymoon talked about the great diving in the area. They even met a couple from Chicago at the bar, and since Zoya had already committed to a cover claiming to be from their city, they asked her questions that would have made Court squirm if he were in her shoes.

But she answered confidently, and the other couple clearly bought into her legend in full.

Court was glad to see that he and the Russian woman had established their bona fides, because he identified one of the two bartenders as a potential informant. The man asked a lot of questions of the foreign guests, Court and Zoya included, and he seemed to be listening in to the conversations of all the English speakers.

Court assumed the man was in the employ of the Chamroon Syndicate, and he had no specific concerns about the American couple, although he might have been ordered to increase his scrutiny in light of what happened two evenings earlier in Bangkok.

After their drink, Court and Zoya were led to a romantic table right out on the sandy beach, and here they both made idle chitchat about the restaurant while their hands felt around under the table and their chairs, subtly as to not draw any attention to their actions. They both felt confident there were no listening devices present, but only when a band started playing on a riser on the beach nearby did they speak openly.

Zoya simply said, "That bartender."

Court nodded. "Yep. He's getting paid to snoop into the guests."

"Right, but do you think he's getting paid by the neighbor?"

"I do."

Zoya had been thinking the same thing. "Pretty sure we satisfied him we were legit."

"You did," Court said. "That was amazing; you really know Chicago."

She shook her head with a smile. "I've never been."

"I don't believe that for a second."

"I'll prove it. Name any one of the top twenty-five largest U.S. cities."

Court shrugged. "Jacksonville."

Her eyes furrowed. "Okay . . . name another."

"Philadelphia."

Zoya slipped effortlessly into her Philly accent, talked about her high school there and how she'd wanted to go to Penn State but ended up having to go to Pitt, and then she dropped the name of the street her apartment was on and talked a little about her view of the Delaware River.

Court realized he would have been fooled if he'd met her on the street.

"You are so completely full of shit." Court said it with an amazed smile on his face.

She took this as a compliment. "Very true. I can do the top cities in the UK, Germany, France, Belgium . . . and a few other places." She added, "I'm working on Australia, as well. UK and Germany are my favorites because people from there don't make you answer a hundred questions about your life. I'd *never* say I was from Dallas or Atlanta, because if I met someone from there they'd probably try to adopt me and I'd never get away."

Court laughed. He noticed her growing ease in talking to him, which was more than likely helped along by the alcohol. She seemed relaxed and in her element here, which was amazing to him considering forty-eight hours earlier she was in the role of a drug-addled human trafficking victim, and a few days before that she'd been ninja-ing her way through a gun battle in Vietnam.

Court was fascinated by Banshee. He could slip into and out of roles as required by his job, of course, but he'd never been around anyone else who could pull it off.

After more wine she seemed comfortable to a point where Court felt he could finally probe a little more, and when their entrées came, Court took a chance. "How did you get into this life?"

Zoya sipped her pinot noir. "Is this where you try to break through my tough exterior?"

"No . . . I tried that yesterday. This is where you see that I'm just making conversation, and you let your walls down just a little."

She smiled, put her glass down, and gave a little shrug. "Military family. A lot of travel. Other kids in the same situation were always complaining about moving all the time, but I loved it. I got to reinvent myself every couple of years. My identity became tied to my ability to change my identity. I'm weird. This is the perfect job for me." She looked off towards the dark ocean. "It *was*, anyway. I don't know what I will do now."

"Only child?"

She turned with a little smile, but the smile faded, and she looked at him for a long time. Court realized he'd said something wrong. To his surprise, though, she answered, and her answer seemed authentic.

"My older brother passed away when I was young. He was in college, studying to be a doctor."

"How did he die?"

"Natural causes. Cancer. Twenty-three years old."

"Christ," Court said. "I'm sorry."

She just sipped more wine with a little nod.

Court tried to get her thinking about *anything* else, so he asked another question. "You went into the military yourself?"

She shook her head. "No. Something about being eighteen and not wanting to give up my freedom." Court wasn't sure if it was true, but he caught himself believing her.

"But you found another way to serve Russia."

Her eyes narrowed a bit now as she cut into her grilled fish, and Court realized he was asking too many questions. As expected, she turned it around on him. "Why do you do what you do?"

Court's real story was more complicated than he was willing to share. The truth was he'd been the son of a police officer and an expert in weaponry who trained CIA officers in firearms tactics. He'd developed incredible skills with guns at a young age. Then, when Court was just eighteen, he'd had a falling-out with his father, and to rebel he'd slipped into the periphery of the criminal underworld as a bodyguard for a drug dealer in Miami. He'd gone to prison at nineteen for killing three of his employer's would-be assassins, but the CIA gave him the option of freedom in exchange for working with them.

No . . . he wasn't going to go into all that. Instead he just said, "It's what I was born to do. I don't always like it, sometimes I hate it, but I don't really question it much anymore."

"Remind me to use that answer next time someone like you asks me the same question," Zoya said coolly.

"Relax, Whitney. You're still one of the most defensive and unforthcoming people I've ever met."

"Likewise, Chad."

They ate in silence for a moment, and Court saw her relaxed mood slipping away quickly. He thought he should reveal something about himself now, if only to keep her from shutting down completely. "I was raised by my dad. A Marine and a cop. My mom died when I was a kid."

Zoya looked him hard in the eyes. After a time it became clear that she believed him. "My mother died when I was six. My father died when I was a teenager."

"Sorry. You suffered a tremendous amount of loss at a young age."

"It made me stronger in some ways."

Court regretted his attempt to refire the conversation. They sat quietly under the torchlights for a while, until they finished their second bottle of wine and Court called for the check.

CHAPTER

FORTY-NINE

They returned to their suite and sat together on their private patio by their private pool, the moonlight the only illumination. Zoya opened a bottle of Australian Shiraz left in the room for them by management, and Court fought a joke about having room service bring a bottle of vodka instead.

Court had planned on calling in to Brewer tonight; it was late morning at Langley, and he wanted her to know he was still in the process of determining if Fan was on the adjacent property. But he realized he didn't want to step out of the room now, worried that the Russian woman might be asleep when he returned.

Suzanne Brewer would have to sit and stew till tomorrow.

They both reclined on deck loungers and sipped wine, and they looked out at the ocean to the southwest. A massive luxury yacht, easily 150 to 200 feet in length, had anchored a mile offshore. Court picked up the binoculars from the table next to him and looked it over. He saw a swimming pool, a helicopter on deck, and a name on the bow. It was the *Medusa*, with a port of registry in Genoa.

He put the binoculars down, then looked to the Russian woman. He could tell she wanted to say something, and he marveled at how comfortable she had become with him in the past day. He attributed it to their shared experiences, and he wondered if she could read him as well as he thought he could read her.

He didn't press her to talk, but when she finally did speak, he found himself disappointed that she was thinking about work.

"There are things you aren't telling me about this operation."

Court looked out to the reflection of moonlight on the sea. "Yes."

Zoya downed the last of her Shiraz. "Well . . . at least you are honest. Answer one more thing for me, then I will let it go."

"Okay."

"The things you aren't telling me . . . if you were in my position, and you found out about them . . . would you run, or would you stay?"

Court reached for his glass. "I'd stay, unquestionably. I'm hiding from you how little I know about what's going on here. It's not as cut-and-dried as I've let on. My country's motivations to get Fan might be muddier than I am comfortable with."

Then he added, "But I'm not hiding anything about us."

She turned to him. "There is an 'us'?"

Court almost spit out his wine. "No . . . I mean . . . I am referring to what we are doing here. Everything I've told you is true." He added, "I wouldn't lie to you." As soon as he said it he regretted it, not because it was a promise he didn't feel he could keep but because he thought it came out sounding cheap, hollow, fake.

After a time, she said, "I think I believe you."

"Good."

Zoya said, "There is something I haven't told you."

"I'm sure there are a lot of things," Court quipped. "I don't even know your name."

"No. You don't."

After a long pause, Court said, "This is where you tell me your name."

"No, this is where I tell you what I did to make this all happen." She sat up and put her glass down. "The only reason the Chamroon Syndicate has Fan in the first place is because I contacted them. In Cambodia. You'd escaped over the border, my task force had been taken away from me, and I needed to somehow get Fan away from you. I had no other options, so I contacted the first organization I could find who had men near that border. They picked Fan up and brought him to Thailand. I thought I was the one person who knew where he was, so I could go get him.

"Then somehow you found out, and my former task force found out."
She shook her head. "I have no idea how that happened."

Court answered this. "Fan sent a message to Taiwanese intelligence. It was picked up by our side somehow. Maybe that's how the Russians—I mean your guys—found out."

Zoya said, "I didn't account for that possibility."

"Don't feel bad. You had a solid plan."

"That's all you are going to say?"

He waved his glass in the air. "It doesn't matter."

"Of course it does. I was willing to let Thai gangsters kill you to achieve my mission. You, on the other hand, cast your entire mission aside to rescue me and a bunch of prostitutes who meant nothing to you."

Court said, "You were close to me during the firefight. Behind a column. But you ran over to the other women, too. You were going to try to save them yourself."

When she did not respond, Court said, "Weren't you?"

Zoya looked out to sea. "I saw that you had Chamroon. I went over to the women just for cover. I was looking for a gun. I would have shot you if I'd found one."

"Well, I am glad things turned out the way they did."

Zoya, still looking into the silvery moonlight, just said, "Tell me why you did it. I want to understand."

Court scratched the back of his head. He didn't know how to explain himself, because normally he would have no need to. But for some reason he wanted her to understand. Not to justify his actions, but instead to help her, because he could tell she was completely adrift, both as an intelligence officer and as a person.

"Occasionally one is presented with moral questions that are different from the mission itself. I don't like it. I would rather keep things simple, but life gets in the way of the job sometimes. At that spa in Bangkok, in that brief moment, you and those other women were the most important thing. The mission is my job, but sometimes I divert a little, for the sake of others." He smiled now. "Doesn't make me a great guy. It doesn't mean I'm not going to shoot some asshole through the forehead five seconds later."

Zoya sighed. "I believe in keeping things simple, too. But it is not always possible." A stray cloud passed in front of the moon, dimming the light on them both. Zoya asked, "Have you ever killed an innocent person?"

From the timing and placement of the question, Court realized she was asking it for her own reasons, not really to elicit information from him. Still, he hesitated a long time before answering, and he answered truthfully: "Yes."

"Under orders?"

"Yes."

"Does that help? That you were ordered to do it?"

Court thought about his answer. "No. Not much. Not enough, anyway."

Zoya nodded now, staring deeply into Court's eyes. "You and I have so much in common."

"I'm very sorry to hear that." Court said it with sincerity. He stood. "We should try to get some sleep."

Court and Zoya each moved bedding from the king-sized bed, as they had the night before. She made a small and neat pallet for herself in the walk-in closet, and Court just tossed a pillow and a blanket on the floor on the far side of the bed from the entrance to the room.

After getting ready for bed they both lay down, fifteen feet apart and unable to see each other, but they continued talking across the room. Mostly they talked about nothing. Every now and then, however, they would discuss some aspect of their plan for the next day.

The conversation trailed off and then picked back up for a few minutes, and it trailed off again.

Court lay there in the dark now, gazing around at the room he could see from his position, using the significant moonlight that poured in from the glass door to the balcony.

For ten minutes he heard only his own breath, his own heartbeat.

And then he sat up.

He didn't think he had made any noise, but he heard a stirring in the closet almost immediately. He climbed to his feet, and a few seconds later he heard Zoya rise, as well.

She whispered, "What is it? You heard something?"

Court moved around the bed, closer to her.

She stepped out of the closet now, revealing herself in the moonlight. She wore a plain white T-shirt and blue cotton track pants; her hair was hooked behind her ears, but a little drooped down in her face. She cocked her head, trying to listen for whatever noise caused the American to get up.

But the American hadn't been stirred by a noise.

He stepped close to her, face-to-face, close enough to where he could feel the warmth of her body. He put his arms around her and pulled her close to him. He kissed her deeply, and for a brief moment, she kissed him back.

Then she pulled away, not out of his grasp, just back a little. With her hands gently on his hips she looked up at him. "This isn't keeping things simple."

Court said, "It is for me. Doing nothing feels impossible."

Zoya said, "I just . . . you remind me of someone. I worry that it is affecting my actions."

"Someone good, I hope?"

She blinked hard, and Court wondered if she was going to cry. It was certainly not the emotion he'd hoped to elicit from her right now.

But she recovered and said, "Someone very good. Someone so good that it worries me that perhaps I am projecting something onto you. Hoping for too much from you. Normally I have a hard time letting my guard down, it is dangerous to do, but . . ."

Court held her tight. "You're safe. Tonight, you're safe."

He kissed her again, and now she brought her hands to the sides of his face, pulled him even closer, and together they stood there in the dark, kissing and touching and breathing each other's air, and then they moved back into the closet, lowered down on the floor, and for now, for tonight, they were both safe, and tomorrow's dangers seemed like they were still far out to sea.

CHAPTER

FIFTY

Court woke well before the first light of dawn. The room was darker now than it had been with the evening's moonlight, and here in the closet it was pitch-black, but he didn't need to see a thing. He was behind her, with his bare chest against her back and his arm around her naked stomach and his nose in her hair at the back of her head. He didn't know where his clothes were—he'd have to do an after-action review later to relive the events of the past several hours, just to reassure himself that it had actually happened.

Court looked out of the closet, waited for his eyes to adjust to the dim. He found everything still in its place and no new threats in the world, a world that felt very different suddenly. He moved his hand from in front of her to rub his eyes, but she lay still. Returning his hand, he brushed his fingertips across her stomach, feeling her abdominal muscles move as she breathed. He retracted his hand a little to her hip, and he felt warm skin over her hip bone. He stroked up a few inches and stopped. There was something there on the skin on her back. A scar, no more than half an inch in diameter. He knew it was a bullet wound instantly, because he had similar marks on his own body. He lingered there, touching it out of curiosity, then realized what an awful thing he was doing and started to move on, angry at himself.

Zoya spoke, and though her voice told Court she'd been sleeping, she displayed neither a hint of shyness nor anger. "That was a 7.62 round. In and out. Three years ago. I was wearing body armor, but not side plates. Stupid."

"Side plates suck," Court said.

"Not as bad as getting shot."

"No argument from me."

She added, "Must have been a ricochet, didn't even break the ribs."

"Where did this happen?"

"Chechnya."

"I hear that place is a hellhole."

She rolled over to face him, though they couldn't see each other at all in the darkness of the closet. "Most every place I've been sent is a hellhole." And with that she kissed him deeply. "But it's not so bad right here."

He started to put his hand on her body again, but she clasped his fingers in hers. He thought she'd had enough of his touch, and he was about to apologize, but she surprised him by saying, "That one is nothing. Feel *this*." She placed his hand on her upper back, between her shoulders and just to the right of her spine. This scar was three times the size of the other.

"What happened there?"

"Knife in the back. I pissed a guy off in a bar. If it hadn't hit my vertebra it would have gone straight into my heart."

"Where did this happen?"

"Can't say."

Court smiled a little. "How is he doing? The guy you pissed off."

"Oh, he's *really* pissed off now."

Court imagined this was an understatement.

Now she reached out and put her hand on Court's rib cage, traced the pink gash there. She must have felt it during their lovemaking, because he knew she couldn't see it now.

Without prompting, Court said, "Nine-millimeter. This one didn't break the ribs, either, but it took off a lot of meat."

"It's pretty fresh."

"Yes."

"Where did this happen?"

"Can't say."

"Who did it?"

He paused a moment. Normally, there was no reason for him to tell the truth. But with this woman, he couldn't think of a reason to lie. He said, "Saudis."

"Assholes."

"These guys were."

They both had other scars, other stories, but the talk of old fights gave way slowly to quiet, to softer touches over untainted skin, and then to new passion. Soon there was no more talking between the two of them. No more past, no more pain. There was just now.

Court figured it was close to nine a.m. now. He could see her face plainly, even in the closet, and he moved a strand of hair out of her eye and behind her ear.

She had been dozing while Court lay there, just thinking, but she woke now, then rose up onto an elbow, her eyes locked on his. She said, "Zoya. That's my name. Zoya Zakharova."

Court smiled. "Zoya."

"It's okay if you don't tell me yours. I just wanted you to know mine."

Court took what she said at face value, and he did not tell her his name. He had been thinking about something else when she spoke, and instead of shifting to follow along with Zoya's train of thought, he said, "Let's say the helicopter comes in today, and we move in to get Fan . . . do you have a plan for after?"

Zoya's eyebrows furrowed; Court could not interpret the meaning behind the expression. Finally she shook her head slowly. "I don't want to jinx today by worrying about tomorrow."

"Maybe you could let me think about tomorrow for you."

"What do you mean?"

He said, "You won't be safe going home, you know that. You won't be safe in a lot of places. SVR has reach, as you know."

She smiled a little, but she'd lost the glow of just a few seconds earlier. "So you are going to protect me?"

"I can help. I can talk to some people. I'm sure they can bring you into the U.S. You'll be safe there."

"You'll talk to people at CIA, you mean."

Court nodded. "They are the ones that can make it happen. I'm sure they'd want to question you . . . but you can come to some sort of an agreement before you commit to anything."

Court thought his idea was solid, and he thought Zoya would immediately agree it was the best plan, so her response surprised him greatly. "What are you doing?"

He cocked his head now. "What do you mean?"

Her body language had changed, her eyes had narrowed precipitously, even her breathing was different.

"Are you trying to recruit me?"

"*Recruit* you? No, of course not. I'm not suggesting you work for the Agency, just that you use them to get into the U.S. After that you can do whatever you want."

Zoya said, "Right, and just think about how important you will be at CIA. You capture a Chinese defector *and* an SVR operative. You can do whatever *you* want."

"*Capture?* I'm just trying to help. I'm worried about what might happen if—"

"Sure you are." She smiled, but Court could plainly see anger in her eyes. "It took me too long, but I've finally got you figured out."

"Meaning?"

"When you bugged Oleg's car you thought you would learn something about Fan, but instead you heard an SVR compromise herself permanently to her organization. You knew I'd be desperate, ready to cling to any lifeline, and you came right in, tricked me by appealing to my sense of the mission. You've brought me along to go after Fan, but from the beginning this was about getting me into the U.S., just like Fan. The last two days have just been to set the trap."

She sat up now, climbed out of the closet, pulled on warm-ups and a T-shirt from her bag. She stormed out of the closet, leaving Court there, staring at the ceiling.

Court was utterly gobsmacked. He truly had no idea how to respond. Finally he just said, "For God's sake, that's ridiculous."

Zoya reappeared back over him a few seconds later. "Is it? Do I have it all wrong?"

"Yes, you do. I'm just trying to help."

Zoya lowered back down, straddling Court now. He looked at her in confusion for an instant, but he kept his hands down.

"What are you—"

She interrupted him. "I'm sorry. As I told you, I have trust issues."

His guard rose quickly, but not quickly enough.

Zoya held the Montblanc pen up into his face, pointing it right at his nose. She depressed the trigger, and the charger exploded in his face with a solid pop.

But nothing came out.

She pulled the pen away slowly. The American stared at her, his own eyes narrow now.

"Do you want to get off me, or would you rather I throw you all the way across the fucking room? It's your call, but make it quick."

Zoya slipped off the man, then walked over to the bed and sat down.

Court stood now, pulled his cargo shorts on, and stepped into the bedroom. He took a chair across from her and sat back down. "The Montblanc was positioned in my pack with the clip facing in and the lid just slightly loose. You put the clip back exactly right, but you tightened the lid. I noticed in Bangkok, just after I left you alone in the room. I removed the powder canister here, the night before last." He pulled it from his pocket and held it up between his thumb and forefinger.

Zoya said, "So much for trust."

Court replied with derision. "Look who's talking."

She got up now, stormed past Court to the patio, then sat on a recliner by the pool. He followed her out. She put her head in her hands, and after a long time she spoke.

"I'm sorry."

Court stood in the doorway. "Yeah. Me, too. I put the blowgun back because I wanted to see if you would try to use it."

She pulled her head out of her hands and looked across the patio at him. "I thought you were too good to be true."

"That's ridiculous."

"You don't know my life."

Court thought about it a moment, then crossed the patio and sat down in front of her. "I think I do. Like you said last night, you and I have a lot in common. We've traveled down the same road, can't you see that? *I* see it, I see what you are up against now, and I was just trying to help."

"*Why?*"

Court looked out to sea. The massive yacht was still there. A brilliant white in the morning sun. "I have my reasons."

"When you said you would talk to the CIA about taking me in, I thought you were trying to do to me what you have been sent to do to Fan. Obviously recruiting me would help your career. Why *wouldn't* you want that?"

"It won't do shit for my career, because I'm not an employee of the CIA."

"Right. That's what everyone in CIA says."

"True. It's also what people who *aren't* in the CIA say. I'm one of those people."

Zoya wasn't buying it; Court could see it on her face.

"I do contract work for them, but only on my terms. I am getting paid for the Fan assignment, but they only knew I would do it because of a personal reason."

"What personal reason?"

"If you'd managed to drug me, you'd already know, because I'd tell you everything." Court stood. "But since your plan failed, I am free to tell you that it's none of your *fucking* business."

Zoya rubbed tears from her eyes.

Court stepped back into the room, grabbed his phone, and slid the Glock into his waistband, covering it with his T-shirt. "I'm going out to make a phone call. If you want to go, you are free to go while I'm gone, or whenever the hell you want to. You are not a captive."

Court went to the door, but Zoya called to him.

"Wait."

He turned back to her but said nothing.

She said, "I've betrayed your trust in me. Trust I did not deserve."

Court did not reply.

She looked away. "Tell your handler I will discuss the terms of my defection at her convenience."

He turned and left the room.

Ten minutes later Court sat at a table in an open-air restaurant between the resort's main swimming pool and the beach. A few guests sat at the nearby open-air bar, a few people were doing morning yoga on the beach, and the bartender was making an espresso for a sleepy elderly man in a sun hat reading a copy of the German magazine *Der Spiegel*. There were a few resort guests at the pool nearby, but Court's immediate area was clear.

A few more guests, mostly families, lay on the sugary sand or splashed in the waters of the bay. In the distance a helicopter took off from the big yacht that had arrived the night before, and then it flew off to the north.

Court took out his phone and dialed Brewer's number, then gave the response to her identity challenge. As soon as his identity was confirmed, Court's CIA handler said, "I've been waiting all damn day for you to call."

Court said, "You'll forgive me when I tell you what I have for you. How would you like to recruit a new foreign asset and score a defection from a tier-one opposition intelligence service at the same time?"

Brewer was taken aback. "What the hell are you talking about?"

"The female I told you about who was working with the Russians."

"What about her?"

"She's here with me in Phuket. She wants to defect and is willing to speak with you about terms."

Brewer was baffled by this. "You flipped her?"

Court had never flipped anyone in his life. He wasn't a case officer; he didn't recruit and run agents. He said, "No, not really. She's in a serious jam with Lubyanka, and they'll kill her if she goes back to Russia. I think she sees us as her only option. Obviously she possesses a lot of intel, considering her position in the SVR."

"Okay, you've got me on the hook. Tell me what you know, but do it quickly, because I have intel for you."

Court filled his handler in on Zoya Zakharova, but he left out the sex and the fact that she'd killed another operative, and he glossed over the fact that she'd attempted to drug him just minutes earlier. There was a lot to his short relationship with this woman, and it was all he could do to give a dispassionate accounting of what had happened without putting in his own spin. At the moment he was pissed at her, and he had decided he wasn't going to let her breach Chamroon's estate with him when he jumped the fence.

Court had his own trust issues, after all.

Brewer took it all in, then said, "Obviously we'd like to speak with her. I'll talk to Matt and see how he wants to proceed."

"Okay."

Brewer added, "And just for the record. You have my permission to pick up as many girls as you like while you are working . . . just as long as they are high-ranking intelligence officers from opposition first-tier agencies who wish to defect."

"Funny," Court said, and he wondered if he'd really given off the impression he'd entered into a relationship with Zoya, or if Brewer was just making a little quip. He pushed the thought away and said, "As far as Fan . . . I am operating on the assumption that the helicopter will arrive at some point, but it hasn't happened yet. I've been around the periphery of the estate, but I was waiting till tonight to breach."

"You can cancel your plans."

"Why would I do that?"

"Because Fan Jiang managed to send a coded message to the U.S. ambassador to Thailand. He is asking for us to rescue him."

Court couldn't believe it. "When did this happen?"

"Our ambassador just got it two hours ago, but it was sent ten and a half hours ago. It got scooped up into a spam folder because it was literally a piece of spam, but somehow the ambassador's secretary found it. Fan says he doesn't know where he is being held, but we were able to use data from the e-mail to pinpoint a cell phone tower that was used to send the message. It's located adjacent to the Chamroon estate there in Phuket, which means Fan is already there."

Court knew he couldn't have missed the helicopter arriving, but perhaps Nattapong Chamroon had been wrong about that indicator of Fan and Kulap's presence. Maybe Fan came overland, arrived by boat, or even got here before Court and Zoya arrived. He asked, "How do you know the e-mail actually came from Fan?"

"He gave specific information only he would have known about his escape from China," Brewer said. "Ground Branch is spinning up right now. They are arranging the helicopters, and they will hit the estate around one a.m."

Court didn't like it. "That's not a good idea. Let me get in there. It's a big building, jungle all around. I can try to pinpoint where they are holding Fan and then—"

"Negative. We've lost him so many times in the past two weeks already. If you go in there early and are detected, he'll be long gone before the operators hit. Either Chamroon will move him or the Chinese will find them."

"The Chinese don't even know about Phuket."

"That can change at any time."

Court wasn't happy about Brewer's decision, but he saw no way to stop her from sending in Ground Branch. "I'll stay on the outside of the compound, but I'll try to get a better fix on his location. I don't trust your intel."

Brewer said, "Nothing wrong with the intelligence that ID'd Fan's location, although I have to say I'm disappointed in the human intelligence asset who picked himself up a Russian girlfriend and is now probably hanging around in his hotel room with no pants on instead of working to acquire his target."

Court's jaw muscles flexed. He took a few breaths before responding, then said, "I'll find where they are keeping Fan if he's here."

Brewer said, "No, you will not. You will check out of your hotel and start heading back to Bangkok by midnight. I can't have you anywhere near the area when the raid comes. Call me back when you are on the road, and by then I'll have instructions for how to proceed with Ms. Zakharova. *She* is your objective now. Let Ground Branch handle Fan Jiang. That op is over for you."

The call ended there; Court didn't like it, of course, but he could make no reasonable excuse to Brewer as to why he had to be the one to rescue Fan.

It seemed to him that at every turn, the one insurmountable hurdle in his own plan for this operation was finding a way to save Donald Fitzroy from Colonel Dai. He owed Fitzroy, and he knew he was Fitzroy's only hope, but it continued to look like saving the life of the Englishman was going to be a bridge too far.

The old man had already had two fingers lopped off, but by this time tomorrow he'd probably be in a shallow grave in the hills over Hong Kong.

Court thought about all this as he climbed the stairs back to the villa, along with the hundred other things running through his mind: the fact that CIA paramilitaries were just hours away from hitting the property east of him and either finding a dry hole, which would be bad, or picking up Fan Jiang, which would be worse for Sir Donald.

Court unlocked the door to his ocean-view suite, walked through the small entryway, and entered the sitting room there. He was surprised to see Zoya sitting on the sofa across from him, especially so because her hair was wet and she wore only a towel.

He had stepped fully into the living room now, passing a wall behind him on his left, and as he did so he focused on Zoya, saw her back ramrod straight, her eyes focused on him, but apprehensive, nervous.

Court sensed danger, close and immediate. He turned his next footfall into a forward roll by lowering his left shoulder and pushing off with his right leg. As he went down to the ground his right hand slipped under his T-shirt and formed around the grip of his Glock jutting there from the waistband of his cargo shorts.

He rolled over on the carpet and came up in a crouch, his pistol out in front of him and pointing back towards the blind spot in the room he'd just passed.

Four Asian men stood there along the wall; they had pistols of their own pointed back his way.

A voice came from the bedroom on Court's right. English with a heavy Chinese accent. "Try it. I'd welcome the opportunity to have you shot right here."

Court turned to look into the bedroom. Three more men stood there. Two held small submachine guns out at hip level, and the third was clearly in charge; this was obvious simply from his body language. He stood there in a suit and tie, his hands clasped behind his back.

Court recognized the man. He was Major Xi, Colonel Dai's second-in-command.

He said, "Engage those four men, so these two men will shoot you down and then shoot your attractive friend here, as well."

Court lowered the Glock, placed it on the floor, and pushed it towards the four men in front of him. As he did this he addressed the one man in the suite he knew spoke English. "I don't guess you guys are just here to work on your tans."

Xi didn't laugh. He said, "We will take you to see Dai."

Court shook his head. "We can't go to Hong Kong. Fan is here."

The man smiled. "The colonel is not in Hong Kong. He is here in Phuket. We will take you to him now."

Court turned back to Zoya, and her expression was clear. *What the hell is going on, who the hell is Colonel Dai, and why did you lie to me?*

Court found her ability to ask three questions with just a glare impressive, if a little disconcerting.

Court turned back to Major Xi. "I'll go, but she stays here. She's not part of this."

"Then you shouldn't have brought her here. You aren't in a position to dictate anything to me, Mr. Gentry. She is coming with us."

Court cringed at the sound of his own name.

To Zoya, Major Xi said, "Get dressed."

She stood from the sofa, and as she walked past Court in the living room to get her clothes from the closet, Court whispered to her.

"I can explain."

She did not break stride. "I can hardly wait."

CHAPTER

FIFTY-ONE

After Zoya Zakharova dressed in dark blue warm-ups and tennis shoes, she and Court were shoved into the back of an SUV and driven up into the hills to the northeast of the resort, with a second SUV full of Chinese operatives trailing behind. Court and Zoya were not hooded or blindfolded, which they appreciated, but men sat on either side of them, and both held pistols jammed into the ribs of their captives. Every bump in the exceedingly bumpy road made Court hold his breath, as the asshole on his right knocked the barrel of his weapon right into Court's right side where he'd been shot the previous month. Court could see that Zoya was equally stressed about the jackass on her left and his gun banging into her side as the SUV bounced along.

Court had been frisked by the Chinese, but they'd missed the tiny vial of scopolamine hydrobromide in his left cargo pocket. He'd done nothing special to conceal it, but it was only an inch long, and the man searching him had squeezed the pocket and found Court's phone, and then moved on to check the other pockets.

It wasn't that Court particularly needed a central nervous system depressant at the moment, but he would keep its presence on his body at the back of his mind.

After less than a ten-minute drive, the two SUVs pulled off the paved rural road and took a gravel drive through a gate opened by two Chinese men in their twenties. This winding drive led to the south, up a steep incline, and ended at a ranch-style home with sweeping views of the ocean. The door next to Court was opened by another young Chinese man in plainclothes, and he and Zoya were directed to go straight into the front door of the home.

Near the entrance to the ranch house, yet another pair of Chinese men dressed in casual wear stood, trying, Court decided, not to look like security officers. He could see the pistols under the men's white shirts and linen pants, and the earpieces in their ears, so they failed in this endeavor, but Court imagined these were Dai's men, from the People's Liberation Army, and playing the role of civilian wasn't really in their bag of tricks.

On a second-floor balcony over the entrance he saw another pair of men. They sat at a table drinking bottled water, but Court had no doubt the men had firearms and orders to keep watch all around.

Inside the walls of the home, Court and Zoya encountered somewhere between twelve and fifteen more men, bringing the total number of operatives around here to over thirty. These wouldn't all be bodyguards for Colonel Dai. No . . . Court was pretty sure he was looking at some sort of paramilitary strike force.

Court and Zoya entered the kitchen of the home, where Colonel Dai Longhai sat alone at a wooden table with a laptop open in front of him and a mobile phone in his hand. His eyes furrowed when he saw Zoya, but he put down the phone and motioned for the two of them to take a seat in front of him.

This was awkward for Court, to say the least. He wanted to speak to Dai outside the earshot of Zoya, but he saw no way to keep her out of it now. He could only hope she had the good sense to play dumb, like she was just a tourist Court had picked up along the way. While in truth she didn't know what was happening right now, surely she was sharp enough to know that admitting to the Chinese that she was a Russian spy who'd been running the task force in charge of kidnapping Fan would *not* go over well in this company.

Court went on the offensive immediately with the colonel. "What the *hell* are you and all your goons doing here?"

Dai said, "Obviously we are here for the same reason you are here. Fan Jiang is inside the walls of the property in the jungle just a few hundred meters away." Dai looked at the attractive brunette with the wet hair, then back to Court. "That *is* why you are here, is it not? Or did you decide to go on vacation right in the middle of our partnership?"

Court said, "Of course that's why I'm here. But that's a big piece of property and I haven't pinpointed Fan Jiang inside it yet. You guys showing up like this will just alert Chamroon's people and cause Fan to escape yet again."

Dai said, "The moment for pinpoint actions has passed, Mr. Gentry. And believe me, we've been very careful in the way we arrived. No one in the Chamroon property knows we are here." Now he looked at Zoya, but he kept his comments directed to Gentry, as if she were unable to speak for herself. "And who is your friend here?"

"She's . . . she's nobody."

"Then you won't mind us eliminating her."

"I *would* mind that, very much," Court said, mustering as much toughness in his words as he could, considering the circumstances. "I met her at my hotel in Bangkok. I couldn't very well come down to this resort by myself. *That* would have stuck out. She's just part of my cover."

Now Dai spoke directly to Zoya. "I understand you are from Chicago?"

Zoya kept the Chicago accent in place, and a twinge of fear in her voice. "Yes, sir. I barely know this guy. I was just looking for a free trip to the beach."

Dai stared her down. "Where is your passport?"

"It was stolen."

"I see."

Court jumped in again. "Colonel, I told you I would contact you when I had a target."

"Yes, you did. A day and a half ago. Your inability to communicate in a timely manner has caused me considerable frustration."

"You hired a private operative, and I am operating privately. Your inability to understand this fact is causing *me* considerable frustration."

Court glanced at Zoya. She was in character, looking at the floor nervously. She'd even generated some sweat on her forehead.

Dai asked, "How did you track Fan here?"

Court said, "I encouraged Nattapong Chamroon to give me the information. He said that his brother, Kulap Chamroon, would bring Fan here via helicopter after hiding out in the capital for a couple of days. I don't know if he is here or not, but I was going into the property to find out. If you get out of here before anyone sees you, then I will have a better chance of—"

Dai heaved a deep breath and blew it out. "Fan Jiang communicated with the American embassy in Bangkok. He said Kulap Chamroon had him under guard. We were able to pinpoint the location from where the e-mail was sent."

Of course Court pretended like this was news to him. "Was there any other intel in the e-mail?"

"No. Nothing more. Only that he hoped America would rescue him."

Court now asked, "And Sir Donald? Where is he?"

Dai smiled a little, a look that gave Court chills. Finally he said, "You can't even pretend like you don't care anymore. That ship has sailed. Yes, your old friend is here. Until this operation is complete, he goes where I go. Don't worry, you will see him shortly."

"Good," Court said. And then he added, "Because I want to beat his ass for hiring me into this fucking job."

Dai smiled. "You have nothing to complain about. I am a man of my word, and you will be paid when we achieve our objective. Look at the facts; the objective is within our grasp. We will raid the Chamroon compound tonight at midnight. We will kill everything that opposes us, and when we find Sergeant Fan, we can all go home."

Court said, "Let me go in with your team."

Dai shook his head vehemently. "No. You will stay here, under guard with Fitzroy. And your friend here, as well. If something should go wrong tonight and Fan makes his escape . . . then I will continue to require your services. As much as it pains me to say it, you just might be the only person working for me who has accomplished much of anything in the past two weeks. The information that Fan was at the Chamroon property next door came from a signals intelligence interception by Beijing. But you already knew, and you were already here."

Despite what Dai had just said, Court knew there was no way the PLA colonel was going to let Zoya walk out of here alive. Dai couldn't kill her now, because he did not know if he'd need Court's compliance in the future. But if this group of paramilitaries around this property was able to assassinate Fan this evening, then the "girl from Chicago" would have to die because she'd seen too much.

Court wondered if Dai just planned on doing away with him when this was over, as well.

Court looked to the colonel. "What about you? Are you going into that estate tonight?"

Dai grinned now. He wasn't quite the cat who caught the canary, but he was the cat who saw that someone had left the canary's cage door open. "I will go in behind the raiding party. I would love to be the last thing Fan Jiang sees before he leaves this world, but I fear he will already be long dead by the time I get to him."

Dai looked up to Major Xi. "The major will take you and your friend here upstairs. You will stay there until our operation is complete."

Court and Zoya were led up a flight of stairs, down a hall, and through a set of doors into a large master suite: a sitting area and a bedroom off to the side. A balcony off the sitting area hung over a cliff, nearly two hundred feet straight down to white waves and jagged shoreline rocks.

Sir Donald Fitzroy was sitting on the sofa, guarded by a single young Chinese officer in a black T-shirt and warm-up pants.

Court saw that Don's right hand was bandaged, and the last two fingers on his hand were clearly gone. He wore a Huntsman & Sons suit and a thin sheen of sweat, obviously from the pain he'd endured in the days since Court's actions had led to Fitzroy's torture.

Before Court could speak to Sir Donald, Xi said, "You will remain in this master suite. If you want water, there is the bathroom sink. You are not to step out onto the balcony. I will have men there with orders to shoot you if you do."

Court looked at Xi. "So . . . no dinner in the oven, and if you go out to look at the view, you die. Some B-and-B you're running here."

Court's gallows humor was an attempt to draw a chuckle from Zoya, but she just stared at him like he was an idiot. Fitzroy didn't seem to be in the mood for jokes, either.

Major Xi just shrugged. "The colonel makes the rules. I wouldn't have brought a *gweilo* in for this operation in the first place, and if I were in charge, I'd put a bullet in each of you now and lead the raid tonight myself."

"You drew the short straw, did you?"

Xi just looked at Court a minute, then said, "I can't go because I have an injury. I was shot in the leg in the spa in Bangkok. It wouldn't surprise me at all if you were the one who did it."

"It *would* surprise me. I didn't shoot anybody but Nattapong Chamroon."

Xi said, "Dai is in a trusting mood because he sees the end of this unfortunate episode for our nation, for our organization. That's why you're alive. If he has a reason to doubt you for an instant, that will change."

Xi turned and stepped out of the room with two of his men, and two more went out to the balcony, shutting the door behind them.

Court looked at his watch and saw that it was four thirty p.m. Dai's operation would kick off in seven and a half hours, and the Americans would arrive an hour after that.

When the three prisoners were left alone, Court greeted Fitzroy, then turned to Zoya. "Obviously you have questions."

Zoya said, "Yeah, like who is this guy?"

"Don, this is Whitney. Whitney, Don."

Fitzroy made a face like he wasn't buying the name, then reached out with his left hand and shook Zoya's hand. "Sorry to meet you under such circumstances."

She just nodded.

Fitzroy looked back and forth between the two. Finally he said, "I've been in this room since the moment the Chinese got here to the villa this morning. They rented the place and entered the same time I did. They didn't plant any bugs. We can talk freely."

Court now winced with the inevitable fallout from what he was about to say. "Whitney . . . would you mind if I spoke with my friend here first? He might be able to clear up some things, so when I try to explain all this to you—"

She got up and left the room without a word, walking into the bedroom. When Zoya shut the door to the bedroom, the older man said, "A girlfriend? *Really*, lad?"

Court rolled his eyes. "She's not a girlfriend." Then softly he said, "SVR."

Fitzroy jerked his head around towards the bedroom, astonishment on his face. Shifting back to Court he said, "*Her?* You're mad."

"This whole thing is mad, Don. I don't understand what the hell is going on."

"She's Russian?"

"Yep."

"And she's with you?"

"Sort of. She trusted me, till it became apparent I was working for the Chinese. I had neglected to mention that to her."

Fitz was still looking at the door to the bedroom. "Incredible. Russian intelligence? What's her angle in all this?"

"She's on my side now."

"Raises the question: whose side are you on?"

Court did not respond directly. "How's the hand?"

Fitzroy held up the bandaged appendage. "It feels quite like some sod cut off two fingers with a straight razor."

"Sorry about that."

Fitzroy reached for a decanter on the coffee table, filled with an amber liquid. "I've been looking at this since I got here. What do you suppose it is?"

"I don't guess it matters; you'll drink it anyway."

"Too true," Fitzroy said as he poured two healthy shots in crystal glasses. Without even smelling it he downed his full portion.

He made a little face. "Whiskey. Nothing special, but not utter shit, either."

He gestured towards Court's glass.

Court shook his head, so Fitzroy lifted it and took a sip. After he swallowed he said, "I don't blame you about the hand. I blame whoever got you into this in the first place. You shouldn't even be involved."

"What does that mean?"

"C'mon, lad. I don't believe for an instant you just fell down from heaven when I got kidnapped by Colonel Dai. No. You were sent in. I'd say by Langley, but since Langley is your sworn enemy, I confess I'm at a loss. Whoever sent you on this little fool's errand, I am quite certain you didn't come to assassinate Fan Jiang just to earn me my freedom. Your aim from the beginning has been to capture Fan and hand him off to a Western power."

Court said, "That was the job I took. But Dai will kill you if I double-cross him."

"Of course he will. If you rescue Fan from all this, Dai will put a bullet in my skull, and then he'll put a bullet in his own, because he can't go back to China without Fan's head on a pike. But now Fan is nearby, and Dai has thirty stone-cold killers readying to raid that property and give poor Fan a terminal overdose of lead. And at that point, it's anyone's bet what Colonel Dai will do to us."

Court spoke low. "The Agency is sending in an SAD team. Oh one hundred hours."

Fitzroy finished his second shot, then rubbed his meaty face with his good hand. "Dear lord. What a mess."

"Yeah."

The Englishman sat back on the couch and looked at Court for a long time.

"What is it?" Court asked.

"I'm trying to figure out how you became involved with Langley."

"The short version is they told me you'd been snatched in Hong Kong and I was to go in and get intel from you and Colonel Dai, something to identify Fan's location."

"And you did just that."

"Damn lot of good it did."

"Don't blame yourself for any of this. If Langley had just stayed out of it from the beginning, we could have avoided the whole thing."

Court cocked his head. "Who is *we*?"

Fitzroy reacted to Court's confusion. "Ah . . . I see. You don't know. Langley just told you I was over in HK working for Dai on the Fan hit."

"That's right. Dai hired you to kill Fan Jiang. Was there something else?"

"I'd been in Hong Kong for weeks before I'd ever heard of Colonel Dai."

"Doing what?"

Fitzroy smiled. "Oh, boy, you really *are* in the dark, lad. I was over here on a job for MI6."

Court raised an eyebrow. "You work for 6?"

"Things come up. You know how it goes."

Court nodded slowly. "Yeah, I guess I do."

"I was hired to oversee the assassination of a man inside mainland China. Damn difficult to do, as it happens."

"Who . . . who did they send you in to kill?"

"A PLA man called Major Song Julong. He was—"

Court interrupted. "He was the personal bodyguard of Fan Jiang's parents."

"That's it. MI6 wanted him dead, so I sent a team in to Shanghai to eliminate him."

"Why would they want to kill the bodyguard of a couple of retirees?"

"It's a tad complicated, but Song was an agent for the West."

Pieces were falling together quickly for Court. "Song sent Fan over the border into Hong Kong because his parents were killed in a car crash. He told Fan he'd be killed if he didn't run."

"Yes," said Fitzroy, and he poured himself another drink.

Court said, "Song tried to arrange for the Taiwanese to help Fan, but the PLA got there first and the defection fell apart."

Fitzroy cocked his head. "No, lad. We . . . I mean whoever in the West that was *really* running Song, found out that *Song's* plan was to kill Fan's parents. So they hired me to go in and stop him. I sent a team in to kill the son of a bitch in Shanghai before he did it, but my lads were themselves killed in Shanghai. By who, I do not know."

"Why did Song want to kill Fan's parents?"

"I was never told. I was just told there was a timeline, because if I didn't get Song, the Fans would end up dead. Which, unfortunately, is exactly what happened."

"How did you get hooked up with Dai?"

"After Fan stumbled over the border with the PLA on his tail and no arms to run into, Colonel Dai came into Hong Kong looking for Fan. Someone told him I was here, and he knew about my network. He knew about you, in fact. It was like that. When he reached out to me, I spoke with MI6, and they realized they had a chance to use me and my network to grab Fan. My teams went looking for him, not to kill him, as Dai thought, but to capture him for the West."

Court said, "But by then Fan had gotten himself hooked up with Wo Shing Wo, and your men got themselves killed."

Fitzroy nodded. "That's when Dai kidnapped me, and that's when you showed up."

Court said, "I was sent by Langley. This was sold to me like they had this once-in-a-lifetime chance to get Fan to the West so they could learn his secrets."

Fitzroy smiled ruefully. "I'd say it was a twice-in-a-lifetime chance. The first time was at the border crossing. If Langley knew about that, which is a safe bet because the Taiwanese knew about it, then it is likely Langley was involved somehow."

Court said, "I wonder if your people were sent in to scare Song. If he knew people were trying to kill him in Shanghai, he would want out of China. His handlers in the West could get him out, but only if he produced something valuable for them."

Fitzroy understood. "It was the push he needed that would show him he was in danger. The catalyst that would get him to act. Someone in the West *wanted* Song to kill Fan's parents so that Fan would run over the border to avoid being put to death for losing his family collateral."

Court looked out past the balcony at the darkness there. "So . . . if this is all true, then the CIA was responsible for the murder of Fan's parents."

"CIA, MI6, Taiwan's NSB, even. A safe bet they were all in it together. Either they conceived of the plan and pushed Song to go along with it, or they sat back and let it happen, happy to be the ultimate beneficiaries of the crime."

Court put his head in his hands. "Well, this blows."

"Exceedingly well put, lad."

Fitzroy drank silently, then held his glass out towards the balcony behind him, towards the big jungle in the distance visible to the east of the ocean. "A cynical plan, to be sure, and a plan that is failing before our eyes. And the final nail in the coffin will take place when the Chinese enter that estate and kill Fan, and then the CIA enter that estate and shoot it out with Chinese intelligence. We are hours away from a nasty incident that could lead to nastier incidents, up to and possibly including war."

Court whispered to himself. "Christ almighty."

Both men sat in silence for a moment. Then Fitzroy said, "There is something you *can* do."

Court lifted his head quickly. "What?"

"Won't be easy."

Court stared Fitzroy down.

Fitz said, "We arrived by boat from the airport this morning, so I saw the layout of the back of this property. I had a nice look around. It's not for me; I'm old, weak, and slow . . . but you could do it. Don't know about the girl, but I'd wager *you* could do it."

"Do *what?*"

"This balcony here. It overhangs a sheer cliff, easily fifty meters of jagged rock down to the sea. It will be no picnic, but it could be done. There are boats there, tied to a dock. You could get in a boat, motor away, and get back to shore where there's a phone. You won't save Fan, but you will save the Agency men on the way."

Court said, "And it won't save you."

Fitzroy shook his head, then held up the glass of whiskey in a toast. "I'm a fuckin' dead man any way you slice it."

Court thought a moment. "If the girl and I can get the guns off the men on the balcony, then maybe we can—"

"Forget it," Fitzroy said. "You might recall I used to be in the game, not as a grumpy old man behind a desk, but as a grumpy young man behind a pistol. Trust me that I've seen the setup. Major Xi will have a dozen men with him here, even while the attack is going on, and the lines of assault to get to them around this house are no good. To get me out of here you'd have to go through the front of the house, which means taking on each and every man on the premises, and they'll all know you are coming once you start shooting.

"No, lad. Making your way down the rock wall in the pitch-black night is your only bloody chance. You'd do well to take that chance and leave me to my fate."

Court knew Fitz was right. He said, "Let me go talk to her."

"I'll warn you again. I've seen you in action, so I feel confident you can make the climb. But I don't know about the woman. It was a straight drop down."

"Trust me, she'll pull it off better than I will."

Fitzroy held his glass up. "Well then, go and live to fight another day."

Court looked at the French doors to the bedroom. "She's pissed at me right now, so if I don't come out in five minutes, send help."

Fitz faked a little smile. "You're on your own there, lad. You have more training against buildings full of armed opposition than you do having a talk with an angry woman. Can't say I'd wager much on you now."

Court looked at the whiskey, then poured himself a healthy shot. "It's not utter shit, you say?"

"Better a mouse in the pot than no meat at all."

Court looked at the glass of booze, then at the Englishman. *"What?"*

"Beggars can't be choosers, lad."

"Oh." Court downed the shot, stood, and headed for the bedroom.

As soon as he entered the bedroom Court closed the French doors behind him, then found Zoya seated on the bed. She was working on something, which surprised Court, but when he saw she had taken the bedsheets and wound them tightly, then tied them together at one end, he realized he should not have been surprised. She added another sheet, making sure the knot was strong enough to hold her weight.

She said, "While you were in there drinking and whispering with the fat guy, I was in here preparing my escape."

"Off the balcony?"

"You have a better plan?"

Court sat on a chair facing the bed. "No. In fact, I had that plan exactly."

Zoya kept working. "Maybe I'll run into you on the cliff."

After a few seconds Court said, "Will you look at me?"

Zoya did turn, though she didn't stop tying off pieces of the sheet. "So . . . the PRC? You are an assassin for the People's Republic of China?"

"Of course not."

"Right."

"It's cover, Zoya. The Agency needed intel on Fan, and they knew I was the one who could get it. I was contracted for this op in the first place because I had a relationship with Donald Fitzroy. He is—"

"I know who Donald Fitzroy is. When I saw him I realized you were not an Agency man, as you said; you were, exactly as you told Colonel Dai, a private operator."

"I've had a long relationship with Fitzroy."

"A *relationship?*"

"Look, I wasn't lying before, but I wasn't exactly letting you in on the whole truth. The truth is, I worked for the Agency for fourteen years. And then one day, I didn't work for them anymore."

She stopped tying the sheets, then slid them under the blanket to hide them in case one of Xi's men came in. Looking at him, she asked, "Does that mean you quit, or does that mean you were let go?"

"Well . . . I didn't exactly get a pink slip. They sent guys to kill me."

Court could see Zoya looking hard at his face, searching for micro-expressions that might give away honesty or deception. "Go on."

"Kind of a long story, actually, but in those years when I wasn't with Langley, I took odd jobs, working for different handlers in the private sector. Fitzroy was one of those employers."

"Doing what, exactly?"

Court did not answer, so Zoya said, "Extrajudicial assassination?"

"Sometimes," he said. And then he amended it with, "Well . . . yes, pretty much exclusively."

There was no judgment from Zoya. No real expression of surprise, for that matter. After several seconds, she said, "I am going to ask you another question. It may be a difficult one for you to answer, but I need to know. Do you *promise* you will tell me the truth?"

Court leaned forward. "I swear it."

Her eyes remained locked on his. "Are you the Gray Man?"

CHAPTER

FIFTY-TWO

When Court just sat there looking at her, Zoya said, "The complete list of possible responses includes 'yes' and 'no.'"

Court struggled for the words. "Well . . . from what I understand, 'the Gray Man' is a term coined by Interpol several years ago. The Gray Man was the guy they blamed when something happened and nobody knew who did it."

"No . . . the Gray Man is a former CIA operations officer who went into the private sector as an assassin after he was targeted by the Agency. The SVR knew that much."

Court continued equivocating. "Right, I'm saying that just because there is an allegation that an assassination was conducted by the Gray Man, that doesn't necessarily—"

"*Yes* or *no?*"

Court hesitated. Then he said, "Yes."

Zoya's mouth opened slightly, and it hung there a moment. Softly she said, "Wow."

Court added, "But when I told you I could connect you with Agency people who will take care of you, I meant it. I talked with someone who would be very interested in speaking with you about coming to the U.S. for asylum. On your terms, of course."

"How is it you are here chasing Fan for the CIA?"

Court said, "The problems between me and the Agency got straightened out, more or less. After that, I agreed to work for them again on a contractual basis. I was sent to Hong Kong because Fitzroy was there working for Colonel Dai, and Dai was holding him hostage, encouraging him to get the job done. The Agency inserted me into the mix, had me go and take the job for Fitz and the Chinese. I was just supposed to gain intel for the Agency so they could get an assault team in to snatch Fan.

"I realized early on that if Fan was taken by the U.S., then Fitzroy would die. I owe Don my life . . . another long story. I was trying to capture Fan myself, to use him to earn Fitzroy's release."

"What was the plan after that?"

"I was going to fuck Colonel Dai over and give Fan to the Americans anyway."

Zoya looked at Court as if he were insane. "That was a pretty ambitious plan."

"When I say it out loud, it sounds a little hokey. And it got even more complicated when Fan told me he didn't want to go to the U.S. He wants to go to Taiwan."

Zoya said, "I hope you can take some constructive criticism."

"Sure."

"It sounds like you are trying to make too many people happy."

Court looked to the carpet a moment. "Welcome to my world."

Zoya said, "But you can't possibly still be considering infiltrating the Chamroon estate now. Can you?"

Court shook his head. "No. If we can get out of here, it will just be purely to save ourselves, and to warn the Agency that the Chinese are here in numbers in Phuket. Dai's men will kill Fan, but maybe I can save the American paramilitaries heading here now. Those guys are assholes, but they're also my friends." He shrugged. "Of course, if we leave, Fitzroy will still be here with Dai, so I am sure he will be killed."

Zoya pulled the fitted sheet off the bed and began tying it with the others. While she worked, she said, "No offense, Mr. Wonderful, but that's only a problem for you and Fitzroy. I don't even know the guy."

"Yeah, I get it." Court cussed under his breath. "*Fucking* Fan. Why did he have to send that damn e-mail? We could have saved him if Dai hadn't shown up."

Zoya continued tying the sheets. She said, "I thought you just said Fan didn't even want to go to the U.S. If that was the case, why would he contact the U.S. ambassador?"

Court walked around the room now, looking for anything he might use to aid them during an escape. "I guess he changed his mind, figured we were the only ones who could save his ass."

"Okay," Zoya said, "but if he's the guy who knows all the Chinese computer hacking secrets, how is it he can't manage to send an e-mail without China not only hacking it but pinpointing where it came from?"

Court stopped looking around. "That's a good question." He sat back down on a chair in the corner, thought it all through. Zoya just watched him while she worked, understanding that he knew more about this entire affair than she did.

Finally he said. "It's a setup."

"What's a setup?"

"The e-mail is a setup. Like you said, Fan doesn't want to go to the USA. He wouldn't have sent that e-mail to the U.S. ambassador on his own, especially not in a way the Chinese could access. My handler told me the e-mail was caught in a spam filter. Fan would know how to get something by a filter. He wanted it to get lost in the spam so the U.S. wouldn't see it, but the Chinese *would* see it."

"The Chinese were the intended recipients."

"That's right. Think about what Kulap Chamroon knows, either from the news or from Fan himself. He knows there are three nations after his prize: Russia, the USA, and China. Russia got wiped out at the Black Pearl, and the USA sent a total of one dumb asshole to rescue him."

Zoya got it. "That leaves China."

Court agreed. "That leaves China. China sent a shitload of gunners to the Black Pearl, set the place on fire, defeated the Russians, and killed a lot of Chamroon's men. Kulap made Fan send that message to an e-mail address Fan knew China had access to. Maybe Chamroon told Fan he'd cut his dick off if the Chinese didn't show in Phuket."

Zoya sighed. "Perhaps it was just his thumb."

"Yeah, maybe. But however he got Fan to comply, there is some kind of a trap waiting for whoever hits that property."

Zoya wasn't buying all of it. "But . . . the colonel just said the e-mail was traced back to Phuket. If it really was Fan who sent it, he'd *have* to be here. Fan is worth a lot of money to Kulap. Would he put him in the middle of the place where he knew the Americans were coming?"

Court thought this over, too, and reflected back on what both Brewer and Colonel Dai had said. "It wasn't traced to a wireless address inside the Chamroon estate; it was traced to a cell tower. Chamroon had Fan send it from somewhere nearby, but somewhere where he wasn't going to be in the middle of a Chinese attack."

"Where could that be?"

Court stood and went to the curtains covering the window out to the balcony. He moved them to the side and peered out. A guard with a pistol in his shoulder holster leaned against the railing of the balcony smoking a cigarette. He pointed angrily to Court, telling him to get away from the sliding balcony door, but Court just looked past the man, down to the ocean far below and out to sea. "Do you know how to spoof a call from a cell phone tower?"

Zoya said, "Of course. You take apart your cell phone and rewire the antenna in it to a directional antenna. Of course, you can't walk around with it, the antenna will be several times larger than the phone itself, but if you point it at a tower you can make the call look like it came from one place when you are someplace else."

Court smiled broadly. Something about this Russian woman's command of tradecraft turned him on, and he was pretty sure that meant he was nuts.

He said, "You're exactly right."

Zoya shook her head now. "But you need line of sight on the tower. That's the only way. This island is mostly jungle. How are you going to find a direct line to—"

Zoya stopped talking, walked quickly over to Court, and looked out past the balcony, to the big, flat ocean to the south.

She said, "That yacht."

Court nodded. "Damn right. The *Medusa*."

"Chamroon owns the yacht?"

"I doubt it. That would be pretty obvious. No . . . it will be owned by someone he controls, or someone he made a deal with. It's registered in Genoa, whatever that's worth. Whoever is on the yacht is holding Fan, and probably protecting Chamroon."

"You are very smart, Mr. Gray Man."

"It's not intelligence. It's mileage. I've seen a lot over the years."

Zoya wasn't listening; she was already thinking about their predicament. "If we got out of here, found a way to make contact with your people to stop them from walking into the trap, and then went to the yacht to grab Fan, you could then use Fan to trade for that old guy in the other room."

Court joked, "Right, that's all we have to do."

Zoya smiled, realizing all she had just said. "You aren't the only one around here who can come up with a crazy plan."

C ourt stepped back into the living room where Fitzroy was seated and found his former employer sitting calmly in the darkness, doing his best to enjoy whiskey he did not truly respect, knowing this might well be his last. Court told Sir Donald they would attempt to break out, and Fitzroy should keep the faith, because they had a plan that might allow him to survive the night.

Fitz didn't seem to believe him, but he kept a stiff upper lip, and he wished Court and his Russian friend Godspeed.

C ourt and Zoya stood together in the dark bedroom right before beginning their operation. Court took her in his arms, and she looked up to him, but he could feel her misgivings. He said, "When you told me your name earlier . . . I should have told you mine. I'm sorry."

"I was upset about that. But I didn't know at the time you were a world-famous secret agent."

Court shrugged. "The most famous secret agent on the planet. What does that get me?"

"Killed, one would assume. Somehow you managed to beat the odds." She added, "Chad."

"It's Court. Court Gentry."

Zoya nodded. "Good luck, Gray Man." She went up on her toes and kissed Court. It was quick and more friendly than romantic, but it was enough to make him feel better.

Court let her go. "Good luck." They separated; Court went to the living room and Zoya stayed in the bedroom.

C ourt and Zoya decided to attempt their escape exactly sixty minutes before the Chinese attacked the Chamroon estate. They reasoned that all the Chinese forces would be moving to their predeployment positions, except, of course, for the ones left behind to guard the prisoners here at the safe house. After dealing with the men on the balcony, Court and Zoya hoped to make it down to the boats at the water by the time the gunfire started nearby, providing them with a slight distraction.

Major Xi had nearly a dozen men at the house with him, but he'd stationed only two on the balcony overhanging the water behind the suite where the captives were being held. Apparently Xi had decided no one would be foolish enough to try to make an escape down the sheer rocky cliff, especially late at night.

Zoya opened the curtains to the balcony, right where Court had done so earlier in the evening. Court was still in the living room, standing at the balcony door there, but he had not moved his curtains yet.

Zoya could see one guard sitting at a small table, facing her direction. A second man was closer to Court's side of the balcony, standing there, hands on his hips.

The seated man saw Zoya, and he stood. He motioned for her to step away from the glass, but she smiled, nodded, and waved, then unlocked the balcony door. Pretending to completely misunderstand the man's gestures, she opened the door, but did not step out.

In her American accent she said, "Sorry, I know to stay inside, but do you speak English?"

"Yes, I speak English. Close the door now!" The man reached for his pistol inside his jacket, but just to put his hand on the grip. He held it there, another indicator for the clueless American woman that he meant business.

As he stepped closer to the woman, his partner had reached into his own jacket for his pistol, and he faced the action twenty feet away.

He never heard the living room door to the balcony slide open.

CHAPTER

FIFTY-THREE

Zoya spoke again to the Chinese guard. "It's okay, sir. Can you get Colonel Dai on the phone? We need to talk to him."

"No! Go back inside or I will—"

The guard closest to Zoya turned to look to his partner, and he saw the bigger American man standing behind him, just now wrapping the cord of a floor lamp around the guard's throat. The American cinched the cord tight enough to lift the man off the ground with one hand, and with the other he reached around and controlled the pistol, holding it tightly in place in its holster, despite the guard's attempts to draw it.

The guard by Zoya spun into action, facing this new threat, pulling his pistol out in a fluid motion and bringing it to bear on the man's head. But before he sighted the weapon he felt a loop of cord around his own neck from behind; it was yanked hard, and then, to his utter astonishment, he saw the legs of the woman out in front of him.

While she held on to the cords around his throat she used the leverage there to kick her legs up, wrap them around the extended weapon, and adroitly disarm the guard by simultaneously kicking forward with her right foot into the slide of the gun and heeling back with her left foot into his hand.

The pistol bounced on the deck of the balcony, and the woman's legs retracted, then cinched around the guard's lower back.

And through all this his windpipe was being crushed by the lamp cord.

He flung himself back to the deck, slamming the woman hard and using his own body to amplify the effects, but she held on, even improving her choke hold by looping a second ring of the cord around the man's neck and pulling it even harder.

After less than thirty seconds the loss of blood to the guard's brain caused him to pass out completely. Zoya quickly pushed him off her, grabbed the pistol, and looked across the balcony to see how Court was doing.

Court already had his guard unconscious on his shoulder, and he walked him to the edge of the balcony. Court let the body fall, dropping the man 150 feet to his death. Zoya saw that the SIG Sauer pistol was already jutting from Court's waistband.

Zoya panted with exertion as she jammed her guard's pistol into the small of her back and retied her warm-ups tightly around it. Then she reached down to lift the body.

Court appeared next to her. Softly he said, "I'll get him."

But Zoya ignored him, took the unconscious man's arm in one hand, then executed a forward roll over the prostrate body. This gave her the momentum she needed to heave the man up onto her shoulder and then stand with him in a fireman's carry.

Court's eyes widened as she walked slowly to the balcony's edge and then let the guard roll off her shoulder and fall away.

Zoya rushed back into the bedroom, grabbed the length of bedsheets she'd turned into a rope with loops at both ends, then made her way back to the edge of the balcony.

Court was there with her and they wasted no time getting off the overhanging balcony, because they had no idea if someone was about to put bullets in their backs from one of the other windows in the big house. They kicked out over the side, lowered slowly till their hands were holding on to the balcony deck itself, and below in the near darkness they found a metal beam support structure holding the balcony away from the home. This they moved along easily, over and under like monkey bars, with Zoya leading the way because of her speed and comfort with the action.

Court thought it was probably a good thing he couldn't even see the ocean below in the low light, but from the sound of the crashing of the waves, the shore was both very far beneath them and very rocky.

When they got to the end of the balcony supports they found themselves at a sheer cement wall, which marked the edge of the foundation of the house. There was almost no moonlight here, but when their eyes adjusted to the darkness, they could see it was eight feet straight down to a narrow ledge of earth that rimmed the top of the rocky cliff. Court hung down and dropped a couple of inches, then moved over to Zoya to help her when she dropped.

She came down on solid footing, not needing him there at all. She said, "I'll be fine. You just worry about yourself and we'll go faster."

"Okay," Court said, completely unaccustomed to working with someone so skilled. He even thought back to his old paramilitary unit in the CIA, Task Force Golf Sierra, known around CIA as the Goon Squad. These were six of the best operators in all of the U.S. military and the intelligence services, mostly former SEALs or Delta Force guys, and Court had been by far the best free climber of the unit.

Now he was completely outclassed by this Russian woman, and he wished he could just sit down and enjoy watching her at work.

They began climbing down the cliff just two minutes after they left the balcony, but within another minute of starting their descent they could hear shouting above them. They soon saw flashlight beams scanning the rocks to the left and right of their position, but unless Xi or one of his men wanted to climb under the balcony itself, there was no way they could be seen from above.

Court and Zoya had discussed moving laterally along the cliff face until they could find a place wide of the Chinese safe house to make their way back up onto smoother ground on the hillside, but Court was glad they'd chosen to descend all the way down to the boats below. If they'd been caught out on the cliff by a flashlight now, they would have only been a few feet away from the balcony, and there would be nothing they could do but hold on to the wall while they were shot to death from above.

They moved along close together with Zoya below Court, and she found ledges, handholds, and small wedges in the rocks where she could jam her tennis shoes in to brace herself. Often she called up to Court softly to give him directions, which he followed carefully. At one point she had to use the makeshift climbing rope over her shoulder to hook it onto a rock and climb out to either side looking for a path. When she found her way she had Court lift the loop of the bedsheets off its outcropping, and then she had Court slide the loop over his own shoulder, while she hooked the other end on a closer rock.

They moved this way for twenty grueling minutes, and by now Court guessed from the sound of the waves they'd made it halfway down. They still had another seventy-five feet or so to go, and he'd just climbed down level with Zoya when she announced that the face of the wall just below her slanted in, and she couldn't find a place for her feet.

"Okay," said Court, straining under a tough handhold. "Do you want me to try?"

"No. Just find a good hold, loop the rope around your head and shoulder, and hang on tight. You're going to have to lower me."

"Right." Court had to move to his left several feet to find a decent spot to hang on, and then he readied himself to take Zoya's weight if she fell. When he was ready, they both hooked into the bedsheets, he around his upper body and she around her waist.

It took every bit of Court's strength to lower Zoya slowly, playing out the bedsheets with his right hand and taking the full weight of her 145-pound, muscular physique. She was aware of Court's strain, and quickly she found a place to get a handhold inside the forty-five-degree inward slope of the wall. This took some of the weight away, and after another minute of work she managed to make contact with the wall with both feet and hands.

She called back up now. "You're going to have to come down the same way, and I'm going to have to hold you."

"Can you do it?" Court asked.

"We'll know in a moment, won't we?"

"Great."

Court took his time, put a hand in one of his footholds, lowered himself, and grabbed on to the other tiny outcropping where his other foot had been. He hung down now, with his legs swaying in open air. Zoya could see them, right in front of her but three feet away. She could grab him by the waist, but from there he'd have to drop, and she didn't know if she could carry both his weight and his momentum.

She called up to him. "Okay, here's what we do. I hang out with one hand and one leg braced. You step down on my shoulder. I lean forward and you step on my lower back. I'll pull myself and you back to the wall while you let go and grab on to me with your hands."

"Jesus," Court said, but he couldn't think of a better plan.

"It's all in the timing," Zoya said. She tightened her left handhold, forced her left foothold tighter to the wall, and then swung out to the right. She fully extended her body away from the wall, and Court began climbing down her slowly. When he had both feet on her butt and one hand on her shoulder, she said, "Okay, one . . . two . . . three."

Court let go with his remaining hand, lowered his head quickly so it didn't smack against the lower edge of the outer wall, and "rode" to the deeper wall on Zoya's back as she swung back in with her right arm and leg. Once there, he got off her as quickly as possible, finding his own foot- and handholds.

"You all right?" He knew that couldn't have been easy for the five-foot, seven-inch woman.

She was clearly reaching exhaustion; he could hear it in her voice. "Fine. Take the rope off and give it to me. I may need both ends to traverse."

Court did as instructed; Zoya put all the bedsheets back over her shoulder, and she started back down.

Court was still thinking about what she'd just had to do. As she lowered her left leg down to a spot far below her, he said, "Why don't I lead? You need a minute to—"

A loud cracking sound in the rock interrupted him and then, to Court's horror, Zoya dropped away suddenly.

Court's mouth bled freely now, dripping onto the wet stone right in front of his face, though he could not see it. His right shin hurt because he'd smacked it on an outcropping as he threw himself forward, and now it was holding up more of his weight than it should have been, considering he had no power to control his shin like he did a hand or foot.

His right wrist and hand hurt, not because he'd hit them as he'd lunged for Zoya, but instead because he was now horizontal to the wall, facing straight down, and three fingers of his right hand were up high and behind his back. Other than his bloody shin, the three fingers were the only part of him taking his body weight because his left foot hung down in open air, and his left arm was hyperextended, his hand gripping the thin fingers of Zoya Zakharova's right hand.

He'd lunged for her, snatching her hand out of free fall in desperation and only then trying to find something of his own to grab on to. He'd banged his face in the process, and his leg, and although he had stopped her from dropping seventy feet to her death, he had no idea what either of them could do now to get out of this situation.

He'd lost hold of her hand almost immediately, but now their fingers were locked tightly together. The position was agonizing for Court, but he knew the woman below him must have been in excruciating pain with the way he held on to her.

Court spit blood into the wall so he could talk. "You okay?"

The voice came from below; he couldn't see any part of her now, only the rock face in front of him. "No. There is another recess here, deeper than the one before. I can't see anything, and my feet can't reach the wall."

"Can you stretch out with your left hand and find the wall?"

"I'll have to spin around, and I'll lose my grip with you. What are you holding on with?"

Court didn't want to tell her, but she was the more experienced climber. If there was a solution to this problem, maybe she could solve it. He said, "Three fingers of my right hand. I can't move my legs without losing my grip."

"Shit," she said, and she said it in English.

"*Der'mo,*" he answered back. He wasn't going to be able to hold her for long.

She asked, "How far down do you think it is to the water?"

"The same distance it is to the rocks."

Zoya said, "You are saying, it doesn't matter."

"Yeah."

Court knew there was only one thing they could possibly try. "Look, I'm going to have to—"

Zoya knew before he finished the sentence. "Do it. Swing me out, then back in towards the cliff, and let me go."

It was a Hail Mary, nothing more. He was going to have to generate some momentum by swinging her back and forth, in and out towards the wall below the underhang. And then, when he'd gotten her moving as fast as possible, he would let go, and she would fly in through the darkness and hope against all reason for three things to go right at the same time: One, that she made it to the wall before she lost momentum and fell to her death. Two, that she would somehow instantly find hand- or footholds that would keep her from sliding off the wall. And three, that he didn't throw her so hard into the wall that she crashed face-first into the rock, knocking her hard enough to where she couldn't grab on to a hold even if it was there for her.

Court knew he couldn't hold on much longer. "I have to start swinging."

"Go."

Slowly at first, he rocked the deadweight in, then out, straining his left shoulder. After three full cycles, Zoya was moving enough for Court to feel significant pull against the three fingers holding him against the wall.

"Court."

"Yes?"

"Do you pray?"

"I'm praying now."

"Then pray for me," she said.

"Okay. Two more swings and then we go. You've got this."

From below he heard her say, "You are a good man. You will rescue Fan and save your Agency friends tonight."

Court said, "Not without your help, spider monkey," and then he swung in with all his might, let go of her fingers, and felt Zoya's hand slip away.

CHAPTER

FIFTY-FOUR

C ourt hefted his numb and nearly useless left arm, and somehow he managed to find a handhold for his left hand. He started pulling himself up, using all his might, even pressing his bloody face into the wet cool rock as he did so. And as he did this he shouted, "Zoya?"

He'd heard her hit the wall, but it sounded way too hard, and then he clearly heard something fall, knocking against the wall as it went down. He didn't know if it was a piece of a rock itself, or if it had been an unconscious woman.

There was no answer. "Zoya!"

For five more seconds he heard nothing. Then her voice, muted by the rock between them. "I'm here."

"Are you hurt?"

"I'll live, but I dropped my gun."

Court closed his eyes, thanked God as relief washed over him, and said, "I'll lend you mine."

After a few more seconds Zoya said, "Good news. I'm feeling the ceiling of this underhang. There are good handholds and footholds. When you get some strength back, you can climb down here and I can reach out and help you position your feet."

"Okay," he said, blinking away misting tears of joy because he was unable to wipe his face with the back of his arm. "I'll need just a second."

The rest of the descent went much faster as the angle of the cliff decreased, and they made it the final twenty feet down to the shoreline by scooting along on their backsides. On the rocky shore they embraced, and both of them wanted to fall over onto the rocks and just lie there, but there was no time. If there were boats here there must have been other ways down to the sand, and while neither Court nor Zoya saw any of Xi's men, the glow of flashlights higher on the hills told them the Chinese guards were out in force and actively searching for them.

"How do you feel?" he asked.

"Pretty beat-up," she admitted. "But I'll make it."

Court felt the same. His left shoulder hurt, his right hand hurt, his lip was fat and sore where he'd smacked it on the cliff, and his right shin was swollen and aching.

The two boats at the dock fifty yards from the cliff were wooden-hulled stern-drive twelve-footers. They clearly belonged to one of the private homes around, and quite possibly the Chinese safe house itself. Court ripped the wiring out of the engine of one boat then hot-wired the simple ignition system on the other in just a couple of minutes, while Zoya held the pistol and watched for trouble.

Finally the engine started, Zoya jumped off the little dock and into the vessel with the line in her hand, and Court went full throttle, fighting his way through both the darkness and the incoming waves.

As they raced off, Court could barely hear the snaps of gunfire over the sound of the engine and the crashing waves, but Xi and his men had been armed with pistols, and they were a couple hundred yards away. It would take a hell of a good shot in this bad light to hit a bouncing and swaying target on the move at that distance.

Zoya and Court raced safely around a rocky point and back to the west, away from the Chamroon estate and back in the direction of their hotel.

Just ten minutes later they came ashore at the Trisara Phuket, docking quietly at the lighted pier and then jogging towards the buildings. It was still ten minutes to midnight, so there were quite a few couples at the bar, and still a few at the beachside restaurant.

Court said, "We need a phone and some diving gear." Both of them had dropped by the dive shop at the resort the day before, and though it would be locked up now, Zoya insisted she could find a way in.

Court raced back to the suite, approached from the patio, and looked inside, making certain Xi hadn't left anyone there. It was exactly as he'd left it, and he used the butt of the SIG pistol to break the window next to the back door so he could slip inside.

Here he changed into black cotton pants and a black T-shirt, then searched through his gear and discovered that one of Xi's men had taken the Glock pistol. The .38 revolver was still in his backpack, however, so he dropped that into his pocket and put the SIG in his waistband.

He returned to the lounge and walked through, then out onto the bar area by the pool. He walked between several tables full of guests, eyeing them carefully. A woman took pictures of her group; one of her friends asked her to dance, and then she covered her phone with her napkin and followed him to the dance floor on the other side of the pool. Several others from the big table also went up to dance, so it was no great feat for Court to merely pass by and slide the napkin and the phone off the table.

Seconds later he stepped into darkness outside the lights of the sedate outdoor nightlife here at the resort, and he dialed Brewer's number. There would be no encryption on his end of this call, which meant he'd have to be careful with what he said.

She answered on the first ring. "Brewer."

"It's me."

"Is this Mr. Cavalcade?"

"No. It's Carlsbad here."

"I'm glad you called early. The time for the party has been moved up an hour."

Court almost choked on his response. "No!"

"Yes. My friends found a ride that would get them there faster, so they—"

Court interrupted. "Bad idea! They need to skip this party, that's why I'm calling."

"Don't be ridiculous, they've been looking forward to it."

Court said, "Listen carefully. My old friend from Hong Kong is here with a huge group of *his* friends, and right now they're walking through the front door of the same party *your* friends are heading to. Not sure there will be enough booze to go around."

There was a long pause. "You're sure?"

"You need to call your friends right now!"

"It's too late."

"Do it! It's a surprise party."

Brewer hesitated, then said, "I don't follow you."

"My friend from Hong Kong will be the surprise guest, and there will be a huge reception waiting for him."

"Where . . . where is the man my friends were hoping to meet?"

"I'm pretty sure he's nearby at another party, on a yacht. You could help me check on that."

"Right. Name and registry?"

"No! Make the call first!"

Brewer put Court on hold. Many times in his career as a CIA paramilitary he'd been one of the guys in the helicopter racing into a target only to get the word to turn around and go home. More than once he was in sight of his objective when the order came. It sucked when it happened, but sometimes it sucked more when it *didn't* happen. When he *wasn't* recalled even after intelligence pointed to a problem at the objective.

Brewer came back on the line. "People are trying to reach my friends now."

"Good." Court couldn't hear any helicopters in the distance, but he knew SAD might be flying in helos with noise reduction technology, so he couldn't say for certain they weren't over the Chamroon property right now.

Brewer next said, "The boat you mentioned?"

"The *Medusa*. Out of Genoa."

There was a pause while Brewer typed that in. It only took a few seconds for her to say, "Got it, running a check on the ownership."

Just then, Court heard the unmistakable sound of helicopter rotors, somewhere in the night. As a warning he said, "I hear a helicopter."

Brewer snapped back, "I've done what I can. The message has been passed."

Court had no idea what was waiting for whoever was the first to breach the Chamroon property, but he was sure whoever entered was not going to swoop in and snatch up Fan Jiang and then skulk away. No, Kulap Chamroon had had two days to prepare a reception for the Chinese.

Now Brewer said, "The boat. Uhh . . . well . . . I hope he's not there."

Court said, "I'm pretty sure he is."

"The boat is owned by some gentlemen from the nation of registry."

Italy? Some gentlemen. Court said, "Any chance these gents would have a business relationship with the people throwing the party on land tonight?"

"There is a significant chance of that. In fact, I'd say it's a given. Cut from the same cloth, if you know what I'm saying." Court realized Brewer was telling him the yacht was owned by the Italian mafia. He remembered from his reading on the Chamroon Syndicate that they had ties to the 'Ndrangheta, one of the largest criminal organizations on the planet. They were based in Calabria, in the toe of the Italian boot. It was the poorest region in the nation, but the 'Ndrangheta controlled a large amount of drug trafficking coming into and through Europe, as well as much of the human-trafficking corridors.

"The Italians. Where in Italy?"

"Tip of the boot."

"Jesus Christ," Court mumbled into the phone.

Brewer seemed momentarily confounded. "I wish I could just tell my friends they need to drop in on the boat party instead of the other one. Especially since it's just a couple of minutes away, and they are already dressed for a night out."

"But?" asked Court. He didn't want SAD hitting the Italian boat, because he'd lose any chance he had at getting Fan himself.

Brewer replied, "I'll have to talk to some other people first, and that will take time."

Court translated this to mean Brewer couldn't just change the target package for the SAD hit. The kidnapping/rescue of Fan Jiang had been okayed when the ones holding him were Thai gangsters, but now that the target was Italian, men that would be known to most as European businessmen, on a massive yacht no less, she couldn't just land a couple of helos on the deck and have the CIA gunning down anyone who got in the way.

The helicopter sounds were louder now; there were multiple birds inbound.

In his utter frustration, Court dropped any pretense of a cover. "Jesus Christ! Do I have to find a *fucking* flare gun?"

Brewer was off the line for several seconds, then came back on. "I've just been told our friends are turning around and heading home."

Court breathed out a long sigh. "Thank you."

"What about you? Are you where you can stay the night without anybody bugging you?"

"No," Court said with finality. "I need to go to the party on the boat."

Brewer's voice lowered an octave. "Disallowed."

Court ignored her. "Sorry you and your friends can't make it. I'll be sure to send all your love to everyone I see."

Brewer shouted into the phone. "You listen to me! You are *not* authorized in any way, shape, or form to—"

Court hung up, partially to save Brewer from continued security breaches over an open line, but mostly because he was tired of getting yelled at.

Above him, the sounds of helicopters began to recede, and he muttered a brief prayer of thanks. He couldn't help but wonder if he knew any of the guys flying overhead, but he also couldn't help but wonder what they might be ordered to do to him tomorrow if this plan of his somehow came together tonight.

He was officially off reservation now, and he figured the SAD helos would probably come after him next.

C ourt met Zoya back at the wooden boat by the dock. She had two scuba rigs as well as flashlights and knives that would strap to their legs, a mesh bag filled with a few tools, duct tape, and other odds and ends she'd picked up in the dive shop. Court was impressed with what she'd accomplished in the past fifteen minutes.

They fired up the boat and took off, probably not too far ahead of the hotel's security realizing someone had stolen a phone and two sets of scuba gear.

As they raced out into the placid bay and away from the lights of the resort, Court and Zoya both turned to look to their left. There, around the rocky point and up the hill not far inland at all, a large flash of light lit up the green canopy of jungle. Within an instant, a second, similar flash came from near the same location as the first. Smaller firefly-like sparkles erupted in the trees. Both Court and Zoya knew this was gunfire, but neither had a clue what had caused the big flashes preceding it.

When the first rumble rolled over the sound of the outboard motor behind them, they both knew a pair of massive explosions and fully automatic gunfire had kicked off the battle at the Chamroon property.

CHAPTER

FIFTY-FIVE

The first explosion confirmed Colonel Dai's fear that he'd walked his force into a trap, but for the past several minutes other clues had led him inexorably towards this conclusion. His men had made their way into positions around the estate after circumventing the most perfunctory police presence on the rural roads nearby, and then they'd made it over the barbed-wire fences in four different locations without seeing patrols at the perimeter. The attackers moved in teams of five, and the first group had reported that they had reached the back door of the main house on the property without encountering a single sentry during their ingress.

Colonel Dai Longhai himself was nestled with a sniper team and the mission commander in an overwatch position higher on the hillside from the front gate of the property, close enough to see for himself that the building in the center of the estate was well lit and appeared to be occupied on all three floors, so he found it odd there was no security at the fence line or in the large clearings around the buildings, but it wasn't until his second squad made it to the front doors of the building, having not seen any sign of a guard, a motion detector, or even a dog, that Dai's level of apprehension reached the point where he articulated his concerns.

He took the radio out of the hand of his ground force commander next to him. "Teams Three and Four? Do you see any movement inside any of the buildings?"

Three and Four were at the edge of the tropical forest that grew on the estate, inside the fence line of the big property, with better vision of the overall scene than the ten men stacked at the doors.

"This is Team Three. We see nothing."

"Team Four. Lights are on, but no movement. It's midnight. Maybe they aren't expecting any trouble."

Dai shook his head there in the dark foliage above the scene. This didn't feel right at all. "No. All units egress quietly."

"This is Team One. We're at the back door now. Confirm you want us to—"

"I said get the fuck out of—"

A simultaneous volley of four rocket-propelled grenades raced out of the jungle to the south and hit the area around the men at the back door, and, within a half second, four more RPGs struck the entrance to the building coming from the northeast, decimating Team Two just as they were stepping down from the large porch.

Ten of Dai's men were dead or horribly wounded in the blink of an eye.

And then, around the cleared portion of the large estate, large wooden boards arced up from the ground on buried hinges, each covered with straw or recently felled brush, and neat rows of camouflaged men stood from hidden trenches and fired Kalashnikovs at the jungle around them.

As Dai watched, some six or seven different groups of men around the property engaged his remaining forces, sending men sprawling, spinning, dying in the clearing or in the jungle, or retreating for their lives back to the fence line.

Up on the overwatch where Dai was positioned, the two sniper teams were preparing to engage with their bolt-action rifles, but Dai called out to them before they fired their first round. "No!" he said. "There must be fifty or more of them. We will just draw fire on ourselves, and we can do nothing for our comrades below."

The battle lasted over ten minutes, but nine of those minutes were just mopping up, because the result had been decided in the opening seconds. Twenty PLA special forces operators were cut down while the six men on the hillside watched: stunned, dismayed, and yet overjoyed to be up on the hill and not down there.

Kulap Chamroon observed it all from the upper stern deck of the *Medusa*, more than a mile and a half to the south of his family compound on Phuket. He had binoculars in his hands, as did several of the Italians at the long table around him, and they drank and ate and enjoyed the show as if they were watching a fireworks display.

They also had wireless cameras set up in both the front and the back of the big home on the estate, and through these views, projected on the large-screen TV in the upper-deck salon there next to the big table full of men, they could all see plainly that the Chinese invaders were being slaughtered.

The fighters dug into Kulap's estate were not Chamroon Syndicate men. No, the syndicate gunmen, other than the security detail used by the Chamroon family, were poorly armed gangsters, great in a bar fight or a back-alley mugging but hopeless for this kind of an affair. No, for tonight he had brought in members of Barisan Revolusi Nasional, the National Revolutionary Front, an insurgent group in southern Thailand and northern Malaysia. BRN had no quarrel with these Chinese, and they knew absolutely nothing of a Chinese computer hacker named Fan Jiang who had been forced into servitude by the Chamroon Syndicate, but they did know the Chamroon Syndicate, because the organization had provided the BRN with weapons and funding over the past few years, as a simple foil to the Thai government.

For tonight Kulap had simply rented fifty-six of the BRN's best fighters, paid their commanders for their services, and moved them up north via a coastal barge here to his compound on Phuket.

The BRN guerrillas dug in with orders to wait for an attack that would surely come.

Two days after they arrived and prepared positions, the Chinese hit and, from all appearances, the Chinese had all either died or retreated.

When it was over, one of the Italians sitting with Kulap at the stern of the yacht turned away from the television and looked at his Thai business associate. "Those savages you hired blew up your house. Was that in your plan?" He said it with unmistakable mirth. He was 'Ndrangheta, a millionaire dozens of times over. The loss of one of his properties would have been nothing to him, and he presumed the same of his little Thai business associate.

Kulap laughed himself, then downed a huge gulp of Sangiovese. "I told them to do what they had to do . . . but you're right, Paolo. It seemed to me like they enjoyed firing those RPGs a little too much!" He laughed again. "Dirty fuckers."

Another man watching the video said, "Looks like the Chinese killed about five of the rebels."

Kulap shrugged. "I have to pay their commanders the same amount of money, no matter how many live or die."

Everyone at the table laughed now.

Half a football field ahead of the conversation at the stern, Zoya Zakharova climbed the anchor chain of the *Medusa*, hanging upside down, her rippling muscles tightening with each pull upwards.

She was a supremely fit woman, but this wasn't an easy task for her. The salt water had taken no time finding its way into every tiny little cut she'd earned descending the cliff face, but she pushed the pain and the ache of her fatigued and bruised muscles out of her mind as she climbed out of the water and towards the hull of the ship where the anchor chain disappeared into the chain locker. She couldn't see up on the bow at all from her position, but she knew Court was floating in the water, just far back enough to see the bow, waiting with the pistol taken from the guard on the balcony at the Chinese safe house. If anyone saw Zoya boarding the *Medusa*, Court would fire on them before they could kill her, giving her time to simply drop from the chain back into the water.

This would ruin tonight's plan, but from the sounds of the small jungle war that was petering out to the north, Zoya thought it likely that Colonel Dai and his men would only continue to be a threat to Sir Donald Fitzroy. Not to Fan, not to her, and not to Court.

This mission was all about getting Fan, and getting Fan was all she cared about now.

Zoya made it to the bow, then turned back to look at Court, hoping to see him in the black water. He was just outside the glow of the yacht's bow lighting, floating with her scuba gear next to him, and he swam forward a few feet and raised his gun arm straight in the air: their signal that all was clear.

She climbed around the chain now and used it to stand on as she looked over the bow itself. It was pitch-black here at the foredeck, but above on the higher decks she could hear voices and see lights. The *Medusa's* bow faced out to sea, clearly so those partying at the stern could see the shoreline and the battle raging inland, but Zoya used the darkness to move silently to a place to hide in front of a forehatch.

Two minutes later Court came over the bow at the anchor chain, rolled onto the deck, and crawled forward to her. She was impressed with his stealth and skill; the Zaslon men she had worked with—on and off—had been some of the best on Earth at clandestine movement, but Court was as good as she'd ever seen.

He knelt next to her, took the pistol out of a mesh bag he'd worn over his shoulder, and let the water drip from the barrel. He whispered, "Two sentries on the top deck. They can't see us from here. The rest of the action on deck is at the stern."

She touched the forehatch in front of her with the tip of her .38 revolver. "Where do you think this leads?"

"Belowdecks will be a hallway, the engine room, quarters for the crew. All the staterooms and public areas will be on the upper decks with all the glass."

Zoya said, "If you were keeping Fan here, do you think you'd keep him down here, or up there?"

Court said, "Let's try below. Even if we don't find Fan there, someone in the crew will know where he is." Court pulled a screwdriver out of the bag and got to work on the forehatch. It was locked from the inside, but he was able to remove the hinges and pull it open just a few inches. Looking down, he saw a dimly lit hall, and he could hear the sounds of electric generators. He looked back to Zoya and nodded, then struggled for another minute to reach in and flip the hatch lever open from the inside with the screwdriver.

Zoya lowered herself down through the hatch, dropped into a crouch, then raised her weapon. Court came down himself a few seconds later, and he found himself in a hallway lined on both sides with doors. He imagined this was all crew living space. He had no idea how many berths there were, but a yacht this size could easily house a crew of twenty-five or more.

After midnight Court didn't expect much action here belowdecks, but he wasn't taking any chances. He felt a little glare from Zoya as he passed her, but he wasn't going to let her take the first bullet that came up this narrow hall.

He thought about checking the doors one by one. But this was a 160-foot yacht, and it was a long hallway, and he decided he needed some intelligence about where to look. He just walked past all the doors and into the engine room beyond.

Court knew the engine room would be the easiest place to find someone working alone, or at least not out in the open.

Directly inside the hatch, electrical panels displayed all the generator battery levels, water tank levels, and other gauges used by the engineers on the crew. They passed several water filters and more control panels, air-conditioning equipment, and the hydraulic pump. The massive Caterpillar engines took up the main part of the room. Court and Zoya passed them by moving low and carefully.

He found a target just thirty seconds later: a man sitting at a desk and eating a piece of chocolate cake. He was in his fifties, wearing blue coveralls and glasses, and he couldn't have been easier to sneak up on with all the noises here in the engine room.

Court tapped him on his back with the pistol, then held it in his face as he turned around.

The man sat stunned, bits of cake hanging out of his beard.

"English?" Court asked.

The man's response came in a hoarse whisper. *"No. Italiano."*

Zoya had been keeping an eye out for others, but when she heard this she stepped in to the desk area and began speaking in rapid-fire Italian.

Court stepped out and began covering the rest of the engine room.

After a minute Zoya leaned out. "He says we can kill him, but he won't talk."

Court pulled the small vial of scopolamine hydrobromide out of a zippered pocket in his wetsuit. He held it in front of the engineer. To Zoya he said, "Tell him what this is, and how fast it works."

She did, and the man listened a minute, drew his shoulders back, and spit at Court.

Zoya reared back to punch him in the face, but Court grabbed her arm. "No. Allow me."

He cracked the little vial in his hand, lunged forward, and shoved it in the man's left nostril. In the shock of the moment the engineer inhaled through his nose, then almost immediately began thrashing.

Court held him down and held his hand over his mouth. He turned to Zoya. "Find a head."

"You mean a bathroom?"

"Yes."

She looked at him with bewilderment. "You have to take a bathroom break *now*?"

"No," he said, "I'm going to lock him in when I get what I need from him."

Ten minutes later the engineer was in his underwear, he had his arms and hands taped behind his back, he had been pushed into the tiny head aft of the engine room, and the door latch was broken off on both the inside and the outside.

The man was conscious but completely out of it. He'd conveyed in Italian that the Thais had come out to the boat yesterday in a party of eight men. He didn't know anything about a Chinese prisoner, but he told Court and Zoya that all the new guests were staying in the five staterooms on the upper deck.

Court realized he was as far as he could be from his target as possible.

After they had him tied and locked in the head, Court turned to Zoya. "One more thing. Ask him where the tenders are."

Zoya spoke again, and the utterly compliant man answered through the door. She looked at Court. "The subdeck below has two fifteen-foot tenders. They can be deployed out through hull hatches."

Court now wore the blue coveralls and tennis shoes he'd taken from the engineer. The coveralls were baggy and the shoes were a full two sizes too large, but Court tightened the laces and wore them anyway, because a barefoot engineer would be an odd sight. He and Zoya went aft out of the engine room to the ladder that led both down to the subdeck and up to the upper decks. Here Court said, "Any chance I can get you to go down to one of the tenders and get ready to deploy it? I might come hard and fast with Fan and we'll need to get out of here in a hurry."

Zoya shook her head. "You'll need me upstairs and you know it." When

Court started to say something else, she added, "Forget about me leaving now. I'm with you all the way."

Court let it go; it was a battle he knew he'd lose before he'd even begun fighting it.

Passing the lower deck, they went through the kitchen. Zoya was still in her wetsuit. All the lights were on and they could hear noises just around the corner.

Zoya peeked out first, then stepped out fully. Court walked out into the passageway and saw Zoya stepping up close behind a female server in black slacks, a black button-down shirt, and a black tie. Her black apron lay on the stainless steel island next to her, and she was well into the process of drinking a glass of wine.

"Long night?" Zoya said, and the woman spun around, sloshing some of the wine on the deck.

The woman spoke with a French accent. "Who are . . ."

She stopped speaking when she saw Court appear behind Zoya, the pistol low in his hand and facing down.

Zoya said, "I'm not going to hurt you. I just need your clothes, and some information." Her voice was soft, friendly, but she had an intensity on her face that made it plain she could be trouble if challenged.

The woman nodded, an expression of terror on her own face.

"How many more working in the kitchen?"

"Two," the French server replied.

"Where are they now?"

"Upper deck, serving at the party." Her eyes then went even wider.

"What is it?" Zoya asked.

"A dishwasher. He went to smoke. He will be back in a moment. I'm sorry. I forgot about him."

"We all make mistakes. How many armed security on the yacht?"

"I don't . . . Maybe ten?"

"Are you asking me or telling me?"

"I'm sorry, I don't know for sure. At least ten. And I think the Thais have guns." The young woman started to cry.

Zoya said, "Calm down, dear. You aren't in trouble." Then she said, "I'll need to borrow your outfit. Let's go somewhere private where we can change."

CHAPTER

FIFTY-SIX

Court waited in a head by the kitchen while Zoya followed the woman down to the berth she shared with two other hostesses. Zoya changed into the dark slacks and dark blouse, and she quickly tied the black tie. All the while the woman stared at her, fighting back some but not all of her tears. Then Zoya tied the woman's hands expertly around one of the bunk rails; as she did this, she leaned into her ear. "The prisoner. Where is he?"

The French crewmember looked to Zoya, blinked away more tears, and said, "I don't know about a prisoner . . . but there is a stateroom on the upper deck. Last one at the end of the hall. We've been told to prepare meals but not to go in. The men from Thailand take the meals into the room. That's all I know."

Zoya said, "That's all I need. You'll be safe right here."

Court and Zoya made it to the upper deck without encountering anyone else, but as soon as they climbed off the ladder they realized their luck would not last much longer. Here armed guards stood around a long table of at least a dozen men.

By turning away from the table at the stern and towards the salon, they avoided having anyone see that they were not, in fact, members of the crew, but as soon as they closed the door to the upper-deck hallway, finding themselves in an ornate area that looked like an Italian wine bar, they encountered two Italian men wearing polo shirts across broad chests. The men were in their thirties, and they definitely had the look of security.

One sat on a sofa with an HK MP5K machine pistol around his neck. The other stood leaning against the door out of the bar and closer to the bow of the yacht; he carried a pistol on his belt, and a pump-action shotgun rested on the little bar next to him. He looked at the two people who entered the room, identified them as crewmembers, and said something in Italian.

Zoya was in front, shielding the pistol she knew Court would be drawing from his coveralls. She answered back in Italian, but she needn't have bothered, because as one the two men realized they didn't recognize either of them.

They both began lifting their weapons.

When Zoya saw them go on the offense, she stepped to her left, and Court raised his weapon with one hand and held his finger over his lips with the other.

The two Italians lowered their guns and slowly raised their hands.

C ourt and Zoya left the two Italians in the room, facedown and hog-tied next to each other, hidden behind the wine bar, with copious amounts of tape over their mouths.

Now Zoya slung the MP5K over her shoulder and tucked it behind her arm, and the new pistol she dropped in a pocket of her little black apron. Court held the shotgun behind his back and rehid his pistol in the pocket of his blue coveralls, and together they entered the dark hallway leading to the five staterooms.

According to both the engineer below and the hostess, all of these rooms were in use by the Thais on board. It seemed as if the Thais were at the dinner party on the aft deck, but as soon as they entered the hall, Court and Zoya encountered a small Thai man leaning against the door at the far end of the hall.

He was clearly a guard, and he clearly was not suspicious of the newcomers. He waved a finger in front of his face and in broken English he said, "No. You no come in here."

Zoya was in the lead again; she had earned her role as the least threatening of the pair, and she smiled at the forty-something Thai man. As she spoke and continued walking forward, she noticed the radio hooked on the man's belt. "Sorry, there is a leak in the air conditioner. Can we just look?"

The Thai started to appear concerned and waved his finger again, while he reached for the radio on his hip. He looked down to unclamp it from his belt, and Zoya launched at him, covering twenty feet in less than two seconds. He cried out just before she went airborne, feetfirst, and she drop-kicked the man in the chest, slamming him hard against the door behind.

The guard buckled and folded straight down to the floor.

Court was still twenty feet back up the hall. "*Damn*," he muttered.

Zoya climbed to her feet and winced with pain as she rubbed her lower back, having landed on the machine pistol hanging from the sling there.

"You okay?" Court asked, but Zoya was already reaching for the door latch.

Court took her hand, pulled it away, and moved in front of her. The shotgun came out in front of him, and then he opened the door.

Fan Jiang sat on a tiny padded ledge and looked out a window into the night. His knees were pulled up to his chest and his hands were cuffed, up by his head, and shackled by a chain to a handrail protruding from the wall behind him. He could slide over to the bed and lie down with his hands over his head, or he could sit here by the ledge to the window, but that was it.

Zoya dragged the unconscious body out of the hall behind Court and got her first close look at Fan Jiang in the flesh. That accomplished, she turned around, took a knee, and held her machine pistol back up the hallway.

Court cleared the little head on his left, then dropped the shotgun on the bed and moved to Fan.

Softly he asked, "Is anyone else in the other rooms up here?"

Fan cocked his head. "How would I know? I have been chained here for two days."

"Right," Court said.

"You left me on the river in Cambodia."

"No options, Jiang. Trust me, I didn't want to do it."

"*Now* what?"

"Now we get out of here."

"I do not want to go to the United States."

"You want to stay here?"

"No . . . but I wish to bargain."

"Let's bust out of here, then we can talk."

"I could make noise. I could get you captured."

Zoya looked over at the conversation going on behind her. She couldn't hear much of it, but any talking and any delay right now bothered her.

She whispered loudly enough to be heard back in the room, "Hey. Can we go?"

Court said, "This shithead is threatening to scream."

Zoya turned back to look up the hallway. "Does he want to die?"

"He thinks the Italians aren't crazy enough to kill him. Just us."

"Tell him about me. *I'm* crazy enough to kill him."

Court looked back to Fan. He mouthed the words *She is* with an emphatic nod.

"Who is that?"

"Russian intelligence. Long story."

"Working with you? With America?"

"Jiang, the whole wide world joined hands just to rescue you, so don't fuck it up. We have to go. We can do this together or I can just knock you out and—"

Zoya couldn't hear from the other side of the room, but she said, "Knock him out and let's go."

Court looked to Fan. "Look. You want to go to Taiwan. I get that. You have my word that I will do everything in my power to get you there."

Fan wiped his face with his hands, restrained by the side of his head. "Really?"

Zoya said, "I'm going to knock you both out if you don't—"

Court turned to Zoya and whispered back, "Hang on a sec." He turned back to Jiang. "Really," Court replied. "Once we get you out of here, you won't be anybody's prisoner anymore. America stands for something, and you'll see that by our actions."

Fan nodded slowly. "I am putting my trust in you, sir."

Court felt like his list of obligations to people, institutions, nations, and ideas had just increased, but only by a little. He'd already planned on doing his best to help this man get what he wanted, because it was the right thing to do.

Court nodded, then looked at the cuffs. "Give me a minute and I'll pick this lock."

Fan replied, "The keys are in the desk drawer over there."

"Even better."

Not five feet from Fan's reach Court pulled open the drawer, then retrieved a pair of keys. He unlocked Fan, and together they moved to Zoya.

"*Finally,*" Zoya muttered. And then she said, "Hold. One of the doors is opening."

Zoya closed the door to Fan's stateroom.

Court realized they had taken too long. He turned and gave Fan an annoyed look.

Kulap Chamroon headed into the Italian wine bar with one of his lieutenants and two of the 'Ndrangheta overbosses so they could sit in the air-conditioned room and talk business while they enjoyed the last of their wine. This had been a successful night for Kulap, to say the least, and now with the Chinese responsible for the Black Pearl attack dead, Kulap's enemies would know that he had avenged his brother's murder, and also that he had the balls to take on a world superpower.

Kulap dreamed big, and although he assumed he'd made an enemy of the Chinese, he knew he'd earned the respect of everyone here in his region, and that was more important.

As he sat down on the leather sofa, he noticed that his Italian friends looked at one another with concern as they stood in the middle of the room. When they exchanged animated words—even more animated than normal for these guys—Kulap sensed a real problem. "What is it?"

Piero, the fatter of the two, turned to the young Thai crime lord. "I don't know where my boys went."

Kulap realized that the two bodyguards who'd remained here in the bar all evening were gone now. Their job had been to keep an eye out to protect the wing of staterooms beyond the wine bar . . . the Chamroon Syndicate's rooms while on the yacht.

Quickly Kulap stood, passed the 'Ndrangheta men, and opened the door to the hall, expecting to see a guard he called Ice standing at his post, just outside the door where the Chinese prisoner was being held.

But the hallway was empty. All the doors seemed to be closed, but Ice was gone, just like the two Italians. Kulap thought for an instant they might have all left their posts to go out to the deck to smoke, but just then one of the Italians shouted out behind him.

Kulap looked back and saw the problem. Two Italians in polo shirts were tied and taped, lying prostrate on the deck behind the little bar he'd just passed on the left.

The rules on the 'Ndrangheta yacht were straightforward. Only 'Ndrangheta men were allowed to carry weapons. His man in the hallway had been armed only with a radio. But he'd never called the other Thais, nor had he called the Italian bodyguards, of which there were easily a dozen on this big yacht.

Kulap closed the door to the hall, turned around, and followed the big Italians back out into the second-deck salon. The overbosses yelled at the four armed guards there, and all the men ran back into the wine bar as they pulled their pistols and submachine guns.

Zoya said, "Might have been a false alarm. The door opened, but now it's closed."

Court said, "No way we're getting Fan out that way. We'll have to get through the window here." He checked to see how it was affixed to the wall. "This will take ten minutes with the tools we have."

Now Zoya turned away from the door.

"Shotgun! Shoot it out!"

Court could hear it in her voice. They didn't have ten minutes. They didn't have ten seconds.

Just then Zoya raised the Heckler & Koch machine pistol up the hall and shouted in Italian, *"Buttalo! Buttalo!"*

Court assumed from the tone that she was telling someone in the hall to drop their weapon. And he could tell by the gunfire that Zoya's demand had been ignored. Rounds crashed through the partially open door, and Zoya fired several short bursts up the hall in the direction of the gunfire there. Two men fell into the hallway from the wine bar. One was dead; the other writhed in the narrow space, clutching his stomach. She dropped down to her knees, then onto her chest, scanning for more guards, and while she did so she shouted back to the American, "We need an exit, *now!*"

CHAPTER

FIFTY-SEVEN

Court raised the shotgun at the sixteen-inch window and fired a blast, blowing out the center. While Fan ran to the bathroom holding his ears to get away from all the gunfire, Court kicked out the rest of the window glass.

Behind him Zoya fired more bursts from her weapon, and between them she shouted again. "Cover!"

Court raced over to the door to the hall and leaned out and over Zoya, just as her weapon went dry. A Thai man had come out of one of the staterooms off to the side, and he reached out for the machine pistol dropped by the injured man. At the same time, another Italian guard with a twelve-gauge shotgun reached around the corner, ready to fire blindly up the hall.

Court fired two shells in quick succession, blasting the man with the shotgun in his hands, severing them instantly, and taking the man leaning out to grab the machine pistol in the chest with his second shot.

Court now yelled into the room behind him, "Take Fan and get all the way down to the subdeck! We're going for the tender!"

Zoya already had Fan by the arm, and then she leaned out the window with her pistol, scanning the foredeck below her. She let go of Fan, brushed away the rest of the window glass, and pulled herself through. Straddling the window, she put her pistol in the small of her back, kicked her other leg out, then slid down to the deck, dropping the last couple of feet.

Back in the stateroom, Fan pushed his head out the window at the same time that Court fired the last two shells in his shotgun, narrowly missing the Italians in the wine bar, all of whom were staying out of the line of fire but reaching around with weapons and firing blindly.

Court stepped to the side, dropped the twelve-gauge, and pulled the SIG pistol out of his coveralls. He looked back to see Fan sliding out of the window, then reached around and fired several rounds back down the hall. At his feet the Thai guard Zoya had knocked out was coming to and crawling up to his feet, but Court kicked the man in the face, spinning him back to the carpet.

Down to a dozen rounds in the pistol, Court took a quick look back up the hall and realized none of the attackers were willing to chance a run his way. He decided this was his chance to go out the portal himself, so he pocketed the weapon again, ran across the stateroom, and grabbed on to the handrail on the wall. Using it for balance he stepped on the ledge, pushed both feet out the window, and slid out.

As soon as he landed on the deck he heard gunfire closer to the bow, just fifty feet away. Looking in that direction, he saw Zoya targeting someone above on the upper deck, forward of the stateroom Court had just slid out from. Court pulled his pistol and was backing up to engage Zoya's target, but a new source of gunfire startled him. It came from the main deck, back at the port quarter near the swimming pool at the stern. He dropped down as automatic fire chattered, and flashes there told him a single shooter was dumping an automatic weapon in his direction.

The safest solution was for Court to dive off the side of the yacht, but he remained flat on the teak deck, firing the SIG pistol over and over at the threat.

After half a dozen rounds, the submachine-gun fire ceased; Court pushed up to his knees, then turned and sprinted for the bow.

As he made it to the forehatch, the same hatch he'd climbed through upon arriving on the yacht a half hour earlier, he saw that Zoya and Fan had already descended. Court kept his weapon trained on the bridge deck, which was where Zoya had been shooting seconds earlier. Just as he slid

456 \ **MARK GREANEY**

into the hatch, shots flashed from right outside the control room, and Court fired a single round in answer before he stumbled down below.

He was back down in the hallway between the crew berths, Zoya and Fan were ahead of him in the hall, and he was glad to see that neither of them appeared to be injured. Court closed the latch above him, but as he'd previously removed the hinges, it wouldn't take much to get it open.

Zoya and Fan took a ladderway down to the subdeck, and just behind them several members of the crew stood in their doorways watching. None of them were armed; they were mostly young women from the kitchen or older male engineers, and they stared in rapt fascination at the progression of wild-eyed, armed, sweat-covered strangers down here belowdecks.

Court, Zoya, and Fan made it down to the tender garage at the lowest level of the ship, and here Court ran straight to a control desk built into the wall. While Zoya covered the ladderway, Court read the various markings on the panel that controlled the door and winches, and he started pushing buttons and flipping levers before he'd completely figured it out.

Court yelled to Fan, "Get in the tender!"

"The what?"

"The boat!"

"*Which* boat?"

It was a fair question; there were two white fifteen-foot tenders, positioned on winches next to each other, but Court figured the first door that opened and the first boat that popped out would be the right one to get into.

The starboard-side garage door began to rise, so Court pointed to the starboard-side tender.

"That one!"

A shotgun boomed from the open hatch above the ladderway, and Zoya fired her pistol back up at whoever was firing down from the lower deck. A body fell through the ladderway to the floor, and an HK submachine gun fell with it. Zoya stepped closer to the hatch in the ceiling to retrieve the weapon, holding her pistol on the opening, but as she reached for the HK a shotgun boomed again above and Zoya lurched back into the tender garage and dropped her pistol on the floor.

As Court spun away from the control panel, Zoya fell onto her back, just feet away from him.

He could see the blood splatter on the deck next to her body.

"Zoya!" Court sprinted the ten feet to her, sliding on his back past her body and firing his pistol straight up at the hatch above. A man leaned his twelve-gauge down into the ladderway and started to pull the trigger without looking.

Court could only see the weapon; he had no target to shoot at.

He also had no time. The shotgun blast straight down through the hatch was certain to hit him here, lying on the floor and looking up at the barrel of the weapon. Court adjusted his aim and squeezed off a single round.

His 9-millimeter bullet struck the steel hatch door, ricocheted at forty-five degrees, and nailed the hidden man holding the shotgun right in the forehead, knocking him back before he could pull the trigger.

The first Court saw of his target was when the man fell half through the hatch and dropped the shotgun from his dead hand, and his head and torso hung down across from the ladder.

Blood drained from a hole in his forehead at his scalp.

Court caught the pistol-grip pump shotgun as it fell, then rolled over and stood up. He grabbed Zoya by the collar of her black crewmember shirt and pulled her out of the line of fire, just as a pistol began firing blindly down the ladderway.

Blood smeared the deck below her.

He lifted her up, then rushed to put her into the tender with Fan, which was still on the winch and just now moving out of the garage and towards the black water.

"I'm okay," she said, but Court took his hand away from behind her back and felt the blood there.

"Just hang on!" he said, but she immediately rolled over and started crawling for the helm.

He spun away from her when he sensed movement at the ladder. He got his gun up in time to see the dead Thai man with the shotgun fall the rest of the way down the ladderway into the tender garage.

The boat hung fully outside at the starboard-side waterline now; Court slammed his hand down on the winch release button, and it dropped into the water. Another weapon fired down into the tender garage through the ladderway; Court fired up as he ran past, then leapt off the yacht and over the gunwale of the tender just as Zoya fired up the boat's engine and jammed the throttle all the way forward.

Court knew they weren't out of danger by any stretch, because he was sure there would be armed men on the decks above, well aware that the tender was about to come into view. He pushed Fan down to the deck of the tender, lay on his back on top of the smaller man, shouldered the submachine gun, and looked through its ghost ring sight. Just as the bridge deck above came into view, he opened fire on a man there with a rifle in his arms.

Court shot the man with a burst of 9-millimeter rounds.

A second target showed itself when an Asian wearing a white silk shirt blasted off rounds from a handgun on the upper deck, and Court raked return fire in the man's direction, sending him and the men around him diving to cover inside the salon.

Zoya was getting everything possible out of the engine of the tender; the boat was banging up and down on the gentle waves already, and Court found it hard to aim. He fired short bursts of suppressive fire at the upper decks now, doing all he could to keep heads down while they made their escape.

He knew he'd be out of ammunition in a few more rounds, but he kept it up until the HK went dry.

"Get off me!" Fan shouted from below.

The tender was far from the lights of the yacht, so Court threw the machine pistol over the side, crawled off Fan, and made his way up to the helm.

Zoya was bleeding heavily from her right shoulder; her black shirt was torn in two places there, but instantly a wave of relief washed over Court. He found entry and exit wounds of two big shotgun pellets, both above her collarbone, but they hadn't hit any major blood vessels or arteries.

She called back to him, "Did I get shot?"

"You weren't bleeding when we got here," Court joked, and she smiled. "In and out, no big deal."

"Damn," she said. "More scars." Then, "How's Fan?"

Court turned around to check on the man he'd come all the way around the world and fought a half dozen different organizations to find. Fan had thrown up on the floor of the tender, but Court just patted him on the back. "You okay, brother?"

"I am okay," he said, and then he looked up at Court. "Brother. Thank you."

Zoya called back to Court now. "You know, we never talked about where we would go after we got him. I guess we didn't really think we'd do it."

Court made his way back to her. "The three of us need to find a place to put the boat in, someplace where we can get a taxi, a pharmacy, and a hotel. In that order, preferably."

They landed at Patong Beach at one forty-five a.m., then walked away from the tender and up a beach road. They squeezed into a *tuk-tuk* returning from taking drunk vacationers from a bar back to their resort, and the driver took them to a pharmacy that was open all night. Court bought everything he needed to tend to a gunshot wound and was surprised to find that the pharmacist would also sell him narcotic pain medicine over the counter. Zoya insisted she didn't need anything, but Court told her he'd been sutured up without anesthesia once himself, and he promised her that the pain from the wound itself paled in comparison to the procedure needed to close up the holes.

Finally she relented, Court bought the drugs, and he also picked up a six-pack of beer for himself and Fan to split while Zoya slept it off. He then grabbed a mobile phone, some packaged food, and several bottles of water.

After another twenty minutes in the *tuk-tuk* they were taken to a jungle guesthouse a couple of miles inland, and here they made their way through a few drunk or stoned young backpackers to the front desk, where the three of them got a room with two double beds and a bathroom.

By four a.m. Court had Zoya's wound professionally bandaged; she slept on one of the beds in the dumpy little hostel while Court and Fan stepped outside, Fan still in the simple cotton T-shirt and cotton warm-up pants given to him by the Chamroon group, and Court still wearing the filthy blue coveralls he'd taken from the engineer on the *Medusa*.

For ten minutes or so Fan told Court everything that had happened to him since the moment Court dove backwards off the boat in the Cambodian river. Clearly Fan was still pissed about being left behind, but Court hadn't second-guessed that move once in the past week.

When Fan finished relaying his story, filling in some answers Court knew he would need in the next few minutes, the young Asian man sat on a bench by the front door of the still and quiet guesthouse. Fan wasn't particularly tired; he hadn't been hanging off cliff faces and battling teams of trained killers like the two Westerners with him, but he'd rather be in bed inside than out here swatting bugs.

But Court asked him to stay outside for a few minutes; the American had a call to make and, at some point, Fan Jiang would be required to take the phone.

CHAPTER

FIFTY-EIGHT

C ourt sat down at a picnic bench outside Fan's earshot and felt the sticky blood on his hands and arms, mostly from Zoya's back wound, but he could tell by the screaming pain in his forearms that they had been scraped and gashed, probably on the cliff face but maybe climbing out the window in the yacht.

His right shin ached and throbbed where he'd cracked it diving for Zoya on the cliff; he needed to ice it but doubted he'd find any ice here, and he needed to check it out, but he told himself it would hurt less if he didn't know what it looked like.

And his mouth. He'd split his lip, and although it wasn't bleeding bad, it was severe enough for Zoya to notice the swelling while she was in the process of getting her shoulder stitched up, partially under the effects of the heavy painkillers.

There'd been no passionate end to tonight's action between the two of them. He and Zoya might have said a nice thing to each other when it was all done; he couldn't even remember now. But his face hurt too bad to kiss her, and her entire body, inside and out, hurt too bad for her to endure the embrace of another human.

No . . . they both just needed sleep—and the recovery time for their bodies that would come with it.

But sleep would have to wait for the American assassin. As he sat at the table he kept his eyes on both Fan and the guesthouse while he set up an account with his new phone and downloaded publicly available encryption software, and soon he was listening to his secure connection as it was answered on the other end.

It was no great surprise to him that Colonel Dai picked up his phone. While Court knew a lot of Chinese must have died tonight, he didn't expect Dai would have been close enough to any real fighting tonight to get his hands dirty.

Court opened the call with, "It's me."

Dai replied, "So . . . you *are* alive? Major Xi insisted you and the girl were shot and killed in the boat you stole as it left the shore below our safe house. He said the boat sank offshore."

"I have a funny feeling Major Xi is about to become Lieutenant Xi."

"The woman who was with you. Obviously she is not a tourist whom you met in Bangkok. Who is she?"

Court thought about sticking with his original story, but he decided against it. "She used to be a Russian spy. Now she is in the private sector, just like me."

"I thought the Gray Man worked alone."

"Yeah, but did you get a look at her?" Court joked.

Dai sighed a little, then said, "She survived as well, I take it?"

"Yes."

"I will do more than demote Xi. I will have him put before a firing squad for his failure."

Court said, "Are you in an executing mood?"

Dai answered, "Very much so, yes. I lost nearly thirty men tonight, and Fan Jiang was apparently not at the compound."

"That's not what I'm asking you. I'm asking if you have already killed Fitzroy."

There was a significant pause. Then, "Not as of yet, but he owes you no favors. Leaving him behind when you and your Russian girlfriend escaped virtually ensured a slow and painful end to him."

Court pumped a fist into the air. If Fitz wasn't dead yet, then Dai wasn't going to kill him. Court hadn't had any leverage against Dai for the last several hours, but he did have leverage, a *lot* of leverage, right now. He said, "You left Fitzroy alive because there was a chance *I* was still alive, and we had a deal."

"You don't think killing my men rendered our agreement null and void?"

"Absolutely not. I never agreed to be kidnapped. You want me alive because I'm the one man who can get you what you want."

"Your stock has fallen to nothing, and you don't even know it. I've lost hope in you. Fan wasn't where I thought he was; it was obviously a trap. But that means he wasn't where *you* thought he was, either."

"Yes, he never was at the estate; I confess I was just as wrong as you about that. But the difference between you and me is that I figured out where he was."

Another long pause. The colonel was unaccustomed to failure, and he was equally unaccustomed to being the man in a conversation chasing the answers. Finally he said, "Are you saying you know Fan's location?"

"He was being kept on board the *Medusa*, the one-hundred-sixty-foot yacht that was anchored south of Trisara. Also on board was Kulap Chamroon, and several men from 'Ndrangheta, the Italian mafia group from Calabria. Apparently a deal had been made to trade Fan to the Italians, but the deal included getting China off Fan's tail. Chamroon used Fan to send an e-mail to the Americans, something they wouldn't necessarily even see, but something he knew cyber experts in China would be certain to immediately intercept. Chamroon knew you would come down to Phuket and raid the Chamroon property, so he filled it up with some militia group from northern Malaysia."

Court added, "And you sent your men right into the trap." He joked now, "And yes, I'll hold while you execute your intelligence chief."

Colonel Dai's voice sounded at once skeptical and suspicious. "How do you know all this?"

"Because Fan Jiang told me."

The Chinese army officer did not hide his astonishment. "You . . . you spoke with Fan Jiang?"

"*Spoke* with him? Right now he's twenty yards away. Wait a second." Court motioned for Fan to come over, which he did, nervously. He took the phone.

"Department Director Dai. You are speaking with Chief Sergeant Class Three Fan Jiang of Unit 61398, Detachment Red Cell. Identification L522678941."

Dai positively growled at the young sergeant. "You have been stripped of all rank and identifiers, Fan. Stop using your title."

Fan spoke subserviently, as he was trained to do. *"Xie de, lujon shang-xiao."* Yes, Colonel.

Court took the phone back and gave the young man a thumbs-up, and Fan shuffled off through the predawn towards the bed waiting for him inside the guesthouse.

Court spoke into the phone. "How 'bout *them* apples?"

"What? I don't understand you." Dai was confused, but he must have worked out it was an American phrase, because he didn't wait for an explanation. "But you are an assassin. Why is he still alive?"

"Listen carefully, Colonel. I will deliver a living and breathing Fan Jiang to a place of my choosing, in exchange for a living, breathing Don Fitzroy. What you do with Fan after the fact is none of my concern."

A pause. Then, "Why is Fitzroy so important to you?"

"Damned if I know, he's a real pain in my ass, but that's the deal."

Dai said, "I think I know. I know why you must have him alive. I watched you in my office in the safe house in Hong Kong. You were hard at work looking out at the skyline, measuring distances to known locations. In that moment I knew you were planning on returning to save Fitzroy.

"Do you know what people say about you?" Dai asked.

"I can imagine."

"Maybe not. Maybe you cannot imagine. They say you are a paladin. That you possess some odd moral code that only you understand, but a code that demands you do what you think to be right. I knew that before I met you, and the way you reacted to Fitzroy convinced me you felt like you owed him some great debt."

Court was too tired to be psychoanalyzed by a man who would probably try to kill him down the road. He just asked, "Do you want Fan or not?"

Dai asked, "How do I know this isn't some sort of a trick?"

"For me to take Fitzroy *and* Fan? I don't want Fan, and I *do* want to get paid at the end of all this. Remember our deal?"

Dai went silent now. Court gave him a moment, then pressed. "If you're scared you will be double-crossed, don't come yourself. Send Major Xi along with Fitzroy. Hell, send every gun you still have in the country with you. It's just me and Fan."

"And the woman," Dai interjected.

Court said, "No."

"Why not?"

Court thought a moment. "She'll have a sniper rifle lined up on Xi's head. If I don't walk away with Fitzroy, we'll kill your men and take Fan directly to the U.S. embassy. I'm sure they'd love to get their hands on him."

Dai said, "I will do as you say. No tricks."

Court smiled a little into the phone. "No tricks. Here are my instructions for the handover."

Ten minutes later, Court still sat at the picnic table, and he waited for a new call to be answered. He picked at the sticky scab on his lip for the first time, and he realized how swollen and sore his face was. He wondered if Zoya thought he looked ugly, or just ridiculous.

"Brewer."

Court couldn't hide his exhaustion. It was five a.m. and his body was utterly worn out. "Yeah, it's me."

Brewer's voice sounded rushed through the protocol. "Identity challenge, Stable."

"Look . . . I don't fucking remember. You can hang up if you want, but—"

"It's fine. Tell me where you were born."

"Glen St. Mary, Florida."

"Confirmed. We know about the fight on the *Medusa*. I presume that was you."

"That was me." Court sniffed. "I've got him. I've got Fan."

There was a long pause. "And we are learning there has been some sort of explosion or series of explosions along with gunfire at the Chamroon estate on Phuket. Police and federal authorities are there now, but—"

Court said, "There were seventy-five guns in that fight. RPGs, too."

"Christ."

"The Chinese lost thirty. Dai is alive, and he still has Fitzroy."

Brewer brushed the comment away. "No one cares about Fitzroy. Fan has been the objective all along."

Court clenched his jaw. "All along. You mean *all along* from the beginning, when CIA and MI6 came up with the plan to arrange the murder of Fan Jiang's parents so that Fan would be forced to defect to avoid his own execution?"

Suzanne Brewer said, "Whoa. You are going way off mission with that talk, Violator."

"Right. I wasn't supposed to figure it out."

"Look . . . I don't know everything. This wasn't my operation. I didn't come up with it. I was thrown on board at the same time you were."

"Maybe so, but you know more than I do."

"I'm the handler; you're the agent. I will *always* know more than you." She was silent a moment, then said, "I was made aware that there was an operation involving a PLA computer cyber intrusion expert's defection, and it became an in extremis situation when he went missing once he was over the border in the New Territories, north of Hong Kong. And yes, I was given *some* background. But most of what you just said I know nothing about. Sounds like one hell of a lot of speculation to me."

Court said, "I want to talk to Hanley."

"*I'm* your handler. You talk to me. Tell me where you are, and I'll have the SAD men from Bangkok come pick up Fan Jiang. And Zoya Zakharova, as well. We'll talk to her; she doesn't have to come back to the States, but we're going to make a very attractive offer to her."

Court drummed his fingers on the picnic table. "Okay . . . Zoya needs medical attention. Shoulder wound, it's stable; just let Ground Branch know that their medics will need to check it out in the helo."

"I'm making a note of it. She'll be taken care of."

"Good." Court gave Brewer the address to the guesthouse, even his room number.

"And Fan? I assume he's there with you?"

Court prepared himself for the fallout of his next comment. "You'll find Zoya here. Fan and I are going to split."

"*What?*"

"I want to talk to Matt. I'll call you back in twelve hours. If Matt Hanley is not on the line, Fan and I are going to do our own thing. Fan has no interest in spying against China, and I have no interest in cleaning up a dirty mission to murder innocent family members for my country's convenience."

Suzanne Brewer almost screamed into the phone, "I've about *fucking* had it with your phony morals, Violator! You've killed so-called innocents in the past, and you know it. It's too late to make peace with God now." She took a breath. "I know all about your failure all those years ago."

"I assumed you did," Court said. "And I don't give a damn." Then he continued, "Pick up Zoya. I'll call you back in twelve hours to speak with Hanley."

Court hung up the phone, then threw it overhand into a garbage can next to the picnic table.

B ack inside the little room, Court knelt over Zoya, checking her wound in the dawn's light coming through the window. He then looked at her face and found her sleeping peacefully. The medication would have her out for a few hours more.

Despite his injured face, he leaned over and kissed her cheek, then nestled his face in her warm neck behind her ear. He kissed her here, too.

She stirred a little, but did not wake up.

Now he stood back up and turned to Fan, who was tucked in the covers in his double bed. Court gave him a shake.

"Sleep well?"

"*What?* I just lay down."

"Gotta go, kid. Shake a leg."

"I . . . Where are we going?"

Court looked out the window a moment, gave a shrug, then said, "Off grid."

"What does that mean?"

"It means you and I are about to disappear."

CHAPTER

FIFTY-NINE

The morning activity was in full swing at the Phuket Backpacker Hostel. The little breakfast room was filled with young men and women from all over the world. Many sat in groups silently, hungover from partying the night before; some of the surfers getting a late start were rushing through their coffee and eggs. A few of the more intrepid guests looked over maps or read details of smartphone destinations to hike in the nearby hills.

The TV was on, but the sound was down, and few if any of the Westerners here knew anything about a shoot-out in the jungle many miles to the north. They were all here on vacation, and it would take an incoming tsunami to draw their attention to the local news.

The breakfast room was open to the lobby, so every head turned when a group of eight men, all bearded Westerners in their thirties and forties, came through the front door, blocking out the harsh morning light with their bodies. They wore sunglasses and ball caps, headsets in their ears, and packs on their backs, and, most notably to every single person in the hostel awake enough to see past their breakfast, all the men had big black and green guns in their hands.

A young lady behind the counter at the entrance said not a word as the men hustled by her, and a couple of young surfers from South Africa moved themselves against the wall quickly as the men approached.

The men shot straight to the back of the hostel and stepped around the door to room twelve, and while three twenty-something backpackers just stood in the hall and stared, some of the intense gunmen opened the door and filed in, while others maintained rear security in the hall.

Zoya Zakharova woke to a shake on her bare arm. She thought it was Court but was surprised to feel that he was wearing gloves. She sat up, rubbed her eyes, and felt the continued effects of the Vicodin in her blood, along with the pain in her shoulder that was even stronger than the narcotic.

When she opened her eyes she saw them. Four men in the room with guns, more men in the hall outside. They were obviously Americans.

The man in front said, "Ma'am, we're friends." And then, "Do you have any weapons on you?"

"*Nyet* . . . No." She rubbed her eyes again and looked around. "Where is . . . where is Court?"

"He sent us to help you, ma'am. We've got transport outside. I understand you're hurt. We have a litter if you can't walk."

"What's your name?" she asked the man.

He hesitated a moment, then said, "I'm Chris. I'm a friend of Court's."

She didn't know if she believed him. "When do we see him?"

The man gave a little smile. "You know Court. You see him when he wants to be seen."

She looked around the room and saw that Fan Jiang was gone. Slowly she understood what had happened. Court had taken off with Fan, and he'd told the CIA where they could pick her up.

And he hadn't even said good-bye.

She was so mad she fought a scream.

She wanted to kill him and she wanted to cry.

Matthew Hanley hated mornings at work: the inevitable new crisis, the never-ending procession of things to sign, people to talk to, fires to put out. Today was the same as the others, other than the fact that the scale was a little larger than usual.

In front of him now was Suzanne Brewer, not his favorite person in the building by a long shot, and not someone he wanted to see waiting in the anteroom of his office when he walked in first thing, a still-warm bagel in a bag in his hand. She had her ubiquitous crutches with her, but her leg had improved enough to where she was putting some weight on it.

Twenty-five minutes later Hanley sat at his desk. The bagel was in the trash can, uneaten, and Hanley was looking at his phone, waiting for it to begin blinking.

Brewer sat in front of him with her ubiquitous tablet computer with which she maintained real-time contact with the communications team in charge of moving Court Gentry's call from her phone to Hanley's office. They'd also be checking that the encryption was maintained throughout the call, as usual, but Gentry was a pro, and he never screwed up.

Hanley's phone finally lit up and Brewer looked down at her pad. "Okay, that's going to be him."

Hanley nodded, watched it ring several times, then snatched it up. "Hey, Court. You okay?"

The pause was brief. "I didn't know if you'd talk to me or not."

"You got me," he said. "Remember, I told you you'd always have a direct feed if you needed it."

"How could I forget? It was just a month ago. Bet you didn't think I'd need it so quickly."

Hanley paused. "Well . . . I had half a guess you might have some concerns on this one."

Court said, "Let's get to it. First concern . . . Zoya Zakharova."

Hanley nodded as he spoke into the phone. "Yep, we got her. Travers and some of the guys picked her up this morning; right now she's in the infirmary at our embassy in Singapore. Doing fine, is what I hear, but I'd be holding out on you if I didn't mention she's pissed about you running out on her."

"Yeah," Court said softly.

Hanley added, "Honestly, dude. I know how she feels. You ran out on us on this one, too."

"Matt . . . tell me we did *not* sanction the murder of Fan Jiang's parents."

There was a silence while Hanley looked for the words. When he found them he knew how they'd be received. "Depends on your definition of the word 'we.'"

"*Dammit!* You are becoming one of them, aren't you? One of the paper pushers who parse every word like a Supreme Court justice. Have you even been in the job a whole month yet?"

"When I came into this office, I found a lot of balls in the air, and they were all coming down. I didn't throw them, but it's my job to catch them. If it weren't me sitting here it would be another guy. And, I remind you, most other guys around here still want you dead."

Court said, "This mission that I came in on the tail end of. This mission I was sent into that I knew nothing about. What is it called?"

Brewer had an earpiece in, so she could hear Violator's side of the conversation. She looked at her boss, obviously wondering how he would answer.

She displayed the shock on her face when her boss answered with the truth.

"It was called Aces High. We had an agent in the PLA, mid-level security guy. His name was—"

Court said, "His name was Song Julong."

Another pause. Then, "Right . . . He wasn't very productive, just an army officer in a dead-end billet. Still . . . he thought the walls were closing in on him. We don't know why; he could never give us anything solid that led us to believe he was in danger. Perhaps there was some security review that shook him, some comment made by a colleague he interpreted to suggest he was in some trouble . . . he never told us."

Court interrupted. "I'll tell you. MI6 hired Donald Fitzroy to send men into Shanghai after Song. Those men scared Song into enacting his escape plan. His escape plan was earning his way out of China by coming up with a big score for the CIA. It was the only way you would pull him out. He did that by killing Fan's parents so Fan would run into the hands of the West."

Hanley did not respond to this.

Court said, "That's right, don't say anything. I'd rather you didn't lie and tell me you didn't know."

"I *didn't* know. I . . . don't know if that is the case. Maybe MI6 was trying to whack Song *before* he did anything stupid."

"Well, that didn't work."

"Look, Court . . . this op was begun by my predecessor. Not me. Shit . . . you think I could have cooked all this up in the time I've been in here?"

Court softened. "No . . . I don't think you thought it up. This smells like Denny Carmichael, working with MI6. Still . . . you're the new guy. This is your watch."

Hanley said, "Right. Pulling a PLA officer out of mainland China isn't easy, as we've all seen in the past couple of weeks. Long ago Song made a deal with Carmichael. If he ever needed to run, he could get us something big, earn the resources we'd put into him over the years. Denny agreed that if that happened, we'd get him out."

"And then?"

"And then a few weeks ago he contacts us, tells us he killed Fan's parents, told Fan he had to run before he was executed, *and* told him how. We used the Taiwanese already in Hong Kong to go pick Fan up. Unfortunately, Colonel Dai got to the crossing, had men on both sides, and the whole thing went south. The Taiwanese missed Fan when he came over the border, and Fan didn't know what to do. He joined up with Wo Shing Wo. Fan did that on his own; Song didn't know that would happen."

"Okay. Then what?"

"The British were aiding us in Hong Kong while we looked for Fan, and they caught a lucky break when known Chinese intelligence cutouts contacted Sir Donald Fitzroy. Fitzroy was already there, as you just mentioned. Frankly, I did not know why he was there. Not sure I ever thought to ask."

Court said, "And Song? Did you get him out?"

Hanley paused. "We tried . . . Three days after Fan came over, Song went to the same crossing to make his run. We were ready and waiting for him, but he was strangled to death in the men's room on the mainland side of the border. One of Dai's men did it. We ID'd the assassin the other day. He was one of the two you killed in the Peninsula hotel in Hong Kong."

"Why didn't I know everything about Aces High from the beginning?" Court demanded.

Hanley snapped at this. "Dammit, son. You aren't still in your little private hit man job. You aren't working for a drug dealer in Sinaloa trying to whack a drug dealer in Guadalajara. You're back in the big leagues now. You don't get to know the whole game anymore. You get what we give you, and you work for us, or you don't. I told you, you were free to take this job or leave it."

"And then you told me the life of a man I owe my own life to was on the line. You *knew* what I'd do. You used that against me. You never used to be so manipulative."

Hanley blew out a sigh. "I agree. I'm an insufferable shit now; comes with the desk I sit at." He shrugged. "If it makes a damn bit of difference to you, I don't enjoy it. Not sure I've looked myself in the mirror since I took this job."

"Give it a try. You might find you look exactly the same as you did *before* you took that job."

Hanley let the comment hang, wash over him, and then he said, "What about Fan? Are you giving him to us, or are we going to have to take him?"

"He doesn't know about the murder of his parents . . . and I'm not going to tell him. Still . . . he doesn't want to work for you. He just wants to be free."

"We'd take care of him."

"By taking away his liberty? Look at what you've accomplished already. He'll no longer work for China, and that's a real body blow to them. Having him out in the wind will hurt them as they try to redo everything he touched, change up everything he knew. They won't be able to trust their own systems. That's a victory for America, Matt. In this particular case, it's more than we deserve, and it's going to have to be enough."

"Look, just think about—"

"See ya around, Matt."

"Court!" Hanley shouted, but the phone call ended.

As soon as Hanley hung up the phone, he looked up and saw Brewer standing up in front of him, off her crutches, tablet computer in her hand, and a wide, wild look on her face.

"What the hell is it?" Matt demanded.

"Violator! His phone! It was new, as always, and his encryption software was set up, as usual, but he'd not enabled the geolocation spoof correctly."

"Meaning?"

"Meaning we have his *exact* location pinpointed. He's at a hotel in Phang Nga City, a couple hours north of Phuket. He's in a room there right now! We moved Ground Branch back to the airport at Phuket. Their helos could be there in less than thirty minutes."

Hanley sniffed. "Well, that's a motherfuckin' trap if I've ever seen one."

"A trap?" Brewer was stunned, almost furious. This was the most excited Hanley had ever seen her, and he'd just popped her bubble.

The director of the National Clandestine Service shook his head now. "Not a trap. He's not going to hurt our guys. But there is something at that location he wants us to know about. Alert Jenner, get his team there, stat, and have them in full load-outs, ready to fight a war if they have to. Stress to them that they are going into a hot LZ."

"You think Fan is there?"

Hanley heaved his big shoulders. "I hope so. I hope there's a pot of gold at the end of the rainbow, too, but I sure as shit wouldn't bet on it."

The three-story-high Thaweesuk Hotel in Phang Nga had a flat roof, which made the CIA pilots of the two Russian helicopters streaking one hundred feet over Phetkasem Road very happy. Phetkasem Road was too narrow to land in, but even if it had been twice as wide, the thick traffic and the jumbled strands of cable, electric, and telephone wires hanging from poles on both sides of the street would have made touching down there a risky proposition.

But the roof of the Thaweesuk Hotel was relatively pristine, so the first CIA helo flared to cut speed right in front of the hotel, spun hard on its X axis, and then flew carefully but quickly towards the building.

It was eight p.m., dark outside, but the streets were full of cars and the sidewalks full of pedestrians. Everyone looked at the two new Russian-built Ka-62s as they flew in tandem, one hovering directly over the street while the other moved above the hotel.

The first Special Activities Division Air Branch pilot maneuvered his craft over the roof three stories above the road and, within two seconds, six armed men leapt off, dropped the three feet to the surface, and ran for the access stairs as a single unit.

The helo didn't wait around. It shot forward, climbed up into the dark, and began circling, with a sniper strapped in on each side scanning the hotel's windows with powerful optics.

Only five seconds after the lead helo left the roof, the second helo flew closer to the building, and three long tactical rappelling ropes dropped out, uncoiling all the way down to the street. Three men on board the Ka-62 attached their terminal descenders to the ropes, then stepped out of the helo and began rappelling down the side of the hotel, facedown, at speeds that made it look as if they were sprinting vertically.

They landed at the front door, freed themselves from their lines, and brought their weapons to bear on men and women fleeing. The operators scanned faces and let everyone pass by, shouting in English and Thai for everyone to get the *fuck* out of the way.

The helo above dropped the lines and flew just five feet over the roof, and then at the back wall of the hotel three more lines flew from the open hatch and spun down to the back door of the hotel, and three black-clad men rappelled down face-first. The CIA paramilitary officers landed on their boots simultaneously, unhooked their lines from the beastly flying machine overhead, and lifted their weapons, pointing them at several men running out the rear door.

The Ka-62 lifted into the night, pulling the three tactical ropes up with it.

Walt Jenner, team leader of the SAD Ground Branch team, was the first to recognize Sir Donald Fitzroy. The portly Englishman was rushing out of the hotel, being pulled along by four other men, Asians in business suits. Jenner had no idea Fitzroy would be here, but the dossier on his mission here in Southeast Asia had mentioned him as a kidnap victim of the Chinese malefactors in the op, and it was known that Court "Violator" Gentry had been attempting to secure Fitzroy's release.

Jenner quickly deduced that if this man coming his way was Fitzroy, then the four Asian men in suits pulling and pushing him along must be Chinese PLA men.

"Freeze!" Jenner put his laser sight on one of the Chinese, and the two Ground Branch paramilitaries with him, Greer and Stapleton, each picked their own target.

The five men stopped. Fitzroy instantly doubled over in exhaustion; clearly they'd been running down the stairs.

Jenner said, "Everybody put your hands up!"

One of the four Chinese men reached quickly into his suit coat. Greer fired three suppressed rounds from his HK MP7 Personal Defense Weapon and struck the man in the chest and solar plexus, and he dropped down dead.

The others raised their hands.

Greer, Stapleton, and Jenner pushed the remaining four men to the ground, and Jenner scanned for more threats while the other two began zip-tying their prisoners, including the Englishman. While this was going on, the voice of CIA officer Chris Travers came through Jenner's headset. "Delta One, this is Two. How copy?"

"Solid copy. Go for One. You got the target?"

Court Gentry's phone was still broadcasting from a room inside the hotel. They'd been able to discern in the helo during their landing that his signal was coming from one of the rooms on the northwest corner. This meant the six-man team that descended from the roof had to search rooms 310, 210, and 110 in order to find Gentry himself.

Travers said, "Negative, no joy. Say again, no joy. I have the phone in room 310, and it's got a note with it, wrapped around it with a rubber band."

Jenner and his two men began walking the prisoners to the hotel's staircase to the roof for extraction.

When he heard there was a note left with the phone, Jenner let out a little sigh. "That dickhead Gentry is always playing games. What's it say?"

Travers's voice crackled through the headset. "'Hi, boys. Thanks for dropping in. The gray-haired Brit missing his fingers is to be handled gently. Any Chinese nationals you find are hostile. Keep an eye out for Colonel Dai Longhai. He is the center of the opposition. Sorry I couldn't make your night with a personal appearance, but if you are reading this, then you probably just kicked some ass, so it was worth gearing up. Get out of here before the local po-po shows up to take you someplace where you'll have to eat fish head soup for the next twenty years.'" Travers added, "He signed it 'Sierra Six.'"

Sierra Six had been Gentry's call sign when he served in CIA's Ground Branch, five years earlier.

Jenner spit on the floor in the stairwell in anger. He could hear the helos getting in position for the extraction. "Fucker," he said into his mic.

Travers said, "I don't know, boss. He's a pain, but you kinda have to appreciate the man's style."

Jenner ignored the comment and looked at Fitzroy. "Which one of these guys is Dai?"

Fitzroy struggled up the stairs with his hands behind his back. "He's not here. The man you shot was Major Xi, second-in-command. The other three are men who work for Dai."

Jenner and the entourage reached the roof a minute later. Sirens approached the hotel from all directions.

The first helo lifted off with half the unit, and the second came in, but slower than Jenner wanted. He called the pilot through his radio to encourage him on. "Delta One to Kilo Alpha One Two; hurry up the exfil, bro. None of us down here want to eat fish head soup for the next twenty years."

Travers was already in the other helo, but he actuated his mic just to laugh into it.

CHAPTER

SIXTY

Three days after Sir Donald Fitzroy was extracted by the CIA, he sat on his bed in his suite at the Mandarin Oriental Singapore and looked down at his injured hand. One of the best orthopedists in Asia had spent an hour with him yesterday, and there would be a surgery at some point to properly address the savage wound, but for now there was no emergency medical treatment necessary, so Sir Donald just treated himself with scotch, luxury, and solitude.

To that end, he sipped a twenty-five-year-old single malt that wasn't half-bad.

He was feeling better now, and the turnaround began with the first thing he did when he left the care of the Americans: he called his daughter in the UK, spoke to her and his granddaughters, and laughed and joked and made funny sounds, and through it all he fought tears, because he could not remember ever being so thankful or happy for anything in his entire life as that damn phone call.

After he arrived he'd had clothes and food and booze all brought to his room, and he'd spent the last forty-eight hours or so looking out the floor-to-ceiling windows at the skyline, and while he wrapped himself in the splendor of comfort and riches and safety, he continuously checked a satellite phone he'd had purchased and delivered the moment he arrived.

He'd left a message with his secretary back at his office in London that she might get a call from a man reticent to give much information about himself. It wasn't much to go on, but his secretary had been with him for years, and she remembered Gentry, his soft American voice, and she knew that he alone was to get Sir Donald's satellite number.

It was noon on the third day when his mobile phone rang. He all but leapt across the expansive suite to get to it, but he answered it warily. "Yes?"

"The boys treated you okay?" It was Court.

"The men in black? Yes, of course. Quiet professionals, all."

"Did they get Dai?"

"No. He was close by, watching the whole thing fall apart in front of him. I considered telling your paramilitaries that he was near, but that would have kept them on the ground longer than I wanted to stick around, and he probably would have run anyway."

Court said, "Fair enough."

Fitz said, "I owe you, lad. I owe you bigger than I can pay."

There was a long hesitation, and then Court said, "You know people in Taiwanese intelligence?"

"Of course I do."

"Good. Fan wants to go to Taiwan. I'd like to make it happen. Of course, the Taiwanese might decline to take him if he refuses to give them information, but he'll probably agree to help them if they agree to let him live on Taiwanese soil. Taiwan intelligence can share his product with America if they want to."

"I'd be happy to set up a handover."

They talked about specifics for a few minutes. Court had a plan in mind; Don just had to connect Fan directly with someone at Taiwan intelligence and then step away, so it was nothing to the well-connected Englishman at all.

When that was organized, Don asked, "Anything else you need?"

"No thanks. I'm thinking about going dark again for a while."

Fitzroy said, "That's what I'm doing at the moment. Or my version of it, anyway. I'm at the Mandarin Oriental in Singapore. Come here, let's get drunk together. Bring your girlfriend. The one you called a spider monkey."

Court said, "CIA has her. It's the best thing for her."

"But not for you. She was good for you. You need friends."

There was an extra long pause, and then Court said, "I wonder, when this is all over, if I end up finding out that you were the one who lied the least."

Fitzroy looked down at his three-fingered hand. "That's a bloody sad measure to use in appraising your friendships."

Court sniffed. "It's not about friendships. That train left the station a long time ago. It's about alliances. It's about making a pact with whoever can help me get through the day."

Fitzroy shook his head. "Bollocks, Court. That's not you. With you it's about doing the right thing, come what may. You'll do it with an ally, you'll do it with an enemy, or you'll do it alone. You'll die before you go against what you believe in. It makes you the one good man in all this."

"It makes me exploitable, and expendable."

"Too true. No argument there, lad."

Court changed the subject. "You are in Singapore? I figured you'd want to get back to the UK."

"Heavens, no. I've got my own trust issues now that I have to deal with. MI6 used me for a job, the job went sideways, and they went home." He smiled. "I am a bit of a man without a country myself after all this."

"Welcome to my world." After a moment he added, "We'll see each other again someday, if it's in the cards."

Fitzroy smiled into the phone. "I'd wager that we will. Good luck to you, lad."

"You, too, Fitz."

Two days later Court Gentry and Fan Jiang stood in the doorway of a hangar at Kuala Lumpur International Airport, and they looked out together at the dull and cloudy morning. An Airbus A330-200 landed on the runway in the distance, taxied in their direction, then rolled to a stop on the tarmac just one hundred yards away. It wore the markings of EVA Air, a Taiwanese national and international carrier, and Court had followed its flight path on the Internet as it took off this morning from Taipei and flew straight here.

As a set of rolling stairs was driven up to the main cabin door, Court put his arm around the smaller Chinese man next to him. The two had spent a lot of time together over the last week, virtually every moment, and Court had found himself wholly enjoying the experience. They'd played first-person shooter video games at a hostel near the Malaysian border, lain in hammocks and drunk beers while watching surfers at the beach, and sat around in hot, cheap hotels in the jungle playing cards. All the while Fan regaled Court with explanations of difficult mathematical concepts, few of which Court understood, but at least it helped the time go by.

The week had been easy and fun and he and Fan Jiang had become friends, but Court did not tell the younger man how nervous he was about today.

There was much that could go wrong here with the handoff to the Taiwanese, but at least the aircraft came from Taiwan and the men getting off the aircraft were Taiwanese intelligence officials. Court had used the Internet to look up the men Fan had been speaking with over the last two days, just to make sure this wasn't some kind of an American double cross.

He couldn't be certain it wasn't, not even now as the Taiwanese officials climbed down from the Taiwanese plane that just arrived directly from Taiwan.

But then again, Court wasn't a terribly trusting guy.

He forced a light tone to his voice. "All right, Jiang. You ready to go to Taipei?"

Fan nodded. "Yes, Chad. I am ready."

Court went with the name Chad, just to give Fan something to call him.

The two Taiwanese spooks stepped forward, shook hands with Fan, and spoke for a moment, then shook Court's hand, as well.

"Thank you for your assistance, sir," one of the men said. "Mr. Fan tells me you have been incredibly helpful."

Court replied, "Take care of him. He's a good man."

Court and Fan embraced.

Fan said, "Good-bye, brother. If you are ever in Taipei, I hope you will find me."

Court smiled. "I hope you are hiding well enough that I won't be able to."

Fan nodded, wiped a tear from his eye, and turned towards the airplane. After bows from the two intelligence officers to Court, they turned and began walking with the defector between them.

Court stood there in front of the doorway watching them leave, then his eyes tracked off into the distance again, beyond the Taiwanese jet, beyond the runway and the airport terminal on the far side. As he stood there the cloudy day darkened even more, the air felt heavier, the gunmetal gray sky suddenly hung low and oppressive, as if all the possibilities of life had been squeezed down to this hundred-yard stretch of hot tarmac between himself and the plane.

From directly behind him he heard a voice. "Sometimes . . . there is no winner. Only losers."

He did not turn around. He recognized the voice of Colonel Dai Long-hai, knew the man had the drop on him, and he did not want to make any sudden moves. Instead he just watched Fan continue along the tarmac with the men, willed him to walk faster or to turn around with the Taiwanese so they could see the danger here at the hangar door.

To Court's surprise Colonel Dai walked up onto Court's left and stopped, his own eyes on Fan Jiang. Dai said, "I lose. *You* lose."

Court turned and looked at Dai, and he realized now that the man's hands were cuffed behind his back.

Now a new voice spoke up from behind. This man spoke American English. Strong, tough, and *very* familiar. "You're gettin' on that bird, too, Six. We all are."

Court turned away from Dai, all the way around, and he found himself facing Zack Hightower, his former team leader with the CIA's Goon Squad. Zack was back working with the CIA, in what capacity Court did not know for certain, but his job clearly had something to do with guns, because he held an HK416 rifle in his hand now, leveled at Court's chest. He stood alone in the small doorway, but now the main hangar door slid open, ten feet off Court's right, and an entire Special Activities Division Ground Branch field team walked out, each man carrying an automatic weapon.

Court scanned them one by one. Jenner, Travers, McClane, Greer, Stapleton, Rogers, Lorenzi, and a couple other assholes Court had never met.

And Hightower. Zack *fucking* Hightower.

Zack said, "Buddy, the U.S. taxpayer just flew me all the way around the motherfuckin' world, just to make sure you didn't do nothin' crazy in the next thirty seconds. I'd really hate to shoot you, but you know me, and you *know* I will if I have to."

"What . . . what the hell is going on, Zack?"

Zack Hightower did not respond to the question. Instead he said, "Chris is gonna frisk you, Court. You try some shit and I'll just stand here and gun you both down."

Travers handed his rifle to Greer, then he stepped forward, looking at Hightower. "Thanks a lot, dick." He moved Dai over to the other men on his team, returned, and patted Court down. He took a phone, a folding knife, some cash, and a pair of keys to a scooter.

He reached up to feel if Court had a knife hanging from a necklace; Court had pulled a similar item off Chris Travers just a couple of months ago, so this felt like a bad dream to Court.

As he did this, Chris spoke softly. "Sorry, man. I'm a friend, but I'm a friend with a job to do."

Court didn't reply; Chris Travers stepped away, and Court turned to look back over his shoulder.

Fan was looking back now. He saw Dai with his hands behind his back; he saw a huge group of tough-looking Americans with guns; he saw "Chad" looking in his direction. The small Chinese man tried to run now, but the two Taiwanese with him tackled him to the tarmac. Court spun to race to help him, but after a shout from Hightower, Travers took Court down at his ankles, and other CIA men jumped onto the pile.

Jenner and Stapleton ran on to where Fan was pinned facedown to the tarmac, and they helped the Taiwanese intelligence officers get control of the small PLA sergeant. Eventually they pulled him back to his feet.

"No!" shouted Court. "No!"

Court was pulled up, as well, and led along by the big group of CIA paramilitaries. When they caught up with Fan and the men holding him, Fan Jiang said, "Chad? Did you know? Did you know this the entire time?"

Court shook his head, still in a state of shock. What came out of his mouth was barely a whisper. "I am *so* sorry."

Everyone started towards the stairs of the huge aircraft, but after just a few more steps Court broke away from the hands holding him and took a step closer to Fan.

Hightower shouted from behind, "Bro . . . don't do it! We have orders to drop you dead and leave you on the tarmac. None of us want to be here and have this go down this way! It's a fucked-up scenario, but you know how this shit goes. We do what we're *fuckin'* told."

Court looked at Jenner, at Travers, at McClane. He wanted to say something, but nothing would come out.

He turned back to Fan. "Look . . . I swear to you, this looks bad, but they will treat you well."

"Forcing me to do something I don't want to do? To go somewhere I have no desire to go? That is treating me well?"

The group walked on. Everyone went up the air stairs; by now the Taiwanese men had peeled away, and it looked to Court like they weren't even going to board the plane.

Probably, he reasoned, because this plane wasn't going to Taiwan.

Court boarded the aircraft along with everyone else, and the door was closed behind him. He entered the first-class section and saw that Fan was being led to a seat; two armed SAD men dropped in next to him, their shoulders to his shoulders.

Colonel Dai was led to the back row of first class; he was seated against the window, and several men positioned themselves around him.

The other SAD guys from the tarmac found seats of their own in first class.

While Court stood there next to Hightower, Suzanne Brewer stepped out of the cockpit. Court had never met her in person, but he'd had a brief video chat with her the moment she became his handler, so he had no trouble recognizing her. She walked up the aisle towards him, and he noticed she had a limp and a little wince when she walked, as if she were in pain.

Brewer looked past Court and to Fan Jiang. "Mr. Fan. My name is Suzanne and I am in charge. You have my word that you will be able to make your own determination if you want to work for us." She smiled a little. "After we get some preliminary information, which, I am afraid, we will require."

"So I work to earn my freedom?" Fan said. "Lady, do you know how many times someone has said that to me in the past month?"

Brewer smiled ruefully, like she really gave a shit what this man had been through. Court saw through it, and knew Fan would, as well. She said, "A week from now you won't know why you were so hesitant to come with us. We will bend over backwards for you."

She turned away, looked to Court, and said, "Follow me."

"I'll stay with Fan," Court said.

"No . . . you will follow me."

Brewer stopped at Dai now. "Colonel, we spoke on the phone yesterday."

Dai nodded. "I only hope you will live up to our agreement."

"Likewise, sir," she said. "We have every intention of rewarding you if you are forthcoming with us. Many people at my agency were skeptical that someone with your background could be persuaded to provide assistance to the United States. I convinced them to give you a chance, and now you have just that." Brewer looked at him with unconcealed skepticism. "A *chance*."

The colonel looked out the window. "If I returned to China, I would be tortured to death. I know that, and you know that, so there is no need for me to engage in a charade that my decision is due to any political awakening on my part. I am here because I place some value on my life. No other reason."

Court and Dai made eye contact, and Dai said, "Interesting. You look even less pleased to find yourself in this situation than I do."

Court said nothing; he just started following Brewer to the curtains to the next section.

Then he stopped. He stood there a moment longer, turned around, and looked hard at all the Americans sitting there with guns on their chests. They all stared back at him, wondering if they'd have to get up and subdue the Gray Man.

Court asked, "Is it always going to be like this? Every time we see each other we have to figure out if anybody is going to pull iron and start shooting?"

Jenner was up front. He stood, turned, and spoke up for the group. "That's your call, tough guy. We can be friendly, or we can be unfriendly. All I know is—"

Court interrupted. "All you know is *jack shit*! Every story has good guys and bad guys. You don't even fucking know it, but on this op, you . . . me . . . Brewer, Hanley . . . *we're* the villains." Court motioned to Fan Jiang. He seemed so small tucked in between all the jocked-up American muscle. "That man's the good guy."

Jenner shrugged, then sat back down.

Court sighed, looking around at all the men. He said, "Treat him right. He's just a kid."

Travers spoke up now. "We got him, Six. Don't worry. Our orders are to let him do anything he wants but run away. White-glove treatment. You have my word."

Court looked at Fan. "I'm sorry, Jiang."

Fan Jiang looked away.

As Court headed towards the next section, Hightower called out from his seat next to Jenner, "Good to see you, brother. Sorry you lost this round. Keep your chin up. You'll get another shot."

Court's eyes were still on Fan. "Fuck you, Zack. You're not my brother." He disappeared through the curtain.

A minute later Court sat alone in an economy seat and watched Brewer talking on the phone. The aircraft started moving as his CIA handler reported in, probably to Hanley, letting him know they were on the way.

A few men and women Court took as analysts, operations officers, and security sat around the large economy cabin, but Court was sequestered from all of them by more than a dozen empty rows; when Brewer finally ended her call she limped over and sat down next to him.

"I'm truly sorry we have to meet face-to-face for the first time under these circumstances."

Court gazed out the portal next to him as the aircraft went to full power and began racing down the runway. "I thought Fan was the pawn in all this. Turns out it was me."

Brewer said, "Take a look at a chessboard. There are lots of pawns." She added, "Why in the hell are you feeling sorry for him? Sure, he'll get a long debrief. Months, for sure, quite possibly a couple of years. But he'll have a nice apartment, whatever he wants to eat, and armed protection from those trying to kill him. And then, at some later date, he'll get witness protection. He'd never get a security clearance from the U.S., but I know there are a dozen agencies, my own, in fact, who would employ him gainfully well past his retirement date forty years from now."

Court said nothing.

"That little bastard up there is going to end up a lot better than me, and a hell of a lot better than you."

Court said, "The whole operation was shit. Killing his parents so he'd be forced to run into our arms."

Brewer replied, "Not my fault."

"No," Court said. "But dragging him back to the U.S. so that a dirty mission ends up as a success. That's all on you."

"You found him for us," she said coolly. "You grabbed him for us. You brought him to us."

Court leaned his head back. "The U.S. flag is supposed to represent something. Not this."

Brewer said, "We saved his life. If Fan Jiang went back to Taiwan, he'd do it with a target on his head. Chinese intelligence has infiltrated Taiwanese intelligence, and there is no way Fan would get to that island without Dai's replacement knowing about it. Fan would be a marked man, and he'd be dead in a year."

"That was his decision to make," Court said. He was barely listening.

"Some people think zoos are terrible places," Brewer said, causing Court to look at her for the first time since he sat down. "And for some species they are. The predators, I mean. Put a lion in a cage, and you've taken everything from him. But the prey? The gazelles and the rabbits? The lemmings and the sea otters? Put them in a zoo and their lives improve. No fighting, no slaughtering, all their needs met. The zoo is the closest thing to utopia that we humans can craft on Earth."

Court glowered at her. "We're doing Fan Jiang a favor? And in so doing, we happen to suck all his intel value from him."

"He chose to work with Unit 61398."

"Actually no, he didn't."

"Well . . . he chose to run from it."

"We fucking set him up!"

"Don't say 'we.' I didn't; you didn't; Hanley didn't. It happened. Yes, it happened, but the person who started the ball rolling was the former head of the National Clandestine Service, and he's not around to answer for it. We cleaned up a mess. That's all."

Brewer was right, Court knew. In this dirty world, Fan Jiang's outcome was as good as it was going to get.

Court just shook his head. "How did you manage to score Colonel Dai?"

"We reached out to him. Got his number off one of his captured men. Told him we were his only lifeline."

Court said, "Still . . . China will kill his family for this."

"We've made it look like you killed him in the field. China is angry at you. Not Dai."

Court's jaw muscles flexed in anger, but he smiled. "You are a bitch."

"You felt bad about Fan's family. But just by you being you, you saved Colonel Dai's family. That should make you feel good."

"And yet I don't."

"You brought us Fan Jiang, and you brought us Zoya Zakharova. You helped us get Colonel Dai. You kept Don Fitzroy alive, and deeply indebted to you, which could be of some use to us in the future. By any measure you've done one hell of a job, even taking into account your insubordination, your double cross, and your general misbehavior."

Court said nothing.

"I would prefer an asset who obeys all directives at all times, but I will settle for one who overdelivers on his objective as an end result."

"So I get a gold star?"

"The only gold stars the CIA gives out are for death in the field, and then only to actual employees, not contracted assets. You get my appreciation." She smiled. "You'll get a gold star in a forgotten file when you die. It will have to wait for now, but I doubt it will wait for too long."

"With friends like you."

"All your friends fucked you over, Court. Face it, you are better off with a straight shooter like me managing you."

Court just stared back at her blankly.

After a moment she leaned back in her chair and crossed her legs. Court saw her wince when she did it. He looked at her leather boots and wondered if they were too tight, or if she had some sort of an injury, which she was trying to hide for some reason.

"So," Court asked. "What now?"

"We're stopping off in Germany for fuel and to pick up some analysts who will help with Fan's initial debrief. We can drop you there. You can drift off into the mist if you want. That's your thing, isn't it? We'll give you cash, documents, whatever you need."

"I figured you'd tell me you had another job for me."

"I do, but I didn't think you'd take it."

"You're right. I won't. You're always right, aren't you?"

Brewer said, "You're getting the idea."

He rubbed his eyes. "What's going on with Zoya?"

Brewer smiled. "Did she tell you her father was Feodor Zakharov?"

Court cocked his head. "I don't know who that is. She just said he was in the military."

"Yeah, like Patton was in the military. Colonel General Feodor Zakharov. The head of GRU. He was killed in Dagestan. The highest-ranking military officer killed in Russia or the Soviet Union since the Second World War."

Court didn't imagine that acclaim had been well received by a teenage girl who had already lost her mother and was soon to lose her brother. He was still thinking about this when Brewer spoke again.

"I can see you have feelings for her. I see it in her eyes, too."

"See *what*?"

"She has feelings for you. More. Hell, she'd jump in front of a train for you." When Court said nothing to this, she added, "She had one request. A demand, really."

"What's that?"

"That she got to see you again before we pulled her in. She knows she will spend the next several months locked in a safe house undergoing vetting." Brewer smiled. "Kind of like Fan. And Dai.

"She's really rather lovely. First ex-SVR operative I've ever met that I didn't want to go have myself steam-cleaned after the conversation. I look forward to working with her once we get her operational."

"Wait. She is going to *work* for you? As an asset?"

"Eventually, yes. If we can get her vetted, she will be a singleton agent under contract, kind of like you."

This bothered Court. He thought it was too dangerous, but he held his tongue.

Brewer, however, vastly misread his silence. "Look, Violator. Don't go getting anything in your head about you and your new girlfriend running around the world together fighting the good fight. If she works for CIA, you'll probably see her once in a blue moon, if ever."

"You mean we won't have annual conferences for singleton assets? Team-building retreats?"

"You joke, but I read people, Violator. Even people like you. I see how you feel about her. I can't see into the future, but I don't envision any operational situation that involves the two of you working in concert."

"I didn't take this job to meet girls."

Brewer laughed. "When we get to Frankfurt, she'll be waiting. She'll get on this plane for the trip to D.C., and you'll be free to melt into Europe."

For the first time since the tarmac in Kuala Lumpur, Court felt better. Not good, just better.

EPILOGUE

The covert CIA flight landed in Frankfurt in the early evening and taxied to a hangar used regularly by U.S. military and intelligence aircraft.

Twenty minutes after touchdown Court walked through the space-age-looking Hilton Frankfurt Airport, opened the door to a small conference space on the second floor, and entered the sterile room.

Zoya sat on the table, her legs hanging off the side.

Court hadn't showered in twenty-four hours and other than a quick washup in the aircraft lavatory he'd done nothing to mitigate the fact he'd been living in cheap guesthouses in the jungles of Southeast Asia for the past week. Zoya Zakharova, in contrast, wore a dark blue business suit; her dark brown hair was pulled back in a short ponytail. He couldn't see her wounded shoulder through the clothing, but her face gave off no hint of the damage and pain she'd suffered six days earlier in Phuket.

She smiled at Court as she slid off the table and walked across the little room.

"How are you?" she asked.

"I'm okay. How about you? Your shoulder is okay?"

"Hurts a little. Not a lot."

"Good."

Zoya said, "I'm sorry, Court." She sat in a chair and Court sat next to her. Close, but not close enough to touch.

Court looked her over. "What did you do that I don't know about?"

"Nothing. I just mean . . . I'm sorry your operation didn't turn out exactly how you wanted it to. Still . . . I agree with Brewer. Fan needs to come to the U.S. The Chinese will kill him in Taiwan, and the West needs the intelligence he has."

After a long time, Court said, "I feel bad for Jiang, though. This isn't his world. He's just a goofy kid who'd rather be playing video games or something."

It was silent for nearly a minute. Court wanted to kiss Zoya, but he wasn't sure if he should.

Finally he said, "I'm sorry. Sorry for leaving you in Thailand."

Zoya nodded. "Brewer explained why you did it. You were protecting me. You were about to run off with Fan Jiang, and you did not want me to be an accomplice to your action."

Court said, "I'm pleasantly surprised Brewer told you the truth and didn't spin that for her own benefit."

Just when he felt like he had to, she turned and looked up at him. Before he could react she took his face in her hands, leaned in, and kissed him hard.

It was another full minute before they pulled back and looked into each other's eyes. She said, "You and I made a good team over there."

"Damn right, we did."

Misty tears formed in her eyes. Court cocked his head; he didn't understand what was wrong.

She understood his look. "Brewer won't let us be together," she said. "I wanted you to come visit while I am held in isolation. Could be for months. She said no. I guess I understand. But still . . . I don't trust her. I think she's hiding something."

"Everyone I've ever met is hiding something," Court said.

Zoya nodded thoughtfully. Wiped her eyes with a tissue she pulled from her pocket. Then she and Court kissed again.

"Where are they taking you?" Court asked.

"Washington, D.C. After that, I'm just along for the ride."

"Ever been there?"

"To Washington? I'd rather not answer that question."

Court repeated himself. "Everyone is hiding something."

Zoya shrugged a little. "Where are you going?"

"I'm a free man as of right now. I can walk out of this hotel and go anywhere I want."

"You didn't answer *my* question."

"Only because I don't know. I might just wander for a while."

"A vacation?"

Court chuckled to himself. "I guess so. Someplace where the beer is good and the people don't get up in your business."

"You've earned a vacation."

Court said, "You should come with me."

Zoya smiled broadly. "No way Brewer would let that happen."

"We could run down to the tarmac and hijack an airplane."

Zoya's laugh filled the conference room. "You are a troublemaker, aren't you?"

"Sometimes, maybe."

There was a quiet knock at the door, and then it opened. A pair of men Court recognized from the flight leaned in. He knew they were CIA National Clandestine Service officers, and he assumed they were here for Zoya.

One said, "Ma'am. It's time to go."

Zoya grabbed Court quickly and kissed him hard, held on tight, but harder with her left than her right, because of the injuries to her right shoulder. When she pulled away she said, "You be careful, whatever you do."

Court smiled. "I will."

"And I'll take a rain check on that hijacking. Next time we're together we are totally flying off into the sunset."

"I like that."

Zoya left the conference room, and Court stepped out a minute later. The hotel lobby was quiet, and he left without anyone in the building ever noticing him at all.

An hour later he stood in the Frankfurt Hauptbahnhof and scanned the massive board of destinations, a hundred or more cities there for his choosing. He could take a train north to Malmo or south to Athens. West to Dublin or east to Moscow.

Like a restaurant's menu, he perused the options for ten minutes.

Finally, he decided it didn't really matter. He made a choice, bought a second-class ticket for the next departure, climbed aboard, and went looking for a quiet compartment to get some sleep while the train took him far away from there.

*TURN THE PAGE FOR A TASTE OF
MARK GREANEY'S
NEXT ELECTRIFYING GRAY MAN THRILLER*

AGENT IN PLACE

*COMING IN HARDCOVER FROM BERKLEY
IN FEBRUARY 2018*

The prisoners were slaughtered one by one, with efficiency as true as a ticking clock. Two dozen dead now, and the executioner was just hitting his stride.

The scene of the massacre was one of abject horror; the stench of fresh blood, the cloying smell of bodies floating in the brown lake, the viscous brain matter splattered and thickening on the sun-blanched pier.

Above the slaughter the rocky hillside sparkled in the midday heat, the reflection of broken glass and twisted metal jutting out of the wreckage of a battle fought months ago. Many had died, and the few vanquished who survived had run for their lives and left the ruined land to the victors.

The black flags of ISIS hung in the town square now, and they waved from the rooftops of the wrecked buildings and whipped in the back of most every pickup truck that rolled through the broken streets; certainly *every* vehicle that was filled to capacity with young bearded men wearing cheap tactical gear and brandishing weapons and eyes wild with the fervency of their sickening death cult.

Here by the lake, between the broken hillside and the water, ran a narrow shoreline of salt flat and brown brush. Forty-three condemned men in orange jumpsuits knelt with hands tied behind their backs, the remainder of the sixty-seven who had been trucked here just twenty minutes earlier. The captives were surrounded by masked fighters holding rifles at the ready.

The prisoners' hands were tied with twine behind their backs and they were all lashed together by a long rope. This removed the chance any one of them would get up and leg it, though it hardly mattered. Nobody was going to run. It was over fifty miles across the dead ground of war-torn Syria to the Turkish border, so what chance would they have if they ran?

No one entwined and kneeling here would resist the fate that awaited him. There was no use to it; and virtually all these men understood their last few moments left on this foul earth would be better spent praying.

The executioner wore a pair of daggers in his belt, but these were just for the camera that filmed the entire event from a position on the shore near the dock. The real weapon of choice for the mass execution was an Avtomat Kalashnikov, model 74U, held in the arms of the hooded man standing at the end of the pier.

As had been the routine for the past twenty minutes, two guards shoved a prisoner to his knees next to the executioner at the end of the pier, the masked man pointed the muzzle of his weapon behind the condemned man's ear and, without a pause or a comment or a moment's hesitation, pulled the trigger.

Sanguine spray erupted from the captive's head, and the body snapped forward, the mangled face leading the way down to the water. It crashed into the surface of the lake, just like so many before it, and just like so many more yet to die.

The shrinking row of prisoners remained passive, kneeling on the lakeside, over a dozen armed men at the ready standing on all sides of them. Some flinched with the rifle's report, others flinched with the sound of the splash, knowing their ruined dead bodies would follow suit in moments, and soon two armed ISIS fighters walked down the fifteen meter long wooden pier, stepped onto the rocky shoreline, and took the closest man in orange by his shoulders. Two more captors had just cut the rope tied around his waist, so the walking crew hefted the condemned from his knees to his feet, guided him back down the pier, shoving him onward if he slowed for an instant. The doomed man prayed softly in Arabic as he walked with his hands secured behind him, his eyes on the wooden planks at his feet, not on the water, not on the dozens of bodies floating just off the end of the pier . . . not on his dead friends and comrades.

The walk was thirty seconds in duration, and then the prisoner's sandaled feet stopped in the pool of blood at the end of the wooden planks. Here the lead executioner waited, the smoking-hot barrel of his Kalashnikov held unslung in his hands.

The executioner said nothing. The prisoner knelt again; he showed no emotion, he only continued to pray, his eyes closed now.

The two men who had delivered him there took a step back, their own boots and pants and even their ammunition racks on their chests were covered in blood splatter, and they kept their weapons raised, barrels just behind their prisoner's ears, but they did not fire. They looked on while the executioner raised his Kalashnikov, glanced toward the cameraman back at the edge of the pier to make certain he was getting all this, and then shot the young man in orange in his right temple.

Half of the man's head exploded, spewed outward three meters above the water, the body spun and tipped forward and dropped into the bloodred lake facefirst with a splash that was identical to the twenty-five other splashes that preceded it.

The escort team had already turned away to take the next man in the rapidly shrinking row of prisoners.

Forty-two now.

There were Iraqis and Syrians and Turks in the row left to be killed this morning on the banks of al-Azzam Lake, and soon the walking team had their hands on the shoulders of a twenty-eight-year-old with matted hair curled in an afro, blood smeared on his face, and a black eye, and they pulled him up and along, beginning his short stroll to his death.

That left forty-one in the row of tied and kneeling men in orange jumpsuits, and the next man to wait his turn looked much the same as the others. Filthy tangled dark hair in his eyes, his head down in supplication, gaze averted from the impossibly horrific scene going on before him. Blood was caked on his bearded face from the beating he took in the makeshift prison the night before, and his nose was swollen; a punch in the jaw had left it scraped and bruised and he was unable to open it fully, but he was not much worse off from the rest of the prisoners still alive.

The main difference between him and them was a small distinction and would serve as no comfort to them. He'd die first, and they'd die after.

The prisoner to the left of the man with the beaten face raised his head now, defying the orders of the captors, and he looked at the horror around him. His name was Abdul Basit Rahal, but everyone just called him Basit. He was Syrian, a rebel soldier in the Free Syrian Army; he had been captured late the evening before along with the prisoner with the beaten face who was next in line to die. Basset was a brave twenty-four-year-old but he was scared; he was human, after all. Still, he took solace in the fact that he would be martyred by his death, like all of the others save for the man on his right. Basit felt sadness for the beaten man at his shoulder, because he had done so much to help, he had been a lion in the battle, a true hero, and now he would die without achieving martyrdom.

Because he was no Muslim.

He was American.

Abdul Basit had just met him the previous day, but already the Syrian thought of the American as a fellow warrior, a kindred spirit, and yes . . . even as a friend.

The Syrian found some peace in the fact that he would share his last few breaths with this great soldier, and peace in the fact the DAESH captors had not learned that this man was a Westerner, because they certainly would have made a bigger show of his death for the camera, and whatever manner they would have chosen, it would have been so much more horrible than a simple rifle shot to the temple.

The American was lucky; he'd get a bullet to the brain and then it would be over.

Basit looked back down at the salty shore before him as the two escorts returned.

The American was cut away from the others, there was a scuffle of boots on the rocks, the shuffle of pants legs through the brush, then the American was grabbed by both shoulders, yanked to a standing position, and pushed away, along the waterline and toward the pier.

Basit called out to him, careful to speak in Arabic, because although he spoke English fluently, doing so would tip off the ISIS monsters of the American's true origins.

"*Habibi!*" Friend! "I swear it has been my great honor to fight and die alongside you."

For his words Basit received a rifle butt to the back of the head, knocking him onto his face and pulling other prisoners down with him by the rope tied around their waists.

But the American either had not heard him, did not understand, or perhaps his jaw was just swollen shut, because he made no reply.

ourtland Gentry's tire-tread sandals thumped along the wooden pier; the coarse twine wrapped around his wrists bit into his skin. The AK barrels held by the men at his sides jabbed against his low back, and he felt the eyes of the other fourteen ISIS gunmen behind him. He'd counted them when they got out of the trucks, and he counted them again as he was brought to the water's edge with the others.

He passed the unarmed cameraman and kept going, glanced up now, focused his eyes on the blood-drenched far edge of the pier. The masked man with the wired-stock AK and the daggers in his belt beckoned him with a bored wave of his rifle; he was a thick man, but even so, Gentry could see the executioner had his chest puffed out, no doubt for the video and the attention paid to him by all on the hillside, confederate and enemy alike.

The American prisoner continued forward; his fate lay at the end of this pier.

The walk was short . . . as if fate was anxious to get on with its day.

One step past the executioner Gentry was forced to his knees; he slipped in the gore coating the wooden planks but recovered. He knelt with his head bowed in supplication and gazed down three feet to the surface of the lake, the water swirling bloodred in the brown. The body of the most recent victim had drifted a few yards away, and this meant the American wouldn't crash into him as he himself went into the lake; not that this gave him any great consolation at all.

The men behind him took a half step back, their gun barrels close to his head, and then Court heard the sling swivels of the executioner's rifle as he lifted the weapon up, trained it right behind his right ear.

This was it.

Courtland Gentry lifted his head, squared his chin, and fixed his eyes in resolution.

"Here we go," he whispered.

A bdul Basit Rahal, the young Syrian who would be the next to die, did not watch the execution of the American warrior. He just closed his eyes and listened for the boom of the rifle. When it came it seemed louder than the all the others now that he was focused fully on the sound, and the report had only just trailed away when the splash came.

Al-Azzam Lake had accepted its newest victim, and the Syrian knew it was now his time to walk to the edge of the bloody pier.

ABOUT THE AUTHOR

Mark Greaney has a degree in international relations and political science. In his research for the Gray Man novels, including *Gunmetal Gray, Back Blast, Dead Eye, Ballistic, On Target,* and *The Gray Man,* he traveled to more than fifteen countries and trained alongside military and law enforcement in the use of firearms, battlefield medicine, and close-range combative tactics. He is also the author of the *New York Times* bestsellers *Tom Clancy Support and Defend, Tom Clancy Full Force and Effect, Tom Clancy Commander in Chief,* and *Tom Clancy True Faith and Allegiance.* With Tom Clancy, he coauthored *Locked On, Threat Vector,* and *Command Authority.* Visit him online at markgreaneybooks.com, facebook.com/MarkGreaneyBooks, and twitter.com/MarkGreaneyBook.